PETER F. HAMILTON

ASPECT

WARNER BOOKS

A
SECOND CHANCE
AT EDEN

$6.99 US / $9.99 CAN.

ISBN 0-446-60671-5

9 780446 606714

50699>

EAN

TO AFFINITY AND BEYOND—FUTURE HISTORY IN THE UNIVERSE OF THE ACCLAIMED BESTSELLER *THE REALITY DYSFUNCTION*

2090
"A Second Chance at Eden"

The now police chief on a new world must solve the ultimate locked-room mystery—how can there be an unsolved murder on a sentient habitat that is linked to the minds of all who dwell within it?

2393
"Candy Buds"

A blind boy, an orphaned girl, and an enigmatic bitek machine are creating edible memories of dreams, fantasies—and nightmares . . .

2447
"The Lives and Loves of Tiarella Rosa"

A fugitive terrorist crosses worlds to find love—and learn the steps one woman will take to protect her destiny.

2586
"Escape Route"

The *Lady Macbeth* discovers an ancient, derelict xenoc starship—now Captain Marcus Calvert must unlock its alien secrets in time to save his crew . . .

more . . .

"His imagination knows no bounds!"
— *Science Fiction Weekly*

"Hamilton puts [sf] back into interstellar over-drive."
— *The Times* (London)

"Hamilton's joy in science-tethered flights of fancy is infectious."
— *Interzone*

A SECOND CHANCE
AT EDEN

ALSO BY PETER F. HAMILTON

The Night's Dawn Trilogy:

The Reality Dysfunction

Part 1: Emergence

Part 2: Expansion

The Neutronium Alchemist

Part 1: Consolidation

Part 2: Conflict

and coming soon

The Naked God

PUBLISHED BY
WARNER BOOKS

PETER F. HAMILTON

A SECOND CHANCE AT EDEN

ASPECT®

WARNER BOOKS

A Time Warner Company

WARNER BOOKS EDITION

Cover design by Don Puckey and Carol Russo
Cover illustration by Jim Burns

Aspect® is a registered trademark of Warner Books, Inc.

This Warner Books edition is published by arrangement with Macmillan Publishers Ltd.

"Sonnie's Edge" first published in *New Moon* magazine September 1991. © Weller Publications 1991.
"Candy Buds" first published in *New Worlds* #2, 1992. © Peter F. Hamilton 1992.
"Deathday" first published in *Fear* magazine, February 1991. © Fear Ltd. 1991.
"The Lives and Loves of Tiarella Rosa" appeared in a different form as "Spare Capacity" in *New Worlds* #3 1993. © Peter F. Hamilton 1993.

Warner Books, Inc.
1271 Avenue of the Americas
New York, NY 10020

Visit our Web site at
www.warnerbooks.com

Ⓦ A Time Warner Company

Printed in the United States of America

First Warner Books Printing: January, 1999

10 9 8 7 6 5 4 3

To David Garnett
because, like many of us, I owe him.

CONTENTS

Introduction

The stories assembled for this collection are set in the universe of my Night's Dawn trilogy. Now, they form a series of snapshot glimpses into the history of the Confederation leading up to the time of Joshua Calvert and Quinn Dexter. It wasn't always so.

During the early nineties I wrote several short stories centred around the affinity technology. They didn't belong to any particular hard and fast version of future history, I was just interested in the potential of the idea. Then along came David Garnett, who had just bought "Candy Buds" for his *New Worlds* anthology, and said: You should turn this into a novel.

Impossible, I told him.

That was back in the days of my foolish youth, before I learned the hard way that the editor is *always* right.

He convinced me to go away and think about it. "Night's Dawn" was the result. OK, so I didn't get the last laugh, but at least I managed to frighten him with the size of volume one, *The Reality Dysfunction*, all 374,000 words of it.

As to the stories themselves, some are new, some have appeared in magazines before, in which case I've altered them slightly so they fit into the Confederation timeline.

Peter F. Hamilton
Rutland, February 1998

Timeline

2020 . . . Clavius base established. Mining of Lunar subcrustal resources starts.

2037 . . . Beginning of large-scale geneering on humans; improvement to immunology system, organ efficency increased.

2041 . . . First deuterium-fuelled fusion stations built; inefficient and expensive.

2044 . . . Christian reunification.

2047 . . . First asteroid capture mission. Beginning of Earth's O'Neill Halo.

2049 . . . Quasi-sentient bitek animals employed as servitors.

2055 . . . Jupiter mission.

2055 . . . Lunar cities granted independence from founding companies.

2057 . . . Ceres asteroid settlement founded.

2058 . . . Affinity symbiont neurons developed by Wing-Tsit Chong, providing control over animals and bitek constructs.

2064 . . . Jovian Sky Power Corporation (JSKP) industrial consortium formed, begins mining Jupiter's atmosphere for He^3, using aerostat factories.

2064 . . . Islamic secular unification.

2067 . . . Fusion stations begin to use He^3 as fuel.

2069 . . . Affinity bond gene spliced into human DNA.

Sonnie's Edge

It was daylight, so Battersea was in gridlock. The M500 motorway above the Thames had taken us right into the heart of London at a hundred and fifty kilometres an hour, then after we spiralled down an off ramp onto the Chelsea Bridge our top speed braked to a solid one kph. Our venue was another three kilometres ahead of us.

We joined the queue of chrome-silver vehicles jamming the street, turning up the reflectivity of our own windscreen against the glare. Bikes slithered through the narrow gaps, their riders in slick-skinned kooler suits. Lighthorns flared and blared in fury as they cut through the two-way tailback, chasing after them like some kind of runway strobe effect. As if that wasn't bad enough, every vehicle on the road was humming urgently, hub motors and air-conditioning vibrating the air at a frequency guaranteed to induce a migraine. Three hours of that.

I hate cities.

Midday, and we rolled into the derelict yard like an old-fashioned circus caravan come to town. I was driver's mate to Jacob, sitting up in the ageing twenty-wheeler's cab, feet up to squash the tideline of McWrappers littering the dash. Curious roadies from the arena were milling about on the fractured concrete, staring up at us. The other two vans in our team's convoy turned in off the road. A big pair of dilapidated metal gates clanged shut behind us.

Jacob locked the wheels and turned off the power cell. I

climbed down out of the cab. The silvered side of the lorry was grimy from the city's airplaque, but my reflection was clear enough. Blond bob hairstyle that needs attention; same goes for the clothes, I guess: sleeveless black T-shirt and olive-green Bermuda shorts I've had for over a year, feet crammed into fraying white plimsolls. I'm twenty-two, though I've got the kind of gaunt figure thirty-year-old women have when they work out and diet hard to make themselves look twenty-two again. My face isn't too bad; Jacob rebuilt it to give me the prominent cheekbones I'd always wanted as a teenager. Maybe it wasn't as expressive as it used to be, but the distorting curves of the lorry's bodywork made it hard to tell.

Outside the cab's insulation, London's sounds hit me square on, along with its heat and smell. The three major waste products of eighteen million consumers determined to preserve their lifestyle by spending and burning their way through domestic goodies and energy at a rate only twenty-first century industry can supply. And even that struggles to keep up with demand.

I can plug straight into that beautiful hive of greed; their need for a byte of the action. I know what they want best of all, and we provide it for them.

Excitement, that's how me and the rest of *Sonnie's Predators* suckle our money. And we've brought a big unique chunk of it here to Battersea. Tonight, there's gonna be a fight.

Beastie-baiting: the all-time blood sport; violent, spectacularly gory, and always lethal. It's new and it's happening; universes away from the sanitized crap of VR games consumers load into their taksuit processor each night. This is real, it ignites the old instincts, the strongest and most addictive of all. And *Sonnie's Predators* are the hottest team to storm ashore in the two years since the contests started. Seventeen straight wins. We've got Baiter groupies howling for us all the way from the Orkney Islands down to Cornwall.

I was lucky, signing up at level one, when all the rage was modifying Rottweilers and Dobermans with fang implants and razor claws. A concept I bet poor old Wing-Tsit Chong never thought of when he invented the affinity bond.

Karran and Jacob were the team's nucleus, fresh out of Leicester University with their biotechnology degrees all hot and promising. They could have gone to any company in the world with those qualifications, plunged straight into the corporate universe of applied research and annual budget squabbles. It's an exchange millions of graduates make each year, zest for security, and the big relief of knowing your student loans will be paid off. But that was about the time when the Pope started appeasing the Church's right wing, and publicly questioned the morality of affinity and the way it was used to control animals. It didn't take long for the mullahs to join the chorus. The whole biotechnology ethics problem became prime topic for newscable studios; not to mention justification for a dozen animal-rights activists to launch terminal action campaigns against biotechnology labs. Suddenly, establishment biotechnology wasn't so enticing.

If they didn't start paying off the student loan within six months of graduation, the bank would just assign them to a company (and take an agency fee from their salary). Baiting was the only financially viable alternative for their talent.

Ivrina was an ex-surgical nurse who had just started helping them with grafting techniques when I arrived. A drifter with little ambition, even less education, but just enough sense to realize this was *different*, something I could immerse myself in, maybe even make a go of. It was new for everybody, we were all beginners and learners. They took me on as a driver and general dogsbody.

Wes joined three months later. A hardware specialist, or

nerd, depending on your prejudice. An essential addition to a sport whose sophistication was advancing on a near-daily basis. He maintained the clone vats, computer stacks, and Khanivore's life-support units, plus a thousand other miscellaneous units.

We were doing all right, *Jacob's Banshees*, as we were known back then, battling hard for cult status. A decent win ratio, pushing sixty per cent. Jacob and Karran were still massively in debt, but they were making the monthly interest payments. The purse money was enough to keep us independent while our contemporaries were scrambling for syndicate backing. Poor but proud, the oldest kick in the book. Waiting for the whole sport to earn cable interest and turn big time. It would happen, all the teams knew that.

Then I had my mishap, and acquired my killer edge.

The buzz from the hub motors on the other two vans faded away, and the rest of the team joined me among the weeds and cat pee of the yard's concrete. According to a London Administration Council sign on the gates the yard had been designated as a site for one of the proposed Central-South dome's support pillars. Though God knows when construction would ever begin. Central-North dome was visible above the razor wire trimming the yard's wall. A geodesic of amber-tinted crystal, four kilometres in diameter, squatting over most of the Westminster district like some kind of display case for the ancient stone buildings underneath. The struts were tiny considering the size of it, a type of superstrong fibre grown in orbit, glinting prismatically in the achingly bright sun. Empty gridworks for the Chelsea and Islington domes were already splintering the sky on either side of it. One day all cities will be like this, sheltering from the hostile climate which their own thermal emission has created. London doesn't have smog any more. Now it just has heat shimmer, the air wobbling in the exhaust vents of twenty-five million conditioning nozzles. The ten largest ones are sitting on the Central-North dome, like black barnacles spewing out the surplus therms in huge fountains of grey haze. London Administration Council won't allow planes to fly over it for fear of what those giant lightless flames will do to airflow dynamics.

Karran came over to stand beside me, setting a wide panama hat over her ruff of Titian hair. Ivrina stood a few paces back, wearing just a halter top and sawn-off jeans; UV proofing treatment had turned her Arctic-princess skin a rich cinnamon. Wes snaked an arm protectively round her waist as she sniffed disapprovingly at the grungy air.

"So how's the vibes, Sonnie?" Karran asked.

They all fell silent, even Jacob who was talking to the roadie boss. If a Baiting team's fighter hasn't got the right hype then you just pack up and go straight home. For all their ingenuity and technical back-up, the rest of the team play no part in the bout. It's all down to me.

"Vibes is good," I told them. "I'll have it wrapped in five minutes."

There was only one time when I'd ever doubted. A Newcastle venue that matched us against the *King Panther* team. It turned into a bitch of a scrap. Khanivore was cut up pretty bad. Even then, I'd won. The kind of bout from which Baiter legends are born.

Ivrina punched a fist into her palm. "Atta girl!" She looked hotwired, spoiling for trouble. Anyone would think she was going to boost Khanivore herself. She certainly had the right fire for it; but as to whether she had the nerve to go for my special brand of killer edge I don't know.

It turned out that Dicko, the arena's owner, was a smooth organizer. Makes a change. Some bouts we've wondered if the place even existed, never mind having backstage gofers. Jacob marshalled the roadies, and got them to unload Khanivore's life-support pod from the lorry. His beefy face was sweating heavily as the opaque cylinder was slowly lifted down along with its ancillary modules. I don't know why he worries so much about a two-metre drop. He does most of the beastie's body design work (Karran handles the nervous system and circulatory network) so more than anyone he knows how tough Khanivore's hide is.

The arena had started life as a vast tubing warehouse before Dicko moved in and set up shop. He kept the corrugated panel shell, stripping out the auto-stack machinery so he could grow a polyp pit in the centre—circular, fifteen metres in diameter, and four metres deep. It was completely surrounded by seating tiers, simple concentric circles of wooden plank benches straddling a spiderwork of rusty scaffolding. The top was twenty metres above the concrete floor, nearly touching the condensation-slicked roof panels. Looking at the rickety lash-up made me glad I wasn't a spectator.

Our green room was the warehouse supervisor's old office. The roadies grunted Khanivore's life support into place on a set of heavy wooden trestles. They creaked but held.

Ivrina and I started taping black polythene over the filthy windows. Wes mated the ancillary modules with the warehouse's power supply. Karran slipped on her Ishades, and began running diagnostic checks through Khanivore's nervous system.

Jacob came in smiling broadly. "The odds are nine to two in our favour. I put five grand on us. Reckon you can handle that, Sonnie?"

"Count on it. The *Urban Gorgons* have just acquired themselves one dead beastie."

"My girl," Wes said proudly, slapping my shoulder.

He was lying, which cut deep. Wes and I had been an inseparable pair for eight months, right up until my mishap. Now he and Ivrina were rocking the camper van's suspension every night. I didn't hold it against him, not consciously anyway. But seeing them walking everywhere together, arms entwined, necking, laughing—that left me cold.

An hour before I'm on, Dicko shows up. Looking at him, you kind of wondered how come he wound up in this racket. A dignified old boy, all formal manners and courteous smile; tall and thin, with bushy silver hair too thick to be entirely natural, and a slightly stiff walk which forced him to use a silver-topped cane. His garb was strictly last century: light grey suit with slim lapels, a white shirt with small maroon bow tie.

There was a girl in tow, mid-teens and nicely proportioned, sweet-faced, too; a fluff-cloud of curly chestnut hair framing a composed demure expression. She wore a simple square-necked lemon-yellow dress with a long skirt. I felt sorry for her. But it's an ancient story; I get to see it countless times at each bout. At least it told me all I needed to know about Dicko and his cultivated mannerisms. Mr Front.

One of the roadies closed the door behind him, cutting off the sounds of conversation from the main hall, a whistling PA. Dicko gave me and the other girls a shallow bow, then handed an envelope to Jacob. "Your appearance fee."

The envelope disappeared into Jacob's sleeveless leather jacket.

Delicate silver eyebrows lifted a millimetre. "You are not going to count it?"

"Your reputation is good," Jacob told him. "You're a pro, top notch. That's the word."

"How very kind. And you, too, come well recommended."

I listened to him and the rest of the team swapping nonsense. I didn't like it, he was intruding. Some teams like to party pre-bout; some thrash and re-thrash tactics. Me, I like a bit of peace and quiet to Zen myself up. Friends who'll talk if I want, who know when to keep quiet. I jittered about, wait-tension making my skin crawl. Every time I glanced at Dicko's girl her eyes dropped. She was studying me.

"I wonder if I might take a peek at Khanivore?" Dicko asked. "One has heard so much . . ."

The others swivelled *en masse* to consult me.

"Sure thing." After the old boy had seen it, maybe he'd scoot. You can't really shunt someone out of their own turf.

We clustered round the life-support pod, except for the girl. Wes turned down the opacity, and Dicko's face hardened into grim appreciation, a corpse grin. It chilled me down.

Khanivore is close on three metres tall, roughly hominoid in that it has two trunklike legs and a barrel torso, albeit encased in a black segmented exoskeleton. After that, things get a little out of kilter. The top of the torso sprouts five armoured tentacles, two of them ending in bone-blade pincers. They were all curled up to fit in the pod like a nest of sleeping boa constrictors. There was a thick twenty-centimetre prehensile neck supporting a nightmare head sculpted from bone that was polished down to a black-chrome gleam. The front was a shark-snout jaw with a double row of teeth, while the main dome was inset with deep creases and craters to protect sensor organs.

Dicko reached out and touched the surface of the pod. "Excellent," he whispered, then added casually: "I want you to take a dive."

There was a moment of dark silence.

"Do what?" Karran squeaked.

Dicko beamed his dead smile straight at her. "A dive. You'll be well paid, double the winning purse, ten thousand CUs. Plus whatever side bets you care to place. That should go a long way to easing the financial strain on an amateur team like yourselves. We can even discuss some future dates."

"Fuck off!"

"And that's from all of us," Jacob spat. "You screwed up, Dicko. We're pros, man, real pros. We believe in beastie-baiting, it's *ours*. We were there at the start, and we're not letting shits like you fuck it over for a quick profit. Word gets out about rigged bouts and we all lose, even you."

He was smooth, I'll give him that, his cocoon of urbanity never flickering. "You're not thinking, young man. To keep on Baiting you must have money. Especially in the future. Large commercial concerns are starting to notice this sport of yours, it will soon be turning professional with official leagues and governing bodies. With the right kind of support a team of your undeniable quality can last until you reach retirement age. Even a beast which never loses requires a complete rebuild every nine months, not to mention the continual refinements you have to stitch in. Baiting is an expensive business, and about to become more so. And business it now is, not some funfair ride. At the moment you are naive amateurs who happen to have hit a winning streak. Do not delude yourselves; one day you are going to lose. You need a secure income to tide you over the lean times while you design and test a new beast.

"This is what I am offering you, the first step towards responsibility. Fighters and promoters feed each other. We always have done, right back to the days of the Roman gladiators. And we always will do. There is nothing dishonest in this. Tonight, the fans will see the tremendous fight they paid for, because Khanivore could never lose easily. Then they will return to watch you again, screaming for victory, ecstatic when you win again. Struggle, heartache, and triumph, that is what demands their attention, what keeps any sport alive. Believe me, I know crowds far better than you ever can; they have been my life's study."

"So is money," Ivrina said quietly. She'd crossed her arms over her chest, staring at him contemptuously. "Don't give us any more of this bullshit about doing us a favour. You run the book in this part of town, you and a few others. A tight, friendly little group who've got it all locked down. *That's the way it is, that's the way it's always been.* I'll tell you what's really happened tonight. Every punter has laid down their wad on *Sonnie's Predators*, the dead cert faves. So you and the boys did a few sums of your own, and worked out how you can profit most from that. Slip us the ten grand for a fall, and you'll walk off with the mega-profit."

"Fifteen thousand," Dicko said, completely unperturbed. "Please accept the offer, I urge you as a friend. What I have said is quite true, no matter what motives you assign me. One day you will lose." He turned to look at me, his expression was almost entreating. "You are the team's fighter, by nature the most practical. How much confidence do you have in your own ability? You are out there in the bouts, you have known moments of doubt when your opponent pulled a clever turn. Surely you do not have the arrogance to believe you are invincible?"

"No, I'm not invincible. What I have is an edge. Didn't it occur to you to wonder how come I always win?"

"It has been the cause of some speculation."

"Simple enough; although nobody else could ever use it. You see, I won't lose to the *Urban Gorgons*, not while they have Simon as their fighter."

"I don't understand, every bout cannot be a grudge match."

"Oh, but they are. Maybe if the *Urban Gorgon* team fronted a female fighter I'd think about taking your money. But I'm virtually unique; none of the other teams I know of use a female to boost their beastie."

"This is your advantage, your legendary edge, women fight better than men?"

"Motivation is the key," I said. "That's why we use affinity to control the beasts. These creatures we stitch together have no analogue in nature. For instance, you couldn't take a brain out of a lion and splice it into Khanivore. For all its hunter-killer instinct a lion wouldn't be able to make any sense of Khanivore's sensorium, nor would it be able to utilize the limbs. That's why we give beasties bioware processors instead of brains. But processors still don't give us what we need. For their program a fight can never be anything more than a complex series of problems, a three-dimensional chess game. An attack would be broken up into segments for analysis and initiation of appropriate response moves. By which time any halfway sentient opposition has ripped them to shreds. No program can ever instil a sense of urgency, coupled to panic-enhanced instinct. Sheer savagery, if you like. Humans reign supreme when it comes to that. That's why we use the affinity bond. Beastie-baiting is a physical extension of the human mind, our dark side in all its naked horror. That's the appeal your punters have come to worship tonight, Dicko, pure bestiality. Without our proxy beasties us fighters would be out there in the pit ourselves. We'd kill each other, no two ways about it."

"And you are the most savage of them all?" Dicko asked. He glanced round the team, their stony faces, hunting confirmation.

"I am now," I said, and for the first time bled a trace of venom into my voice. I saw the girl stiffen slightly, her eyes round with interest.

"A year or so back I got snatched by an estate gang. No reason for it, I was just in the wrong place at the wrong time. Know what they do to girls, Dicko?" I was grinding the words out now, eyes never leaving his face. His mask was cracking, little fissures of emotion showing through.

"Yes, you do know, don't you. The gang bang wasn't so bad, there was only two days of that. But when they finished they started on me with knives. It's a branding thing, making sure everyone knows how fucking hard they are. So that is why, when the *Urban Gorgons* send their Turboraptor out in the pit tonight, I am going to shred that bastard to pieces so small there's going to be nothing left but a fog of blood. Not because of the money, not even for the status; but because what I'm really doing is carving up that *male* shit Simon." I took a step towards Dicko, arm coming up to point threateningly. "And neither you nor anyone else is going to stop that happening. You got that, shitbrain?"

One of Khanivore's tentacles began to uncoil, an indistinct motion beneath the murky surface of the life-support pod.

Dicko snatched a fast glance at the agitated beastie and gave another of his prissy bows. "I won't press you any further, but I do ask you to think over what I proposed." He turned on a heel, snapping his fingers for the girl to follow. She scampered off through the door.

The team closed in on me with smiles and fierce hugs.

Time for the bout, they formed a praetorian guard to escort me out to the pit. The air around the arena was already way too hot, and becoming badly humid from the sweat and breath of the crowd. No conditioning. Naturally.

My ears filled with the chants rising from the seats, slow handclaps, whistles, hoots, catcalls. The noise rumbled sluggishly round the dark empty space behind the stand.

Under the scaffolding, reverberating with low-frequency harmonics. Then out into an unremitting downpour of harsh blue-white light and gullet-rattling noise. Cheering and jeering reached a crescendo. Every centimetre of wooden seating was taken.

I sat in my seat on the edge of the pit. Simon was sitting directly opposite me, naked from the waist up; lean, bald, and sable black. A stylistic ruby-red griffin tattoo fluoresced on his chest, intensity pulsing in time to his heartbeat. Big gold pirate earrings dangled from mauled lobes. He stood to give me the grand fuckittoyou gesture. *Urban Gorgons* fans roared their delight.

"You OK, Sonnie?" Ivrina whispered.

"Sure." I locked eyes with Simon, and laughed derisively. Our side's supporters whooped rapturously.

The ref bobbed to his feet halfway round the side of the pit. The PA came on with a screech, and he launched into his snappy intros. Standard soundbite fodder. Actually, he's not so much a ref as a starter. There aren't too many rules in beastie baiting—your creature must be bipedal, no hardware or metal allowed in the design, no time limit, the one left alive is the winner. It does tend to cut out any confusion.

The ref was winding up, probably afraid of getting lynched by an impatient crowd. Simon closed his eyes, concentrating on his affinity link with Turboraptor.

An affinity bond is a unique and private link. Each pair of cloned neuron symbionts is attuned to its twin alone; there can be no interception, no listening in. One clump is embedded in the human brain, the other is incorporated in a bioware processor. It's a perfect tool for Baiting.

I closed my eyes.

Khanivore was waiting behind the webwork of scaffolding. I went through a final systems check. Arteries, veins, muscles, tendons, fail-soft nerve-fibre network, multiple-redundant heart-pump chambers. All on line and operating at a hundred per cent. I had the oxygenated blood reserves to fight for up to an hour.

There wasn't anything else. Vital internal organs are literally that: vital. Too risky to bring into the pit. One puncture and the beastie could die. One! That's hardly a fair fight. It's also shoddy combat design. So Khanivore spends most of its time in a life-support pod, where the ancillary units substitute functions like the liver, kidneys, lungs, and all the other physiological crap not essential to keep it fighting.

I walked it forward.

And the crowd goes *wild*. Predictable as hell, but I love

them for it. This is my moment, the only time I am truly alive.

Turboraptor was already descending into the pit, the makeshift wooden ramp sagging under its weight. First chance for a detailed examination.

The *Urban Gorgons* team had stitched together a small bruise-purple dinosaur, minus tail. Its body was pear-shaped with short dumpy legs—difficult to topple. The arms were weird, two metres fifty long, five joints apiece—excellent articulation, have to watch that. One ended in a three-talon claw, the other had a solid bulb of bone. The idea was good, grip with the talon and punch with the bone fist. Given the arm's reach, it could probably work up enough inertia to break through Khanivore's exoskeleton. A pair of needle-pointed, fifty-centimetre horns jutted up from its head. Stupid. Horns and blade fins might make for good image, but they give your opponent something to grab; that's why we made Khanivore ice-smooth.

Khanivore reached the pit floor, and the roadies hauled the wooden ramp away behind it. There was silence again as the ref stretched out his arm. A white silk handkerchief dangled from his fingers. He dropped it.

I let all five tentacles unroll halfway to the floor, snapping the pincers as they went. *Sonnie's Predators* fans picked up the beat, stamping their feet, clapping.

Turboraptor and Khanivore circled each other, testing for speed and reflexes. I lashed a couple of tentacles, aiming to lasso Turboraptor's legs. Impressed by how fast it dodged with those stumpy legs. In return its talon claw came dangerously close to the root of a tentacle. I didn't think it could cut through, but I'd have to be vigilant.

The circling stopped. We began to sway the beasties from side to side, both tensing, waiting for either an opening or a charge. Simon broke first, sending Turboraptor at me in a heavy run, arm punching the bone fist forward. I pirouetted

Khanivore on one foot, whipping the tentacles to add spin-momentum. Turboraptor sliced past, and I caught it across the back of the head with a tentacle, sending it slamming into the pit wall. Khanivore regained its footing, and followed. I wanted to keep Turboraptor pinned there, to hammer blows against it which it would be forced to absorb. But both of its arms came slashing backwards—the bastards were pivot hinged. One of my tentacle tips was caught in its talon claw. I brought more tentacles up to fend off the punch from the bone fist, simultaneously twisting the captured tentacle. Turboraptor's punch slapped into a writhing coil of tentacle, muting the impact. We staggered apart.

The tip of my tentacle was lying on the pit floor, flexing like an electrocuted snake. There was no pain; Khanivore's nerves weren't structured for that. A little jet of scarlet blood squirted out of the severed end. It vanished as the bioware processors closed off the artery.

The crowd was on its feet, howling approval and demanding vengeance. Slashes of colour and waving arms; the roof panels vibrating. All distant.

Turboraptor sidestepped hurriedly, moving away from the danger of the pit wall. I let it go, watching intently. One of its pincer talons seemed misaligned; when the other two closed it didn't budge.

We clashed again, colliding in the centre of the pit. It was a kick and shove match this time. Arms and tentacles could only beat ineffectually on armoured flanks while we were pressed together. Then I managed to bend Khanivore's head low enough for its jaws to clamp around Turboraptor's shoulder. Arrow-head teeth bit into purple scales. Blood began to seep out of the puncture marks.

Turboraptor's talon claw started to scrape at Khanivore's head. Simon was using the dead talon like a can opener, gouging away at the sensor cavities. I lost a couple of retinas and an ear before I decided I was on a hiding to nothing.

Khanivore's mouth had done as much damage as possible, it wouldn't close any further. I let go, and we fell apart cleanly.

Turboraptor took two paces back, and charged at me again. I wasn't quick enough. That pile-driver bone fist struck Khanivore's torso full on. I backpedalled furiously to keep balance, and thudded into the pit wall.

Bioware processors flashed status graphics into my mind, red and orange cobwebs superimposed over my vision, detailing the damage. Turboraptor's fist had weakened the exoskeleton's midsection. Khanivore could probably take another couple of punches like that, definitely no more than three.

I slashed out with a couple of tentacles. One twined round Turboraptor's bone fist. The second snared the uppermost segment of the same arm. An inescapable manacle. No way could Simon manoeuvre another punch out of that.

I shot an order into the relevant control processors to maintain the hold. Controlling five upper limbs at once isn't possible for a human brain. We don't have the neurological programming for it, that's why most beasties are straight hominoids. All I could ever do with Khanivore was manipulate two tentacles; but for something simple like sustaining a grip the processors can take over while I switch to another pair of tentacles.

Turboraptor's talon claw bent round to try and snip the tentacles grasping its arm. I sent another two tentacles to bind it, which left me the fifth free to win the war.

I'd just started to bring it forwards, figuring on using it to try and snap Turboraptor's neck when Simon pulled a fast one. The top half of the talon claw arm started to pull back. I thought Khanivore's optical nerves had gone haywire. My tentacles' grip on the arm was rock solid, it couldn't possibly be moving.

There was a wet tearing sound, a small plume of blood. The tentacles were left wrapped round the last three segments of the arm, while the lower section, the one which had separated, was a sheath for a fifty-centimetre sword of solid bone.

Simon stabbed it straight at Khanivore's torso, where the exoskeleton was already weakened. Fear burned me then, a stimulant harder than any adrenalin or amphetamine, accelerating my thoughts to lightspeed. Self-preservation superseded reticence, and I swiped the fifth tentacle downwards, knowing it would get butchered and not caring. Anything to deflect that killer strike.

The tentacle hit the top of the blade, an impact which nearly severed it in two. A fountain of blood spewed out, splattering over Turboraptor's chest like a scarlet graffiti bomb. But the blade was deflected, slicing downwards to shatter a hole in the exoskeleton of Khanivore's right leg. It slid in deep enough for the display graphics to tell me the tip was touching the other side. Simon levered it round, decimating the flesh inside the exoskeleton. More cobweb graphics flowered, reporting severed nerve fibres, cut tendons, artery valves closing. The leg was more or less useless.

I was already throwing away the useless section of Turboraptor's trick arm. One of the freed tentacles wove around the sword hilt, contracting the loop as tight as it would go, preventing the blade from moving. It was still inside me, but prevented from causing any more havoc. Our bodies were locked together. None of Turboraptor's squirming and shaking could separate us.

With a care that verged on the tender, I slowly wound my last tentacle clockwise round Turboraptor's head, avoiding its snapping jaw. I finished with a tight knot around the base of a horn.

Simon must have realized what I was going to do. Turboraptor's legs scrabbled against the bloody floor, frantically trying to unbalance the pair of us.

I began pulling with the tentacle, reeling it in. Turboraptor's head turned. It fought me every centimetre of the way, straining cords of muscle rippling under the scales. No good. The rotation was inexorable.

Ninety degrees, and ominous popping sounds emerged from the stumpy neck. A hundred degrees and the purple scales were no longer overlapping. A hundred and ten degrees and the skin started to tear. A hundred and twenty, and the spine snapped with a gunshot crack.

My tentacle wrenched the head off, flinging it triumphantly into the air. It landed in a puddle of my blood, and skidded across the polyp until it bumped into the wall below Simon. He was doubled up on the edge of his chair, hugging his chest, shaking violently. His tattoo blazed cleanly, as if it was burning into his skin. Team-mates were swooping towards him.

That was when I opened my own eyes, just in time to see Turboraptor's decapitated body tumble to the ground. The crowd was up and dancing, rocking the stand, and crying my name. Mine! Minute flecks of damp rust from the roof panels were snowing over the whole arena.

I stood up, raising both my arms, collecting and acknowledging my due of adulation. The team's kisses stung my cheeks. *Eighteen*. Eighteen straight victories.

There was just one motionless figure among the carnival frenzy. Dicko, sitting in the front row, chin resting on his cane's silver pommel, staring glumly at the wreckage of flesh lying at Khanivore's feet.

Three hours later, and the rap is still tearing apart Turboraptor's trick arm. Was it bending the rules? Should we do something similar? What tactics were best against it?

I sipped my Ruddles from a long-stemmed glass, letting the vocals eddy round me. We'd wound up in a pub called the Latchmere, local *it* spot, with some kind of art theatre upstairs where the cosmically strange punters kept vanishing. God knows what was playing. From where I was slumped I could see about fifteen people dancing listlessly at the far end of the bar, the juke playing some weird acoustic Indian metal track.

Our table was court to six Baiter fans, eyes atwinkle from the proximity to their idols. If it hadn't been for the victory high, I might have been embarrassed. Beer and seafood kept piling up, courtesy of a local merchant who'd been at the pit side, and was now designer-slumming at the bar with his pouty mistress.

The girl in the yellow dress came in. She was alone. I watched her and a waitress put their heads together, swapping a few furtive words as her haunted eyes cast about. Then she wandered over to the juke.

She was still staring blankly at the selection screen a minute later when I joined her.

"Did he hit you?" I asked.

She turned, flinching. Her eyes were red-rimmed. "No," she said in a tiny voice.

"Will he hit you?"

She shook her head mutely, staring at the floor.

Jennifer. That was her name. She told me as we walked out into the sweltering night. Lecherous grins and Karran's thumbs-up at our backs.

It was drizzling, the minute droplets evaporating almost as soon as they hit the pavement. Warm mist sparkled in the hologram adverts which formed rainbow arches over the road. A team of servitor chimps were out cleaning the street, glossy gold pelts darkened by the drizzle.

I walked Jennifer down to the riverfront where we'd parked our vehicles. The arena roadies had been cool after the bout, but none of us were gonna risk staying in Dicko's yard overnight.

Jennifer wiped her hands along her bare arms. I draped

my leather jacket over her shoulders, and she clutched it gratefully across her chest.

"I'd say keep it," I told her. "Except I don't think he'd approve." The studs said *Sonnie's Predators* bold across the back.

Her lips ghosted a smile. "Yes. He buys my clothes. He doesn't like me in anything which isn't feminine."

"Thought of leaving him?"

"Sometimes. All the time. But it would only be the face which changed. I am what I am. He's not too bad. Except tonight, and he'll be over that by morning."

"You could come with us." And I could just see me squaring that with the others.

She stopped walking and looked wistfully out over the black river. The M500 stood high above it, a curving ribbon of steel resting on a line of slender buttressed pedestals that sprouted from the centre of the muddy bed. Headlights and brakelights from the traffic formed a permanent pink corona across it, a slipstream of light that blew straight out of the city.

"I'm not like you," Jennifer said. "I envy you, respect you. I'm even a little frightened of you. But I'll never be like you." She smiled slowly. The first real one I'd seen on that face. "Tonight will be enough."

I understood. It hadn't been an accident her turning up at the pub. A single act of defiance. One he would never know about. But that didn't make it any less valid.

I opened the small door at the rear of the twenty-wheeler, and led her inside. Khanivore's life-support pod glowed a moonlight silver in the gloom, ancillary modules making soft gurgling sounds. All the cabinets and machinery clusters were monochrome as we threaded our way past. The tiny office on the other side was quieter. Standby LEDs on the computer terminals shone weakly, illuminating the foldout sofa opposite the desks.

Jennifer stood in the middle of the aisle, and slipped the jacket off her shoulders. Her hands traced a gentle questing line up my ribcage, over my breasts, onto my neck, rising further. She had cool fingertips, long fuchsia nails. Her palms came to rest on my cheeks, fingers splayed between earlobes and forehead.

"You made Dicko so very angry," she murmured huskily. Her breath was warm and soft on my lips.

Pain exploded into my skull.

• • •

My military-grade retinas flicked to low-light mode, banishing shadows as we trooped past the beast's life-support pod in the back of the lorry. The world became a sketch of blue and grey, outlines sharp. I was in a technophile's chapel, floor laced with kilometres of wire and tubing, walls of machinery with little LEDs glowing. Sonnie's breath was quickening when we reached the small compartment at the far end. Randy bitch. Probably where she brought all her one-nighters.

I chucked the jacket and reached for her. She looked like she was on the first night of her honeymoon.

Hands in place, tensed against her temples, and I said: "You made Dicko so very angry." Then I let her have it. Every fingertip sprouted a five-centimetre spike of titanium, punched out by a magpulse. They skewered straight through her skull to penetrate the brain inside.

Sonnie convulsed, tongue protruding, features briefly animated with horrified incomprehension. I jerked my hands away, the metal sliding out cleanly. She slumped to the floor, making a dull thud as she hit. Her whole body quaked for a few seconds then stilled. Dead.

Her head was left propped up at an odd angle against the

base of the sofa she was going to screw me on. Eyes open. Eight puncture wounds dribbling a fair quantity of blood.

"Now do you think it was worth it?" I asked faintly. It needed asking. Her face retained a vestige of that last confused expression, all sad and innocent. "Stupid, dumb pride. And look where it got you. One dive, that's all we wanted. Why don't you people ever learn?"

I shook my hands, wincing, as the spikes slowly telescoped back into their sheaths. They stung like hell, the fingertip skin all torn and bleeding. It would take a week for the rips to heal over, it always did. Price of invisible implants.

"Neat trick," Sonnie said. The syllables were mangled, but the words were quite distinct. "I'd never have guessed you as a *spetsnaz*. Too pretty by far."

One eyeball swivelled to focus on me; the other lolled lifelessly, its white flecked with blood from burst capillaries.

I let out a muted scream. Threat-response training fired an electric charge along my nerves. And I was crouching, leaning forward to throw my weight down, fist forming. Aiming.

Punch.

My right arm pistoned out so fast it was a smear. I caught her perfectly, pulping the fat tissue of the tit, smashing the ribs beneath. Splintered bone fragments were driven inwards, crushing the heart. Her body arched up as if I'd pumped her with a defibrillator charge.

"Not good enough, my cute little *spetsnaz*." A bead of blood seeped out of the corner of her mouth, rolling down her chin.

"No." I rasped it out, not believing what I saw.

"You should have realized," the corpse/zombie said. Its speech had decayed to a gurgling whisper, words formed by sucking down small gulps of air and expelling them gradually. "You of all people should know that hate isn't enough to give me the edge. You should have worked it out."

"What the sweet shit are you?"

"A beastie-baiter, the best there's ever been."

"Tells me nothing."

Sonnie laughed. It was fucking hideous.

"It should do," she burbled. "Think on it. Hate is easy enough to acquire; if all it took was hate then we'd all be winners. Dicko believed that was my edge because he wanted to. Male mentality. Couldn't you smell his hormones fizzing when I told him I'd been raped? That made sense to him. But you've gotta have more than blind hate, *spetsnaz* girl, much more. You've gotta have fear. Real fear. That's what my team gave me: the ability to fear. I didn't get snatched by no gang. I crashed our van. A dumb drifter kid who celebrated a bout win with too much booze. Crunched myself up pretty bad. Jacob and Karran had to shove me in our life-support pod while they patched me up. That's when we figured it out. The edge." Her voice was going, fading out like a night-time radio station.

I bent down, studying her placid face. Her one working eye stared back at me. The blood had stopped dripping from her puncture wounds.

"You're not in there," I said wonderingly.

"No. Not my brain. Just a couple of bioware processors spliced into the top of my spinal column. My brain is elsewhere. Where it can feel hundred-proof fear. Enough fear to make me fight like a berserk demon when I'm threatened. You want to know where my brain is, *spetsnaz* girl? Do you? Look behind you."

A metallic clunk.

I'm twisting fast. Nerves still hyped. Locking into a karate stance, ready for anything. No use. No fucking use at all.

Khanivore is climbing out of its life-support pod.

Timeline

2075 . . . JSKP germinates Eden, a bitek habitat in orbit around Jupiter, with UN Protectorate status.

2077 . . . New Kong asteroid begins FTL stardrive research project.

2085 . . . Eden opened for habitation.

2086 . . . Habitat Pallas germinated in Jupiter orbit.

A Second Chance at Eden

The *Ithilien* decelerated into Jupiter orbit at a constant twentieth of a gee, giving us a spectacular view of the gas giant's battling storm bands as we curved round towards the dark side. Even that's a misnomer, there is no such thing as true darkness down there. Lightning forks whose size could put the Amazon tributary network to shame slashed between oceanic spirals of frozen ammonia. It was awesome, beautiful, and terrifyingly large.

I had to leave the twins by themselves in the observation blister once *Ithilien* circularized its orbit five hundred and fifty thousand kilometres out. It took us another five hours to rendezvous with Eden; not only did we have to match orbits, but we were approaching the habitat from a high inclination as well. Captain Saldana was competent, but it was still five hours of thruster nudges, low-frequency oscillations, and transient bursts of low-gee acceleration. I spent the time strapped into my bunk, popping nausea suppressors, and trying not to analogize between *Ithilien*'s jockeying and a choppy sea. It wouldn't look good arriving at a new posting unable to retain my lunch. Security men are supposed to be unflappable, carved from granite, or some such nonsense anyway.

Our cabin's screen flicked through camera inputs for me. As we were still in the penumbra I got a better view of the approach via electronically amplified images than eyeballing it from the blister.

Eden was a rust-brown cylinder with hemispherical end-caps, eight kilometres long, twenty-eight hundred metres in diameter. But it had only been germinated in 2075, fifteen years ago. I talked to Pieter Zernov during the flight from Earth's O'Neill Halo, he was one of the genetics team who designed the habitats for the Jovian Sky Power corporation, and he said they expected Eden to grow out to a length of eleven kilometres eventually.

It was orientated with the endcaps pointing north/south, so it rolled along its orbit. The polyp shell was smooth, looking more like a manufactured product than anything organic. Biology could never be that neat in nature. The only break in Eden's symmetry I could see were two rings of onion-shaped nodules spaced around the rim of each endcap. Specialist extrusion glands, which spun out organic conductor cables. There were hundreds of them, eighty kilometres long, radiating out from the habitat like the spokes of a bicycle wheel, rotation keeping them perfectly straight. It was an induction system; the cables sliced through Jupiter's titanic magnetosphere to produce all the power Eden needed to run its organs, as well as providing light and heat for the interior.

"Quite something, isn't it?" I said as the habitat expanded to fill the screen.

Jocelyn grunted noncommittally, and shifted round under her bunk's webbing. We hadn't exchanged a hundred words in the last twenty-four hours. Not good. I had hoped the actual sight of the habitat might have lightened the atmosphere a little, raised a spark of interest. Twenty years ago, when we got married, she would have treated this appointment with boundless excitement and enthusiasm. That was a big part of her attraction, a delighted curiosity with the world and all it offered. A lot can happen in twenty years, most of it so gradual you don't notice until it's too late.

I sometimes wonder what traits and foibles I've lost, what

attitude I've woven into my own personality. I like to think I'm the same man, wiser but still good-humoured. Who doesn't?

Eden had a long silver-white counter-rotating docking spindle protruding out from the hub of its northern endcap. *Ithilien* was too large to dock directly; the ship was basically a grid structure, resembling the Eiffel Tower, wrapped round the long cone of the fusion drive, with tanks and cargo pods clinging to the structure as if they were silver barnacles. The life-support capsule was a sixty-metre globe at the prow, sprouting thermal radiator panels like the wings of some robotic dragonfly. In front of that, resting on a custom-built cradle, was the seed for another habitat, Ararat, Jupiter's third; a solid teardrop of biotechnology one hundred metres long, swathed in thermal/particle impact protection foam. Its mass was the reason *Ithilien* was manoeuvring so sluggishly.

Captain Saldana positioned us two kilometres out from the spindle tip, and locked the ship's attitude. A squadron of commuter shuttles and cargo tug craft swarmed over the gulf towards the *Ithilien*. I began pulling our flight bags from the storage lockers; after a minute Jocelyn stirred herself and started helping me.

"It won't be so bad," I said. "These are good people."

Her lips tightened grimly. "They're ungodly people. We should never have come."

"Well, we're here now, let's try and make the most of it, OK? It's only for five years. And you shouldn't prejudge like that."

"The word of the Pope is good enough for me."

Implying it was me at fault, as always. I opened my mouth to reply. But thankfully the twins swam into the cabin, chattering away about the approach phase. As always the façade clicked into place. Nothing wrong. No argument. Mum and Dad are quite happy.

Christ, why do we bother?

• • •

The tubular corridor which ran down the centre of Eden's docking spindle ended in a large chamber just past the rotating pressure seal. It was a large bubble inside the polyp with six mechanical airlock hatches spaced equidistantly around the equator. A screen above one was signalling for *Ithilien* arrivals; and we all glided through it obediently. The tunnel beyond sloped down at quite a steep angle. I floated along it for nearly thirty metres before centrifugal force began to take hold. About a fifteenth of a gee, just enough to allow me a kind of skating walk.

An immigration desk waited for us at the far end. Two Eden police officers in smart green uniforms stood behind it. And I do mean smart: spotless, pressed, fitting perfectly. I held in a smile as the first took my passport and scanned it with her palm-sized PNC wafer. She stiffened slightly, and summoned up a blankly courteous smile. "Chief Parfitt, welcome to Eden, sir."

"Thank you," I glanced at her name disk, "Officer Nyberg."

Jocelyn glared at her, which caused a small frown. That would be all round the division in an hour. The new boss's wife is a pain. Great start.

A funicular railway car was waiting for us once we'd passed the immigration desk. The twins rushed in impatiently. And, finally, I got to see Eden's interior. We sank down below the platform and into a white glare. Nicolette's face hosted a beautiful, incredulous smile as she pressed herself against the glass. For a moment I remembered how her mother had looked, back in the days when she used to smile—I must stop these comparisons.

"Dad, it's supreme," she said.

I put my arm around her and Nathaniel, savouring the moment. Believe me, sharing anything with your teenage children is a rare event. "Yes. Quite something." The twins were fifteen, and they hadn't been too keen on coming to Eden either. Nathaniel didn't want to leave his school back in the Delph company's London arcology. Nicolette had a boy she was under the impression she was destined to marry. But just for that instant the habitat overwhelmed them. Me too.

The cyclorama was tropical parkland, lush emerald grass crinkled with random patches of trees. Silver streams meandered along shallow dales, all of them leading down to the massive circumfluous lake which ringed the base of the southern endcap. Every plant appeared to be in flower. Birds flashed through the air, tiny darts of primary colour.

A town was spread out around the rim of the northern endcap, mostly single-storey houses of metal and plastic moated by elaborately manicured gardens; a few larger civic buildings were dotted among them. I could see plenty of open-top jeeps driving around, and hundreds of bicycles.

The way the landscape rose up like two green tidal waves heading for imminent collision was incredibly disorientating. Unnerving too. Fortunately the axial light-tube blocked the apex, a captured sunbeam threaded between the endcap hubs. Lord knows what seeing people walking around directly above me would have done to my already reeling sense of balance. I was still desperately trying to work out a viable visual reference frame.

Gravity was eighty per cent standard when we reached the foot of the endcap, the funicular car sliding down into a plaza. A welcoming committee was waiting for us on the platform; three people and five servitor chimps.

Michael Zimmels, the man I was replacing, stepped forward and shook my hand. "Glad to meet you, Harvey. I've scheduled a two-hour briefing to bring you up to date. Sorry to rush you, but I'm leaving on the *Ithilien* as soon as it's been loaded with He^3. The tug crews here, they don't waste time." He turned to Jocelyn and the twins. "Mrs Parfitt, hope you don't mind me stealing your husband away like this, but I've arranged for Officer Coogan to show you to your quarters. It's a nice little house. Sally Ann should have finished packing our stuff by now, so you can move in straight away. She'll show you where everything is and how it works." He beckoned one of the officers standing behind him.

Officer Coogan was in his late twenties, wearing another of those immaculate green uniforms. "Mrs Parfitt, if you'd like to give your flight bags to the chimps, they'll carry them for you."

Nicolette and Nathaniel were giggling as they handed their flight bags over. The servitor chimps were obviously genetically adapted; they stood nearly one metre fifty, without any of the rubber sack paunchiness of the pure genotype primates cowering in what was left of Earth's rain forests. And the quiet, attentive way they stood waiting made it seem almost as though they had achieved sentience.

Jocelyn clutched her flight bag closer to her as one of the chimps extended an arm. Coogan gave her a slightly condescending smile. "It's quite all right, Mrs Parfitt, they're completely under control."

"Come on, Mum," Nathaniel said. "They look dead cute." He was stroking the one which had taken his flight bag, even though it never showed the slightest awareness of his touch.

"I'll carry my own bag, thank you," Jocelyn said.

Coogan gathered himself, obviously ready to launch into a reassurance speech, then decided chiding his new boss's wife the minute she arrived wasn't good policy. "Of course. Er, the house is this way." He started off across the plaza, the twins plying him with questions. After a moment Jocelyn followed.

"Not used to servitors, your wife?" Michael Zimmels asked pleasantly.

"I'm afraid she took the Pope's decree about affinity to heart," I told him.

"I thought that just referred to humans who had the affinity gene splice?"

I shrugged.

• • • •

The Chief of Police's office occupied a corner of the two-storey station building. For all that it was a government-issue room with government-issue furniture, it gave me an excellent view down the habitat.

"You got lucky with this assignment," Michael Zimmels told me as soon as the door closed behind us. "It's every policeman's dream posting. There's virtually nothing to do."

Strictly speaking I'm corporate security these days, not a policeman. But the Delph company is one of the major partners in the Jovian Sky Power corporation which founded Eden. Basically the habitat is a dormitory town for the He^3 mining operation and its associated manufacturing support stations. But even JSKP workers are entitled to a degree of civilian government; so Eden is legally a UN protectorate state, with an elected town council and independent judiciary. On paper, anyway. The reality is that it's a corporate state right down the line; all the appointees for principal civil posts tend to be JSKP personnel on sabbaticals. Like me.

"There has to be a catch."

Zimmels grinned. "Depends how you look at it. The habitat personality can observe ninety-nine per cent of the interior. The interior polyp surface is suffused with clusters of specialized sensitive cells; they can pick up electromagnetic waves, the full optical spectrum along with infrared and ultraviolet; they can sense temperature and magnetic fields, there are olfactory cells, even pressure-sensitive cells to pick up anything you say. All of which means nobody does or says anything that the habitat doesn't know about; not cheating on your partner, stealing supplies, or beating up your boss after you get stinking drunk. It sees all, it knows all. No need for police on the beat, or worrying about gathering sufficient evidence."

"Ye gods," I glanced about, instinctively guilty. "You said ninety-nine per cent? Where is the missing one per cent?"

"Offices like this, on buildings which have a second floor, where there's no polyp and no servitors. But even so the habitat can see in through the windows. Effectively, the coverage is total. Besides which, this is a company town, we don't have unemployment or a criminal underclass. Making sure the end-of-shift drunks get home OK is this department's prime activity."

"Wonderful," I grunted. "Can I talk to this personality?"

Zimmels gave his desktop terminal a code. "It's fully interfaced with the datanet, but you can communicate via affinity. In fact, given your status, you'll have to use affinity. That way you don't just talk, you can hook into its sensorium as well, the greatest virtual-reality trip you'll ever experience. And of course, all the other senior executives have affinity symbiont implants—hell, ninety per cent of the population is affinity capable. We use it to confer the whole time, it's a heck of a lot simpler than teleconferencing. And it's the main reason the habitat administration operates so smoothly. I'm surprised the company didn't give you a neuron symbiont implant before you left Earth, you just can't function effectively without one up here."

"I told them I'd wait until I got here," I said, which was almost the truth.

The terminal chimed melodically, then spoke in a rich male euphonic. "Good afternoon, Chief Parfitt, welcome to Jupiter. I am looking forward to working with you, and hope our relationship will be a rewarding one."

"You're the habitat personality?" I asked.

"I am Eden, yes."

"Chief Zimmels tells me you can perceive the entire interior."

"That is correct. Both interior and exterior environments are accessible to me on a permanent basis."

"What are my family doing?"

"Your children are examining a tortoise they have found in the garden of your new house. Your wife is talking to Mrs Zimmels, they are in the kitchen."

Michael Zimmels raised his eyebrows in amusement. "Sally Ann's cutting her in on the local gossip."

"You can see them, too?"

"Hear and see. Hell, it's boring; Sally Ann's a sponge for that kind of thing. She thinks I don't look after my advancement prospects, so she plays the corporate social ladder game on my behalf."

"Do you show anybody anything they ask for?" I asked.

"No," Eden replied. "The population are entitled to their privacy. However, legitimate Police Department observation requests override individual rights."

"It sounds infallible," I said. "I can't go wrong."

"Don't you believe it," Zimmels retorted knowingly. "I've just given you the good news so far. You're not just responsible for Eden, the entire JSKP operation in Jupiter orbit comes under your jurisdiction. That means a lot of external work for your squads; the industrial stations, the refineries, inter-orbit ships; we even have a large survey team on Callisto right now."

"I see."

"But your biggest headache is going to be Boston."

"I don't remember that name in any of my preliminary briefings."

"You wouldn't." He produced a bubble cube, and handed it over to me. "This contains my report, and most of it's unofficial. Supposition, plus what I've managed to pick up from various sources. Boston is a group of enthusiasts—radicals, revolutionaries, whatever you want to call them—who want Eden to declare independence, hence the name. They're quite well organized, too; several of their leading lights are JSKP executives, mostly those on the technical and scientific side."

"Independence from the UN?"

"The UN and the JSKP, they want to take over the whole Jupiter enterprise; they think they can create some kind of technological paradise out here, free of interference from Earth's grubby politicians and conservative companies. The old High Frontier dream. Your problem is that engaging in free political debate isn't a crime. Technically, as a UN policeman, you have to uphold their right to do so. But as a JSKP employee, just imagine how the board back on Earth will feel if Eden, Pallas, and Ararat make that declaration of independence, and the new citizens assume control of the He³ mining operation while you're here charged with looking after the corporation's interests."

• • •

The PNC wafer's bleeping woke me. I struggled to orientate myself. Strange bedroom. Grey geometric shadows at all angles. A motion which nagged away just below conscious awareness.

Jocelyn shifted around beside me, twisting the duvet. Also unusual, but the Zimmels had used a double bed. Apparently it would take a couple of days to requisition two singles.

My questing hand found the PNC wafer on the bedside dresser. I prayed I'd programmed it for no visual pick-up before I went to bed. "Call acknowledged. Chief Parfitt here," I said blearily.

The wafer hazed over with a moiré rainbow which shivered until a face came into focus. "Rolf Kümmel, sir. Sorry to wake you so early."

Detective Lieutenant Kümmel was my deputy, we'd been introduced briefly yesterday. Thirty-two and already well up the seniority ladder. A conscientious careerist, was my first impression. "What is it, Rolf?"

"We have a major crime incident inside the habitat, sir."

"What incident?"

"Somebody's been killed. Penny Maowkavitz, the JSKP Genetics Division director."

"Killed by what?"

"A bullet, sir. She was shot through the head."

"Fuck. Where?"

"The north end of the Lincoln lake."

"Doesn't mean anything. Send a driver to pick me up, I'll be there as soon as I can."

"Driver's on her way, sir."

"Good man. Wafer off."

• • •

It was Shannon Kershaw who drove the jeep which picked me up, one of the station staff I'd met the previous afternoon on my lightning familiarization tour, a programming expert. A twenty-eight-year-old with flaming red hair pleated in elaborate spirals; grinning challengingly as Zimmels introduced us. Someone who knew her speciality made her invaluable, giving her a degree of immunity from the usual sharpshooting of office politics. This morning she was subdued, uniform tunic undone, hair wound into a simple tight bun.

The axial light-tube was a silver strand glimpsed through frail cloud braids high above, slightly brighter than a full Earth moon. Its light was sufficient for her to steer the jeep

down a track through a small forest without using the headlights. "Not good," she muttered. "This is really going to stir
people up. We all sort of regarded Eden as . . . I don't know.
Pure."

I was studying the display my PNC wafer was running, a
program correlating previous crime incident files with
Penny Maowkavitz, looking for any connection. So far a
complete blank. "There's never been a murder up here before, has there?"

"No. There couldn't be, really; not with the habitat personality watching us the whole time. You know, it's pretty
shaken up by this."

"The personality is upset?" I enquired sceptically.

She shot me a glance. "Of course it is. It's sentient, and
Penny Maowkavitz was about the closest thing to a parent it
could ever have."

"Feelings," I said wonderingly. "That must be one very
sophisticated Turing AI program."

"The habitat isn't an AI. It's alive, it's conscious. A living
entity. You'll understand once you receive your neuron symbiont implant."

Great, now I was driving round inside a piece of neurotic
coral. "I'm sure I will."

The trees gave way to a swath of meadowland surrounding a small lake. A rank of jeeps were drawn up near the
shoreline; several had red and blue strobes flashing on top,
casting transient stipples across the black water. Shannon
parked next to an ambulance, and we walked over to the
group of people clustered round the body.

Penny Maowkavitz was sprawled on the grey shingle four
metres from the water. She was wearing a long dark-beige
suede jacket over a sky-blue blouse, heavy black cotton
trousers, and sturdy ankle boots. Her limbs were askew, the
skin of her hands very pale. I couldn't tell how old she was,
principally because half of her head was missing. What was

left of the skull sprouted a few wisps of fine silver hair. A wig of short-cropped dark-blonde hair lay a couple of metres away, stained almost completely crimson. A wide ribbon of gore and blood was splashed over the shingle between it and the corpse. In the jejune light it looked virtually black.

Shannon grunted, and turned away fast.

I'd seen worse in my time, a lot worse. But Shannon was right about one thing, it didn't belong here, not amongst the habitat's tranquillity.

"When did it happen?" I asked.

"Just over half an hour ago," Rolf Kümmel said. "I got out here with a couple of officers as soon as Eden told us."

"The personality saw it happen?"

"Yes, sir."

"Who did it?"

Rolf grimaced, and pointed at a servitor chimp standing passively a little way off. A couple of uniformed officers stood on either side of it. "That did, sir."

"Christ. Are you sure?"

"We've all accessed the personality's local visual memory to confirm it, sir," he said in a slightly aggrieved tone. "But the chimp was still holding the pistol when we arrived. Eden locked its muscles as soon as the shot was fired."

"So who ordered it to fire the pistol?"

"We don't know."

"You mean the chimp doesn't remember?"

"No."

"So who gave it the pistol?"

"It was in a flight bag, which was left on a polystone outcrop just along the shore from here."

"And what about Eden, does it remember who left the bag there?"

Rolf and some of the others were beginning to look resentful. Lumbered with a dunderhead primitive for a boss, blundering about asking the obvious and not understanding a word spoken. I was beginning to feel isolated, wondering what they were saying to each other via affinity. One or two of them had facial expressions which were changing minutely, visible signs of silent conversation. Did they know they were giving themselves away like that?

My PNC wafer bleeped, and I pulled it out of my jacket pocket. "Chief Parfitt, this is Eden. I'm sorry, but I have no recollection of who placed the bag on the stone. It has been there for three days, which exceeds the extent of my short-term memory."

"OK, thanks." I glanced round the expectant faces. "First thing, do we know for sure this is Penny Maowkavitz?"

"Absolutely," a woman said. She was in her late forties, half a head shorter than everyone else, with dark cinnamon skin. I got the impression she was more weary than alarmed by the murder. "That's Penny, all right."

"And you are?"

"Corrine Arbury, I'm Penny's doctor." She nudged the corpse with her toe. "But if you want proof, turn her over."

I looked at Rolf. "Have you taken the *in situ* videos?"

"Yes, sir."

"OK, turn her over."

After a moment of silence, my police officers gallantly shuffled to one side and let the two ambulance paramedics ease the corpse onto its back. I realized the light was changing, the mock-silver moonlight deepening to a flaming tangerine. Dr Arbury knelt down as the artificial dawn blossomed all around. She tugged the blue blouse out of the waistband. Penny Maowkavitz was wearing a broad green nylon strap around her abdomen, it held a couple of white plastic boxes tight against her belly.

"These are the vector regulators I supplied," Corrine Arbury said. "I was treating Penny for cancer. It's her all right."

"Video her like this, then take her to the morgue, please," I said. "I don't suppose we'll need an autopsy for cause of death."

"Hardly," Corrine Arburry said flatly as she rose up.

"Fine, but I would like some tests run to establish she was alive up until the moment she was shot. I would also like the bullet itself. Eden, do you know where that is?"

"No, I'm sorry, it must be buried in the soil. But I can give you a rough estimate based on the trajectory and velocity."

"Rolf, seal off the area, we need to do that anyway, but I want it searched thoroughly. Have you taken the pistol from the chimp?"

"Yes, sir."

"Do we have a Ballistics Division?"

"Not really. But some of the company engineering labs should be able to run the appropriate tests for us."

"OK, get it organized." I glanced at the chimp. It hadn't moved, big black eyes staring mournfully. "And I want that thing locked up in the station's jail."

Rolf turned a snort into a cough. "Yes, sir."

"Presumably we do have an expert on servitor neurology and psychology in Eden?" I asked patiently.

"Yes."

"Good. Then I'd like him to examine the chimp, and maybe try and recover the memory of who gave it the order to shoot Maowkavitz. Until then, the chimp is to be isolated, understood?"

He nodded grimly.

Corrine Arburry was smiling at Rolf's discomfort. A sly expression which I thought contained a hint of approval, too.

"You ought to consider how the gun was brought inside the habitat in the first place," she said. "And where it's been stored since. If it had ever been taken out of that flight bag the personality should have perceived it and alerted the police straight away. It ought to know who the bag belonged to, as well. But it doesn't."

"Was the pistol a police weapon?" I asked.

"No," Rolf said. "It's some kind of revolver, very primitive."

"OK, run a make, track down the serial number. You know the procedure, whatever you can find on it."

• • •

The start of the working day found me in the Governor's office. Our official introductory meeting, what should have been a cheery getting-to-know-you session, and I had to report the habitat's first ever murder to him. I tried to tell myself the day couldn't get worse. But I lacked faith.

The axial light-tube had resumed its usual blaze, turning the habitat cavern into a solid fantasy ideal of tropical wilderness. I did my best to ignore the view as Fasholé Nocord waved me into a seat before his antique wooden desk.

Eden's governor was in his mid-fifties, with a frame and vigour which suggested considerable genetic adaptation. I've grown adept at recognizing the signs over the years; for a start they all tend to be well educated, because even now it's really only the wealthy who can afford such treatments for their offspring. And health is paramount for them, the treatments always focus on boosting their immunology system, improving organ efficiency, dozens of subtle metabolic enhancements. They possess a presence, almost like a witch's *glamour*; I suppose knowing they're not going to fall prey to disease and illness, that they'll almost certainly see out a century, gives them an impeccable self-confidence. Given their bearing, cosmetic adaptation is almost an irrelevance, certainly it's not as widespread. But in Fasholé Nocord's case I suspected an exception. His skin was just too black, the classically noble face too chiselled.

"Any progress?" he asked straight away.

"It's only been a couple of hours. I've got my officers working on various aspects; but they aren't used to this type of investigation. Come to that, there's never been a large-scale police investigation in Eden before. With the habitat's all-over sensory perception there's been no need until today."

"How could it happen?"

"You tell me. I'm not an expert on this place yet."

"Get a symbiont implant. Today. I don't know what the company was thinking of, sending you out here without one."

"Yes, sir."

His lips twitched into a rueful grin. "All right, Harvey, don't go all formal on me. If ever I needed anyone on my side, then it's you. The timing of this whole thing stinks."

"Sir?"

He leant forward over the desk, hands clasped earnestly. "I suppose you realize ninety per cent of the population suspect I have something to do with Penny's murder?"

"No," I said cautiously. "Nobody's told me that."

"Figures," he muttered. "Did Michael brief you on Boston?"

"Yes, the salient points; I have a bubble cube full of files which he compiled, but I haven't got round to accessing any of them yet."

"Well, when you do, you'll find that Penny Maowkavitz was Boston's principal organizer."

"Oh, Christ."

"Yeah. And I'm the man responsible for ensuring Eden stays firmly locked in to the JSKP's domain."

I remembered his file; Nocord was a vice-president (on sabbatical) from McDonnell Electric, one of the JSKP's parent companies. Strictly managerial and administration track, not one of the aspiring dreamers, someone the board could trust implicitly.

"If we can confirm where you were prior to the murder, you should be in the clear," I said. "I'll have one of my officers take a statement and correlate it with Eden's memory of your movements. Shouldn't be a problem."

"It would never be me personally, anyway, not even as part of a planning team. JSKP would use a covert agent."

"But clearing your name quickly would help quell any rumours." I paused. "Are you telling me JSKP takes Boston seriously enough to bring covert operatives into this situation?"

"I don't know. I mean that, I'm not holding out on you. As far as I know the board is relying on you and me to prevent things from getting out of control up here. We know you're dependable," he added, almost in apology.

I guess he'd studied my file as closely as I'd gone over his. It didn't particularly bother me. Anyone who does access my history isn't going to find any earthshaker revelations. I used to be a policeman, I went into the London force straight from university. With thirty-five million people crammed together in the Greater London area, and four million of them unemployed, policing is a very secure career, we were in permanent demand. I was good at it, I made detective in eight years. Then my third case was working as part of a team investigating corruption charges in the London Regional Federal Commission. We ran down over a dozen senior politicians and civil servants receiving payola for awarding contracts to various companies. Some of the companies were large and well known, and two of the politicians were sitting in the Greater Federal Europe congress. Quite a sensation, we were given hours of prime facetime on the newscable bulletins.

The judge and the Metropolitan Police Commander congratulated us in front of the cameras, handshakes and smiles all round. But in the months which followed none of my colleagues who went up before promotion boards ever seemed successful. We got crappy assignments. We pulled the night shifts for weeks at a time. Overtime was denied. Expenses were queried. Call me cynical, I quit and went into corporate security. Companies regard employee loyalty and honesty as commendable traits—below board level anyway.

"I like to think I am, yes," I told the Governor. "But if you're expecting trouble soon, just remember I haven't had time to build any personal loyalties with my officers. What did you mean that the murder's timing stinks?"

"It looks suspicious, that's all. The company sends a new police chief who isn't even affinity capable; and, *wham*, Penny is murdered the day after you arrive. Then there's the cloudscoop lowering operation in two days' time. If it's successful, He^3 extraction will become simpler by orders of magnitude, decreasing Jupiter's technological dependence on Earth. And the *Ithilien* delivered the Ararat seed, another habitat, safeguarding the population if we do ever have a major environmental failure in Eden or Pallas. It's a good time for Boston to try and break free. Ergo, killing the leader is an obvious option."

"I'll bear it in mind. Do you have any ideas who might have killed her?"

Fasholé Nocord sat back in his chair and grinned broadly. "Real police are never off the case, eh?"

I returned a blank smile. "You have been emphasizing your own innocence with a great deal of eloquence."

It wasn't quite the response he was looking for. The professional grin faltered. "No, I don't have any idea. But I will tell you Penny Maowkavitz was not an easy person to work with; if pushed I'd describe her as stereotypically brash. She was always convinced everything she did was right. People who didn't agree with her were more or less ignored. Her brilliance allowed her to get away with it, of course; she was vital to the initial design concept of the habitats."

"She had her own biotechnology company, didn't she?"

"That's right, she founded Pacific Nugene; it's basically a softsplice house, specializing in research and design work rather than production. Penny preferred to deal in concepts; she refined the organisms until they were viable, then licensed out the genome to the big boys for actual manufacture and distribution. She was the first geneticist JSKP approached when it became obvious we needed a large dormitory station in Jupiter orbit. Pacific Nugene was pioneering a microbe which could digest asteroid rock; initially the board wanted to use those microbes to hollow out a biosphere cavern in one of the larger ring particles. It would be a lot cheaper than shipping mining teams and all their equipment out here. Penny proposed they use a living polyp habitat instead, and Pacific Nugene became a minor partner in JSKP. She was a board member herself up until five years ago; even after she gave up her seat she retained a non-executive position as senior biotechnology adviser."

"Five years ago?" I took a guess. "That would be when Boston formed, would it?"

"Yes," he sighed. "Let me tell you, the JSKP board went ballistic. They considered Penny's involvement as a total betrayal. Nothing they could do about it, of course, she was essential to develop the next generation of habitats. Eden is really only a prototype."

"I see. Well, thanks for filling me in on the basics. And if you do remember anything relevant . . ."

"Eden will remember anyone she ever argued with." He shrugged, his hands splaying wide. "You really will have to get a symbiont implant."

"Right."

I drove myself back to the station, sticking to a steady twenty kilometres an hour. The main road of naked polyp which ran through the centre of the town was clogged with bicycle traffic.

Rolf Kümmel had set up an incident room on the ground floor. I didn't even have to tell him; like me he'd been a policeman at one time, four years in a Munich arcology. I walked in to a quiet bustle of activity. And I do mean quiet, I could only hear a few excitable murmurs above the whirr of the air conditioning. It was eerie. Uniformed officers moved round constantly between the desks, carrying fat files and cases of bubble cubes; maintenance techs were still installing computer terminals on some desks, their chimps standing to attention beside them, holding toolboxes and various electronic test rigs. Seven shirtsleeved junior detectives were loading data into working terminals under Shannon Kershaw's direction. A big hologram screen on the rear wall displayed a map of Eden's parkland. Two narrow lines—one red, one blue—were snaking across the countryside like newborn neon streams. They both originated at the Lincoln lake, which was about a kilometre south of town.

Rolf was standing in front of the screen, hands on hips, watching attentively as the lines lengthened.

"Is that showing Penny Maowkavitz's movements?" I enquired.

"Yes, sir," Rolf said. "She's the blue line. And the servitor chimp is red. Eden is interfaced with the computer; this is a raw memory plot downloaded straight from its neural strata. It should be able to tell us everyone who came near the servitor in the last thirty hours."

"Why thirty hours?"

"That's the neural strata's short-term memory capacity."

"Right." I was feeling redundant and unappreciated again. "What was the servitor chimp's assigned task?"

"It was allotted to habitat botanical maintenance, covering a square area roughly two hundred and fifty metres to a side, with the lake as one border. It pruned trees, tended plants, that kind of thing."

I watched the red line lengthening, a child's crayon-squiggle keeping within the boundary of its designated area. "How often does it . . . go back to base?"

"The servitor chimps are given full physiological checks every six months in the veterinary centre. The ones allotted to domestic duties have a communal wash-house in town where they go to eat, and keep themselves clean. But one like this . . . it wouldn't leave its area unless it was ordered to. They eat the fruit, their crap is good fertilizer. If they get very muddy they'll wash it off in a stream. They even sleep out there."

I gave the screen a thoughtful look. "Did Penny Maowkavitz take a walk through the habitat parkland very often?"

He rewarded me a grudgingly respectful glance. "Yes, sir. Every morning. It was a kind of an unofficial inspection tour, she liked to see how Eden was progressing; and Davis Caldarola said she used the solitude to think about her projects. She spent anything up to a couple of hours rambling round each day."

"She walked specifically through this area around Lincoln lake?"

His eyelids closed in a long blink. A green circle started flashing over one of the houses on the parkland edge of the town. "That's her house; as you can see it's in the residential zone closest to Lincoln lake. So she would probably walk through this particular chimp's area most mornings."

"Definitely not a suicide, then; the chimp was waiting for her."

"Looks that way. It wasn't a random killing, either. I did think the murderer might have simply told the chimp to shoot the first person it saw, but that's pretty flimsy. Whoever primed that chimp put a lot of preparation into this. If all you want to do is kill someone, there are much easier ways."

"Yes." I gave an approving nod. "Good thinking. Who's Davis Caldarola?"

"Maowkavitz's lover."

"He knows?"

"Yes, oir."

The "of course" was missing from his voice, but not his tone. "Don't worry, Rolf, I'm getting my symbiont implant this afternoon."

He struggled against a grin.

"So what else have we come up with since this morning?"

Rolf beckoned Shannon Kershaw over. "The gun," he said. "We handed it over to a team from the Cybernetics Division's precision engineering laboratory. They say it's a perfect replica of a Colt .45 single-action revolver."

"A replica?"

"It's only the pistol's physical template which matches an original; the materials are wrong," Shannon said. "Whoever made it used boron-reinforced single-crystal titanium for the barrel, and berylluminium for the mechanism, even the grip was moulded from monomolecule silicon. That was one very expensive pistol."

"Monomolecule silicon?" I mused. "That can only be produced in microgee extruders, right?"

"Yes, sir." She was becoming animated. "There are a couple of industrial stations outside Eden with the necessary production facilities. I think the pistol was manufactured and assembled in the habitat itself. Our Cybernetics Division factories could produce the individual components without any trouble; and all the exotic materials are available as well. I checked."

"It would go a long way to explaining why Eden never saw the pistol before," Rolf said. "Separately, the components wouldn't register as anything suspicious. Then after manufacture they could have been put together in one of the areas where the habitat personality doesn't have total perception coverage. I'd say that was easier than trying to smuggle one through our customs inspection; we're pretty thorough."

I turned to Shannon. "So we need a list of everyone authorized to use the cyberfactories, and out of that we need those qualified or capable of running up the Colt's components without anyone else realizing or querying what they were doing."

"I'm on it."

"Any other angles?"

"Nothing yet," Rolf said.

"What about a specialist to examine the chimp?"

"Hoi Yin was recommended by the habitat Servitor Department, she's a neuropsychology expert. She said she'll come in to study it this afternoon. I'll brief her myself."

"But you must be very busy, Rolf," Shannon said silkily. "I can easily spare the time to escort her."

"I said I'd do it," he said stiffly.

"Are you quite sure?"

"OK," I told them. "That'll do." I clapped my hands, and raised one arm until I had everyone's attention. "Good morning, people. As you ought to know by now, I'm Chief Harvey Parfitt, your new boss. I wish we could have all had a better introduction, Christ knows I didn't want to start with this kind of pep talk. However . . . there are a lot of rumours floating round Eden concerning Penny Maowkavitz's murder. Please remember that they are just that, rumours. More than anyone, we know how few facts have been established. And I expect police officers under my command to concentrate on facts. It's important for the whole community that we solve this murder, preferably with some speed; the habitat residents must have confidence in us, and we simply cannot allow this murderer to walk around free, perhaps to kill again.

"As to the investigation itself; as Eden's personality seems unable to assist us at this point, our priority is to search back through Penny Maowkavitz's life, both private and professional, to establish some kind of motive for the murder. I want a complete profile assembled on her physical movements going back initially for a week, after that we'll see if it needs extending any further. I want to know where she went, who she met, what she talked about. On top of that I want any long-time antagonisms and enemies listed. Draw up a list of friends and colleagues to interview. Remember, no detail is too trivial. The reason for her death is out there somewhere." I looked round the dutifully attentive faces. "Can anyone think of a line of inquiry I've missed?"

One of the uniformed officers raised her hand.

"Yes, Nyberg."

If she was embarrassed that I remembered her name, she didn't show it. "Penny Maowkavitz was rich. Someone must inherit Pacific Nugene."

"Good point." I'd wondered if they'd mention that. Once you can get them questioning together, working as a team in your presence, you've won half the battle for acceptance. "Shannon, get a copy of Maowkavitz's will from her lawyer, please. Anything else? No. Good. I'll leave you to get on with it. Rolf will hand out individual assignments; including someone to take a statement from the Governor about his whereabouts over the last few days. Apparently we have one or two conspiracy theorists to placate." Several knowing grins flashed round the room. Rolf let out a dismayed groan.

I let them see my own amusement, then signalled Shannon over. "It might be a good idea to check out that theory of yours about the pistol being manufactured up here," I told her. "Get on to the Cybernetics Division, ask them to put a Colt .45 pistol together using exactly the same materials as the murder weapon was built from. That way, we'll see if it is physically possible, and if so what the assembly entails."

She agreed with a degree of eagerness, and hurried back to her desk.

I would have liked to hang around, but harassing the team as they got to work wasn't good policy. At this stage the investigation was the pure drudgery of data acquisition. To assemble a jigsaw, you first have to have the pieces—old Parfitt proverb.

I went upstairs to my office, and started in on routine administration datawork. What joy.

• • •

The hospital was a third of the way round the town from the police station, a broad three-storey ring with a central courtyard. With its copper-mirror glass and mock-marble façade it looked the most substantial building in the habitat.

I was ushered into Corrine Arburry's office just after two o'clock. It was nothing like as stark as mine, with big potted ferns and a colony of large purple-coloured lizards romping round inside a glass case in the corner. According to her file, Corrine had been in Eden for six years, almost since the habitat was opened for residency.

"And how are you settling in?" she asked wryly.

"Well, they haven't gone on strike yet."

"That's something."

"What were they saying about me out at the lake?"

"No chance." She wagged a finger. "Doctor/patient confidentiality."

"OK, what were the pathology findings?"

"Penny died from the bullet. Her blood chemistry was normal . . . well, there was nothing in it apart from the prescribed viral vectors and a mild painkiller. She hadn't been drugged; and as far as I can tell there was no disabling blow to the head prior to the shooting, certainly no visible bruising on what was left of her skull. I think the personality memory of her death is perfectly accurate. She walked out to the lake, and the chimp shot her."

"Thanks. Now what can you tell me about Penny Maowkavitz herself? So far all I've heard is that she could be a prickly character."

Corrine's face puckered up. "True enough; basically, Penny was a complete pain. Back at the university hospital where I trained we always used to say doctors make the worst patients. Wrong. Geneticists make the worst patients."

"You didn't like her?"

"I didn't say that. And you should be nicer to someone who's scheduled to cut your skull open in an hour. Penny was just naturally difficult, one of the highly strung types. It upset a lot of people."

"But not you?"

"Doctors are used to the whole spectrum of human behaviour. We see it all. I was quite firm with her, she respected that. She did argue about aspects of her treatment. But radiation sickness is my field. And a lot of what she said was due to fear."

"You're talking about her cancer treatment?"

"That's right."

"How bad was it?"

Corrine dropped her gaze. "Terminal. Penny had at most another three months to live. And that last month would have been very rough on her, even with our medical technology."

"Christ."

"Are you sure it wasn't a suicide?" she asked kindly. "I know what it looked like, but—"

"We did consider that, but the circumstances weigh against it." I thought of the chimp, the bag, putting the pistol together in stealthy increments, the sheer amount of effort involved. "No, it was too elaborate. That was a murder. Besides, surely Penny Maowkavitz would have had plenty of available options to kill herself that were a damn sight cleaner than this?"

"I would have thought so, yes. She had a whole laboratory full of methods to choose from. Although a bullet through the brain is one of the quickest methods I know. Penny was a very clever person, maybe she didn't want any time for reflection between an injection and losing consciousness."

"Had she talked about suicide?"

"No, not to me; and normally I'd say she wasn't the suicide type. But she would know exactly what that last month was going to be like. You know, I've found myself thinking about it quite a lot recently; if I knew that was going to happen to me, I'd probably do something about it before I lost my faculties. Wouldn't you?"

It wasn't something I liked to think about. Christ. Even death from old age is something we manage to deny for most of our lives. Always, you'll be the marvel who lives to a hundred and fifty, the new Methuselah. "Probably," I grunted sourly. "Who knew about her illness?"

"I'd say just about everyone. The whole habitat had heard about her accident."

I sighed. "Everyone but me."

"Oh, dear." Corrine grinned impetuously. "Penny was exposed to a lethal radiation dose eight months ago. She was on a review trip to Pallas, that's the second habitat. It was germinated four years ago, and trails Eden's orbit by a thousand kilometres. Her division is responsible for overseeing the growth phase. And Penny takes her duty very seriously. She was EVA inspecting the outer shell when we had a massive ion flux. The magnetosphere does that occasionally, and it's completely unpredictable. Jupiter orbit is a radiative hell anyway; the suits which the crews here wear look more like deep-sea diving rigs than the kind of fabric pressure envelopes they use in the O'Neill Halo. But even their shielding couldn't protect Penny against that level of energy." She leant back in the chair, shaking her head slowly. "That's one of the reasons I was chosen for this post, with my speciality. Those crews take a terrible risk going outside. They all have their sperm and ova frozen before they come here so they don't jeopardize their children. Anyway . . . the spaceship crew got her back here within two hours. Unfortunately there wasn't anything I could do, not in the long term. She was here in hospital for a fortnight, we flushed her blood seven times. But the radiation penetrated every cell, it was as if she'd stood in front of a strategic-defence X-ray laser. Her DNA was completely wrecked, blasted apart. The mutation—" Breath whistled painfully out of Corrine's mouth. "It was beyond even our gene therapy techniques to rectify. We did what we could, but it was basically just making her last months as easy as possible while the tumours started to grow. She knew it, we knew it."

"Three months at the most," I said numbly.

"Yes."

"And knowing that, somebody still went ahead and murdered her. It makes no sense at all."

"It made a lot of sense to somebody." The voice was challenging.

I fixed Corrine with a level gaze. "I didn't think you'd give me a hard time over being a company man."

"I won't. But I know people who will."

"Who?"

Her grin had returned. "Don't tell me Zimmels didn't leave you a bubble cube full of names."

My turn to grin. "He did. What nobody has told me is how widespread Boston's support is."

"Not as much as they'd like. Not as little as JSKP would like."

"Very neat, Doctor. You should go into politics."

"There's no need to be obscene."

I stood up and walked over to her window, looking down into the small courtyard at the centre of the hospital. There was an ornate pond in the middle which had a tiny fountain playing in it; big orange fish glided about below the lily pads. "If the company did send a covert agent up here to kill Maowkavitz, he or she would have to be very biotechnology literate to circumvent the habitat personality's observation. I mean, I couldn't do it. I don't even understand how it was done, nor do most of my officers."

"I see what you mean. It would have to be someone who's been up here before."

"Right. Someone who understands the habitat surveillance parameters perfectly, and who's one hundred per cent loyal to JSKP."

"My God, you're talking about Zimmels."

I smiled down at the fish. "You have to admit, he's a perfect suspect."

"And would you have him arrested if he is guilty?"

"Oh, yes. JSKP can have me fired, but they can't deflect me."

"Very commendable."

I turned back to find her giving me a heartily bemused stare. "But it's a little too early to be making allegations like that; I'll wait until I have more data."

"Glad to hear it," she muttered. "I suppose you've also considered it could have been a mercy killing by some sympathetic bleeding-heart medical practitioner, one who was intimate with Penny's circumstances."

I laughed. "Top of my list."

•   •   •

Before I went for the implant, they dressed me in a green surgical smock, and shaved off a three-centimetre circle of hair at the base of my skull. The operating theatre resembled a dentist's surgery. A big hydraulic chair at the centre of a horseshoe of medical consoles and instrument waldos. The major difference was the chair's headrest, which was a complicated arrangement of metal bands and adjustable pads. The sight triggered a cascade of unpleasant memories, newscable images of the more brutal regimes back on Earth. What one party states did to their opposition members.

"Nothing to worry about," Corrine said breezily, when the sight of it slowed my walk. "I've done this operation about five hundred times now."

The nurse smiled and guided me into the chair. I don't think she was more than a couple of years older than Nicolette. Should they really be using teenagers to assist with delicate brain surgery on senior staff?

Straps around my arms, straps around my legs; a big strap, like a corset, around my chest, holding me tight. Then they started immobilizing my head.

"How many survived?" I asked.

"All of them. Come on, Harvey, it's basically just an injection."

"I hate needles."

The nurse giggled.

"Bloody hell," Corrine grunted. "Men! Women never make this fuss."

I swallowed my immediate short-and-to-the-point comment. "Will I be able to use the affinity bond straight away?"

"No. What I'm going to do this afternoon is insert a cluster of neuron symbiont buds into your medulla oblongata. They take a day or so to infiltrate your axons and develop into operational grafts."

"Wonderful." Sickly grey fungal spores grubbing round my cells, sending out slender yellow roots to penetrate the delicate membrane walls. Feeding off me.

Corrine and the nurse finished fixing my head in place

and stood back. The chair slowly tilted forwards until I was inclined at forty-five degrees, staring at the floor. I heard a hissing sound; something cold touched the patch of shaved skin. "Ouch."

"Harvey, that's the anaesthetic spray," Corrine exclaimed with some asperity.

"Sorry."

"Once the symbionts are functioning you'll need proper training to use them. It doesn't take more than a few hours. I'll book your appointment with one of our tutors."

"Thanks. Exactly how many people up here are affinity capable?"

She was busy switching on various equipment modules. Out of the corner of my eye I could see a holographic screen light up with some outré false-colour image of something which resembled a galactic nebula, all emerald and purple.

"Just about all seventeen thousand of us," she said. "They have to be, there's no such thing as a domestic or civic worker up here. The servitor chimps perform every mundane task you can think of. So you have to be able to communicate with them. The first affinity bonds to be developed were just that, bonds. Each one was unique. Clone-analogue symbionts allowed you to plug directly into a servitor's nervous system; one set was implanted in your brain, and the servitor got the other. Then Penny Maowkavitz came up with the idea of Eden, and the whole concept was broadened out. The symbionts I'm implanting in you will give you what we call communal affinity; you can converse with the habitat personality, access its senses, talk to other people, order the servitors around. It's a perfect communication system. God's own radio wave."

"Don't let the Pope hear you say that."

"Pope Eleanor's a fool. If you ask me, she's a little too desperate to prove she can be as traditionalist as any male. The Christian Church has always been antagonistic to science, even now, after the reunification. You'd think they'd learn from past mistakes. They certainly made enough of them. If her biotechnology commission would just open their eyes to what we've achieved up here."

"There's none so blind . . ."

"Damn right. Did you know every child conceived up here for the last two years has had the affinity gene spliced in when they were zygotes, rather than have symbiont implants? They're affinity capable from the moment their brain forms, right in the womb. There was no pressure put on the parents by JSKP, they insisted. And they're a beautiful group of kids, Harvey, smart, happy; there's none of the kind of casual cruelty you normally get in kindergartens back on Earth. They don't hurt each other. Affinity has given them honesty and trust instead of selfishness. And the Church calls it ungodly."

"But it's a foreign gene, not one God gave us, not part of our divine heritage."

"You support the Church's view?" Her voice hardened.

"No."

"God gave us the gene for cystic fibrosis, He gave us haemophilia, and He gave us Down's syndrome. They're all curable with gene therapy. Genes the person didn't have to begin with, genes we have to vector in. Does that make those we treat holy violations?"

I made a mental note never to introduce Corrine to Jocelyn. "You're fighting an old battle with the wrong person."

"Yeah. Maybe. Sorry, but that kind of medieval attitude infuriates me."

"Good. Can we get on with the implant now, please?"

"Oh, that?"

The chair started to rotate back to the vertical. Corrine was flicking off the equipment.

"I finished a couple of minutes ago," she said with a contented chuckle. "I've been waiting for you to stop chattering."

"You . . ."

The smiling nurse began to unstrap me.

Corrine pulled off a pair of surgical gloves. "I want you to go home and relax for the rest of the afternoon. No more work today, I don't want you stressed; the symbiont neurons don't need to be drenched in toxins at this stage. And no alcohol, either."

"Am I going to have a headache?"

"A hypochondriac like you, I wouldn't be at all surprised." She winked playfully. "But it's all in your mind."

• • •

I walked home. The first chance I'd had to actually appreciate the real benefit of the habitat. I walked under an open sky, feeling zephyrs ripple my uniform, smelling a mélange of flower perfumes. A strange experience. I'm just old enough to remember venturing out under open skies, taking backpack walks through what was left of the countryside for pleasure. That was before the armada storms started bombarding the continents for weeks at a time. Nowadays, of course, the planet's climate is in a state of what they call Perpetual Chaos Transition. You'd have to be certifiable to wander off into the wilderness regions by yourself. Even small squalls can have winds gusting up to sixty or seventy kilometres an hour.

It was the heat which did it. The heat from bringing the benefits of an industrial economy to eighteen billion people. Environmentalists used to warn us about the danger of burning hydrocarbons, saying the increased carbon dioxide would trigger the greenhouse effect. They were wrong about that. Fusion came on-line fairly early into the new century; deuterium tritium reactions at first, inefficient and generating a depressing quantity of radioactive waste for what was heralded as the ultimate everlasting clean energy source. Then He^3 started arriving from Jupiter and even those problems vanished. No more carbon dioxide from chemical combustion. Instead people developed expectations. A lot of expectations. Unlimited cheap energy was no longer the province of the Western nations alone, it belonged to everybody. And they used it; in homes, in factories, to build more factories which churned out more products which used still more energy. All over the planetary surface, residual machine heat was radiated off into the atmosphere at a tremendous rate.

After a decade of worsening hurricanes, the first real mega-storm struck the Eastern Pacific countries in February 2071. It lasted for nine days. The UN declared it an official international disaster zone; crops ruined over the entire region, whole forests torn out by the roots, tens of thousands made homeless. Some idiot newscable presenter said that if one butterfly flapping its wings causes an ordinary hurricane, then this must have taken a whole armada of butterflies to start. The name stuck.

The second armada storm came ten months later, that one hit southern Europe. It made the first one seem mild by comparison.

Everybody knew it was the heat which did it. By then more or less every home on the planet had a newscable feed, they could afford it. To prevent the third armada storm all they had to do was stop using so much electricity. The same electricity which brought them their newly found prosperous living standard.

People, it seems, don't wish to abandon their wealth.

Instead, they started migrating into large towns and cities, which they fortified against the weather. According to the UN, in another fifty years everybody will live in an urban area. Transgenic crops were spliced together which can withstand the worst the armada storms throw at them. And the amount of He^3 from Jupiter creeps ever upwards. Outside the urban and agricultural zones the whole planet is slowly going to shit.

Our house was near the southern edge of Eden's town, with a long back lawn which ran down to the parkland. A stream marked where the lawn ended and the meadowland began. The whole street was some tree-festooned middle-class suburb from a bygone age. The house itself was made from aluminium and silicon sandwich panels, a four-bedroom L-shape bungalow ranch with broad patio doors in each room. Back in the Delph arcology we had a four-room flat on the fifty-second floor which overlooked the central tiered well, and we could only afford that thanks to the subsidized rent which came with my job.

I could hear voices as soon as I reached the fence which ran along the front lawn, Nicolette and Jocelyn arguing. And yes, it was a picket fence, even if it was made from spongesteel.

The front door was ajar. Not that it had a lock. Eden's residents really did have absolute confidence in the habitat personality's observation. I walked in, and almost tripped on a hockey stick.

The five white composite cargo pods from the *Ithilien* had been delivered, containing the Parfitt family's entire worldly goods. Some had been opened, I guessed by the twins, boxes were strewn along the length of the hall.

"It's stupid, Mother!" Nicolette's heated voice yelled out of an open door.

"And you're not to raise your voice to me," Jocelyn shouted back.

I went into the room. It was the one Nicolette had claimed. Cases were heaped on the floor, clothes draped all over the bed. The patio door was open, a servitor chimp stood placidly outside.

Jocelyn and Nicolette both turned to me.

"Harvey, will you kindly explain to your daughter that while she lives in our house she will do as she's told."

"Fine. I'll bloody well move out now, then," Nicolette squealed. "I never wanted to come here anyway."

Great, caught in the crossfire, as always. I held up my hands. "One at a time, please. What's the problem?"

"Nicolette is refusing to put her stuff away properly."

"I will!" she wailed. "I just don't see why I have to do it. That's what it's here for." She flung out an arm to point at the servitor.

I fought against a groan. I should have realized this was coming.

"It'll pack all my clothes away, and it'll keep the room neat the whole time. You don't even need bloody affinity. The habitat will hear any orders and get the chimps to do as you say. They told us that in the orientation lecture."

"That *thing* is not coming in my house," Jocelyn said flatly. She glared at me, waiting for back-up.

"Daddy!"

The headache I wasn't supposed to be having was a hot ache five centimetres behind my eyes. "Jocelyn, this is her room. Why don't we just leave her alone in here?"

The glare turned icy. "I might have known you'd be in favour of having those creatures in the house." She turned on a heel and pushed past me into the hall.

I let out a long exhausted breath. "Christ."

"I'm sorry, Daddy," Nicolette said in a small voice.

"Not your fault, darling." I went out into the hall. Jocelyn was pulling clothes from an open pod, snatching them out so sharply I thought they might tear. "Look, Jocelyn, you've got to accept that using these servitor creatures is a way of life up here. You knew about the chimps before we came."

"But they're *everywhere*," she hissed, squeezing her eyes

shut. "Everywhere, Harvey. This whole place must be ringing with affinity."

"There is nothing wrong with affinity, nothing evil. Even the Church agrees with that. It's only splicing the gene into children they object to."

She turned to face me, clasping a shirt to her chest, her expression suddenly pleading. "Oh, Harvey, can't you see how corrupt this place is? Everything is made so easy, so luxurious. It's insidious. It's a wicked lie. They're making people dependent on affinity, bringing it into everyday life. Soon nobody will be free. They'll give the gene to their children without ever questioning what they're doing. You see if they don't. They'll create a whole generation of the damned."

I couldn't answer, couldn't tell her. Christ, my own wife, and I was too stricken to say a word.

"Please, Harvey, let's leave. There's another ship due in ten days. We can go back to Earth on it."

"I can't," I said quietly. "You know I can't. And it's unfair to ask. In any case, Delph would fire me. I'm nearly fifty, Jocelyn. What the hell would I do? I can't make a career switch at my age."

"I don't care! I want to leave. I wish to God I'd never let you talk me into coming here."

"Oh, that's right; it's all my fault. My fault the children are going to live in a tropical paradise, with clean air and fresh food. My fault they're here in a world where they don't have to take a stunpulse with them every time they step outside the house in case they're raped or worse. My fault they're going to have an education we could never afford to give them on Earth. My fault they're going to have a chance at *life*. And you want to take it away because of your stupid blind prejudice. Well, count me out of your proud poverty of existence, Jocelyn. You go running back to that ball of disease you call a world. I'm staying here, and the children are staying with me. Because I'm going to do the best job of being a parent I can, and that means giving them the opportunities which only exist here."

Her eyes narrowed, staring hard at me.

"Now what?" I snapped.

"What's that on the back of your neck?"

My anger voided into some black chasm. "A dermal patch," I said calmly. "It's there because I had an affinity symbiont implant this afternoon."

"How could you?" She simply stared at me, completely expressionless. "How could you, Harvey? After all the Church has done for us."

"I did it because I have to, it's my job."

"We mean so little to you, don't we?"

"You mean everything."

Jocelyn shook her head. "No. I won't have any more of your lies." She put the clothes down gently on one of the pods. "If you want to talk, I shall be in the church. Praying for all of us."

I didn't even know there was a church in Eden. It seemed a little strange given the current state of relations between the Vatican and the habitat. But then there's always that *more rejoicing in heaven over one sinner* piousness to consider.

I really ought to make an effort not to be so bitter.

Nicolette had slumped down onto the bed when I went back to her.

"You had a row," she said without looking up.

I sat on the mattress beside her. She's a lovely girl; perhaps not cable starlet beautiful, but she's tall, and slim, and she's got a heart-shaped face with shoulder-length auburn hair. Very popular with the boys back in the arcology. I'm so proud of what she is, the way she's growing up. I wasn't going to let Earth stunt her, not with Eden able to offer so much more. "Yes, we had a row." Again.

"I didn't know she was going to be so upset over the chimps."

"Hey, what happens between me and your mother isn't your fault. I don't want to hear you blaming yourself again."

She sniffed heavily, then smiled. "Thanks, Dad."

"Use the chimps in here all you want, but for God's sake don't let them into the house."

"OK. Dad, did you really have a symbiont implant?"

"Yes."

"Can I have one? The orientation officer said you can't really expect to live here without one."

"I expect so. But not this week, all right?"

"Sure, Dad. I think I want to fit in here. Eden looks gorgeous."

I put my arm round her shoulders and kissed her cheek. "Do you know where your brother is?"

"No, he went off with some boys after the orientation lecture."

"Well, when he comes in, warn him not to allow the chimps into the house."

I left her to herself and went into the lounge. The bubble cube Zimmels had given me was in my jacket pocket. I settled down in the big settee, and slotted it into my PNC wafer. The menu with the file names appeared; there were over a hundred and fifty of them. I checked down them quickly, but there was no entry for Corrine Arburry.

Content I had at least one sympathetic ally, I started to review the masters of the revolution.

●　●　●

My second day started with Penny Maowkavitz's funeral. Rolf and I attended, representing the police, both of us in our black dress uniforms.

The church was a simple A-frame of polished aluminium

girders with tinted glass for walls. I estimated nearly two hundred people turned up for the service, with about eighty more milling outside. I sat in the front pew along with the Governor and other senior Eden staff from the UN and JSKP. Father Cooke conducted the service, with Antony Harwood reading a lesson from the Bible: Genesis, naturally. I knew him from Zimmels's files, another of Boston's premier activists.

Afterwards we all trooped out of the church and down a track into a wide glade several hundred metres from the town. Fasholé Nocord led the procession, carrying the urn containing Penny's ashes. Anyone who dies in Eden is cremated; they don't want bodies decomposing in the earth, apparently they take too long, and as Eden hasn't quite finished growing there's always the chance they'll come to the surface again as the soil layer is gradually redistributed.

A small shallow hole had been dug at the centre of the glade. Pieter Zernov stepped up to it and put a large jet-black seed in the bottom; it looked like a wrinkled conker to me.

"It was Penny's wish that she should finish up here," he said loudly. "I don't know what the seed is, except it was one of her designs. She told me that for once she had forgone function, and settled for something that just looks damn pretty. I'm sure it does, Penny."

As Pieter stood back an old Oriental man in a wheelchair came forwards. It was a very old-fashioned chair, made from wood, with big wheels that had chrome wire spokes, there was no motor. A young woman was pushing him over the thick grass. I couldn't see much of her; she had a broad black beret perched on her head, a long white-blonde ponytail swung across her back, and her head was bowed. But the old man . . . I frowned as he scooped up a handful of ash from the urn Fasholé Nocord held out.

"I know him, I think," I whispered to Rolf.

That earned me another of those looks I was becoming all too familiar with. "Yes, sir; that's Wing-Tsit Chong."

"Bloody hell."

Wing-Tsit Chong let Penny's ashes fall from his hand, a small plume of dry dust splattering into the hole. A geneticist who was at least Penny Maowkavitz's equal, the inventor of affinity.

• • •

Father Leon Cooke cornered me on the way back to town. Both genial and serious in that way only priests know how. He was in his late sixties, wearing the black and turquoise vestments of the Unified Christian Church.

"Penny's death was a terrible tragedy," he said. "Especially in a closed community like this one. I hope you apprehend the culprit soon."

"I'll do my best, Father. It's been a hectic two days so far."

"I'm sure it has."

"Did you know Penny?"

"I knew of her. I'm afraid that relations between the Church and most of the biotechnology people have become a little strained of late. Penny was no exception; but she came to a few services. When confronted with their approaching death, people do tend to show a degree of curiosity in the possibility of the divine. I didn't hold it against her. Everyone must come to faith in their own way."

"Did you hear her confession?"

"Now, my son, you know I can never answer that. Even more than doctors, we priests hold the secrets of our flock close to our hearts."

"I was just wondering if she ever mentioned suicide?"

He stopped beside a tree with small purple-green serrated leaves, tufty orange flowers bloomed at the end of every branch. Dark grey eyes regarded me with a humorous compassion. "I expect you have been told Penny Maowkavitz was a thorny character. Well, with that came a quite monstrous arrogance; Penny did not run away from anything life threw at her, not even her terrible illness. She would not commit suicide. I don't think anybody up here would."

"That's a very sweeping statement."

The tail end of the mourners filed past us; we were earning quite a few curious glances. I saw Rolf standing fifteen metres down the track, waiting patiently.

"I'll be happy to discuss it with you, perhaps at a more appropriate time."

"Of course, Father."

A guilty smile flickered over Leon Cooke's face. "I talked to your wife, yesterday."

I tried to maintain an impassive expression. But he was a priest . . . I doubt he was fooled. "I don't expect she painted a very complimentary picture of me. We'd just had a row."

"I know. Don't worry, my son, it was a very modest row compared to some of the couples I've had to deal with."

"Deal with?"

He ignored the irony. "You know she doesn't belong in this habitat, don't you?"

I shifted round uncomfortably under his gaze. "Can you think of a better place for our children to grow up?"

"Don't dodge the issue, my son."

"All right, Father, I'll tell you exactly why she doesn't care for Eden. It's because of the Pope's ludicrous proclamation on the affinity gene. The Church turned her against this habitat and what it represents. And I have to tell you, in my opinion the Church has made its biggest mistake since it persecuted Galileo. This is my second day here, and I've already started to think how I can make my posting permanent. If you want to help, you might try and convince her that affinity isn't some satanic magic."

"I will help the two of you any way I can, my son. But I can hardly contradict a papal decree."

"Right. It's funny, most couples like us would have divorced years ago."

"Why didn't you? Though I'm glad to see you haven't, that's an encouraging sign."

I smiled wryly. "Depends how you read it. We both have our reasons. Me; I keep remembering what Jocelyn used to be like. My Jocelyn, she's still in there. I know she is, if I could just find a way of reaching her."

"And Jocelyn, what's her reason?"

"That's a simple one. We made our vows before God. Richer or poorer, better or worse. Even if we were legally separated, in God's eyes we remain husband and wife. Jocelyn's family were Catholics before the Christian reunification, that level of devotion is pretty hard to shake off."

"I get the impression you blame the Church for a lot of your situation."

"Did Jocelyn tell you why she places so much weight on what the Church says?"

"No."

I sighed, hating to bring up those memories again. "She had two miscarriages, our third and fourth children. It was pretty traumatic; the medical staff at the arcology hospital were convinced they could save them. God, it looked like she was being swallowed by machinery. It was all useless, of course. Doctors don't have half as much knowledge about the human body as they lay claim to.

"After the second time she . . . lost faith in herself. She became very withdrawn, listless, she wasn't even interested in the twins. A classic depression case. Everything the hospital did was orientated on the physical, you see. That's their totem, I suppose. But we were lucky in a way. Our arcology had a good priest. Quite a bit like you, actually. He gave us a lot of his time; if he'd been a psychiatrist I'd call it counselling. He made Jocelyn believe in herself again, and at the same time believe in the Church. I'm very grateful for that."

"Only in word, I suspect," Leon Cooke said softly.

"Yeah. You're a very insular institution, very conservative. Did you know that, Father? This fuss over affinity is a good example. Jocelyn used to have a very open mind."

"I see." He looked pained. "I shall have to think about what you've told me. It saddens me to see the Church forming such a wedge between two loving people. I think you've both drifted too far from each other. But don't give up hope, my son, there's no gulf which can't be bridged in the end. Never give up hope."

"Thank you, Father. I'll do my best."

• • • •

There appeared to be a fair amount of honest toil going on in the incident room when Rolf and I walked in. Most of the CID staff were at their desks; a chimp was walking round carrying a tray of drinks. I claimed a large spongesteel desk at the front of the room, and slung my dress uniform jacket over the chair. "OK, what progress have we made?"

Shannon was already walking towards me, a PNC wafer in her hand, and a cheerful expression on her face. "I retrieved a copy of Maowkavitz's will from the court computer." She dropped the wafer on the desk in front of me, its display surface was covered with close-packed lines of orange script.

"Give me the highlights," I said. "Any possible suspects? A motive?"

"The whole thing is a highlight, boss. It's a very simple will; Maowkavitz's entire estate, including Pacific Nugene, gets turned into a trust. Initial estimates put the total value at around eight hundred million wattdollars. She left no guidelines on how it was to be used. Monies are to be distributed in whatever way the trustees see fit, providing it is a majority decision. That's it."

Rolf and I exchanged a nonplussed glance. "Is that legal?" I asked. "I mean, can't the relatives challenge it?"

"Not really. I consulted the Eden attorney's office. The will's very simplicity makes it virtually unchallengeable. Maowkavitz recorded a video testimony with a full polygraph track to back it up; and the witnesses are real heavyweights, including—would you believe—the ex-Vice-President of America, and the current Chairwoman of the UN Bank. And Maowkavitz's only relatives are some very distant cousins, none of whom she's ever had any contact with."

"Who are the trustees?"

Shannon's fingernail tapped the wafer. "There are three. Pieter Zernov, Antony Harwood, and Bob Parkinson. Maowkavitz also lists another eight people should any of her initial choices die."

I studied the list of names. "I know all of these." I pushed the wafer over to Rolf who scanned it quickly, and gave me a reluctant nod.

"Boston's leadership," I mused.

Shannon's grin was pure wickedness. "Prove it. There's no such thing as Boston. It isn't entered in any databank; there are no records, no listings of any kind. Technically, it doesn't exist. Even Eden's surveillance can only turn up bar talk."

I toyed with the wafer on my desk. "What do they want the money for? Harwood and Parkinson are both rich in their own right. In fact I think Harwood is actually richer than Maowkavitz."

"They're going to buy guns," Shannon said. "Arm the peasants so they can storm the Winter Palace."

I gave her a censorious stare. "This is a murder inquiry, Shannon. Contribute, or keep silent, please."

She gave an unrepentant shrug. "The modern equivalent

of guns. However they figure on bringing off their coup, it won't be cheap."

"Good point. OK, I want to speak to these three trustees. We won't bring them in for questioning, not yet. But I do want to interview them today, ask them what they're planning on doing with the money. Rolf, set it up, please." I fished my own PNC wafer from my jacket pocket, and summoned up a file I'd made the previous evening. "And Shannon, I want you to access the wills of everyone on this list, please. I'd like to see if they've made similar arrangements to hand over their wealth after they die."

She read the names as I downloaded the file into her wafer, then let out a low whistle. "You're well informed, boss."

"For someone who told me Boston doesn't exist, so are you."

She sauntered back to her desk.

"Hoi Yin examined the servitor chimp yesterday," Rolf said. "She hasn't had any luck recovering the memory of who gave it the order to shoot Penny."

"Bugger. Does she think she'll ever be able to get at the memory?"

"I don't think so, from what she told me. But she said she'd come in again this morning, after the funeral. You could ask her."

"I'll do that; I need the background information anyway. What have we assembled on Penny Maowkavitz's last few days?"

"Purely routine stuff, I'm afraid. She wasn't letting her illness interfere with her work. The JSKP Biotechnology Division has been busy preparing for Ararat's arrival, which she was supervising. And Davis Caldarola says she was still performing design work for Pacific Nugene. She was working ten-, twelve-hour days. Nothing out of the ordinary for her. She never did a lot of socializing, and she'd been cutting back on that recently anyway. According to the people we've interviewed so far she aidn't have any really big rows with anybody, certainly not in the last few weeks. They were all treating her with kid gloves because of the cancer."

It sounded to me like Penny Maowkavitz was someone who had come to terms with her fate, and was trying to get as much done as possible in what time she had remaining. "That's her work. What about her Boston meetings?"

"Sir?"

"She must have had them, Rolf. She was supposed to be their leader. Were they argumentative? I can't imagine them being particularly smooth, not when you're discussing how to take over an entire city-state."

"There's no way of knowing. You see, Shannon was right about not having any evidence against Boston, their leadership would never have met in the flesh, not for that. All their discussions would have taken place using affinity. Nobody can intercept them."

"I thought affinity up here was communal."

"It is, but we have what we call singular engagement mode. It means you can hold private conversations with anyone inside a fifteen-kilometre radius."

"Oh, wonderful. OK, what about these genetic designs she was working on when she died? What were they? Anything a rival company would kill to prevent her from finishing?"

"I don't know. The Pacific Nugene laboratory up here wasn't working on anything radical; mostly transgenic crops for Eden's Agronomy Division, and some sort of servitor which could operate effectively in free fall. If she was working on anything else, we haven't uncovered it yet. She did a lot of the initial softsplice work on her home computer, then turned it over to a lab team to refine and develop up to commercial standard. We haven't been able to access many of her files so far. She used some very complex entry guard codes. It'll take time to crack them. I'll give it to Shannon when she's finished with the wills, it's her field."

"Fine, keep me informed."

•   •   •

Hoi Yin was the most beautiful woman I'd ever seen—the most beautiful I imagine it's possible to see. She came into my office half an hour after I finished in the incident room. I didn't just stare, I gawped.

She was still in the demure black dress she had worn at the funeral. And that was the second surprise, she was the one I'd seen pushing Wing-Tsit Chong's wheelchair.

Her figure was spectacular enough; but it was the combination of diverse racial traits which made her so mesmerizing. Fine Oriental features defined by avian bones, with dark African lips, and the fairest Nordic hair, tawny eyes which appeared almost golden. She had to be the greatest cosmetic gene-adaptation ever put together. She wasn't genetic engineering, she was genetic artistry.

I guessed her age at around twenty-two—but with honey-brown skin that clear how can you tell?

She took off the black beret as she sat in front of my desk, letting her rope of hair hang down almost to the top of her hips. "Chief Parfitt?" she said pleasantly; the tone was light enough, but there was a hint of weariness in it. Hoi Yin, I got the impression, looked down from a great height at common mortals.

I did my best to appear businesslike—waste of time really, she must have known what she did to men. "I understand you've had no success with the servitor chimp?"

"Actually, it was a most enlightening session, I have learnt a considerable amount from the event, some of which I found disturbing. But unfortunately nothing which is immediately helpful to solving your case."

"Fine, so tell me what you have got."

"Whoever instructed the servitor chimp to shoot Penny Maowkavitz was almost my equal in neuropsychology. The method they employed was extremely sophisticated, and ingenious."

"Somebody in your department?"

"I work as an independent consultant. But I believe most of the Servitor Division staff would have the ability, yes. If they had sufficient experience in instructing a chimp, they could probably determine how to circumvent the habitat's safeguards. So too would most of the Biotechnology Division staff. However, I cannot provide you with any likely names, it would be your job to establish a motive."

I made a note on my PNC wafer. "How many people work in the Servitor and Biotechnology Divisions?"

Hoi Yin closed her eyes to consult the habitat personality, assuming a fascinating dream-distant expression which would have left Mona Lisa floundering in envy.

"There are a hundred and eighty people employed in the Servitor Division," she said. "With another eight hundred working in the Biotechnology Division. Plus a great many others in fringe professions, such as agronomy."

"Fine. And what are these safeguards?"

"It is difficult to explain without using affinity to demonstrate the concept directly." She gave me a small apologetic moue. "Forgive me if the description is muddy. Although the servitors are nominally independent, any order given to one by a human is automatically reviewed by the habitat personality. It is a question of neural capacity and interpretation. A chimp's brain has just enough intelligence to retain orders and perform them efficiently. For example, if you were to give one a general order to pick up litter along a certain road, it would be quite capable of doing so without further, more explicit, instruction. Also, if you tell one to put a plate into a dishwasher, there is no problem. It will pick up the object indicated and place it where instructed; even though it does not know the name for "plate" or "dish-washer", nor what they are for. The image in your mind contains sufficient information for it to recognize the plate. So as you can see, we had to protect them from deliberate abuse, and the kind of inevitable misuse which comes from children ordering them around."

"I think I understand. I couldn't order a chimp to carry someone into an airlock and cycle it."

"Exactly. By itself the chimp wouldn't know that what it was doing was wrong. It lacks discrimination, that ability we call sentience. So every order is reviewed by the personality to ensure it is not harmful or illegal. Therefore, although you could tell a chimp to pick up *this* particular object, and point it at *that* person's head, then pull this small lever at the bottom, it would not perform the act. The chimp does not know the object is a pistol, or that pulling the trigger is going to fire it, nor even the consequences such an action would result in. But the habitat personality does, and its neural strata has the capacity to review every single order as it is issued. The order to murder would be erased, and the police would be informed immediately."

"So what went wrong this time?"

"This is what I find most worrying about the incident. You understand that the habitat personality is what we call a homogenized presence?"

"I crammed biotechnology for three months before I came here, but it was just basic stuff. I know Eden has a large neural strata. But that's about all."

Hoi Yin crossed her legs. Distracting, very distracting.

"If you look at a cross-section of the habitat shell you will see it is layered like an onion," she said. "Each layer has a different function. On the outside we have dead polyp, several metres thick, protecting us from cosmic radiation, and gradually ablating away in the vacuum. Inside that is a layer of living polyp which gradually replaces it. Then there is a very complex mitosis layer. More polyp containing nutrient-fluid arteries. A layer for water passages. Another with waste-extraction tubules and toxin-filter glands. And so on. Until finally the innermost layer, landscaped, smeared with soil, and laced with sensitive cells. But the layer just below that surface one is what we call the neural strata. It is nearly a metre thick, and connected to the sensitive cell clusters via millions of nerve strands. Consider that, Chief Parfitt, a strata of neural cells, a brain, measuring one metre thick, and covering almost sixty-four square kilometres."

I hadn't thought of it in quite those terms before. Too unnerving, I suppose. "It ought to be infallible."

"Yes. But Eden's thoughts work on parallel-processing principles. A neural network this large could not function in any other fashion. There is only one personality, yet its mind is made up from millions of semi-autonomous subroutines. Think of it as analogous to a hologram; if you cut up a hologram each little piece still contains a copy of the original image; no matter how small the fragment, the whole pattern is always there. Well, that is how the personality works, complete homogeneity. It can conduct a thousand—ten thousand—conversations simultaneously, and the memory of each one is disseminated throughout its structure so that it is available as a reference everywhere in the habitat. Indeed, all its knowledge is disseminated in such a fashion. When I converse with it through affinity, I am actually talking to a subroutine operating in the neural strata more or less directly below my feet. The amount of the strata given over to running that subroutine is dependent purely on the complexity of the task it is performing. If I were to ask it an exceptionally difficult question, the subroutine would expand to utilize more and more cells until it reached a size appropriate to fulfil the request. Sometimes the subroutines are large and sophisticated enough to be considered sentient in their own right, sometimes they are little more than computer programs."

"The murderer got at the safeguard subroutine, not the chimp," I blurted.

Her eyebrows rose in what I hoped was admiration. "Precisely. Somehow the murderer used his or her affinity to suspend the subroutine responsible for monitoring the orders given to that particular chimp. Then while it was inactive, the order to collect the pistol and stalk Penny Maowkavitz was issued to the chimp. The monitoring subroutine was then brought back on-line. Eden was not aware of the rogue order in the chimp's brain until it actually observed the chimp shooting the pistol. By then it was too late."

"Clever. Can you prevent it from happening again?"

She looked at the floor, her lips pulled together in a delicious pout. "I believe so. Eden and I have been considering the problem at some length. The servitor monitoring subroutines will have to be reconfigured to resist such tampering in future; indeed all of the simpler subroutines will have to be hardened. Although it is of no comfort to Penny Maowkavitz, we have gained considerable insight into a vulnerability which we never previously knew existed. As with all complex new systems, methods of abuse can never be fully anticipated; Eden is no exception. This has given us a lot to think about."

"Fine. What about extracting a memory of the murderer from the chimp? What he or she looks like, how big, anything at all we could work with."

"If there was a visual image, I expect I could retrieve it given time. But I do not believe there is one. In all probability the murderer was nowhere near the chimp when the order was loaded. Whoever they are, they have demonstrated a considerable level of understanding with regards to how the habitat servitors work; I don't think they would make such an elementary mistake as allowing the chimp to see them. Even if they did need to be near the chimp in order to suppress the monitor subroutine, they only had to stay behind it."

"Yeah, I expect you're right."

Hoi Yin gave a small bow, and rose to her feet. "If there is nothing else, Chief Parfitt."

"There was one other thing. I noticed you were with Wing-Tsit Chong at the funeral."

"Yes. I am his student."

And did I hear a defensive note in her voice? Her expression remained perfectly composed. Funny, but she was the first person so far who hadn't said how much they regretted Penny's death. But, then, Hoi Yin could give an ice maiden a bad case of frostbite.

"Really? That's auspicious. I would like to study under him as well. I wondered if you could ask him for me."

"You wish to change your profession?"

"No. My neuron symbionts should be working by tomorrow. Dr Arburry said I'd need tutoring on their use. I would like Wing-Tsit Chong to be my tutor."

She blinked, which for her seemed to be the equivalent of open-mouthed astonishment. "Wing-Tsit Chong has many very important tasks. These are difficult times, both for him and Eden. Forgive me, but I do not believe he should spend his time on something quite so trivial."

"None the less, I'd like you to ask him. At most it will take a second of his valuable time to say no. You might tell him that I wish to perform my job to the best of my ability; and to do that I must have the most complete understanding of affinity it is possible for a novice to have. For that, I would prefer to be instructed by its inventor." I smiled at her. "And if he says no, I won't take offence. Perhaps then you'd consider the job? You certainly seem to have a firm grasp of the principles."

Her cheeks coloured slightly. "I will convey your request."

    •   •   •

Shannon called me just after Hoi Yin walked out.

"I think you're psychic, boss," she said. The image on the desktop terminal screen showed me her usual grin was even broader than normal.

"Tell me."

"I've just finished running down the wills of all those Boston members you gave me. And, surprise surprise, they all follow exactly the same format as Maowkavitz's; a trust fund to be administered in whatever way the trustees see fit. And they all nominate each other as trustees. It reads like financial incest."

"If they were all to die, what would the total sum come to?"

"Christ, boss; half of them are just ordinary folks, worth a few grand; but there's a lot of them like Penny: multimillionaires. It's hard to say. You know the way rich people tangle up their money in bonds and property deals."

"Try," I urged drily. "I expect you already have."

"OK, well you got me there, boss; I did some informal checking with Forbes Media corp for the biggies. I'd guess around five billion wattdollars. Purely unofficial."

"Interesting. So if their wills aren't changed, the last one left alive will inherit the lot."

"Holy shit, you think someone's going to work down the list?"

"No, I doubt it. Too obvious. But I still want to know what Boston intends to do with all that money."

    •   •   •   •

It was Nyberg who drove me to my interview with Antony Harwood. From the way she acted I thought she might be angling for some kind of executive-assistant role. She told me how she'd sorted out my interviews with the three trustees nominated in Maowkavitz's will. I also got a résumé on her career to date, and how she was studying for her detective exams. But she was a conscientious officer, if a little too regimented, and obviously trying to advance herself. No crime.

I did wonder idly if she was a covert agent for JSKP security, assigned to keep tabs on me. It seemed as though she was always there when I turned round. Paranoid. But then it was a growing feeling, this awareness of constant observation. The more I had Eden explained to me, the more conscious I was of how little privacy I had from it. Did it watch me sleeping? On the toilet? Eating? Did it laugh at my spreading gut when I took my uniform off at night? Did it have a sense of humour, even? Or did it, with its cubic-kilometre brain, regard us all as little more than insignificant gnats flittering round? Were our petty intrigues of the slightest interest? Or were we merely tiresome?

I think I had the right to be paranoid.

Antony Harwood's company, Quantumsoft, had a modest office building in what aspired to be the administration and business section of town. A white and bronze H-shaped structure surrounded by bushy palm trees which seemed a lot bigger than five years of growth could account for. It was all very Californian, quite deliberately.

Quantumsoft was a typical Californian vertical. After the Big One2 quake in AD 2058 a lot of the high-tech companies resident in Los Angeles quietly shut up shop in the old city and moved up to High Angeles, a new asteroid that had been shunted into Earth orbit by controlled nuclear explosions. The asteroid project had been sponsored by the California legislature; always Green-orientated, the state wanted the raw materials from the rock to replace all its environmentally unsound groundside mining operations. A laudable notion, if somewhat late in the day. The kind of companies which ascended tended to be small, dynamic research and software enterprises, with a core of highly motivated, very bright, very innovative staff. And, ultimately, very wealthy staff. The verticals were geared towards producing and developing cutting edge concepts, a pure, Green, cerebral industrial community; leaving their groundside subsidiary factories with the grubby task of actually manufacturing the goods they thought up.

High Angeles itself was one of the largest asteroids in the O'Neill Halo after New Kong, although even its central biosphere cavern wasn't a fifth of the size of Eden's verdant parkland. After the miners finished extracting its ore and minerals, and the verticals moved in, it developed into little more than a giant spaceborne Cabana club for clever millionaires. Millionaires who made no secret of their resentment with the unbreakable fiscal ties which bound the asteroid to Earth. They no longer had to endure quakes, and gangs, and ecowarriors, and crime, and pollution, but their physical safety came with a price: specifically Californian taxes.

However distant it might be from the battered Pacific coast, High Angeles was still owned by the state. With its vast mineral reserves and its dynamic verticals the asteroid remained the single largest source of revenue for the legislature. After pouring billions of wattdollars into its capture and starting up its biosphere, the Earthside senators weren't about to let its privileged occupants cheat ordinary taxpayers out of their investment by turning it into an independent tax haven, no matter how much bribe money they were offered.

Ironically, as High Angeles siphoned off talent and wealth from Earth, so Eden drew the cream of the O'Neill Halo.

The challenge Jupiter presented proved an irresistible attraction to the corporate aristocracy. Pacific Nugene was a prime example. Quantumsoft was another.

Antony Harwood rose from behind his desk to greet me as I entered his office: an overweight fifty-five-year-old with a thick black beard. He had changed out of his mourning suit since the funeral, wearing designer casuals as if they were a uniform, open-neck silk shirt and glossy black jeans, along with a pair of hand-tooled cowboy boots.

Some people, you just know right from the moment you clap eyes on them that you're not going to like them. No definable reason, they just don't fit your sensibilities. For me, Harwood was one such.

"I can give you a couple of minutes, but I am kinda busy right now," he said as we shook hands. As generous and jovial as his size suggested, but with a quality of steel.

"Me too, someone got murdered a couple of days ago. And, understandably, I'm rather anxious to find out who did it."

Harwood gave me a second, more thorough, appraisal, his humour bleeding away. He indicated a crescent sofa and table conversation area next to the window wall. "I heard what they say about you: the honest policeman. JSKP should have put you in a museum, Chief, the rarity value oughta haul in a pretty good crowd."

"Along with the honest businessman, I expect."

There was a flash of white teeth in the centre of his beard. "OK, bad start. My mistake. Let's backtrack and begin fresh. What can I do for you?"

"Penny Maowkavitz. You knew her quite well."

"Sure I knew Penny. Sharp character, her tongue as well as her mind."

"You must have spent a lot of time with her, the two of you were contemporaries. So firstly, did she ever say anything, drop any hint, that she thought she might be in danger?"

"Not a thing. We had disagreements. It was kinda inevitable, the way she was, but they were all professional differences. Penny never got personal in any way, not with anyone."

"What does Boston intend to do with her money? Your money too, come to that?"

He smiled again, showing an expression of polite bafflement. "Boston? What's that?"

"What does Boston want the money for?"

The smile tightened. "Sorry. *No comprende, señor*."

"I see. Well, let me explain. For an act of premeditated murder to be committed, logically there must be a motive. Right now I have exactly three suspects: Bob Parkinson, Pieter Zernov, and yourself. You three have the only motive my investigative team has been able to uncover so far. You have been placed in sole charge of a trust fund worth eight hundred million wattdollars, with absolutely no legal constraints or guidelines on how you spend it. So unless you can convince me right here and now in this office that you don't intend to simply split it three ways and disappear into the sunset, you're going to find yourself sleeping in my department's unpleasantly small hospitality suite, with no room service, for the rest of your life. *Comprende?*"

"No way. You can't make that bunch of crap stick, and you know it. This is just blatant intimidation, Chief. My legal boys will put blisters on your ass, they'll kick you so hard."

"You think so? Then try this. I wasn't joking when I said you're a murder suspect. That officially makes you a potential hazard to other residents. And as the lawful civil security officer of an inhabited space station I have the right to expel anyone I regard as a possible endangerment to the population of said station or its artificial ecosphere environment. Check it out: clause twenty-four in the revised UN Space Law Act of 2068, to which Eden is a signatory. Boston will just have to start the revolution without you."

"All right, let's try and remain calm here, shall we? We both want the same thing: Penny's killer behind bars."

"We do indeed. I'm perfectly calm, and I'm also waiting."

"I'd like a minute to myself."

"Confer with whoever you want. You're not going anywhere."

He glowered, then pressed his fingertips to his temple, concentrating hard.

Despite my initial misgivings I was becoming impatient for my symbionts to start working. What must it be like to call on friends and colleagues for support whenever you wanted? Must do wonders for the ego.

My gaze wandered round the office. Standard corporate glitz; tastefully furnished in some Mexican/Japanese fusion, expensive art quietly on show. It seemed all very cold and functional to me. I stared at a picture on the wall behind Harwood. Surely it must be a copy? But then again I couldn't imagine Harwood settling for copies of Picasso.

He surfaced from his trance, shaking his shoulders about like a wrestler preparing for a difficult grapple. "OK, why don't we take a hypothetical situation."

I groaned, but let it pass.

"If an independent nation were to nationalize the property of a company which was in its domain, the international courts would disallow the legality of the move, and seize the assets of that nation as compensation for the owners. There was a rock-solid precedent set in the Botswana case of 2024; when Colonel Matomie's new government confiscated the Stranton corp's car factory. Colonel Matomie thought he was in a nineteen-sixties timewarp, back when all the new ex-colonial governments were grabbing any foreign asset for themselves. Stranton hauled him into the UN International Court; it took them a couple of years, but the ruling was unequivocally in their favour. The factory was their property, and Matomie's government was guilty of theft. Stranton applied for a sequestration injunction. Botswana's airliners were impounded as soon as they touched down on foreign soil, power from South Africa's grid was shut off, all non-humanitarian imports were embargoed. Matomie had to back down and return the factory. Ever since then, Marxist regimes have had a real problem nationalizing foreign enterprises. Sure, there's nothing to stop them from harassing the workforce, or shut businesses down with phoney health regulations, impose ludicrous taxes, or simply refuse to grant operating licences. But they can't *own* the property, not if the original owners don't want to sell."

"Yes, I can see how that would cause problems for you people. The only bona fide economic asset out here is the He^3 mining operation. Even if the people of Eden declared independence there's nothing to stop the JSKP from housing its workers in another habitat. Eden by itself would become financially unviable; you couldn't compete in the microgee industry market because of the transport costs. Anything you build can also be built in the O'Neill Halo, and for far less. You have to have the mining operation as well as the habitat if you are to succeed."

Harwood gave an indifferent shrug. "So you say. But my hypothetical government already has a small stake in the foreign factory it wants to take into national ownership. That changes the entire legal ball game; the whole concept of ownership and rights becomes far more ambiguous."

"Ah!" I clicked my fingers as the full realization hit me. "You're going to engineer a leveraged buyout from the existing shareholders, and probably try to oust the existing board members as well. No wonder you need all that money." I stopped, recalling the briefing files I'd studied on the JSKP. "But even that can't be enough. You only have a few billion available. JSKP is a multi-trillion-wattdollar venture; it won't break even for another fifty years."

"No government on Earth is going to disrupt the flow of goods from this hypothetical nationalized factory. They can't afford to, the product it manufactures is unique and extraordinarily valuable. Ultimately, the courts and the financial community will permit this proposed managerial restructuring, especially as full compensation will be paid. Nobody is trying to cheat anyone out of anything. A large proportion of the money which Penny and other philanthropists have pledged to this hypothetical government will be spent on legal battles; which are shaping up to be very violent and depressingly prolonged."

"Yes, I see now." I stood up. "Well, providing I can verify this *hypothesis*, I think you and the other trustees can be removed from my suspect list. Thank you for your time."

Harwood lumbered to his feet. "I hope you find Penny's killer soon, Chief Parfitt."

"I'll do my best."

"Yeah, I guess so." His expression turned confidently superior. "But don't count on having too much time. You might just find you ain't gonna be here for very much longer."

I stopped in the open door, and gave him a genuinely pitying look. "Do you really think that Boston won't need a professional police force if you ever do manage to form a government here? If so, you're more of a daydreaming fool than I thought."

• • • •

Pieter Zernov was a lot more cordial than Harwood; but then we'd got to know each other quite well on the *Ithilien*. A modest man, quietly intelligent, who kept most of his opinions to himself; but when he did talk on a subject which interested him he was both coherent and well informed. It was his nomination as a trustee which made me inclined to believe Harwood's explanation about what Boston intended to do with the money. I trusted Pieter, mainly because he was one person who couldn't have killed Penny. The way it looked at the moment, the murderer had to have been in the habitat for at least a couple days prior to the murder.

A time when Pieter was on the *Ithllen* with me. Good alibi.

I found him in the JSKP's Biotechnology Division headquarters, supervising Ararat's germination.

"It ought to be Penny doing this," he said mournfully. "She put in so much work on Ararat, especially after her accident. It's a tremendous improvement on Eden and Pallas."

We were standing at the back of a large control centre; five long rows of consoles were arrayed in front of us, each with technicians scanning displays and issuing streams of orders to their equipment. Big holoscreens were fixed up around the walls, each showing a different view of Ararat as the large seed floated fifteen kilometres distant from Eden. The foam which protected it during the flight from the O'Neill Halo had been stripped away, allowing the base to be mated to a large support module.

"It looks like an old-style oil refinery," I said.

"Not a bad guess," Pieter said. "The tanks all hold hydrocarbon compounds. We'll feed them into the seed over the next two months. Then if we're happy that the germination is progressing normally, the whole thing gets shifted to its permanent orbital location, leading Eden by a thousand kilometres. We have a suitable mineral-rich rock there waiting for it."

"And Ararat will just start eating it?"

"Not quite, we have to process the raw material it consumes for a further nine months, until its own absorption and digestion organs have developed. After that it'll be attached directly onto the rock. We are hoping that the next generation habitats are going to be able to ingest minerals straight out of the ore right from the start."

"From tiny acorns," I murmured.

"Quite. Although, this isn't one unified seed like you have for trees. Habitat seeds are multisymbiotic constructs; we don't know how to sequence the blueprint for an entire habitat into a single strand of DNA. Not yet, anyway. And, regrettably, biotechnology research is slowing down on Earth, there's too much association with affinity. That's why Penny was so keen to move her company out here, where she could work without interference."

"Speaking of which . . ."

He bowed his head. "Yes, I know. Her will."

"If you could just confirm what Antony Harwood told me."

"Oh, Antony. You shook him up rather badly, you know. He's not used to being treated like that. His employees are a great deal more respectful."

"You were hooked in?"

"Most of us were."

I found I quite liked that idea, silent witnesses to Mr Front knuckling under at the first touch of pressure. Most unprofessional, Harvey. "The will," I prompted.

"Of course. What Antony told you is more or less true. The money will be channelled into fighting legal cases on Earth. But we're aiming for more than just a leveraged buyout, that would simply entail replacing the current JSKP board members with our own proxies. Boston wants the He^3 mining industry to be owned collectively by Eden's residents. We're prepared to purchase every share in the enterprise, even though it will take decades, maybe even a century, to pay off the debt. If Eden's independence is to be anything other than a token, we must be in complete control of our own destiny."

"Thank you." I could sense how much it hurt him to talk about it, especially to someone like me. Yet he was proud, too. When he talked of "Boston" and "us", I could see he was totally committed to the ideal. What a strange umbrella organization it was; you could hardly find two more disparate people than Pieter Zernov and Antony Harwood.

"I'm rather honoured Penny named me," he said. "I hope I live up to her expectations. Perhaps she wanted one moderate voice to be heard. I do tend to feel slightly out of place amongst all these millionaire power players. Really, I'm just a biotechnology professor from Moscow University on a three-year sabbatical with the JSKP. Think of that, a Muscovite living in a tropical climate. My skin peels constantly and I get headaches from the axial light-tube's brightness."

"Will you be going back?"

He gave me a long look, then shook his head ponderously. "I don't think so. There is a lot of work to be done here, whatever the outcome. Even the JSKP has offered me a permanent contract. But I would like to teach again some day."

"What's the appeal, Pieter? I mean, does the composition of the JSKP board membership really make that much difference? People here at Jupiter are still going to live and work in the same conditions. Or are you that committed to the old collective ideal?"

"You ask this of a Russian, after all we've been through? No, it's more than a blind grasp for collectivism in the name of workers' liberation. Jupiter offers us a unique opportunity; there are so many resources out here, so much energy, if it can be harvested properly we can build a very special culture. A culture which thanks to affinity will be very different from anything which has gone before. That chance to do something new happens so rarely in human history; which is why I support the Boston group. The possibility, the fragile hope, cannot be allowed to wither; any inaction on my part would be criminal, I could never live with the guilt. I told you the next generation of habitats will be able to ingest minerals right away; but they are also capable of much, much more. They will be able to synthesize food in specialist glands, feed their entire population at no cost, with no machinery to harvest or prepare or freeze. How wonderful that will be, how miraculous. The polyp can be grown into houses, into cathedrals if you want. And our children are already showing us how innately kind and decent people can be when they grow up sharing their thoughts. You see, Harvey? There is so much potential for new styles of life here. And when you combine it with the sound economic foundation of the He^3 mining, the possibilities become truly limitless. Biotechnology and super-engineering combining synergistically, in a way they have never been allowed to do back on Earth. Even the O'Neill Halo suffers limits imposed by fools like the Pope, and restrictions issued by its own jealous population, fearful of changing the status quo, of letting in the masses. That would not happen here, Harvey, out here we can expand almost without limit. This is the frontier we have lacked for so long, a frontier for both the physical and spiritual sides of the human race."

Despite myself (I should say my official self), I couldn't help feeling a strong admiration for Boston and its goals. There's something darkly appealing about valiant underdogs going up against those kind of odds. And don't be fooled into thinking anything else, the odds were *huge*, the corporations wielded an immense amount of power, most of it unchecked. International courts could be bought from their petty-cash funds. It started me thinking again about the possibility that Penny Maowkavitz was deliberately eliminated. Her death, particularly now, was terribly convenient for JSKP.

Pieter had been right about one thing, though, Eden was a special entity; the nature of the society which was struggling to emerge out here was as near perfect as I was ever likely to see. Its people deserved a chance. One where they weren't squeezed by the JSKP board to maximize profits at the expense of everything else.

"You talk a great deal of sense," I told him ruefully.

His meaty hand gripped my shoulder, squeezing fondly. "Harvey, what you said to Antony came as a surprise to many of us. We were expecting the JSKP to appoint someone . . . shall we say, more dogmatic as Chief of Police. I would just like to say that Antony does not have a deciding vote, we are after all attempting to build an egalitarian democracy. So for what it's worth, we welcome anyone who wishes to stay and do an honest day's work. Because unfortunately I suspect you were right; people are going to need policemen for a long time to come. And I know you are a good policeman, Harvey."

• • • •

I made the effort to get home for lunch. I don't think I'd spent more than a couple of hours with the twins since we arrived.

We ate at a big oval table in the kitchen, with the patio doors wide open, allowing a gentle breeze to swim through the room. There were no servitor chimps in sight. Jocelyn must have prepared the food herself. I didn't ask.

Nathaniel and Nicolette both had damp hair. "We've been swimming in the circumfluous lake at the southern endcap," Nathaniel told me eagerly. "We caught a monorail tram down to a water sports centre in one of the coves. They've got these huge slides, and waterfalls where the filter organs vent out through the endcap cliff, and jetskis. It's great, Dad. Jesse helped us take out a full membership."

I frowned, and glanced up at Jocelyn. "I thought they were due in school."

"Dad," Nicolette protested.

"Next week," Jocelyn said. "They start on Monday."

"Good. Who's Jesse?"

"Friend of mine," Nathaniel said. "I met him at the day club yesterday. I like the people here; they're a lot easier going than back in the arcology. They all know who we are, but they didn't give us a hard time about it."

"Why should they?"

"Because we're a security chief's children," Nicolette said. I think she learnt that mildly exasperated tone from me. "It didn't make us real popular back in the Delph arcology."

"You never told me that."

She made a show of licking salad cream off her fork. "When did you ask?"

"Oh, of course, I'm a parent. I'm in the wrong. I'm always in the wrong."

Her whole face lit up in a smile. For the first time I realized she had freckles.

"Of course you are, Daddy, but we make allowances. By the way, can I keep a parrot, please? Some of the red parakeets I've seen here are really beautiful, I think they must be gene-adapted to have plumage like that, they look like flying rainbows. There's a pet shop in the plaza just down the road which sells the eggs. Ever so cheap."

I coughed on my lettuce leaf.

"No," Jocelyn said.

"Oh, Mum, it wouldn't be affinity bonded. A proper pet."

"No."

Nicolette caught my eye and screwed her face up.

"How's the murder case coming on?" Nathaniel asked. "Everyone at the lake was talking about it."

"Were they, now?"

"Yes. Everyone says Maowkavitz was an independence rebel, and the JSKP had her killed."

"Is that right, Dad?" Nicolette looked at me eagerly.

Jocelyn had stopped eating, also focusing on me.

I toyed with some of the chicken on my plate. "No. At least, not all of it. Maowkavitz was part of a group discussing independence for Eden; people have been talking about that for years. But the company didn't kill her. They've had plenty of opportunities during the last few years to eliminate her if they wanted to, and make it seem like an accident. She was back on Earth eighteen months ago, if the JSKP board wanted her dead, they would've had it done then, and nobody would have questioned it. Her very public murder up here is the last thing they need. For a start, they're bound to be considered as prime suspects, by public rumour if not my department. It will inevitably make more people sympathetic to her cause."

"Have you got a suspect, then?" Nathaniel asked.

"Not yet. But the method indicates that it's just one person, acting alone. There was a large amount of very secretive preparation involved. It has to be someone who's clever, above-average intelligence, familiar with Eden's biotechnology structure, and also the cybersystems, we think. Unfortunately that includes about half of the population. But the murderer must have an obsessive personality as well, which isn't so common. Then there's the risk to consider; even with the method they came up with—which admittedly is very smart—there was still a big chance of discovery. Whoever did it was prepared to take that risk. This is one very cool customer, because murder up here is a capital crime."

"The death penalty?" Nicolette asked, her eyes rounded.

"That's right." I winked. "Something to think about when you're considering joyriding one of the jeeps."

"I wouldn't!"

"What about a motive?" Nathaniel persisted. Tenacious boy. I wonder where he got it from?

"No motive established so far. I haven't compiled enough information on Maowkavitz yet."

"It's got to be personal," he said decisively. "I bet she had a secret lover, or something. Rich people always get killed for personal reasons. When they fight about money they always do it in court."

"I expect you're right."

• • •

One thing all Penny Maowkavitz's nominees had in common, they were industrious people. I caught up with Bob Parkinson in the offices of the He^3 mining mission centre, the largest building in Eden, a four-storey glass and composite cube. An archetypal company field headquarters, the kind of stolid structure designed to be assembled in a hurry, and last for decades.

His office didn't have quite the extravagance of Harwood's, it was more how I imagined the study of a computer science professor would look like. The desk was one giant console, while two walls were simply floor to ceiling holoscreens displaying orbital plots and breathtaking views of Jupiter's upper cloud level, relayed directly from the aerostats drifting in the gas-giant's troposphere. A hazed ochre universe that went on for ever, flecked by long streamers of ammonia cirrus that scudded past like a time-lapse video recording. The JSKP currently had twenty-seven of the vast hot-hydrogen balloons floating freely in the atmosphere; five hundred metre diameter spheres supporting the filtration plant which extracted He^3 from Jupiter's constituent gases, and liquified it ready for collection by robot shuttles.

He^3 is one of the rarest substances in the solar system, but it holds the key to commercially successful fusion. The first fusion stations came on-line in 2041, burning a mix of deuterium and tritium; second-generation stations employed a straight deuterium–deuterium reaction. Those combinations have a number of advantages: ignition is easy, the energy release is favourable, and the fuels are available in abundance. The major drawback is that both reactions are neutron emitters. Although you can use this effect to breed more tritium, by employing lithium blankets, it's a messy operation, requiring more complex (read: expensive) reactors, and a supplementary processing facility to handle the lithium. Without lithium blankets the reactor walls become radioactive, then have to be disposed of; and you require additional shielding to protect the magnetic confinement system. The costs in both monetary and environmental terms weren't much of an improvement on fission reactors.

Then in 2062 the JSKP dropped its first aerostat into Jupiter's atmosphere, and began extracting He^3 in viable quantities. There are only minute amounts of the isotope present in Jupiter. But minute is a relative thing when you're dealing with a gas giant.

The fusion industry—if you'll pardon the expression—went critical. Stations burning a deuterium–He^3 mix produced one of the cleanest possible fusion reactions, a high-energy proton emitter. It also proved an ideal space drive, cutting down costs of flights to Jupiter, which in turn reduced the costs of shipping back He^3, which led to increased demand.

An upward spiral of benefits. He^3 was every economist's fantasy commodity.

Bob Parkinson was the man charged with ensuring a steady supply was maintained; a senior JSKP vice-president, he ran the entire mining operation. It wasn't the kind of responsibility I would ever want, but he appeared to handle it stoically. A tall fifty-year-old, with a monk's halo of short grizzled hair, and a heavily wrinkled face.

"I was wondering when you were going to get round to me," he said.

"They told me it would have to be today."

"God, yes. I can't delay the lowering, not even for Penny. And I have to be there." A finger flicked up to one of the screens showing a small rugby-ball-shaped asteroid which seemed to be just skimming Jupiter's cloud tops. Fully half of its surface was covered with machinery; large black radiator fins formed a ruff collar around one conical peak. A flotilla of industrial stations swarmed in attendance, along with several inter-orbit transfer craft.

"That's the cloudscoop anchor?" I asked.

"Yes. Quite an achievement; the pinnacle of our society's engineering prowess."

"I can't see the scoop itself."

"It's on the other side." He gave an instruction to his desk, and the view began to tilt. Against the backdrop of salmon and white clouds I could see a slender black line protruding from the side of the asteroid which was tide-locked towards the gas giant. Its end was lost somewhere among the rumbustious cyclones of the equatorial storm band.

"A monomolecule silicon pipe two and a half thousand kilometres long," Bob Parkinson said with considerable pride. "With the scoop head filters working at full efficiency, it can pump a tonne of He^3 up to the anchor asteroid every day. There will be no need to send the shuttles down to the aerostats any more. We just liquify it on the anchor asteroid, and transfer it straight into the tanker ships."

"At one-third the current cost," I said.

"I see you do your homework, Chief Parfitt."

"I try. What happens to the aerostats?"

"We intend to keep them and the shuttles running for a while yet. They are very high-value chunks of hardware, and they've got to repay their investment outlay. But we won't be replacing them when they reach the end of their operational life. JSKP plans to have a second cloudscoop operational in four years' time. And, who knows, now we know how to build one, we might even stick to schedule."

"When do you start lowering?"

"Couple of days. But the actual event will be strung out over a month, because believe me this is one hyper-complicated manoeuvre. We're actually decreasing the asteroid's velocity, which reduces its orbital height, and pushes the scoop down into the atmosphere."

"How deep?"

"Five hundred kilometres. But the trouble starts when it begins to enter the stratosphere; there's going to be a lot of turbulence, which will cause flexing. The lower section of the pipe is studded with rockets to damp down the oscillations, and of course the scoop head itself has aerodynamic surfaces. Quantumsoft has come up with a momentum-command program which they think will work, but nobody's ever attempted anything like this before. Which is why we need a large team of controllers on site. The time delay from here would be impossible."

"And you're leading them."

"That's what they pay me for."

"Well, good luck."

"Thanks."

We stared at each other for a moment. Having to conduct a direct interview with someone who was technically my superior is the kind of politics I can really do without.

"As far as we can ascertain at this point, Penny Maowkavitz didn't have any problems in her professional life," I said. "That leaves us with her personal life, and her involvement with Boston. The motive for her murder has to spring from one of those two facets. You are one of the trustees named in her will, she obviously felt close to you. What can you tell me about her?"

"Her personal life, not much. Everyone up here works heavy schedules. When we did meet it was either on JSKP business, or discussing the possibilities for civil readjustment. Penny never did much socializing anyway. So I wouldn't know who she argued with in private."

"And what about in the context of Boston? According to my information you're now its leader."

His tolerant expression cooled somewhat. "We have a council. Policies are debated, then voted on. Individuals and personality aren't that important, the overall concept is what counts."

"So you're not going to change anything now she's gone?"

"Nothing was ever finalized before her death," he said unhappily. "We knew why Penny had the views she did, and made allowances."

"What views?"

It wasn't the question he wanted, that much was obvious. A man who took flying an asteroid in his stride, he was discomforted by simply having to recount the arguments that went on in what everyone insisted on describing to me as a civilized discussion forum.

He ran his hands back through the hair above his ears, concern momentarily doubling the mass of creases on his face. "It's the timing of the thing," he said eventually. "Penny wanted us to make a bid for independence as soon as the cloudscoop was operational. Six to eight weeks from now."

I let out a soft whistle. "That soon?" That wasn't in Zimmels's briefing. I'd gathered the impression they were thinking in terms of a much longer timescale.

"Penny wanted that date because that way she'd still be alive to see it happen. Who can blame her?"

"But you didn't agree."

"No, I didn't." He said it almost as a challenge to me. "It's too soon. There's some logic behind it, admittedly. With an operating cloudscoop we can guarantee uninterrupted deliveries of He^3 to Earth. It's a much more reliable system than sending the shuttles down to pick up fuel from the aerostats. Jupiter's atmosphere is not a benign environment; we lose at least a couple of shuttles each year, and the aerostats take a real pounding. But the cloudscoop—hell, there are virtually no moving parts. Once it's functioning it'll last for a century, with only minimal maintenance. And we have now established the production systems to keep on building new cloudscoops. So when it comes to He^3 acquisition technology we're completely self-sufficient, we don't have to rely on Earth or the O'Neill Halo for anything."

"And biotechnology habitats are also autonomous," I observed. "You don't need spare parts for them either."

"True. But it's not quite that simple. For all its size and cost and technology, the JSKP operation here is still very much a pioneering venture; roughly equivalent to the aircraft industry between the last century's two World Wars. We're at the propeller-driven monoplane stage."

"That's hard to credit."

"You've talked to Pieter Zernov, I believe. He's full of dreams of what the habitats can eventually evolve into. We need money for that, money and time. Admittedly not much in comparison to the cost of a cloudscoop; but nor is it a trivial sum. Then there's Callisto. At this moment I've got a team there surveying the equator for a suitable mass driver site. JSKP is planning to start construction in 2094, and use it to fire tanks of He^3 at Earth's L3 point. There will be a whole string of tanks stretching right across the solar system. It'll take three years for them to arrive at L3, but once they start, delivery will be continuous. A mass driver will eliminate the need for ships like the *Ithilien* to make powered runs every month."

"So what are you worried about? That Earth won't supply the parts for a mass driver? They'll be acting against their own interest. Besides, you'll always find one company willing to oblige."

"It's not the availability of technology. It's the cost. The next decade is going to see JSKP investment in Jupiter triple if not quadruple. And it's only after that, when there are several cloudscoops operational, and the mass driver is flinging He^3 at Earth on a regular basis, when you'll start to see the cash flow reversing. Once we've established a He^3 delivery operation sophisticated enough to function with minimum maintenance and minimum intervention, the real profits are going to start rolling in. And that's when we can start thinking about buying out the existing shareholders."

"I see what you mean. If you try and buy them out now, you won't have the money for expansion you need."

He nodded, pleased I was seeing his viewpoint. "That's right. All this talk of independence is really most impulsive and premature. It can happen, it should happen, but only when the moment is right to assure success."

Company line, that's what it sounded like to me. Which left me thinking: would a JSKP vice-president really be an unswervingly committed member of a rebellion against the board? Whatever the outcome, independence or otherwise, Bob Parkinson would keep the same job, probably for the same pay. Christ, but he'd manoeuvred himself into a superb position to play both ends against the middle. Just how shrewd was he?

"From what you've just told me, Boston actually benefited from Penny Maowkavitz's death."

"That's way out of line, Chief, and you know it."

"Yeah. Sorry. Thinking out loud; it's a bad habit. But I have to run through the process of elimination."

"Well, I'd say you can eliminate any Boston members. Pieter told you what kind of ideals drive us. If it had come to a vote, Penny would have abided by the majority decision, as would I."

"You mean you haven't decided yet?"

"There is a line, Chief Parfitt, and you are not on our side of it. I've put myself in a most dangerous position confiding in you. One word to the board from you, and my role out here is finished, along with my career and my pension and my future. But I talked to you anyway, honestly and openly, because I can see you genuinely want to find Penny's murderer, and I believe you're capable of doing so. But informing you of anything more than our general intentions, things which you could pick up in any bar in the habitat, that's out of the question. You see, you've been making some very ingratiating sounds towards us, words we like to hear, words we're flattered to hear, especially from your lips. But we don't know if they're real, or if they're just an excellent interview technique. So why don't you tell me; will the Eden police try to prevent Boston from achieving independence?"

I looked into his hooded eyes, searching for the depth which must surely come from being augmented by other minds. There was a great deal of resolution, but nothing much else. Bob Parkinson was a man alone.

So I had to ask myself, did he really think the board didn't know of his membership? Or if they did, and he was their provocateur, why wouldn't he tell me?

"It's like this," I said. "I would never fight a battle, unless I knew I'd already won."

• • •

My third day started with a dream. I was completely naked, standing on Jupiter's delicate ring. Clouds swirled eternal below me, perfectly textured mountains of frozen crystals glittering in every shade of red, from deep magenta to a near-dazzling scarlet. Close enough that I could reach out and touch them, fingertips stirring the interlocking whorls, bathing my skin in a sensation of powder-fine snow. It tingled. The planet was crooning plaintively, a bass whalesong emerging from depths beyond perception. I watched, entranced, as its energy shroud was revealed to me, the magnetosphere and particle wind, embracing it like the milk-white folds of an embryo membrane. They palpitated slowly, long fronds streaming out behind the umbra.

Then the palpitations began to grow, becoming more frenzied. Long tears opened up, spilling out a precious golden haze. A ripping sound grew into thunder, and the ring quaked below my feet.

I knifed up on the bed. Clean sober awake. Heart racing, sweaty. And for some reason, expectant. I glanced round the darkened room. Jocelyn was stirring fitfully. But *someone* was watching me.

A faint mirage of a man sitting up in bed, staring round wildly.

"What is this?"

Please relax, Chief Parfitt, there is nothing to worry about. You are experiencing a mild bout of disorientation as your symbiont implants achieve synchronization with my neural strata. It is a common phenomenon.

It wasn't a spoken voice, the room was completely silent. The hairs along my spine prickled sharply as though someone was running an electric charge over my skin. It was the memory of a voice, but not my memory. And it was happening in real-time.

"Who?" I asked. But my throat just sort of gagged.

I am Eden.

"Oh, Christ." I flopped back on the mattress, every muscle knotted solid. "Do you know what I'm thinking?" The first thing which leapt into my mind was that last row with Jocelyn. I felt my ears burning.

There is some random overspill from your mind, just as you perceived some of my autonomic thought routines. It is a situation similar to a slightly mistuned radio receiver. I apologize for any upset you are experiencing.

The effect will swiftly fade as you grow accustomed to affinity.

Jupiter again; a bright vision of the kind which might have been granted to a prehistory prophet. Jupiter floated passively below me. And space was awash with pinpricks of microwaves, like emerald stars. Behind each one was the solid bulk of a spacecraft or industrial station.

"That's what you see?"

I register all the energy which falls upon my shell, yes.

I risked taking a breath, the first for what seemed like hours. "The inside. I want to see the inside. All of it."

Very well. I suggest you close your eyes, it makes perception easier when your brain doesn't have two sets of images to interpret.

And abruptly the habitat parkland materialized around me. Dawn was coming, washing the rumpled green landscape with cold pink-gold radiance. I was seeing all of it, all at once. Feeling it stir as the light awoke the insects and birds, its rhythm quickening. I knew the axial light-tube, a slim cylindrical mesh of organic conductors, their magnetic field containing the fluorescent plasma. I sensed the energy surging into it, flowing directly from the induction pick-off cables spread wide outside. Water surged along the gentle valleys, a cool pleasing trickle across my skin. And always in the background was the mind-murmur of people waking, querying the habitat personality with thousands of mundane requests and simple greetings. Warmth. Unity. Satisfaction. They were organic to the visualization.

"My God." I blinked in delighted confusion at the thin planes of light stealing round the sides of the curtains beyond the end of the bed. And Jocelyn was staring at me suspiciously.

"It's started, hasn't it?"

I hadn't heard her sound so wretched since the last miscarriage. Guilt rose from a core of darkness at the centre of my mind, staining every thought. How would I react if she ever went ahead and did something I considered the antithesis of all I believed in?

"Yes."

She nodded mutely. There wasn't any anger in her. She was lost, totally rejected.

"Please, Jocelyn. It's really just a sophisticated form of virtual reality. I'm not letting anyone tinker with my genes."

"Why do you do that? Why do you treat me as though my opinions don't matter, or they're bound to be wrong? Why must you talk as if I'm a child who will understand and thank you once you've explained in the simplest possible terms? I lost our children, not my mind. I gave up my life for you, Harvey."

Right then, if I could have pulled the symbionts out, I think I would have done it. I really do. Christ, how do I land myself into these situations?

"All right." I reached out tentatively, and put my hand on her shoulder. She didn't flinch away, which was something, I suppose. "I'm sorry I did that, it was stupid. And if you've been hurt by coming here, by me having the symbiont implant, then I want you to know it was never deliberate. Christ, I don't know, Jocelyn; my life is so straightforward, all mapped out by the personnel computer at Delph's headquarters. I just do what they tell me, it's all I can do. Maybe I don't take the time to think like I should."

"Your career is straightforward," she said softly. "Not your life. We're your life, Harvey, me and the twins."

"Yes."

A faint resigned smile registered on her lips. "They like it here."

"I really didn't know the other kids in the arcology were tough on them."

"Me neither."

"Look, Jocelyn . . . I saw Father Cooke yesterday."

"What about him?"

"He's a smart old boy; that's what. Perhaps I should go and see him again. I'm not too proud to ask for help."

"You'd do that?" she asked, uncertainty gave her voice a waver.

"Yes, I'd do that."

"I don't want us to be like this, Harvey. It was good before."

"Yeah. Which means it can be again, I suppose. I'll go and see Cooke, then, find out what he's got to say about us. Uh, I'm not sure if I can do it today."

"I know. The Maowkavitz case."

"Her and Boston. Everything always comes at once, doesn't it?"

"And at the worst time. But that's something I knew even before I married you."

•   •   •

It was Eden which guided me to Wing-Tsit Chong's residence, that echo of a voice whispering directions into my brain. I drove myself there right after breakfast, it was too early for Nyberg to be on duty. I didn't feel like her company anyway. But I had a rising sense of satisfaction as I steered the jeep along a track through the parkland; at least Jocelyn and I were talking again.

The old geneticist lived some way out of the town itself, a privilege not many people were granted. The Agronomy and Domestic Maintenance divisions wanted to keep all the buildings in one neat and tidy strip. If everyone was allowed a rustic cottage in the woodlands the whole place would have been crisscrossed with roads and power cables and utility pipes. But for Wing-Tsit Chong they made an exception. I expect even administration types held him in the same kind of reverence that I did. Whether you approved of it or not, affinity was such a radical discovery.

His residence was a simple bungalow with a high, steeply curved blue slate roof which overhung the walls to form an all-round veranda. Very Eastern in appearance, to my untutored eye it resembled a single-storey pagoda. There was none of the metal and composite panelling which was used in most of the habitat's buildings, this was made from stone and wood. It had been sited right on the edge of a small lake, with the overlooking veranda standing on stilts above the vitreous water. Black swans glided imperiously across the surface, keeping just outside the thick band of large pink and white water lilies which skirted the entire lake. The whole area seemed to siphon away every sound.

Wing-Tsit Chong and Hoi Yin were waiting for me on the wooden lakeside veranda. She was dressed in a simple sleeveless white-cotton robe, standing behind her mentor, as stern and uncompromising as ever. Wing-Tsit Chong however smiled welcomingly as I came up the short flight of steps from the lawn. He was sitting in his ancient wheelchair, dressed in a navy-blue silk jacket, with a tartan rug wrapped round his legs. His face had the porcelain delicacy of the very old; my file said he was in his early nineties. Almost all of his hair had gone, leaving a fringe of silver strands at the back of his head, long enough to come down over his collar.

It is most gratifying to meet you, Chief Parfitt. The habitat rumour band has talked of no one else for days. He chuckled softly, small green eyes alight with a child's mischief.

"It was very good of you to agree to tutor me. As you can see, I still haven't got a clue about affinity."

This we shall change together. Come, sit here. Hoi Yin, some tea for our guest.

She flashed me a warning glance as she went inside. I sat

in a wicker chair opposite Wing-Tsit Chong. Dulled copper wind chimes hanging along the edge of the eaves tinkled quietly. I really could imagine myself attending some spiritual guru back in Tibet.

A good girl. But somewhat overprotective of me. I ought to be grateful to have anyone so attentive at this time in my life.

"*She thinks I'm wasting your time.*"

The chance to offer guidance towards understanding is not one I can lightly refuse. Even an understanding as simple as this one. All life is a steady progression towards truth and purity. Some achieve great steps in their quest to achieving spiritual clarity. Others are doomed to remain less fortunate.

"That's Buddhist philosophy, isn't it?"

Indeed. I was raised in that fashion. However, I diverged from the training of Patimokkha traditions many years ago. But then arrogance is my vanity, I acknowledge this with great sadness. But still I persist. Now then; the task in hand. I wish you to talk to me without using your voice. Subvocalization is the talent you must master. The focus, Chief Parfitt, that is the key to affinity, the focusing of your mind. Now, a simple greeting: Good morning. Look at me. Nothing else, only me. Form the words, and deliver.

• • •

I sat on that veranda for two hours. For all his smiling frailty, Wing-Tsit Chong was unrelenting in pursuing my education. The whole session put me in mind of those adolescent martial arts series on the entertainment cables, stumbling pupil and wise old master.

I did indeed learn how to focus my thoughts. How to flick a mental switch that allowed me to use affinity when I wanted rather than that initial erratic perception which I'd experienced. How to recognize individual mental signatures and use singular engagement. I eavesdropped on the general bands which filled the habitat's ether, the gossips who discussed every subject under the sun; not so dissimilar from the net bulletins on Earth. Communion with Eden was the most fascinating, having its entire mental and sensory facilities available at a whim—using them time and again until the commands became instinctive. Instructing servitors. Sending my own optical images, receiving other people's.

Only then did I realize how restricted I had been until that moment. Earth was the kingdom of the blind, and Eden the one-eyed man.

• • •

This is a priceless gift, I told Wing-Tsit Chong. I thank you.

I am pleased you think it useful.

Whatever gave you the original idea for affinity?

A fusion of disciplines. My spiritual precepts told me that all life is in harmony. As a scientist I was fascinated by the concept of nonlocal interaction, a mathematical explanation for atomic entanglement. Quantum theory permits us to consider a particle as a wave, so the wave function of one particle may overlap another even though they are at distance. An effect once described as atomic telepathy. The original neural symbionts I developed allowed me to exploit this loophole and produce instantaneous communication. Identical cloned cells are able to sense the energy state in their twin. They are in harmony.

But if affinity confirmed your Buddhist principles, why have you rejected it? I asked.

I have not rejected the Buddha's basic tenets; rather I

seek a different road to dhamma, or the law of the mind, which is the goal of the Buddhist path.

How?

I consider the nature of thought itself to be spiritual. Human thought is our mystery, it is our soul. All states of existence are contained within our own minds. Buddhists believe that thoughts should be cleansed and simplified to bring about progress along the path. For myself, I consider every thought to be sacred, they should all be treasured and revered, no matter what they are; only the wealth of experience can bring about enrichment of the soul. You cannot achieve this by meditation alone. By purifying your mind, you become nothing more than a machine for thinking, a biological computer. We are meant for more than that.

Hoi Yin was rocking her head in agreement with everything he said. She had sat in on the whole affinity training session, helping Wing-Tsit Chong to drill me in the essentials. Her attitude towards me hadn't changed; and affinity showed me her thoughts were as hard and cold as her expression. But she remained quite devoted to the old man. I was becoming very curious about the underlying nature of their relationship. At first I'd thought she might be a relative, a granddaughter or a niece, but now I could see it wasn't that sort of attachment. She called herself his student. I'd say it was more like his acolyte.

Is this what you believe, as well? I asked her.

Alert tawny eyes regarded me for a full second, searching for treachery in the question. Of course. I have learnt to order my thoughts rationally. To accept what I am, and be thankful for it. I savour the essence of life.

So why do you never smile? I asked myself.

Hoi Yin has accomplished much in the time she has been with me, Wing-Tsit Chong said. But it is Eden itself which is my greatest pupil, and my greatest challenge.

I couldn't stop the amazed grin from spreading over my face. **You're teaching Eden to be a Buddhist?** The image that brought up was ridiculous; I hoped to hell that I genuinely had learnt how to internalize my flights of fantasy.

No. I simply teach Eden to think. That is why I am here. This technophile conquest of Jupiter holds no interest for me, other than a purely academic admiration for the accomplishments of the JSKP's engineering teams. It is the habitat's intellectual nurturing which I consider important enough to devote my last days to. My final work.

I developed affinity symbionts for the Soyana corporation back in 2058, and they made a great deal of money from selling bonded servitors before the worsening social and religious situation on Earth virtually closed down the market. It was on my insistence that they joined the JSKP consortium. I pointed out to the Soyana board that with a single modification to the proposed design of the habitats they could develop a whole new market here in Jupiter orbit where the population was uniformly educated, and largely immune to popular prejudice. I could see how the most effective utilization of servitors could be brought about, and advocated incorporating what is now termed the neural strata into Eden. Prior to this, it was envisaged the habitat would have only a small cluster of neural cells, possessing a limited sentience to regulate its functions. Penny Maowkavitz and I collaborated to design the cells and structure of the neural strata. And afterwards, while she devoted her energies to refining the design of new habitats, I assisted with the birth of Eden's consciousness.

You mean it wasn't sentient to start with? I asked. **How could something this smart not be self-aware?**

Wing-Tsit Chong smiled fondly out over the lake. **The consciousness which is every human's birthright is a** gift often overlooked. It is brought about over many years by responding to stimuli, by parental devotion in imparting language and example. Now consider a habitat seed; already its neural kernel is orders of magnitude larger than a human brain. Hoi Yin has explained to you how the neural strata is a homogeneous presence operating innumerable thought routines simultaneously. Well, those principal thought routines were all designed by me, and entered into the seed as growth was initiated. I have remained here almost ever since, guiding Eden through the inevitable confusion which awakening engenders in any living entity, and assisting it in refining those routines as required. There was, after all, so much I could not possibly foresee.

Penny Maowkavitz was the creator of my physical structure, Eden said, Wing-Tsit Chong is the father of my mind. I love them both.

Hoi Yin was watching me closely, waiting for my reaction.

You can love? I asked.

I believe so.

Any entity with a soul can love, Wing-Tsit Chong said. It is only the fault of our flawed society that not all are given the chance to love. For only by showing love can you receive love in return. This is what I consider to be the most fundamental act of dana, the Buddhist practice of giving. In its purest state, dana is a sacrifice of self which will allow you complete understanding of the needs of others. And in doing so you transform yourself. A supreme state of Nibbana achievable only with unselfish love. Sadly so few are capable of such munificence.

I expect you're right. I was getting out into waters way beyond my depth. Philosophy doesn't figure very heavily on the Hendon Police College's training courses. I wondered what Father Cooke would have to say on the subject of Eden having a soul.

You worked with Penny Maowkavitz? I asked.

For many years, Wing-Tsit Chong said. As a geneticist she was peerless. So many fine ideas. So much energy and single-minded determination. Given the diversity of our respective cultural backgrounds our temperaments were not conjunctive, but even so we achieved much together. Eden alone is testament to that. I await with some eagerness to see what it is that will bloom from her grave. To experience eagerness at my age is remarkable. Only she could bring about such a thing.

Did she confide in you at all?

Alas no. Our union was conducted on a professional level. I was filled with sorrow at her radiation accident, and I grieve her death. To suffer so is a tragedy. But both of these incidents can only be understood in the greater nature of Kamma; our past actions create our present life.

You mean she deserved it? I asked, surprised.

You misunderstand; there is no cruelty involved with the law of Kamma, which is given as: knowledge of the ownership of deeds. The nearest Western interpretation of this would be controlling your own destiny. Only you are responsible for your own future. And the future is determined by the past.

Reap as ye shall sow, I said.

Again this is too literal, it demonstrates a Western inclination towards belief in preordained fate. You are rooted in the physical world. The determinative actions to which Kamma refer are acts of will.

Right. I could see myself developing another headache if this went on much longer. Now that's fate, action and reaction. So you don't know of anyone who would wish to harm her?

No, I regret I can shed no light on the perpetrator for you.

What about Boston? I asked. You're not listed as a member in the files I have been given. Do you support its aims?

You asked to come here to learn about affinity, Hoi Yin interjected sharply. You outstay your welcome, Chief Parfitt.

Patience. Wing-Tsit Chong held up a hand, still smiling softly. Chief Parfitt has a job to do. We will assist in any way we can, and in doing so honour the memory of Penny Maowkavitz.

Hoi Yin slouched down further in her chair. For someone who claimed to embrace rational thought, she could be amazingly petulant.

I have taken no active role in the Boston group's activities, Wing-Tsit Chong said. As you see, Chief Parfitt, I am no longer as robust as I once was. I chose to devote my remaining time to Eden, Pallas, and now Ararat. They still need nurturing; intellectually they remain children. I have been asked to endorse the Boston group, of course, several times. My name, they feel, will add weight to their campaign. I declined because I do not wish the indignity of becoming a meaningless symbol. Boston conducts its campaigns in what I see as very much a materialistic arena, who owns what, who has the right to issue orders. I do not condemn economics nor their ideological pursuit of national self-determination; but these causes must be seen in the context of the greater reality. The people of Eden already build and control the industrial facilities in Jupiter orbit. What is, is. Everything else is book-keeping, the chosen field of contest for those who lead the movement. JSKP and Boston are two armies of accountants, waging war in boardrooms.

A storm in a teacup, I said.

Wing-Tsit Chong gave a thin laugh. **You are an interesting man, Chief Parfitt. You see more than you admit. If there is any other question arising from your investigation, please do not hesitate to contact me. You have the skill to do this, now.**

I do. And again I thank you for it.

Hoi Yin and I stood up together. She fussed round Wing-Tsit Chong for a moment, tucking his blanket under his knees, straightening his silk jacket. I looked out over the lake. There was a small waterfall at the far end, its spray acting as a cage for rippling rainbows. The swans had all vanished. When I turned back, Hoi Yin was already pushing the wheelchair through a door into the house. I just couldn't work that girl out.

•   •   •

I drove the jeep halfway back towards the town, then pulled off the track and stopped. A subliminal query, and I knew that no one else was using the track, nor was there anyone walking through the surrounding parkland. I shook my head in bemusement when I realized what I'd done.

I closed my eyes and settled back comfortably on the seat. This was something I'd known I would have to do right from the moment I got the call saying Maowkavitz had been murdered.

Eden?

Yes, Chief Parfitt.

Show me your memory of Penny Maowkavitz's death.

It was a composite of memories, taken from the various sensitive cells around Lincoln lake—mock-rock outcrops along the shore, small polyp-sided gullies, affinity-bonded birds and field mice, even smooth stones apparently jutting from the soil at random were polyp. Eden blended the viewpoints together, making it seem as though I was an invisible ghost floating beside Penny Maowkavitz as she took her morning walk.

Just by looking at her I knew that had we ever met we would never have got on. There was no sympathy in the way her face was set; she had a core of anger that burned far darker than Hoi Yin's inner demon. The way she walked, legs striding on purposefully through the thick grass, belayed any impression of a casual stroll. She didn't drink down the view on her inspections; the wild flowers and the tangled trees had no intrinsic aesthetic value, they were simply aspects of design, she was hunting for faults and flaws.

She came to the side of the lake, and made her way along the fine shingle around the edge. Beads of sweat were appearing on her face, glinting softly in the silver glimmer of the axial light-tube. I could smell their muskiness in the air. She undid the front of her long jacket, a spasm of irritation crossing her face as her hand touched the vector regulators strapped to her belly.

Ten metres away the servitor chimp was walking across the grass, heading at a slight angle towards the lake. It had a dark utility bag to carry its gardening implements, the fabric stained and fraying, bulging with odd shapes. Penny Maowkavitz never paid it the slightest attention.

I focused on her face. The wig wasn't on quite straight. Her lips were twitching, the way they do when people are lost in thought. What I'm sure was a frown had just started to crease her forehead when the chimp put its hand in the bag. Whatever problem Penny Maowkavitz was working on, its solution was eluding her. The chimp pulled out the pistol, its arm swinging round to point at her. Surprise flamed in her eyes, and her mouth started to open. Below her feet, Eden's general observation routines registered the object in the chimp's hand. Pattern recognition procedures were enacted immediately. Penny Maowkavitz's first flare of alarm impinged upon the neural strata. It ended abruptly as the chimp pulled the trigger.

Blood and brain erupted as her skull blew open.

The chimp froze as Eden's frantic command overrode every nerve impulse. Although even the habitat couldn't stop its teeth from chittering in fright. Primitive emotions whirled through its simple brain: terror, regret, panic, the last remnants of its animal origin fighting for recognition.

If I had a more developed instinct I would have seized control of the servitor chimp much sooner, Eden said sorrowfully. **As it was, I took too long to identify the pistol for what it was. Penny Maowkavitz might have been alive today if I had not taken so long.**

Self-recrimination is unhealthy, I told it. Christ, nursemaid to a habitat. But its thoughts had a timbre that made me think of a knowing child. I could hardly be angry, or even sarcastic. **You have learnt from the incident. That's as much as any intelligent creature can hope for.**

You sound like Wing-Tsit Chong.

Then I must be right.

Instinct is a hard concept for me. So much of what I think is logical, precise.

Finding out the world is neither kind nor well ordered is all part of growing up. Painful but necessary.

I wish it was different.

Believe me, we all do. How come you can't remember any further back? This happened more than thirty hours ago.

I have two memory levels. The first is short term, a thirty-hour storage for every impression gathered by my sensitive cells. If something untoward occurs which I did not initially realize the importance of, such as who placed the bag with the pistol for the chimp to collect, then it can be recovered providing I am informed before the thirty hours are up. Other than that, memory is point-

less. Why would I wish to memorize years of parkland in which no activity is occurring? If every sensitive cell impression were to be placed immediately into long-term memory, my total capacity would quickly be filled. So these observation memories dissipate quite naturally. Long-term memory is a conscious act, whereby I transfer over events from the short term for permanent record.

That makes sense, I suppose. That short-term facility is like a security camera recording they use in the public areas back in the arcologies. I paused, recalling what I had reviewed. **I want the memory again, but just the end section this time. After the chimp shoots her.**

The gunshot, shockingly loud to the chimp's unsuspecting ears. Eden's affinity orders slamming into its brain. A moment when the ether reverberated with their thoughts. Then the chimp's mind was engulfed by the habitat's glacial control. I could actually feel every muscle in in its body locked solid; looking through its eyes, seeing the grisly body toppling over.

Again, please.

But I already knew. In the instant between firing the shot, and being captured, a single thought-strand of regret had slithered through the chimp's mind. Where the hell had that come from?

•   •   •   •

Rolf was rising from his chair to greet me as soon as I walked into the incident room. "We had a positive result from Wallace Steinbauer over at the cyberfactory," he said. "They've managed to put together a Colt .45 pistol. I said we'll come over and see for ourselves."

Excellent.

The corner of his mouth lifted in sardonic acknowledgement. **Welcome aboard, Chief.**

Thanks. By the way, I've been reviewing Eden's memory of the murder. Has anyone noticed the chimp's emotional outburst after it shot Maowkavitz?

That earned me some blankly puzzled looks from around the room.

No, sir, Rolf said cautiously.

Another point to the good guys. **Then I suggest you all review it again. The chimp experiences quite a degree of regret immediately after pulling the trigger. I'd like some ideas why that should be, please. How are we doing with the other lines of enquiry?**

Still nothing in Maowkavitz's immediate past. No arguments, no disputes. And we've just about finished interviewing all the people she came into contact with. Oh, and the Governor is in the clear. We've more or less confirmed he didn't leave the pistol for the chimp. His schedule's been pretty hectic for weeks, he hasn't had the time to put together the pistol or wander out into the parkland.

I ignored the jeer from the back of the room. Through Eden's sensitive cells in the polyp floor I knew it was Quinna. I wasn't even aware I'd enquired. This was going to take some getting used to. **You do surprise me. Well, that snippet isn't to be considered confidential.**

Yes, sir.

Shannon, how are you doing on accessing Maowkavitz's computer files?

Some progress, boss. She gave me a thumbs-up from behind her terminal, then ducked her head down again. **I've recovered about twenty per cent of the files stored in her home system. It's all been genetic work so far, beyond me. Rolf said to turn it over to Pacific Nugene for assessment. I haven't heard anything back from them yet.**

Those files were fairly easy to crack. But there's a whole series of files which use a much higher level of entry encryption techniques; stuff she didn't leave any keys for, not even in her will. That's real strange, because the files are quite large. They obviously contain a lot of work.

OK, prioritize that, please, I want to know what's in them. Today if possible.

Her head came up again, giving me a martyred look. I'm organizing some decryption architecture now.

Good grief, an officer with initiative. Whatever next?

An officer with decent pay, she shot back.

I gave up. Any luck with the bag which the pistol was left in? I asked Rolf.

No. It's a standard issue flight bag, made in Australia, been in production for six years. JSKP distributes them to every family which is given an assignment here, they're automatically included with the cargo pods we're sent to pack everything in. Ninety per cent of the habitat population have one sitting at home somewhere. Impossible to trace. The medical lab at the hospital ran some forensic tests on it for us. No fingerprints, naturally. It had been wiped with a paper tissue; they found traces of the fibre, identified as a domestic kitchen towel. They also found some hair which they confirm came from the chimp. But nothing to tell us who put it there.

Nobody said it was going to be easy, Rolf. I made an effort not to show how worried I was becoming. Two days of solid investigation, with a fairly dedicated team putting in a lot of effort, and we were still no nearer to solving it than we were the minute Maowkavitz was killed. That wasn't good. A worldlet where surveillance is total, an effective organization for collecting and correlating data. And *nothing*. Nobody was that good. There is no such thing as a professional murderer. Sure, you get assassins, snipers, contract killers; but like I told Nathaniel, I didn't believe this was a paid hit. This was an act of vengeance, or revenge, or—remote possibilities—passion and jealousy. A one-off, planned in isolation.

That means a mistake was made. You cannot cover everything, every angle, because at the very heart of the crime lies your reason to murder. Once the police have that, they have you, no matter how well you camouflage your tracks with regards to the method.

And with all I knew, I couldn't think of a reason why anyone in Eden would want to kill Penny Maowkavitz. Nobody I'd spoken to had actually admitted to liking her, but everyone respected her, it was like one of those universal constants.

The only person left who could conceivably cast any light on the problem was Davis Caldarola. I'd held off interviewing him out of an old-fashioned sense of sympathy; according to Zimmels's ubiquitous files he and Penny had been together for seven years, her death would have hit him hard. He had certainly looked pretty shaken up when I glimpsed him at the funeral.

Sorry, Davis.

• • •

Rolf drove the jeep down to the southern endcap, taking one of the five equidistantly spaced roads which ran the length of the habitat. A tram monorail ran down the outside of each lane. Two of the automatic vehicles passed us, coming in the opposite direction; bullet-nosed aluminium cylinders painted a bright yellow. They had seats for forty passengers, although I only saw five or six people using them. I couldn't work out why they'd been streamlined, either; their top speed was only forty-five kilometres an hour. Something Victorian would have been more appropriate, more pleasing to the eye as well. But that's modern designers for you, image junkies.

We were halfway to the cyberfactory when the Governor called me. It was like a sixth sense made real; I *knew* someone wanted to talk to me, swiftly followed by a subliminal image of Fasholé Nocord sitting at his desk.

Yes, Governor?

About time you became affinity capable, he said. His mind-tone was as grumpy as his voice. How is the investigation going?

I sent you a progress update file last night, sir.

Yes, I accessed it. It's not what I'd call progress. You haven't found shit so far.

It's only been two days, sir.

Look, Harvey, I've got the board breathing acid fire down my neck. The newscable reporters are jamming half the uplinks from Earth demanding statements. Even the Secretary General's office is pressing for a result; they want to show how efficient and relevant the UN's administration of Eden is. I've got to have something to tell them all.

What can I say, enquiries are continuing.

Damn it, Harvey, I've given you time without any pressure; now I want results. Have you even got a suspect yet?

No, sir, I haven't. Perhaps you'd care to take charge of the investigation yourself if you're that dissatisfied with my progress.

Don't try pulling that smartarse routine on me, Harvey, it doesn't work. Come on, man, you should have some kind of lead by now. Nobody can hide in Eden.

Really? Somebody is making a pretty good job of it.

Harvey!

Yeah, all right. Sorry. Tell them we expect to make an arrest in the near future. Usual crap; they know it is and we know it is, but it should satisfy the press for the moment. In any case, it's almost true; my team have eliminated quite a few possibilities, we're narrowing the field. But we have to have more time to correlate the information we've acquired. Nobody ever issued a set schedule for solving murder inquiries.

Two days. I want a positive result which I can announce in two days, Harvey. Someone under arrest or in custody. Understand?

Yes, sir.

The contact ended.

Who was that? Rolf asked.

The Governor. He's graciously given me two days to find the murderer.

"Arsehole," Rolf grunted. He pressed his toe down on the accelerator, and sent the jeep racing over the causeway that traversed the circumfluous lake.

• • •

Eden's cyberfactories were installed in giant caverns inside the base of the southern endcap. Apart from the curving walls, they didn't look any different from the industrial halls back in the Delph arcology: row after row of injection moulders, machine tools, and automated assembly bays with waldo arms moving in spider-like jerks. Small robot trolleys trundled silently down the alleys, delivering and collecting components. Flares of red and green laserlight strobed at random, casting looming shadows.

We found Wallace Steinbauer in a glass-walled office on one side of the cavern. The JSKP Cybernetic Manufacturing Division's manager was in his late thirties; someone else I suspected had been gene-adapted. Above-average height, with a trim build, and a handsome, if angular, face that seemed to radiate competence. You just knew he was the right man for the job—any job.

He shook my hand warmly, and hurriedly cleared some carbon-composite cartons from the chairs. His whole office was littered with intricate mechanical components, as though someone had broken open half a dozen turbines and not known how to reassemble them.

Don't get many visitors here, he said in apology.

I let my gaze return to the energetic rows of machinery beyond the glass. **This is quite an operation you've got here.**

I like to think so. JSKP only posted me here a couple of years ago to troubleshoot. My predecessor couldn't hack it, which the company simply couldn't afford. Cybernetics is the most important division in Eden, it has to function perfectly. I helped get it back on stream.

What do you make here?

The smart answer is everything and anything. But basically we're supposed to provide all the habitat's internal mechanical equipment; we're also licensed by the UN Civil Spaceflight Authority to provide grade-D maintenance and refurbishment on spacecraft components and the industrial stations' life-support equipment; and on top of that lot we furnish the town with all its domestic fundamentals. Anything from your jeep to the water-pumping station to the cutlery on your kitchen table. We've got detailed templates for over a million different items in our computer's memory cores. Anything you need for your home or office, you just punch it in and it'll be fabricated automatically. The system is that sophisticated. In theory there's no human intervention required, although in practice we spend sixty per cent of our time troubleshooting. It's taken eighteen months to refine, but I've finally got us up to self-replication level. Any piece of machinery you see out in that cavern can now

be made here. Except for the electronics, which are put together in one of the external industrial stations.

Doesn't Eden import anything? I asked.

Only luxury items. JSKP decided it would be cheaper for us to produce all our own requirements. And that includes all the everyday consumables like fabrics, plastics, and paper. My division also includes recycling plants, which are connected to the habitat's waste tubules. Eden's organs consume all the organic chemicals, but we reclaim the rest.

What about the initial raw materials? Surely you can't make everything from recycled waste. Suppose I needed a dozen new jeeps for my officers?

No problem. Eden digests over two hundred thousand tonnes of asteroid rock each year in its maw; it is still growing, after all. His mind relayed a mental image of the southern endcap, supplied directly from the integral sensitive cells. Right at the hub was the maw; a circular crater lined with tall red-raw spines resembling cilia. The largest spines were arrayed round the rim, pointing inwards and rippling in hour-long undulations, giving the impression that some giant sea anemone was clinging to the shell. The arrangement was an organic version of a lobster pot; chunks of ice and rubble, delivered from Jupiter's rings by tugs, were trapped inside. They were being broken down into pebble-sized granules by the slow, unrelenting movement of the spines, and ingested through mouth pores in the polyp.

That was when the process became complex. Sandwiched between the endcap's inner and outer layers were titanic organs; first, enzyme filtration glands which distilled and separated minerals and ores into their constituent compounds. Anything dangerously toxic was vented back out into space through porous sections of the shell. Organic chemicals were fed into a second series of organs where they were combined into nutrient fluids and delivered to the mitosis layer to sustain Eden's growth. Inorganic elements were diverted into deep storage silos buried in the polyp behind the cyberfactory caverns, glittery dry powders filling the cavities like metallic grain.

We have huge surpluses of metals and a host of other minerals, Wallace Steinbauer said. And they're all available in their purest form. We send the metal powder out to a furnace station to get usable ingots and tubing. The minerals we shove through a small chemical-processing plant.

So you're totally self-sufficient now? I said. My admiration for Penny Maowkavitz had returned with a vengeance after I viewed the maw and its associated organs. That woman had ingenuity in abundance.

I like to think so. Certainly we'll be able to provide Pallas and Ararat with their own cyberfactories. That's our next big project. Right now we're just ticking over with maintenance and spares for our existing systems.

So a simple pistol is no trouble.

That's right. Wallace Steinbauer rifled through some boxes at the side of his desk, and pulled out the Colt with a triumphant grin. No major problem in putting it together, he said. But then I never thought it would be. We could build you some weapons far more powerful than this if you asked.

I took it from him, testing the weight. It struck me as appallingly primitive; looking from the side the grip jutted almost as though it was an afterthought. There was an eagle emblem on the silicon, its wings stretched wide. Interesting point. If you could build any gun you wanted, why choose a weapon like this, why not something more modern?

I'd suggest your murderer chose it precisely because of its simplicity, Wallace Steinbauer said. The Colt .45 has been around since the late eighteen-hundreds. Don't let its age fool you, it's an effective weapon, especially for close-range work. And from a strictly mechanical point of view it's a very basic piece of machinery, which means it's easy to fabricate, and highly reliable, especially when made out of these materials. I'd say it was an excellent choice.

But why an exact replica? Rolf asked. Surely you can come up with something better using the kind of CAD programs we have these days? My kid designs stuff more complicated than this at school, and he's only nine. In fact why bother with a revolver at all? The chimp was only ever going to be able to fire a single shot.

I can give you a one-word answer, Wallace Steinbauer said. Testing. The Colt is tried and tested, with two hundred years of successful operation behind it. The murderer knew the components worked. If he had designed his own gun he would need to test it to make absolutely sure it was going to fire when the chimp pulled the trigger. And you can hardly test a gun in Eden.

I handed the pistol over to Rolf. Everyone keeps talking about templates, and original components, I said. Where did they come from? I know any reference library memory core would have video images of a Colt. But where did actual templates come from? How did you make this one?

Wallace Steinbauer scratched the back of his head, looking faintly embarrassed. My division has the templates for quite a few weapons. It's the potential, you see. If the police or the Governor ever really needed heavy duty firepower, like if those Boston bastards turn violent, I could provide you with the relevant hardware within a few hours. Those stun guns and lasers you're issued with are only adequate providing you don't come up against anything more powerful.

And the Colt is one of the templates? I said wearily.

Yes, I'm afraid so. I didn't know myself until your department came to me with this request. It looks like someone back on Earth just downloaded an entire *History of Armaments* almanac for our reference source.

Who else has accessed the Colt's file?

Wallace Steinbauer grimaced apologetically. There's no record of any aooooo prior to my request. Sorry.

Has your computer been compromised?

I thought it was a secure system, but I suppose it must have been. There are only five people in the division including me who have the authority to access the weapons files anyway. So the murderer must have hacked in; if they have the skill for that, erasing access records wouldn't pose any problem.

I used singular-engagement mode to tell Rolf: We'll need alibis for Steinbauer and the other four who can access the weapons file. Also check to see if any of them ever had any contact with Maowkavitz.

Yes, sir.

What about records for machine time? I asked Steinbauer. Do you know when the original pistol's components were fabricated?

Again, nothing, he said, cheerlessly. We're going to have to strengthen our whole computer system after this. I didn't realize it was quite so open to abuse. It worries me.

So there won't be any record of the materials being taken out of storage either, I concluded glumly.

No. Hiding a kilogram loss would be absurdly easy. We're used to dealing in ten-tonne units here. Unless it's larger than that we wouldn't even notice it's gone.

Great. OK, Rolf, I want Shannon over here to examine the computer system. See if she can find any signs of tampering.

He pulled a sardonic face. **We'll be popular. Do you want her to do that before she tries to crack the rest of Maowkavitz's files?**

I winced as I tried to sort out a priority list in my mind. **No, Maowkavitz's files must come first. The Cybernetics Division computer is a long shot, but I would like it covered today. Do we have someone else who could run through it?**

I could try, if you like. I took software management as my second subject at university.

OK, see what you can come up with. And also run a check through any other memory cores you can think of, see if the Colt's template was on file anywhere else. I gave Wallace Steinbauer a tight smile. **I'd like you to install some stronger safeguards in your computer procedures as soon as possible, please. The idea of people being able to walk in here any time they like and load a template for an artillery piece isn't one I enjoy. I am responsible for Eden's overall security, and this seems like a gaping flaw.**

Sure, I'll ask Quantumsoft if they can supply us with a more secure access authority program.

Good. Did you know Penny Maowkavitz?

He inflated his cheeks, and let out an awkward breath. Definitely a question he really did not want to be asked. **I knew her. We had to keep the Biotechnology Division informed about the raw material produced by the digestive organs, especially if there were any problems. It was strictly an inter-department contact.**

Penny was intractable, I suggested.

You've heard.

Yeah.

We didn't get on terribly well. But there was no point in making an issue out of it. I'm due back to Earth in another four months. And there was her illness . . .

I think you're the first person I've met that doesn't like it here.

I do like Eden, he protested lightly. **It's interesting work, challenging. But the Snecma company has offered me a vice-presidential post in the New Kong asteroid. Better pay, more responsibility. I couldn't turn that down.**

* * *

I left Rolf in Wallace Steinbauer's office to review the Cybernetics Division computer, and drove myself over to Penny Maowkavitz's house. By Eden's standards it was lavish, though nothing like as ostentatious as she could afford. She had built herself a U-shaped bungalow, with the wings embracing an oval swimming pool. It was set in a large garden which was shielded by a hedge of tall fuchsia bushes. I guessed Maowkavitz had designed the bushes herself; the topaz and jade flowers were larger than my fist, looking like origami snowflakes. Quite beautiful.

Davis Caldarola was sitting in a chair at the poolside, slouched down almost horizontally. He was in his fifties, just starting to put on weight. A ruby-red sports shirt and baggy shorts showed me limbs with dark tanned skin and a mass of fine greying hair. A tall glass was standing on the table beside him, rapidly melting ice cubes bobbing about near the bottom. I guessed at vodka and tonic. A second guess that it wasn't his first today. I made a conscious effort not to check with Eden.

He gestured roughly at a nearby chair, and I dragged it over to him.

"Ah, Eden's Chief of Police, himself. I'm honoured. I was wondering when you'd come calling," he said. The voice was furry, not quite slurred, but close. In his state, I don't suppose he wanted to try holding his thoughts steady enough to use the affinity symbionts. "Your people have been barging round in the house for days."

"I'm sorry if they're getting in your way. They were told to be as quiet as possible."

"Ha! You're running a murder investigation. You told them to do whatever they have to, and bugger what—" He broke off and pressed his fists to his forehead. "Shit. I sound like the all-time self-pitying bastard."

"I think you're entitled to feel whatever the hell you like right now."

"Oh, very good; very clever. Christ Almighty." He snatched the glass off the table and glared at it. "Too much of this bloody stuff. But what else is there?"

"I need to know what you can tell me about Penny, but I can come back later."

He gave a loud snort. "I wouldn't if I were you. I'll be even worse then." The last of the vodka was downed in a swift gulp. "What can I tell you? She was awkward, argumentative, obstinate, she wouldn't tolerate fools at all, let alone gladly. They all knew that, they all tiptoed around her. 'Making allowances for her brilliance.' Like bollocks. They were jealous, all of them; her colleagues, her company staff, even that yogi master fruitcake Chong. She wasn't brilliant, she was a fucking genius. They don't call this Eden for nothing, you know, and it's her creation."

"You're saying people resented her?"

"Some of them, yeah."

"Anyone in particular?"

"God, I don't know. They're all the same, fawning over her in public, then stabbing her in the back once she's out of earshot. Bastards. None of them are sorry she's gone, not really. The only one who was ever honest about hating her guts was Chong's bimbo. The rest of them . . . they ought to hand out Oscars for the acting at that funeral."

A servitor chimp came out of the house, carrying another

tall glass. It put it on the table beside Davis Caldarola, and picked up the empty one. Davis gave the new glass a guilty look, then squinted over at me. "Have you got any idea who did it?"

"Not a specific suspect, no. But we've eliminated a lot of possibles."

"You haven't got a fucking clue, have you? Jesus, she's murdered in full view, and you don't have one single idea who did it. What kind of policeman are you?"

I steeled my expression, and said: "A persistent one. I'll find the culprit eventually, but I'll do it a lot quicker with your cooperation."

He wilted under the rebuke, just as I expected. Davis was a grieving drunk prone to tantrums, not an anti-establishment rebel.

"I want to know about her," I said more gently. "Did she talk to you about her work?"

"Some. We were a stimulus to each other. I listened to her describe her genetics projects; and I explained my own field to her. She was interesting and interested. That's why our relationship worked so well, we were compatible right across the board."

"You're an astronomer?"

"Astrophysicist." He grinned savagely. "Get it right. There's some in my profession who'd be badly offended by that. Think yourself lucky I'm so easygoing."

"Does the JSKP pay for your work?"

"Some of it, my position is part-funded by the University of Paris. I'm supposed to be studying Jupiter's gravitational collapse. Interesting field."

"You don't sound very enthusiastic."

"Oh, there's enough to captivate me. But there's a lot else going on up here, more provoking puzzles. Even after all this time observing Jupiter at close range, and dropping robot probes into the atmosphere, there's very little we know about it, certainly what goes on within the deeper levels, below the altitude which the probes can reach. Our solid-state sensor drones implode long before they reach the semi-solid layers. All we've got on the interior is pure speculation, we don't understand what happens to matter at those sort of compression factors, not for sure. And Christ alone knows what's actually taking place at the core. There's a hundred theories."

"And Penny was interested?"

He picked the glass of vodka up, swirled the ice, then put it down without drinking any. "Yeah. Academically, anyway. She could follow the arguments."

"What did she tell you about her work?"

"Whatever she wanted. What bugged her, what was going well, new ideas. Christ, she would come up with some bizarre concepts at times. Balloon fish that could live in Jupiter's atmosphere, mythological creatures, webs of organic conductors which could fly in the Earth's ionosphere."

"Anything really radical?"

"What? Those not enough for you? Don't you want to see dragons perching on the mountaintops again?"

"I meant something which could upset national economies, or put companies out of business."

"No, nothing like that. Penny wasn't an anarchist. Besides, ninety per cent of her time was still tied up with developing the next generation of habitats. She was determined to do as much as she could before ..." He trailed off helplessly.

"So, no secret projects, no fundamental breakthrough to crown her achievements?"

"No. The habitats were enough for her."

"Did she ever mention anyone she was having trouble with?"

He gave the glass another covetous look. "No individuals.

She was narked with some of the Boston crowd—" He stopped. Flinched. "You know about them?"

"Oh, yes. I know all about you."

He grunted dismissively. "Big deal."

"I take it the Boston argument was over the timing of independence?"

"Christ, some secret society we are. Yes. OK. All right, everyone knows it. Penny wanted the declaration as soon as the cloudscoop was operational. She was trying to talk people round, those that supported Parkinson. Which wasn't a good idea, she's not the diplomatic type. I was doing what I could, trying to help. She deserved to see independence." His eyes narrowed on my uniform's UN insignia. "The old order overthrown."

"What about you and her, did you ever argue?"

"You shit. You think I'd do that? I'd kill Penny? You fucked-up Gestapo bastard." He hurled the glass of vodka towards me in an unsteady lurch. I didn't even have to duck, the aim was so wild. It splashed into the pool and sank, leaving just the ice cubes floating about.

I wanted to tell him. That it was just procedure. That he shouldn't take it personally. And that, no, I didn't think he killed her. But his whole face was contorted into abject misery, on the verge of tears.

Instead, I stood up and mumbled something vaguely apologetic. I don't suppose he even heard. Another servitor chimp carrying a fresh glass was already heading over to him when I slid open a patio door and stepped into Penny Maowkavitz's study.

Nice going, boss, Shannon said. She was sitting in a luxurious scarlet swivel chair in front of a computer console, registering moderate exasperation.

You know I had to ask.

Yes. And I could have told you what reaction you would get.

Yeah.

But then that's what Davis would do even if he was guilty.

I looked at her in surprise. **Do you think he's guilty?**

No.

You're a big help.

How did it go at the Cybernetics Division?

Not good. Their computer security is a shambles. How are you making out with this one? I gazed at Maowkavitz's computer; it was a powerful hypercube marque, with enough capacity to perform genesplice simulations. Shannon had removed three panels from the side of the console, exposing the neat stack of slim processor blocks inside. A rat's nest of fibre-optic ribbons wormed their way through the databuses, plugging the system into several customized electronic modules lying on the carpet.

Shannon shoved some of her loose copper hair back from her forehead, and pointed to her own laptop terminal balanced on the edge of the console. **Tough going, but I think I'm making progress.**

I frowned round the study; it was almost depersonalized. A white-wall cube with a few framed holograph stills of various animals and plants I suspected where Maowkavitz's own gene-adaptions. **How come Eden doesn't know the codes?**

It can't see in. The whole room is made of composite, even the floor, and the patio door is silvered.

Funny. Not allowing her own creation to see what she was up to.

You think that's significant?

Insufficient data, which you're going to rectify for me. Today, remember?

If Boston includes police unionization and improved working conditions on its manifesto, they'll get my vote.

• • •

After that interview with Caldarola, which I can only describe as badly bungled, I drove back to the police station with the first chill of depression souring my thoughts. Or maybe it was plain honest guilt. I should have gone easier on Davis Caldarola; I knew full well he wasn't in any state to answer difficult personal questions. Then again, Shannon was quite right saying what she had: if he was guilty, that's exactly how he would behave.

Eden.

Yes, Chief Parfitt?

Did Maowkavitz and Caldarola argue very often?

They disagreed over many things. But their discussions were mainly conducted on a rational level. I would judge that they debated rather than argued. Although I do recall several rather intense rows over the years; but none of these occurred during the last eight months. His attitude towards her was one of complete devotion.

Thanks.

I didn't really suspect him. But, Christ, you've got to go by the book. Without that, without the law, nothing would function, society would cease to exist. Police work is more than tracking down lone lunatics. But I didn't expect Davis Caldarola would be too interested in a sociology lecture right then.

I was right. I did feel guilty.

• • •

I still hadn't unpacked the small box of personal items I'd brought with me to the office. There wasn't much in it, holograms of Jocelyn and the twins, paper books, some carved quartz we'd picked up on a holiday—God knows where, the memory was long gone. I sat at the desk and stared at it. I

simply couldn't be bothered to make the effort to unpack.
Besides, if Boston did make a bid for independence after the
cloudscoop was lowered, I might be packing it up again real
soon. If I didn't stop them. If the police wouldn't follow orders to stop them. If I didn't join them.

Christ.

I put my head in my hands and allowed myself a long
minute of self-indulgent pity. It was no practical help, but
wallowing in misery can feel great on occasion. Almost re-
freshing.

Eden.

Yes, Chief Parfitt?

**Give me the identity signature for Lynette Mendelson,
please.**

The memory wasn't quite a visual image, more like an
emotional sketch. I carefully ran through the procedure for
singular engagement—it would never do for this conversation to be public property—and called her, projecting that
unique mental trait which encapsulated her essence.

The response was more or less what I expected when I
identified myself.

**Oh, shit, I might have known you'd dump yourself into
my life sooner or later,** Lynette Mendelson groused. **What
did that bastard Zimmels tell you about me?**

**Only that he caught you trying to sell copies of the
genomes for some new transgenic vegetables grown up
here.** I tactfully didn't mention what else was in her file.
Lynette Mendelson worked for the JSKP in Eden's Agronomy Division as a soil chemistry specialist. It put her in a
position where she had access to each batch of Pacific Nugene's new crop designs as they came out of the laboratory
for field testing. It was a position which subjected her to a
great deal of temptation. Especially as she had a record for
fencing prototype DNA splices back on Earth. Technically,
she should never have been allowed up here; JSKP didn't

employ anyone with a less than spotless record. But Zimmels had vetoed the Personnel Department's rejection. A deceptively wily man, Zimmels. Because, sure enough, after twenty fascinating months spent analysing lumps of soil Mendelson reverted, true to form. As an entrapment exercise, it was damn near perfect.

Zimmels made her the inevitable offer: join Boston, or get shipped back to Earth where JSKP will probably have you prosecuted, and certainly have you blacklisted. Unemployment and the dole for life.

Boston gained an ardent new supporter.

That was a long time ago, Lynette Mendelson said.

It certainly was. And I'm willing to overlook it, I told her magnanimously. **But how do you think your Boston friends will react to knowing you've been supplying the Police Department, and indirectly the JSKP, with the names of their members, and information on their activities for the last two years? Eden has already had its first murder, so I suppose a lynching is inevitable at some point.**

You bastard!

You knew perfectly well what you agreed to, Lynette; being a police informer is the same as paying taxes and becoming one of the undead, it lasts for ever.

Zimmels was paying me.

I doubt it.

Well, go ahead and blow me to Boston, then. Fat lot of use I'll be to you then.

Fat lot of use you are if I'm not kept regularly updated. I paused; in this game you have to know when to allow a little slack. I'd run enough informers in my own time. **But I do have a small discretionary fund available.**

You'd better not be shitting me.

Would I?

All right; but I want real money, not some poxy taxi-driver tip. I'm taking risks for you.

Thank you, Lynette. I want to know about the argument on the timing of when Eden should declare independence. Just how heated was it?

It wasn't heated at all, not on the surface. These people are born-again politicians, everything they say is smooth and righteous. Policy discussions are all very civilized.

But there was some objection to declaring independence right after the cloudscoop is lowered. Parkinson wanted to wait, I know, he told me. According to him, you wouldn't have enough money from a single cloud-scoop's revenue to fund the buyout.

That was Bob's big justification, yes. Penny's argument was that everything is relative. If today's operation can buy out today's shares, she said, then it makes no sense to wait a decade until the profits go up, because the equity base will increase proportionally. If anything, it makes the situation worse, because investors will be far more reluctant to let go of a sizeable ultra-stable successful He_3 mining operation, which is what JSKP will be with more cloudscoops and the Callisto mass driver. By waiting you're just adding to the complexity of the leveraged buyout. But if Boston launched its buyout now, they'll still be able to attract investment for all the planned expansion projects, because the bankers don't care who's calling the shots as long as revenue keeps coming in. The whole point of the Boston takeover is to ensure the He_3 mining doesn't become invalid, they can't afford to do without it. If you ask me, the whole timing issue was a clash of personalities between Penny and Bob. They got on pretty well before, then she started accusing him of only joining Boston to help JSKP delay independence, maybe even postpone it indefinitely. That he was a straight company man.

Have they taken a vote yet?

No. It's all been pushed off until after the cloudscoop lowering is complete. Parkinson, Harwood, and a few other big guns from Boston's council are down on the anchor asteroid for the next few weeks supervising the mission. If it's successful they'll start the debate for real.

I see. Tell me, do you know if Boston ever tried to recruit Wallace Steinbauer?

He was asked. But Snecma offered him a good position back in the O'Neill Halo. Eden and the JSKP are just opportunities for him, he's exploiting his success with the Cybernetics Division to put himself way ahead of his contemporaries on the corporate ladder. He's an ambitious little bastard. Everyone knows that. So he turned Boston down flat; frightened he'd be tarred with the brush of the revolution. That would kill his promotion chances stone dead. Snecma have a seven per cent stake in JSKP, he's one of their most senior people here.

OK, thanks for your help. I'll be in touch.

Can't wait.

•   •   •

My watch said it was gone five when Nyberg drove me over to the hospital. Not that I could tell, the day-long noon of the light-tube was dousing the town and parkland in the same glaring corona as it always did. Corrine hadn't been exactly enthusiastic about my visit, but I'd come over all official, so she acquiesced with a minimum of fuss.

Bicycles filled the streets again. Everyone on their way home. Affinity allowed me to soak up the general buzz of expectation they radiated. When I asked Nyberg if that was always how it was, she told me people were optimistic about the cloudscoop lowering, eager for it to begin. I suppose I hadn't really been paying attention to the impending mission and what it meant. But of course, to Eden's population it was the dawn of a whole new era. Almost as if the habitat was coming of age. Boston or no Boston, this was what they were here to achieve.

It was only people like me who were mired in the mundane.

Corrine was sitting working at her desk, with a pile of bubble cubes beside her terminal. "Be with you in a minute," she said, without looking up.

Fine.

She grinned wolfishly, and slipped another cube into the terminal's slot. **Your session with Chong went well, then?**

Yes. Quite a remarkable man. Makes me feel glad I threw my rank about; someone like me doesn't often get the chance to talk to a living legend.

Make the most of it.

What's that supposed to mean?

Corrine held her hand up, concentrating hard on the terminal's holographic screen. Then she let out a satisfied grunt, and flicked the terminal off. The bubble cube was ejected from its slot. **Amazing. The kids born up here just don't have psychological problems. I'm going to have to recommend we release two of our paediatric psychiatrists from their contracts and send them back to Earth. They're just wasting their time in Eden.**

Yes, you told me before, the kids who grow up with affinity are better adjusted.

So I did. But the degree to which they've involved themselves in this consensus mentality is astounding. You'd normally expect one or two unable to cope, but we haven't found one single case. Maybe I should keep the psychiatrists on after all, they make a fascinating study.

Sure. You were talking about Wing-Tsit Chong.

She gave a miscreant smile. **No. It's you who's interested.**

Corrine!

OK. Spare me the third degree. You saw how frail he was?

Yeah. I felt a sudden chill. **Not another terminal illness?**

Not exactly an illness, just something we all suffer from eventually: old age. He is over ninety, after all. I could keep him alive for several more years, maybe even stretch it out for over a decade. We have the appropriate life-support techniques nowadays, especially for someone as important as him. But he turned down all my offers. I can hardly insist; and he's quite happy doing what he does, sitting and thinking all day long. I hope I go like that when it's my turn; out there in the clean air watching the swans paddle about, rather than in a hospital bed smothering in machinery.

How long has he got?

Sorry, detective, that's something I can't give you a precise answer to. I'd say anything up to a couple of years, providing he doesn't overtax himself. Fortunately Hoi Yin makes sure he doesn't.

Yes, I said emphatically, **so I noticed. Do you know how the two of them met?**

She's his student, so she always told me. They were both already here when I arrived four years ago. And in all that time she's never been involved with anyone. Surprisingly, because enough have tried. Was that what you came over to ask me about? Gossip on Hoi Yin? There's no need to turn up in person, that's what affinity is for. Bloody marvellous faculty, isn't it? You'll have to practise using it. A lot of people experiment once they've had their symbionts implanted. Sex is a popular field of exploration with the teenagers, and the teenagers at heart.

Sex?

Yes. Affinity is the only true way to find out what it really feels like from the other side.

Christ. As Chief of Police I think it's my duty to access your record; how you were ever granted a practitioner's licence to minister to the sick is beyond me.

Dear oh dear, I do believe our hardened criminologist is blushing. Aren't you the remotest bit curious?

No.

Liar. I was. It's . . . interesting. Knowing exactly how to please your partner.

I'll take your word for it. The damnedest thing was, now she had mentioned it the notion seemed to have lodged in my mind. Curiosity is a terrifying weapon.

So if it isn't sex, and it isn't how to meet the divine Miss Hoi Yin socially, what did you come here for?

I went to the window wall behind her, and shut the louvre blinds. Silver-grey light cast dusky shadows across the office.

What are you doing? Corrine asked.

Eden, can you perceive the inside of this office?

It is difficult, Chief Parfitt. I see the silhouette of someone standing behind the blinds, that is all.

Thank you. "What about hearing? Can you hear what's being said in here?"

The question was met with mental silence.

Corrine was giving me a speculative look.

I backed away from the window. "There's a question I've wanted to ask you. I don't know if I'm being paranoid, or if I'm misunderstanding affinity, but I'd value your opinion on this."

"Go on."

"You told me that the children share their thoughts quite openly. So that set me to thinking, is it possible for the servitor chimps to develop a communal intelligence?"

"Is it . . . ?" Corrine trailed off in shock, then gave a nervous little laugh. "Are you serious?"

"Very. I was thinking of an insect hive mind. Individually the chimps are always subsentient, but what if all those minds are linked up by affinity and act in tandem? That's a lot of brain power, Corrine. Could it happen?"

She was still staring at me, thunderstruck. "I . . . I don't know. No. No, I'm sure that couldn't happen." She was trying to sound forceful, as if her own conviction would make it certain. "Intelligence doesn't work like that. There are several marques of hypercube computers which have far more processing power than the human brain, yet they don't achieve sentience when you switch them on. You can run Turing AI programs in them, but that's basically just clever response software."

"But these are living brains. Quantum wire processors can't have original thoughts, inspiration and intuition; but flesh and blood can. And it's only brain size which is the barrier to achieving full sentience. Doesn't affinity provide the chimps with a perfect method of breaking that barrier? And worse, a secret method."

"Jesus." She shook her head in consternation. "Harvey, I can't think of a rational argument to refute it, not straight off the top of my head. But I just can't bring myself to believe it. Let me go through it logically. If the chimps developed intelligence, then why not tell us?"

"Because we'd stop them."

"You are paranoid. Why would we put a stop to it?"

"Because they are servitors. If we acknowledge their intelligence they stop working for us and start competing against us."

"What's so terrible about that? And even if the current generation were to stop performing the habitat's manual labour, people like Penny would just design new ones incapable of reaching . . . Oh shit, you think they killed her."

"She created them; a race born into slavery."

"No. I said people *like* her. Penny didn't create them; Pacific Nugene has nothing to do with the servitors. Bringing them to Eden was all Wing-Tsit Chong's idea. It's the Soyana company which supplies JSKP with servitors, they clone the chimps up here, along with all the other affinity capable servitor creatures. Soyana and Chong are responsible for them living in servitude, not Penny."

"Oh. I should check my facts more thoroughly. Sorry."

"Hell, Harvey, you frightened me. Don't do things like that."

I managed a weak smile. "See, people would be afraid if the chimps developed intelligence. There's a healthy xenophobic streak running through all of us."

"No, you don't. That wasn't xenophobia. Shock, maybe. Once the initial surprise wore off, people would welcome another sentient species. And only someone with a nasty suspicious mind like yours would immediately assume that the chimps would resort to vengeance and murder. You judge too much by your own standards, Harvey."

"Probably."

"You know you're completely shattering my illusions about policemen. I thought you were all humourless and unimaginative. God, sentient chimps!"

"It's my job to explore every avenue of possibility."

"I take it this means you don't have a human suspect yet?"

"I have a lot of people hotly protesting their innocence. Although the way everyone keeps claiming they overlooked Penny Maowkavitz's infamous Attitude because of who she was is beginning to ring hollow. Several individuals had some quite serious altercations with her."

Corrine's face brightened in anticipation. "Like who?"

"Now, Doctor, the medical profession has its confidentiality; we humble police have our sub judice."

"You mean you don't have a clue."

"Correct."

●   ●   ●

I wasn't back in the house thirty seconds when the twins cornered me.

"We need you to authorize our implants," Nicolette said. She held up a hospital administration bubble cube. Her face was guileless and expectant. Nathaniel wasn't much different.

Fathers have very little defence against their children, especially when they expect you to be a combination knight hero and Santa Claus.

I glanced nervously at the kitchen, where I could hear Jocelyn moving about. "I said, next week," I told Nicolette in a low voice. "This is too soon."

"You had one," Nathaniel said.

"I had to have one, it's my job."

"We need them," Nicolette insisted. "For school, for talking with our friends. We'll be ostracized again if we're not affinity-capable. Is that what you want?"

"No, of course not."

"It's Mum, isn't it?" she asked, sorrowfully.

"No. Your mother and I both agree on this."

"That's not fair," Nathaniel blurted hotly. "We didn't want to come here. OK, we were wrong. Bringing us to Eden was the greatest thing you've ever done for us. People live here, really live, not like in the arcologies. Now we want to belong, we want to be a part of what's going on here, and you won't let us. Well, just what do you want us to do, Dad? What do you want from us?"

"I simply want you to take a little time to think it through, that's all."

"What's to think? Affinity isn't a drug, we're not dropping out of school, the Pope's an idiot. So why can't we have the symbiont implants? Just give us one logical reason."

"Because I don't know if we're staying here," I bellowed. "I don't know if we're going to be *allowed* to stay here. Got that?"

I couldn't remember the last time I'd raised my voice to them—years ago, if I ever had.

They both shrank back. The shame from watching them do that was excruciating. My own kids, fearful. Christ.

Nathaniel rallied first, his expression hardening. "I'm not leaving Eden," he snapped. "You can't make me. I'll divorce you if I have to. But I'm staying." He very deliberately put his bubble cube down on a small table, then turned round and stalked off to his room.

"Oh, Daddy," Nicolette said. It was a rebuke that was almost unbearable.

"I did ask you to wait. Was one week so difficult?"

"I know," she said forlornly. "But there's a girl; Nat met her at the water sports centre."

"Great. Just great."

"She's lovely, Dad. Really pretty, and she's older than him. Sixteen."

"Pension age."

"Don't you see? She doesn't mind that he's a few months younger, that he's not as sophisticated as she is, she still likes him. That never happened to him before. It couldn't happen to him, not back on Earth."

Sex, the one subject every parent dreads. I could see Corrine's face, leering knowingly. Eden teenagers use affinity to experiment. Thoroughly.

I must have groaned, because Nicolette was resting her hand on my arm, concern sculpted into her features.

"Dad, are you all right?"

"Bad day at the office, dear. And what about you? Is there a boy at the sports centre?"

Her smile became all sheepish and demure. "Some of them are quite nice, yes. No one special, not yet."

"Don't worry, they won't leave you alone."

She blushed, and looked at her feet. "Will you speak to Mum about the symbionts? Please, Dad?"

"I'll speak to her."

Nicolette stood on tiptoes, and kissed me. "Thanks, Dad. And don't worry about Nat, his hormones are surging, that's all. Time of the month." She put her bubble cube on the table next to Nathaniel's, and skipped off down the hall to her room.

Why is it that children, the most perfect gift we can ever be given, can hurt more than any physical pain?

I picked the two bubble cubes up and weighed them in my palm. Sex. Oh, Christ.

When I turned round, Jocelyn was standing in the kitchen doorway. "Did you hear all that?"

Her lips quirked in sympathy. "Poor Harvey. Yes, I heard."

"Divorced by my own son. I wonder if he'll expect alimony?"

"I think you could do with a drink."

"Do we have any?"

"Yes."

"Thank Christ for that."

I flopped down in the lounge's big mock-leather settee, and Jocelyn poured me a glass of white wine. The patio doors were open wide, letting in a balmy breeze which set the big potted angel-trumpet plants swaying.

"Now just relax," Jocelyn said, and fixed me with a stern look. "I'll get you something to eat later."

I tasted the wine—sweet but pleasant. Shrugged out of

my uniform jacket, and undid my shirt collar. Another sip of the wine.

I fished about in the jacket for my PNC wafer, and accessed the JSKP's personnel file on Hoi Yin, or Chong's bimbo, as Caldarola had called her. I'd been curious about that ever since.

Surprisingly, my authority code rating was only just sufficient to retrieve her file from the company memory core; its security classification was actually higher than Fasholé Nocord's. And there I was thinking my troubles couldn't possibly get any worse.

· · ·

My fourth day started with a re-run of the third. I drove myself out to Wing-Tsit Chong's lakeside retreat. Eden confirmed Hoi Yin was there, what it neglected to mention was what she was doing.

I parked beside the lonely pagoda and stepped down out of the jeep. The wind chimes made a delicate silver tinkling in the stillness. Chong was nowhere to be seen. Hoi Yin was swimming in the lake, right out in the middle where she was cutting through the dark water with a powerful crawl stroke.

I would like to talk with you, I told her. **Now, please.**

There was no reply, but she performed a neat flip, legs appearing briefly above the surface, and headed back towards the shore. I saw a dark-purple towel lying on the grass, and walked over to it.

Hoi Yin stood up just before she reached the fringe of water lilies, and started wading ashore. She wasn't wearing a swimming costume. Her hair flowed down her back like a slippery diaphanous cloak.

There's an old story which did the rounds while I was at the Hendon Police College: when Moses came down from the mount carrying the tablets of stone he said, "First the good news, I managed to get Him down to ten commandments. The bad news is, He wouldn't budge on adultery."

Looking at Hoi Yin as she rose up before me like some elemental naiad, I knew how the waiting crowd must have felt. Men have killed for women far less beautiful than her.

She reached the edge of the lake and I handed her the towel.

Does nakedness bother you, Chief Parfitt? You seem a little tense. She pulled her mass of hair forwards over her shoulder, and began towelling it vigorously.

Depends on the context. But then you'd know all that. Quite the expert, in fact.

She stopped drying her hair, and gave me a chary glance. **You have accessed my file.**

Yes. My authority code gave me entry, but there aren't many people in Eden who could view it.

You believe I am at fault for not informing you what it contained?

Bloody hell, Hoi Yin, you know you're at fault. Christ Almighty, Penny Maowkavitz designed you for Soyana, using her own ovum as a genetic base. She altered her DNA to give you your looks, and improve your metabolism, and increase your intelligence. It was almost a case of parthenogenesis; genetically speaking, she's somewhere between your mother and your twin. And you think that wasn't important enough to tell me? Get real!

It was not a relationship she chose to acknowledge.

Yeah. I'll bet. Quite a shock for her, I imagine, finding you up here with Chong. She ignored nearly all of California's biotechnology ethics regulations to work on that contract; and indenture is pretty dodgy legal ground even in Soyana's own arcology. Your file says you were created exclusively as a geisha for all those middle-aged executives, that's why you were given Helen of Troy's

beauty. Maowkavitz considered you an interesting organism, nothing more. You were a job that paid well, and twenty-eight years ago Pacific Nugene needed that money quite badly. Everything which came later, her success and fortune, was all founded on the money which came from selling you right at the start, you and Christ knows how many other sisters like you. Then you came back to haunt her.

Hoi Yin wrapped the towel around her waist, and tied a knot at the side, just above her right hip. Droplets of water were still glistening across her torso and breasts. Oh yes, I noticed. Christ, she was magnificent. And completely composed, as if we were discussing some kind of financial report on the newscable. Emotionally divorced from life.

I did not haunt Penny Maowkavitz. I made precisely one attempt to discuss my origin with her. As soon as I told her who and what I was, she refused to speak to me. A situation I found quite acceptable.

I don't doubt it. Your mother, your creator, the woman who breathed life into you so that you could be condemned to an existence of sexual slavery. Then when you do meet, she rejects you utterly. And yet she made you more intelligent than herself, compounding her crime. Even when you were young you must have been smart enough to know how much more you could be, a knowledge which would grow the whole time you were with Soyana, all those years gnawing at you. I don't think I could conceive of a situation more likely to breed resentment than that. It wouldn't even be resentment at the end, just loathing and dire obsession.

Do you believe I murdered Penny Maowkavitz, Chief Parfitt?

You're the alleged psychology expert. Why don't you tell me what a girl with your history would feel about

Penny Maowkavitz? Have you got a candidate with a better motive?

I can tell you exactly what I thought about her. If I had met her ten years ago I would have killed her without even hesitating. You cannot even begin to imagine how vile my life was, although you were correct about my heightened intellect. My mind was the supreme punishment Penny Maowkavitz inflicted upon me, it set me aloof, forcing me to watch the uses to which my body was put by Soyana, understanding that there was never to be any escape, and that every thought which I had for myself was utterly irrelevant. Ignorance and stupidity would have been a blessing, a kindness. I should have been a dumb blonde. But instead she gave me intelligence. The other girls and I were kept out of the way in an arcology crèche until we reached puberty, and our education covered just one topic. Was that in my file, Chief Parfitt? Did you read how the joyful spirit of a five-year-old girl was meticulously broken to prepare me for the life I was to lead? I only learnt to read when I was fourteen. I found an entertainment deck's instruction booklet at the home of my master, and asked him to explain it to me. It was in German, the first written words I had ever seen. He taught me the meaning of the letters because he thought it was amusing to have me talk in German, another trick in my repertoire. In one month I could read and speak the language better than he. Her back was held pridefully rigid, shoulders squared. But those wonderful gold-brown eyes weren't seeing anything in this universe, they were boring straight into the past. Tears had begun to trickle down her cheeks.

"Oh, Christ." I was beginning to regret ever coming out here. You just can't imagine anything bad happening to someone so beautiful. The data was all there in her file, but that's all it was: data. Not living pain. **And Chong took you away**, I said gingerly.

Yes. When I was sixteen, I was assigned to the Vice-President of Soyana's Astronautics Division. Wing-Tsit Chong was his guest for dinner on several occasions. This was the time when Eden's seed was being germinated out here, his last trip to Earth. He was kind, for I was so ignorant, yet I thirsted for knowledge. It surprised him, that a simple geisha should understand the concepts of which he spoke. I had learnt how to operate a terminal by then, it was my way of exploring the world beyond my master's house, beyond the Soyana arcology. The only window my mind had.

Ten days after he met me, Wing-Tsit Chong asked that I be assigned to him. Soyana could not offer me to him fast enough; after all, the company fortune was built on the foundation stone of affinity.

And you've been with him ever since, I said.

I have. He told me later he accessed my record, and saw what I was. He said he was angered that a life such as mine should be so wasted. It is he who birthed me, Chief Parfitt, not Penny Maowkavitz. My mind is free now thanks to him. He is my spirit father. I love him.

Hoi Yin, all you've told me . . . it just makes you look even more guilty.

I am guilty of one thing, Chief Parfitt; I have not yet reached the purity of thought to which Wing-Tsit Chong has tried to raise me. I will never be worthy of his patronage, because I hate. I hate Penny Maowkavitz in a fashion which shames me. But I can never exorcize the knowledge of what she did. And that is why I would never kill her.

I don't follow.

Hoi Yin wiped the tears with the back of her hand. It was such a delicate childish action, betraying her terrible vulnerability, that I ached to put my arms round her. I wanted, needed, to draw the hurt out of her. Any male would.

I would not kill Maowkavitz, because she was dying of cancer, Hoi Yin said. Her last months of life were to be spent screaming as her body rotted away. That, I thought, was Kamma. She would have suffered through it all, for she is a soulless inhuman selfish monster, and she would have fought her decay, stretching out her torment at the hands of those clinically caring doctors. If today I could save her from that bullet wound I would do so, in order that she might undergo that horrendous final ordeal which was her ordained destiny. Penny Maowkavitz never deserved anything so quick and clean as a bullet through the brain. Whoever did that cheated me. "They cheated me!" she yelled, face screwed up in passionate rage.

I stepped up to her as she started sobbing, cradling her as I often did Nicolette. She was trembling softly in my embrace. Her skin below my hands was textured as smooth as silk, I felt the warmth of her, the residual dampness. She clung to me tightly, open mouth searching blindly across my chin. Then we were kissing with an almost painful urgency.

She pulled my uniform off as we tumbled onto the thick grass. Her towel came free with one fast tug from my hand. Suddenly we were locked together, rolling over and over with her hair flying free around us. She was strong, and magnificently supple, and dangerously knowledgeable. And affinity was blinding me with desire; I could feel my hands squeezing her breasts and stroking her thighs, and at the same time I could taste the rapture each movement brought her as she surrendered her thoughts to me. All I could think of was doing whatever I could to bring her more ecstasy. Then I let her discover my enjoyment. The whole world detonated into orgasm.

• • •

I woke to find myself lying on my back in the grass beside the lake. Hoi Yin was snuggled up beside me, one finger stroking my chin.

She smiled lazily, which was like watching sunrise over Heaven. "I haven't done that for twelve years," she said huskily.

"I know the feeling." Christ, what was I saying.

"And I have never been with a man from my own choice before. Not once. How strange that it should be you." She kissed me lightly, and ran her finger along the line of my jawbone. "Don't be guilty. Please. This is Eden, only one step down from paradise."

"And I'm one step from hell. I am married, Hoi Yin."

"I won't spoil your happiness. I promise, Harvey."

First time you've called me that.

Because this is the first time you have been Harvey to me. I'm not entirely sure I like Chief Parfitt. He can be cold. Her lips started to work down my throat.

"You don't love me, do you?" I'm not quite sure for whose benefit the hopeful tone was included in that question. The confusion raging round in my mind made clear thinking very difficult.

No, Harvey. I enjoy you. At this moment we are right for each other. Yesterday we were not. Tomorrow, who knows? But now is perfect, and should be rejoiced. That is the magic of Eden, where human hearts are open to each other. Here honesty rules.

Ah.

Do you enjoy me, Harvey?

I'm old enough to be your father.

A very young father. Her tongue put in an impish appearance at the corner of her mouth. **I accessed your file long before you accessed mine. Wing-Tsit Chong's authority can open any JSKP file for me.**

Christ.

So answer the question, do you enjoy me?

Yes.

Good.

She swung a leg over my belly, and straddled me. Her corona of wild blonde hair caught the light, shimmering brightly. A splendidly erotic angel.

I'm on duty, I protested.

She laughed, then held herself perfectly still. Her mind released a surge of desire, revealing the places where she adored to be touched.

My hands moved up to caress her, seemingly of their own accord.

• • • •

When it comes to guilt, who better to consult than a priest? Except for the fact that I would never ever dream of telling Father Cooke about me and Hoi Yin.

Christ. Jocelyn and I have our first pleasant civilized evening together for I don't know how long, and first thing next morning I'm making love to the most beautiful girl the world has ever known. And not just twice, either. Her youth and voracity proved a powerful aphrodisiac.

We had parted without any promises of commitment. All very bohemian and fashionable. In one respect she was right about Eden, or at least affinity; we could see right into each other's hearts. There and then our emotions had harmonized. She desperate and anguished; me appalled, wanting to comfort, and weighted down with a sense of isolation. There and then, what we did was right.

Only in Eden.

Where else would I make love in a field like some uncontrollably randy teenager? Where else would I make love to a girl who is physical perfection?

Who also happens to be my principal suspect. Whose expertise the police had called upon to examine, in private, the chimp which pulled the trigger. Who reported back that there was no visual memory of the murderer, nor could ever be one.

Oh, crap.

•   •   •

There was no one in the main section of the church, but Eden directed me to the small suite of rooms at the back where Father Cooke lived. I found the priest sitting in his lounge, watching the cloudscoop-lowering operation on a hologram screen.

"It's supposed to be my morning for Bible class at school," he said with a contrite grin. "But the kids are like everyone else today, watching the cloudscoop. It gives me an excuse to tune in like the rest of them." He indicated a chair, then frowned. "Did you fall over, Chief?"

I brushed self-consciously at the smear of mud on the sleeve of my jacket. My trousers still had some broken blades of grass clinging to them. And the fabric was a mass of creases. The whole uniform had been cleanly pressed when I left the house that morning.

"Yes. But nothing broken." I sat hurriedly and pointed at the large wall-mounted screen. "How's it going?"

The screen showed a picture of the anchor asteroid traversing Jupiter's choppy cloudscape. A thin spear of stellar-bright fusion plasma was emerging from the centre of the radiator panels. It looked as though it could be braided, but the screen's resolution wasn't sharp enough for me to be sure. Cooke had turned the sound down, muting the newscable commentator's voice to a monotonous insect buzz.

"It's going fine by all accounts," he said. "Look at that clustered fusion drive unit, ten thousand tonnes of thrust. Imagine that! Sometimes I think we're challenging the

Almighty Himself with these stunts. Rearranging the cosmos to suit ourselves. What boldness."

"You don't approve?"

"On the contrary, my son, I love this aspect of being up here, right out where the cutting edge of engineering is happening. Spaceflight and high technology have always fascinated me. That's one of the main reasons Eden was given to me as my parish. The bishop thought I was unhealthy on the subject, but my enthusiasm works to the Church's advantage."

"But you don't have neural symbionts."

"Of course not, but I talk to Eden through my PNC wafer. And the servitor chimps respond to verbal orders when I need any tasks performed round the house. The only thing I miss out on is this glorified mental telephone ability to converse with someone away down the other end of the habitat. But then, when people need to talk to me, I prefer it to be face to face. There are some traditions which should be maintained." He was smiling with soft expectancy, a thousand lines crinkling his humane face.

"Jocelyn and I talked last night," I began lamely. "We haven't done that for quite a while."

"That's good, then. That's encouraging."

"Possibly. You see, the twins told us in no uncertain terms how much they enjoy being in Eden. They want to stay."

"Well, I could have told you that was going to happen; I've seen it a hundred times. Do you know why the majority of the population supports Boston? It's because if Eden becomes an independent nation, they will be its legal citizens. In other words, they won't be sent back to Earth when their contract with the JSKP runs out."

I hadn't considered that aspect of grassroots support. Trust a priest to see the true motivation factor behind all the fine words about destiny and liberty. "The thing is, the twins want neuron symbiont implants. They say they'll be left out if they're not affinity capable."

"Which they will, and you know that. Your children especially, I don't suppose they had it easy back on Earth."

"Christ, you must be psychic."

"No, my son, I'm not. I wish I were, it would make my job a lot simpler, given the way people hedge and squirm in the confessional. What I have is a terrible weight of experience. I know the way police and company security men are regarded on Earth. It's becoming clear to me that the price of an industrialized society is an almost total collapse of civil and moral behaviour. Urbanization blunts our responsibilities as citizens. Eden is a complete reversal of that, the pastoral ideal."

"Yeah, I expect you're right. But what do we do, Jocelyn and me? She's completely torn; more than anything she wants the twins to be happy, but she doesn't want them to be happy here."

"And you do."

"I don't mind where they are as long as they have that chance at happiness. But I can't imagine them ever being happy back on Earth, not now they've seen Eden, seen how it doesn't have to be like the arcology."

"That's understandable. When urban kids are let loose to run around up here, they really do believe it's paradise."

"You're saying it again, how much you approve of Eden."

"Like every human society, there is much to admire, and much to regret. Physically, materialistically, Eden is far superior to Earth. I suspect your children really won't be swayed by arguments of spiritual fulfilment. People under fifty rarely are."

"If it was just me, I'd stay," I told him earnestly. "I'd love to stay. You know that. But what about Jocelyn? Affinity is the biggest barrier between us, ironic as that sounds. I just can't ever see her fitting in here. Not now. I had it all planned out so beautifully before we came. She was going to take a job in the Governor's office; she used to work in the Delph arcology administration back in London. JSKP are quite good about that kind of thing, finding family partners employment. But she's obviously not going to be able to do that now, because you need affinity for any job where you have to interface with other people. If I've learned nothing else in the last couple of days, I've learned that. And she won't have the implant, which means she'll have to sit around at home all day long. Imagine how demeaning that will be for her, not to mention depressing."

"Yes, I see your problem," he said. "Your children won't leave, your wife can't stay. And you love them both. It's a pretty fix you've got yourself in, my son, and no mistake."

"So what do you think? Should I keep on trying to persuade Jocelyn to have an implant? Or could you do it, convince her that the symbionts are harmless, that they don't violate the Pope's declaration?"

"Alas, I'm not sure about that, my son," he said regretfully. "Not at all. Perhaps the Pope was wrong to concentrate on the affinity gene itself rather than the whole concept. I came here with the first batch of people to live in the habitat, five years ago. I've seen how they've changed thanks to this communal affinity. It almost abrogates my role entirely. They don't need to confide in me any more, they have each other, and they are totally honest about their feelings, affinity allows that."

"You don't like it because it's putting you out of a job?" I asked, annoyed at him for what seemed almost like conceit. I wanted my problem solved, not his regrets about falling service attendance.

"They are not turning from me, my son, rather what I represent. The Church. And not just Christians either; there is a small Muslim community in Eden as well, they too are turning from their teachings, and as a rule of thumb they tend to be even more devout than the old Catholics. No, affinity is taking people from God, from faith. Affinity is making them psychologically strong together."

"Surely that's good?

"I wish it were so, my son. But to have so much self-faith borders on hubris. The absolute denial of God. I cannot endorse what I see happening here. I urge you with all my heart to talk with your children again, try and convince them how ultimately shallow their lives would be if they were to spend them here."

I stared at him for a long minute, too shocked to speak. What the hell could he know about affinity? What gave him the right to pass judgement? All my misgivings about the Church and its blind dogma were beginning to surface again. "I'm not sure I can do that, Father," I said levelly.

"I know, my son. I'll pray that you are given guidance in this matter. But I genuinely feel that Eden is being emptied of divine spirit. In His wisdom our Lord gave man a multitude of weaknesses so we might know humility. Now these people are hardening their souls." For a second his face showed an immense burden of regret, then he mustered his usual placid smile. "Now, before you go, do you have anything to confess, my son?"

I stood, putting on a front of steely politeness. Why is it that you can never manage to be rude to men of the cloth? "No, Father, I have nothing to confess."

• • •

Did you hear all that? I asked Eden when I was back in the jeep.

I did.

The intimation of immense calmness behind the thought mollified me. Slightly. **What do you think? Are we all** using you and affinity like some kind of cephalic valium?

What can I say, Chief Parfitt? I believe the priest is wrong, yet he is a decent man who means well.

Yeah, and God preserve us from them.

What do you intend to do about your family?

Christ, I don't know. I suppose you saw me and Hoi Yin?

Yes. Your association registered with my sensitive cells.

Association, I mused. **I don't think I've ever heard it called that before.**

Wing-Tsit Chong explained that there are some human subjects which should be approached with extreme caution. Sex is one of them.

He's certainly right about that. I turned the jeep onto the road leading to the police station. There was a locker room there, I could have a shower, wash the smell of her away. That was probably what clued Father Cooke in. Nothing I could do about the messed up uniform, though. Unless I sent a servitor chimp sneaking into my bedroom.

Almost without conscious thought I could see the house. Jocelyn was in the lounge, watching the cloudscoop lowering on the newscable. Two servitor chimps were cleaning the street pavements a hundred metres away from the front garden. Sending one in unnoticed would be easy. My three spare uniforms were hanging up in a closet—memory of yesterday: Jocelyn hanging them up, taking care not to crease them.

No.

I wasn't going to resort to that. But I wasn't going to confess, either.

That wasn't the answer.

Boss? Shannon called.

Hello, and I think I conveyed just a bit too much boisterous relief in my response. There was a slight recoil.

Er, I've cracked Maowkavitz's remaining files, boss.

Great, what's in them?

**I think you ought to come out to the house and have a
look for yourself.**

On my way. There was a suppressed excitement in her
thought. I did a U-turn, and sent the jeep racing towards the
plush residential sector on the edge of town.

Davis Caldarola greeted me when I came in through the
front door. He was wearing very dark sunglasses, every
move measured and delicate. Classic hangover case.

Sorry about yesterday, he said humbly. **I'm not like that
normally.**

**Don't worry about it. In my job I meet too many be-
reaved people. You were remarkably restrained, believe
me.**

Thanks.

Where's Officer Kershaw?

In the study.

Shannon was lounging indolently in the big scarlet chair,
a very smug expression in place. Three screens were illuminated on the top of the console, each displaying a vast
amount of fine blue text.

Have you been here all night? I asked.

**Almost. Someone was pretty insistent about wanting
to know what was in her files, remember?**

**OK, enjoy your moment of glory. What have you
found?**

**According to her access log record, the last fifty-two
files she was working on contained Cybernetics Division
records. They're pretty comprehensive, too. She's been
downloading them from their computer for the last six
weeks.**

I don't get it. I gave Davis Caldarola a puzzled glance, meeting equal bafflement. **Did she tell you she was working on this?** I asked him.

No. Never. Penny never showed the slightest interest in the Cybernetics Division, certainly not after Wallace Steinbauer took over a couple of years ago. It was one of her jokes that ultimately she could replace all the mechanical systems inside the habitat with biological equivalents, and put the whole division out of work. She said they were a temporarily necessary anachronism. She always resented using the jeeps and the funicular railways.

I studied the screens again. The tabulated data was simply list after list of mechanical components and domestic items which the factories had manufactured, each one with an index cataloguing the date, time, material composition, energy consumption, quality control inspections, what it was used for, who requested it . . . "What did she want it all for?" I mumbled. **And more importantly, why didn't Wallace Steinbauer tell me she had been downloading all his division's files? He claimed there was very little contact between him and Maowkavitz.**

Because he didn't know? Shannon suggested sagely.

Good point. The Cybernetics Division computer system was poorly managed. Could Maowkavitz download these records without anyone in the Cybernetics Division knowing?

Shannon pouted. **I certainly could. And Maowkavitz probably knew the system management command codes; she was a JSKP director, after all. Hacking in would be very simple for her.**

OK. So tell me, Shannon, what is the point of acquiring this much data on anything? What can you actually do with it?

Data? Two things, sell it or search it.

Penny wouldn't sell it, Davis Caldarola said emphatically.

There's nothing here to sell anyway, Shannon said. **The actual assembly bay control programs use a form of flexible fuzzy logic which is quite sophisticated, they might be reasonably valuable to a rival manufacturing company, but they're hardly exclusive. And in any case,** she waved an arm at the console, **they're not here. These files are just manufacturing records.**

Which leaves us with a search, I said.

You got it, boss.

OK, genius, search it for what?

She flashed a smile, and started typing rapidly on a keyboard. **Her programs don't have restricted access, only the files. So let's see.** The data on the screens began to change as she called up various system menus. Her head swivelled round like a vigilant owl as she checked the ever-changing display formats. "Gotcha!" A sharply pointed fingernail tapped one of the screens. **This is the one. According to the log record she was using it the day before she died.** Long columns of purple and green numbers fell down the screen. Shannon blinked, and peered forwards eagerly. **Holy shit. Boss, it's a tracer program which looks for gold.**

Gold? I queried.

Davis Caldarola gave a small start. I only just caught it out of the corner of my eye. And he covered fast, turning it into a perplexed scowl. Interesting.

Yes, Shannon said. **It's a fairly basic routine; it just runs through the files and pulls any reference for gold.**

And Penny Maowkavitz was using it to search the Cybernetics Division files? Which file has the same log-on time as the search program?

Way ahead of you, boss. The screens were running

through menu displays again, too fast for the data to be anything other than a fluorescent smear.

In my own mind I was starting to assemble a theory, segments of the puzzle manoeuvring round each other, slotting together. There was a strong sense of conviction rising, buoying up my flagging confidence. Progress was coming too fast for it to be mere coincidence. **Eden.**

Yes, Chief Parfitt

Tell me about the asteroid rock you digest; does it contain gold?

Yes.

And other precious metals?

Yes. Silver and platinum are also present in small quantities.

"But everything is relative," I whispered. Eden digests over two hundred thousand of tonnes of rock each year, that's what Wallace Steinbauer told me. And had been doing so ever since it was germinated.

Davis Caldarola had turned even paler. **Do you separate these precious metals out and store them in the silos in the southern endcap?** I asked.

Yes.

What is the current quantity stockpiled in the silos?

I am holding one thousand seven hundred and eighty tonnes of silver; one thousand two hundred and thirty tonnes of gold, and eight hundred and ninety tonnes of platinum.

"I never knew that," Shannon said. She had stopped typing to look at me in astonishment.

Me neither, I said. **It wasn't in any briefing I received. In fact, I doubt the JKSP board even knows about it. I expect the information that Eden could extract precious metals as well as ordinary ones was hidden away in some technical appendix that nobody ever looked at, that's if Maowkavitz ever bothered to mention it at all.**

Why? Shannon demanded.

Well, Davis? I said heavily. **Why don't you tell us?**

I didn't know, he blurted.

I don't believe you, Davis. It was an extremely subtle deception; and one which must have been planned right from the very start. In other words, it was Penny Maowkavitz's idea.

His jaw worked silently, then he slowly lowered his head into his hands. "Oh God, you've got this all wrong."

So put us straight, I said.

It was never for personal gain. It was all for Boston, everything she did was for us.

She was going to reveal the existence of the precious metal stockpile after independence, I said. **Then it could be used for Boston's buyout of JSKP shares.**

You know? he asked in surprise.

It seems logical.

Yes. It was all so beautifully simple. Only Penny could be this elegant. Nobody has ever attempted to extract precious metals from asteroid rock before. Sure, precious metals are present in the O'Neill Halo asteroids, but the quantities simply aren't large enough to warrant building specialist extraction units on to the existing furnaces. Given the mass of ore involved, it isn't cost-effective. But in Eden's case it costs nothing for the digestive organs to extract them from the ore. Like you said, she never told the JSKP board the metals were being automatically refined; and nobody ever thought in those terms. The board never expected to receive gold from Jupiter.

And what you don't know, you can't act upon, I said. **Neat.**

She just wanted what was best, he insisted staunchly.

How many other people knew? I asked.

Only the four of us. Penny thought that it would be a very hard secret to keep. People would be tempted.

I expect she's right. So you and she knew; who were the others?

Antony Harwood and Eric McDonald.

Not Bob Parkinson? He is Boston's leader now, after all.

Davis Caldarola let out a contemptuous snort. No way! She said she didn't trust him any more. Not since this row over the timing. She said he was showing his true loyalties now the crunch was coming. I know she didn't want him as a trustee any more, she was going to replace him.

OK, I know Harwood. Who's Eric McDonald?

He used to be in charge of the Cybernetics Division, before JSKP brought in their management whiz-kid Steinbauer. Eric is still up here; he got shunted sideways into the cloudscoop operation, supervising the microgee industrial stations which produced the pipe.

Steinbauer didn't know?

No. Hell, he's not even a Boston member.

I looked enquiringly at Shannon. I'd guess that Penny Maowkavitz has been checking up on Steinbauer. If anyone was likely to find out about the stockpile, it would be him. Blowing that subterfuge to the JSKP board really would guarantee his promotion.

Most likely, yes, boss.

So what was the last file Maowkavitz reviewed?

She consulted one of the screens. Now that's a funny one; strictly speaking it isn't a Cybernetics Division file. It's the maintenance log for a Dornier SCA-4545B two-man engineering capsule. JSKP has about sixty of them up here, tending the industrial stations and the He_3 operations. But, boss, this log hasn't got the UN Civil

Spaceflight Authority codes; I'd say it was some kind of bootleg copy.

The data on the screen didn't mean anything to me. **Run the gold search program**, I told her.

Her finger stabbed down on the enter key.

Bingo.

•   •   •

Can you actually see Steinbauer yourself? I asked Rolf.

Yes, sir; he's in his office, two down from the one I'm using.

What's he doing?

Using the computer, I think. He's sitting at the desk, anyway.

OK, under no circumstances are you to approach him. I turned the jeep onto one of the main roads running the length of the habitat. At the back of my mind I was aware of Eden clearing all other traffic from the road ahead of me, and diverting people away from the cyberfactory cavern where Steinbauer had his office. I twisted the accelerator, pushing the jeep up to fifty kilometres an hour, top speed.

Boss, Shannon called, **I make that over two hundred and twenty modifications to the capsule systems; he's been replacing everything from wiring to thermal foil.**

Have they all been substituted?

Yes.

OK, thanks, Shannon. Nyberg?

Yes, sir.

What's your ETA?

We're leaving the station now, sir. We should be there in eight minutes.

I saw a mirage of three police jeeps pulling out onto the street, each with five officers dressed in black lightweight flex-armour. The trouble was, people were huddled on the pavement watching the little convoy speed past. They would be telling their friends, who would tell their friends. The whole habitat would be blanketed with the news in a matter of minutes. Someone was bound to inform Steinbauer in all innocence. And there wasn't a thing I could do about it.

What worried me was the kind of weapons the armed response team might be facing. Steinbauer could have built anything in that bloody factory, from a neutron beam rifle to a guided missile. We wouldn't know until he hit us with it.

I toyed with the idea of just calling him and telling him we knew, point out that he couldn't escape. It might save lives, especially if he panicked when the team crashed into the office. But then again he might just use the time to prepare. Command decisions, what I get paid for.

Eden.

Yes, Chief Parfitt?

Can you see anything which might be a weapon in Steinbauer's office, or anywhere else in the cyberfactory for that matter?

No. But I'm still reviewing the mechanical objects whose function isn't immediately clear to me.

Shunt the images straight to Rolf, he ought to be able to speed up the process.

Sir, Rolf said. **Steinbauer has just asked me what's happening. I've told him it's just a readiness exercise.**

Shit. Is he buying it?

He is asking me to confirm, Eden said. **Which I have done.**

I looked through the sensitive cells in Steinbauer's office, seeing him sitting at his desk, frowning out at the ranks of machinery in the cavern. He gave Rolf a concerned glance, then stood up.

A wave of trepidation from Rolf flooded back to me. **If he makes a move towards you, I'll tell him the response team will be issued with shoot to kill orders**, I told him.

Thanks, sir.

Steinbauer was leaning over his desk, typing furiously on his computer console.

Hey! Rolf protested.

What is it?

The computer memory is erasing. God damn, he's wiping the whole Cybernetics Division system clean.

Steinbauer picked up a small box, and left his office. Outside, the machines were coming to a halt in a crescendo of squealing metal. Red strobes began to flare in warning, turning the whole cavern into a lurid grotto of oscillating shadows. Trolleys braked suddenly, some of them spilling their loads. Alarm klaxons added to the din of abused machinery.

Rolf's hands gripped the armrests of his chair. I could feel the tendons taut in his forearms as Steinbauer walked past the glass wall in front of him.

Eden, are there any servitor chimps in the cavern?

No, Chief Parfitt, I'm afraid not, the noise and machinery upsets them.

Damn. I had thought we could send a scrum of them to overpower him.

Steinbauer had reached the back of the cavern. The sensitive cells showed me tiny beads of sweat pricking his forehead. He opened the box and took out the Colt .45 pistol. It was the one we had asked him to build.

"Bugger," I spat. My jeep had just reached the start of the causeway. **Eden, did he make any bullets for it?**

Yes. You did ask for a complete evaluation.

Rolf, get out. Now. Eden, pull everyone else from the cavern; steer them clear of Steinbauer as they go.

I watched impotently as Steinbauer checked the revolver's barrel, and pulled the safety catch back.

Steinbauer?

No answer, although he did cock his head to one side. He carried on walking along the rear wall.

Steinbauer, this is pointless. We know about the gold and the Dornier capsule. Put the pistol down. You're not going anywhere. This is a habitat, for Christ's sake, there's nowhere to hide.

Steinbauer stopped in front of a circular muscle membrane in the wall. He stood there with both hands on his hips, glaring at it.

He has ordered it to open, Eden said. But I won't allow it.

Where does it lead to?

It is one of the entrances to the inspection tunnels which run through my digestive organs.

I was abruptly aware of the tunnels, a nightmare topology which twined round the titanic organs. The entire southern endcap was riddled with them. Steinbauer tilted his head back, peering curiously at the polyp roof. Then the image vanished from my mind, colour streaks imploding like a hologram screen that had been fused.

Eden, what's happening?

I do not know, Chief Parfitt. My input from the sensitive cells at the rear of the cavern has failed. I cannot account for it. Something seems to be affecting my interpretation routines.

"Christ!" The jeep had reached the entrance to the cavern. A dozen cyberfactory staff were milling round outside, uncertainty etched on their faces. I braked sharply, and tapped out my code on the small weapons locker between the jeep's front chairs. The lid flipped open, and I pulled out the Browning laser carbine.

Everybody back, I ordered. Get on the next tram, I don't want any of you left on this side of the circumfluous lake.

Rolf was elbowing his way through them.

Have you seen Steinbauer? I asked.

No. He hasn't tried to come out.

I gave the entrance to the cavern a jaundiced look; it resembled a railway tunnel that had been lined in marble. There were no doors, no way of sealing it. **Eden, how many entrances to the inspection tunnels are there?**

Eleven.

Oh great. OK, I want the entire southern endcap evacuated. Get everyone back across the lake. Nyberg, I want the response team distributed round all the tunnel entrances. If Steinbauer emerges without warning, they are to shoot on sight. Christ knows what he's got stashed away in the tunnels.

Yes, sir, she acknowledged.

Rolf, get the rest of our people kitted out with armour and issued with weapons. I think we might have to go into those tunnels and flush him out.

I'm on it, sir, he said, grim-faced.

Chief Parfitt, Eden called. **I am losing my perception inside the inspection tunnel leading away from the back of the cyberfactory cavern.**

There's over eighty kilometres of tunnels, Rolf exclaimed in dismay. **It's a bloody three-dimensional maze in there.**

Clever place to hide, I said. **Or perhaps not. If he can't consult Eden about his location, he's going to wind up wandering round in circles.** I started to walk into the cavern, the Browning held ready. Red light was flickering erratically. The chemical smell of coolant fluid was strong in the air.

Wing-Tsit Chong?

Yes, Harvey, how may I help you? I have been informed that armed police have been deployed in the habitat; and now Eden tells me it is suffering a disturbingly powerful glitch in its perception routines.

That's where I'd like your advice. Wallace Steinbauer has come up with some sort of disruption ability. Pre-

sumably it's based on the same principles he used to fox the chimp's monitoring routine. Have you and Hoi Yin come up with any sort of counter yet?

Wallace Steinbauer?

Yes, the Cybernetics Division manager. It looks like he's Penny's murderer.

I see. One moment, please.

I edged round the corner of the assembly bay access to the entrance, and scanned the long aisle ahead of me. Several trolleys had stopped along its length, two of them had collided, producing a small avalanche of aluminium ingots. There was no sign of Steinbauer.

Eden, can you perceive me?

Only from the sensitive cells around the entrance, the rest of the cavern is blocked to me.

OK. I crouched low and scuttled along the aisle. The flashing red light made it hellish difficult to spot any genuine motion on the factory floor. Funnily enough, the one thing which kept running through my mind as I made my way to the rear of the factory was the thought that if Steinbauer had murdered Penny Maowkavitz, then Hoi Yin was in the clear.

Incredibly unprofessional.

Harvey, Wing-Tsit Chong called. **I believe we can offer some assistance. The dysfunctional routines Steinbauer leaves behind him can be wiped completely, and fresh ones installed to replace them.**

Great.

However, the ones in his direct vicinity will simply be glitched again. But that in itself will enable us to track his position, to around fifteen or twenty metres.

OK, fine. Do it now.

A blinked glimpse of the placid lake beyond the veranda. Hoi Yin bending over towards him, long rope of blonde hair brushing his knee rug, her face compressed with worry. His thin frame was trembling from the effort of countering Steinbauer's distortion, a heavy painful throbbing had started five centimetres behind his temple.

I am regaining perception of the cavern, Eden informed me. **Steinbauer is not inside. He must be in the inspection tunnel.**

I started running for the rear of the cavern. The muscle membrane was half-open, quivering fitfully. As I approached it the lips began to calm.

It is not just the perception routines Steinbauer is glitching, Wing-Tsit Chong said with forced calmness. **Every segment of the personality in the neural strata around him is being assaulted.**

A wicked smell of sulphur was belching out of the inspection tunnel. I coughed, blinking against the acrid vapour. **What the hell is that?**

The muscle membrane promptly closed.

It must be a leakage from the enzyme sacs, Wing-Tsit Chong said. **The duct network which connects them to the organs is regulated by muscle membranes. Steinbauer is wrecking their autonomic governor routines.**

Christ. I stared helplessly at the blank wall of polyp. **Have you located him yet?**

He is approximately two hundred metres in from the cavern, thirty metres above you, Eden said.

Rolf, do we have gas masks?

No, sir. But we could use spacesuits.

Good idea, though they're going to restrict—

The cry which burst into the communal affinity band was awesome in its sheer volume of anguish. It contained nameless dread, and loathing, and a terrified bewilderment. The tormented mind pleaded with us, wept, cursed.

Wallace Steinbauer was standing, slightly stooped, in a cramped circular tunnel. It was illuminated in a gloomy green hue, a light emitted by the strip of phosphorescent cells running along the apex. Its polyp walls had a rough wavy texture, as if they'd been carved crudely out of living rock.

He was retching weakly from the appalling stench, hands clutching his belly. Lungs heaved to pull oxygen from the thick fetid air. The floor was inclined upwards at a gentle angle ahead of him. Wide bugged eyes stared at the tide of muddy yellow sludge which was pouring down the tunnel. It reached his shoes and flowed sluggishly around his ankles. Immediately he was struggling to stay upright, but there was no traction; the sludge was insidiously slippery. Cold burned at his shins as the level rose. Then blowtorch pain was searing at his skin, biting its way inwards. His trousers were dissolving before his eyes.

He lost his footing, and fell headlong into the sludge. Pain drenched every patch of naked skin, gobbling through the fatty tissue towards the muscle and bone beneath. He screamed once. But that simply let the rising sludge into his mouth. Fire exploded down his gullet. Spastic convulsions jerked his limbs about. Sight vanished, twisting away into absolute blackness.

Coherent thoughts ended then. Insanity blew some tattered nerve impulses at us for a few mercifully brief seconds. Then there was nothing.

Minds twinkled all around me, a galaxy misted by a dense nebula. Each one radiating profound shock, shamed and guilty to witness such a moment. The need for comfort was universal. We instinctively clung together in sorrow, and waited for it to pass.

Father Cooke was quite right: sharing our grief made it that much easier to endure. We had each other, we didn't need the old pagan symbols of redemption.

•   •   •   •

The fifth day was mostly spent sorting out the chaos which came in the wake of the fourth; for the Governor, for the newscable reporters, (in a confidential report) for the JSKP board, for the police, and for the rest of the shocked population. Pieter Zernov and I organized a combined operation to clear the inspection tunnels and recover the body. I let his team handle most of it—they were welcome to the job.

Fasholé Nocord was delighted the case had been solved. The general public satisfaction with my department's performance added complications to Boston's campaign. We had proved beyond any shadow of doubt the effectiveness and impartiality of the UN administration. Not even a senior JSKP employee could escape the law.

Congratulations all round. Talk of promotions and bonuses. Morale in the station peaked up around the axial light-tube.

The one sour note was sounded when Wing-Tsit Chong collapsed. Corrine told me he had badly overstressed himself in helping us overcome Steinbauer's distortion of Eden's thought routines. She wasn't at all confident for his recovery.

All in all, it allowed me to, quite justifiably, postpone making any decisions about Jocelyn and the twins.

•   •   •

I used the same excuse at breakfast on the sixth day, as well. Nobody argued.

At midday I took a funicular railway car up the northern endcap, and headed down the docking spindle to inspect Steinbauer's dragon hoard. The pressurized hangar I had requisitioned was just a fat cylinder of titanium, ribbed by monomolecule silicon spars, with an airlock door at the far end large enough to admit one of the inter-orbit tugs. A thick quilt of white thermal blankets covered the metal, preventing the air from radiating its warmth off into space. Thick bundles of power and data cables snaked about in no recognizable pattern. I glided through the small egress airlock which connected the hangar to Eden's docking spindle, tasting a faint metallic tang in the air.

The Dornier SCA-4545B hung in the middle of the yawning compartment, suspended between two docking cradles that had telescoped out from the walls. It was a fat cone shape with two curving heavily shielded ports protruding from the middle of the fuselage. Every centimetre had been coated in a layer of ash-grey carbon foam which was pocked and scored from innumerable dust impacts. An array of waldo arms clustered round its nose were fully extended; with their awkward joints and spindly segments they looked remarkably like a set of insect mandibles.

Equipment bay panels had been removed all around the fuselage, revealing ranks of spherical fuel tanks, as well as the shiny intestinal tangle of actuators, life-support machinery, and avionics systems. Shannon Kershaw and Susan Nyberg were floating over one open equipment bay, both wearing navy-blue one-piece jump suits, smeared with grime. Nyberg was waving a hand-held scanner over some piping, while Shannon consulted her PNC wafer.

I grabbed one of the metal hand hoops sprouting from the Dornier's fuselage, anchoring myself a couple of metres from them. **How's it going?**

Tough work, boss, Shannon replied. She glanced up and gave me a quick impersonal smile. **It's going to take us days to recover all the gold if you don't appoint someone to assist us. We're not really qualified to strip down astronautics equipment.**

You're the closest specialist I've got to a spacecraft technician, I can hardly give this job to a regular maintenance crew. And you should think yourself lucky I gave you this assignment. I was in the cyberfactory cav-

ern yesterday evening when the recovery team finished flushing the enzyme goop out of the inspection tunnels. It took Zernov's biotechnology people eight hours to restore the organ and its ancillary glands to full operability. Then we had to wait another hour while the tunnel atmosphere was purged.

Did you get the body? Nyberg asked.

Most of it. The bones had survived, along with the bulk of the torso viscera. We also found the pistol, and some of the buttons from his tunic. Those enzymes were bloody potent; the organ employs them to break down bauxite, for Christ's sake. We were lucky to find as much of him as we did.

Shannon screwed up her face in disgust. "Yuck!" I think you're right, we'll just carry on here.

Excellent. How much gold have you collected so far?

Nyberg pointed to a big spherical orange net floating on the end of a tether. It was stuffed full of parts from the Dornier capsule—coils of wire, circuit boards, sheets of foil. About a hundred and fifty kilos so far. He substituted it everywhere he could. In the circuitry, in thermal insulation blankets, in conduit casing. We think the radiator panel surfaces might be pure platinum.

I shifted my gaze to the mirror-polished triangular fins jutting from the rear of the Dornier's fuselage. The billion-wattdollar spacecraft. Christ.

I don't understand how he ever hoped to get it all back to Earth, Nyberg said.

He probably planned to assign the Dornier to one of the tanker spaceships on a run back to the O'Neill Halo, Shannon said. Plausible enough. Nobody seemed to query this capsule being withdrawn for maintenance so often. I checked its official UN Civil Spaceflight Authority log; the requests to bring it into the drydock hangars all originate from the Cybernetics Division. We all regard computers as infallible these days, especially on something as simple as routine maintenance upgrades. Which is what these were listed as. She held up an S-shaped section of piping, wrapped in the ubiquitous golden thermal foil.

What's the total, do you think? I asked.

Not sure. Now Steinbauer has wiped the Cybernetics Division computer, all we have left to go on is that bogus log Maowkavitz downloaded earlier. I'd guesstimate maybe seven hundred kilos altogether. You'd think the Dornier's crew would notice that much extra mass. It must have played hell with their manoeuvring.

Yeah. I took the piping from her, and scratched the foil with my thumbnail. It was only about a millimetre thick, but it still had that unmistakable heavy softness of precious metal.

Shannon was burying herself in the equipment bay again. I hauled in the orange net, and shoved the piping inside.

Harvey, Corrine called.

The subdued mental timbre forewarned me. **Yes?**

It's Wing-Tsit Chong.

Oh crap. Not him as well?

I'm afraid so. Quarter of an hour ago; it was all very peaceful. But the effort of countering Steinbauer's distortion was just too much. And he wouldn't let me help. I could have given him a new heart, but all he'd allow was a mild sedative.

I could feel the pressure of damp heat building around her eyes. **I'm sorry.**

Bloody geneticists. They've all got some kind of death wish.

Are you OK?

Yeah. Doctors, we see it all the time.

You want me to come around?

Not now, Harvey, maybe later. A drink this evening?

That's a date.

• • •

The road out to the pagoda was becoming uncomfortably unfamiliar. I found Hoi Yin sitting in one of the lakeside veranda's wicker chairs, hugging her legs with her knees tucked under her chin. She was crying quite openly.

Second time in a week, she said as I came up the wooden steps. **People will think I'm cracking up.**

I kissed her brow, then knelt down on the floor beside her, putting our heads level. Her hand fumbled for mine.

I'm so sorry, I said. **I know how much he meant to you.**

She nodded miserably. **Steinbauer killed both of Eden's parents, didn't he?**

Yes. I suppose he did, ultimately.

His death . . . it was awful.

Quick, though, if not particularly clean.

People can be so cruel, so thoughtless. It was his greed which did this. I sometimes think greed rules the whole world. Maowkavitz created me for money. Steinbauer killed for money. Boston intends to fight Earth over self-determination, which is just another way of saying ownership. Father Cooke resents affinity because it's taking worshippers from him—even that is a form of greed.

You're just picking out the big issues, I said. **The top one per cent of human activity. We don't all behave like that.**

Don't you, Harvey?

No.

What are you going to do about the stockpile? Give it to the board, or let Boston keep it?

I don't know. It's still classified at the moment, I haven't even told the Governor. I suppose it depends on

what Boston does next, and when. After all, possession is nine-tenths of the law.

My dear Harvey. Her fingers stroked my face. **Torn so many ways. You never deserved any of this.**

You never told me; do you support Boston?

No, Harvey. Like my spirit father, I regard it as totally irrelevant. In that at least I am true to him. She leant forwards in the choir, and put both arms around me. **Oh, Harvey; I miss him so.**

Yes, I know I shouldn't have. I never intended to. I went out to the pagoda purely because I knew how much she would be hurting, and how few people she could turn to for comfort.

So I told myself.

Her bedroom was spartan in its simplicity, with plain wooden floorboards, a few amateur watercolours hanging on the walls. The bed itself only just large enough to hold the two of us.

Our lovemaking was different from the wild exuberance we had shown out in the meadow. It was more intense, slower, clutching. I think we both knew it would be the last time.

We lay together for a long time afterwards, content just to touch, drowsy thoughts merging and mingling to create a mild euphoria.

There is something I have to say to you, Hoi Yin said eventually. **It is difficult for me, because although you have a right to know, I do not know if you will be angry.**

I won't be angry, not with you.

I will understand if you are.

I won't be. What is it?

I am pregnant. The child is ours.

"What!" I sat up in reflex, and stared down at her. "How the hell can you possibly know?"

I went for a scan at the hospital yesterday. They confirmed the zygote is viable.

"Fuck." I flopped back down and stared at the thick ceiling beams. I have a gift, the ability to totally screw up my life beyond either belief or salvation. It's just so natural, I do it without any effort at all.

After twelve years of celibacy, contraception was not something I concerned myself over any more, Hoi Yin said. **It was remiss of me. But what happened that morning was so sudden, and so right . . .**

Yes, OK, fine. We were consenting adults, we're equally responsible. She was watching me closely, those big liquid gold eyes full up with apprehension. My lips were curving up into a grin, like they were being pulled by a tidal force or something. **You're really pregnant?**

Yes. I wanted to be sure as soon as possible, because the earlier the affinity gene is spliced into the embryo, the easier it is.

"Ah." **Yes, of course.**

I feel there is a rightness to this, Harvey. A new life born as one dies. And a new life raised in a wholly new culture, one where my spirit-father's ideals will hold true for all eternity. I could never have borne a child into the kind of world I was born into. This child, our child, will be completely free from the pain of the past and the frailty of the flesh; one of the first ever to be so.

Hoi Yin, I'm not sure I can tell Jocelyn today. There's a lot we have to sort out first.

She looked at me with a genuine surprise. **Harvey! You must never leave your wife. You love her too much.**

I . . . Guilty relief was sending shivers all down my skin. Christ, but I can be a worthless bastard at times.

You do, Hoi Yin said implacably. **I have seen it in your heart. Go to her, be with her. I never ever intended to lay claim to you. There is no need for that simplicity and**

selfishness any more. Eden will be a father, if a father
figure is needed. And perhaps I will take a lover, maybe
even a husband. I would like some more children. This
will be a wonderful place for children.

Yeah, so my kids tell me.

This is farewell, you know that, don't you, Harvey?

I know that.

Good. She rolled round on top of me, hunger in her eyes.
Hoi Yin in that kind of kittenish mood was an enrichment of
the soul. Then we had better make it memorable.

• • •

My seventh day in Eden was profoundly different from any
which had gone before, in the habitat or anywhere else. On
the seventh day I was woken up by the human race's newest
messiah.

Good morning, Harvey, said Wing-Tsit Chong.

I wailed loudly, kicked against the duvet, and nearly fell
out of bed. "You're dead!"

Jocelyn looked at me as if I had gone insane. Perhaps she
was right.

A distant mirage of a smile. No, Harvey, I am not dead.
I told you once that thoughts are sacred, the essence of
man; it is our tragedy that their vessel should be flesh,
for flesh is so weak. The flesh fails us, Harvey, for once
the wisdom that comes only with age is granted to us, it
can no longer be used. All we have learnt so painfully is
lost to us for ever. Death haunts us, Harvey, it condemns
us to a life of fear and hesitancy. It shackles the soul. It
is this curse of ephemerality which I have sought to lib-
erate us from. And with Eden, I have succeeded. Eden
has become the new vessel for my thoughts. As I died I
transferred my memories, my hopes, my dreams, into
the neural strata.

"Oh my God."

No, Harvey. The time of gods and pagan worship is over. We are the immortals now. We do not need the crutch of faith in deities, and the wish fulfilment of pre-ordained destiny, not any more. Our lives are our own, for the very first time. When your body dies, you too can join me. Eden will live for tens of thousands of years, it is constantly regenerating its cellular structure, it does not decay like terrestrial beasts. And we will live on as part of it.

"Me?" I whispered, incredulous.

Yes, Harvey, you. The twins Nicolette and Nathaniel. Hoi Yin. Your unborn child. Shannon Kershaw. Antony Harwood. All of you with the neuron symbionts, and all who possess the affinity gene; you will all be able to transfer your memories over to the neural strata. This habitat alone has room for millions of people. I am holding this same conversation simultaneously with all the affinity-capable. Like all the thought routines, my personality is both separate and integral; I retain my identity, yet my consciousness is multiplied a thousandfold. I can continue to mature, to seek the Nibbana which is my goal. And I welcome you to this, Harvey. This is my dana to all people, whatever their nature. I make no exception, pass no judgement. All who wish to join me may do so. It is my failing that I hope eventually all people will come to seek enlightenment and spiritual purity in the same fashion as I. But it is my knowledge that some, if not most, will not; for it is the wonder of our species that we differ so much, and by doing so never become stale.

You expect me to join you?

I offer you the opportunity, nothing more. Death is for ever, Harvey, unless you truly believe in reincarnation. You are a practical man, look upon Eden as insurance. Just in case death is final, what have you got to lose?

And if, afterwards, you reconfirm your Christian beliefs, you can always die again, only with considerably less pain and mess. Think about it, Harvey, you have around forty years left to decide.

Think about it? The biological imperative is to survive. We do that through reproduction, the only way we know how. Until now.

I knew there and then that Wing-Tsit Chong had won. His salvation was corporeal, what can compete against that? From now on every child living in Eden, or any of the other habitats, would grow up knowing death wasn't the end. My child among them. What kind of culture would that produce: monstrous arrogance, or total recklessness? Would murder even be considered a crime any more?

Did I want to find out? More, did I want to be a part of it?

Forty years to make up my mind. Christ, but that was an insidious thought. Just knowing the option was there waiting, that it would always be there; right at the end when you're on your deathbed wheezing down that last breath, one simple thought of acquiescence and you have eternity to debate whether or not you should have done it. How can you not contemplate spirituality, your place and role in the cosmos, with that hanging over you for your entire life? Questions which can never be answered without profound thought and contemplation, say about four or five centuries' worth. And it just so happens . . .

Whatever individuals decided, Wing-Tsit Chong had already changed us. We were being forcibly turned from the materialistic viewpoint. No bad thing. Except it couldn't be for everybody, not the billions living on Earth, not right away. They couldn't change, they could only envy, and die.

An enormous privilege had been thrust upon me. To use it must surely be sinful when so many couldn't. But then what would wasting it achieve? If they could do it, they would.

Forty years to decide.

• • •

The events of the tenth day were virtually an anticlimax. I think the whole habitat was still reeling from Wing-Tsit Chong's continuation (as people were calling it). I couldn't find anyone who would admit to refusing the offer of immortality. There were two terminal patients in the hospital, both of them were now eager for death. They were going to make the jump into the neural strata, they said; they had even begun transferring their memories over in anticipation. It was going to be the end of physical pain, of their suffering and that of their families.

Corrine was immersed in an agony of indecision. Both patients had asked for a fatal injection to speed them on their way. Was it euthanasia? Was it helping them to transcend? Was it even ethical for her to decide? They both quite clearly knew what they wanted.

The psyche of the population was perceptibly altering, adapting. People were becoming nonchalant and self-possessed, half of them walked round with a permanent goofy smile on their face as if they had been struck by an old-fashioned biblical revelation, instead of this lashed-up technobuddhist option from life. But I have to admit, there was a tremendous feeling of optimism running throughout the habitat. They were different, they were special. They were the future. They were immortal.

Nobody bothered going to Father Cooke's church any more. I knew that for a fact, because I accompanied Jocelyn to his services. We were the only two there.

Seeing the way things were swinging, Boston's council chose to announce their intentions. As Eden was *ipso facto* already diverging from Earth both culturally and by retaining the use of advanced biotechnology, then the habitat should naturally evolve its own government. The kind of true consensual democracy which only affinity could provide. Fasholé Nocord didn't get a chance to object. Boston had judged the timing perfectly. It was a government which literally sprang into being overnight. The people decided what they wanted, and Eden implemented it; a communal consensus in which everybody had an equal say, everyone had an equal vote, and there was no need for an executive any more. Under our aegis the habitat personality replaced the entire UN administration staff; it executed their jobs in half the time and with ten times the efficiency. The neural strata had processing capacity in abundance to perform all the mundane civic and legal regulatory duties which were the principal function of any government. It didn't need paying, it was completely impartial, and it could never be bribed.

An incorruptible non-bureaucratic civil service. Yes, we really were boldly different.

Boston's hierarchy also announced they were going to launch a buyout bid for all the JSKP shares. That was where the ideological purity broke down a little, because that aspect of the liberation was handed over to the teams of Earthside corporate lawyers Penny Maowkavitz and her cohorts had been grooming for the court battle. But confidence was still high; the cloudscoop-lowering mission was progressing smoothly; and I had formally announced the existence of the precious metal stockpile, which our consensus declared to be the national treasury.

On the twelfth day, the old religion struck back.

I was out on the patio at the time, swilling down some of the sweet white wine produced by Eden's youthful vineyard. I'd acquired quite a taste for it.

And I still hadn't decided what to do about my family. Not that it was really a decision as such, not handing down the final verdict for everyone to obey. The twins were going to stay in Eden. Jocelyn wanted to leave, now more than ever; the non-affinity-capable had no place at all in Eden. It was a question of who to support, whether to try and browbeat Jocelyn over affinity.

My position wasn't helped by the offer I received from the consensus. It had been decided that—sadly—yes, the habitat did still need a police force to physically implement the laws which consensus drafted to regulate society. People hadn't changed that much, there were still drunken fights, and heated disputes, and order to be maintained in industrial stations and the cloudscoop anchor asteroid. The consensus had asked me to continue as Chief of Police and organize the new force on formal lines.

"Harvey," Jocelyn called from the lounge. "Harvey, come and see this." There was a high-pitched anxiety in her voice.

I lumbered up from my chair. Jocelyn was standing behind the settee, hands white-knuckled, clasping the cushions as she stared at the big wallscreen. A newscable broadcast from Earth was showing.

"What is it?" I asked.

"The Pope," she said in a daze. "The Pope has denounced Eden."

I looked at the blandly handsome newscable presenter. "The statement from Her Holiness is unequivocal, and even by the standards of the orthodox wing of the Church, said to have her ear on doctrinal matters, it is unusually drastic," he said. "Pope Eleanor has condemned all variants of affinity as a trespass against the fundamental Christian ethos of individual dignity. This is the Church's response to the geneticist, and inventor of affinity, Wing-Tsit Chong transferring his personality into the biotechnology habitat Eden when his body died. Her Holiness announced that this was a quite monstrous attempt to circumvent the divine judgement which awaits all of us. We were made mortal by the Lord, she said, in order that we would be brought before Him and know glory within His holy kingdom. Wing-Tsit Chong's flawed endeavour to gain physical immortality is an obscene blasphemy; he is seeking to defy the will of God. By himself he is free to embark upon such a course of devilment, but by releasing the plague of affinity upon the world he is placing an almost irresistible temptation in the path of even the most honourable and devout Christians, causing them to doubt. The Pope goes on to call upon all Christian persons living in Eden to renounce this route Wing-Tsit Chong is forging.

"In the final, and most dramatic, section of the statement, Her Holiness says that with great regret, those Christians who do not reject all aspects of affinity technology will be excommunicated. There can be no exceptions. Even the so-called harmless bond which controls servitor animals is to be considered a threat. It acts as an insidious reminder of the sacrilege which is being perpetrated in orbit around Jupiter. She fears the temptation to pursue this false immortality will prove too great unless the threat is ended immediately and completely. The Church, she says, is now facing its greatest ever moral crisis, and that such a challenge must be met with unswerving resolution. The world must know that affinity is a great evil, capable of sabotaging our ultimate spiritual redemption."

"She can't be serious," I said. "There are millions of affinity-bonded servitor animals on Earth. She can't just excommunicate their owners because they won't give them up. That's crazy."

"The use of servitors on Earth was already declining," Jocelyn said calmly. "And people will support her, because they know they will never be given the chance to live on as part of a habitat. That's human nature."

"You support her," I said, aghast. "After all you've seen up here. You know these people aren't evil, that they simply want the best future for themselves and their children. Tell me that isn't human."

She touched my arm lightly. "I know that you are not an evil man, Harvey, with or without affinity. I've always known that. And you're right, the Pope's judgement against this technology is far too simplistic; but then she has to appeal to the masses. I don't suppose we can expect anything more from her; these days she has to be more of a populist than any of her predecessors. And in being so, she has cost me my children, too. I know they will never come back with me to Earth, not now. The only thing I wish is that events hadn't been so sudden. It's almost as if the Church has been forced into opposing Eden and Wing-Tsit Chong's continuance."

"You really are going to go back to Earth, aren't you?"

"Yes. I don't want to be a ghost in a living machine. That isn't immortality, Harvey. It's just a recording, like a song that's played over and over long after the singer has died. A memory. A mockery. Nothing more. Chong is simply a clever old man who wants to impose his vision of existence on all of us. And he's succeeded, too." She looked at me expectantly. There was no anger or resentment left in her. "Are you coming home with me?"

•   •   •

Day twenty; one of the worst in my life. Watching Jocelyn and the twins saying goodbye at the foot of the funicular lift was a torture. Nicolette was crying, Nathaniel was trying not to and failing miserably. Then it was my turn.

Don't go, Dad, Nicolette pleaded as she hugged me.

I have to.

But you'll die on Earth.

I'll be a part of your memories, you and Nat. That's

good enough for me. Nathaniel flung his arms around me. **Take care, son.**

Why are you doing this? he demanded. **You don't love her this much.**

I do, I lied. **This is best for all of us. You'll see. You're going to have a wonderful future here, you and all the other Edenists. I don't belong.**

You do.

No, you have to cut free of the past if you're to have any chance of success. And I am most definitely the past.

He shook his head, tightening his grip.

The ship is leaving in another twelve minutes, Eden reminded me gently.

We're going.

I kissed the twins one last time, then guided Jocelyn into the funicular railway car. It rose smoothly up the track, and I looked down the length of the habitat, trying to commit that incredible sight to memory.

You're actually doing it, Hoi Yin said. There was a strand of utter incomprehension in her mental voice.

Yes. I won't forget you, Hoi Yin.

Nor I you. But my memory will last for ever.

No. That's a uniquely human conceit. Although it will certainly be for a very long time.

I don't think I ever did understand you, Harvey.

You didn't miss much.

Oh, but I did.

Goodbye, Hoi Yin. I wish you the best possible life. And someday, tell my child about me.

I will. I promise.

 • • •

The *Irensaga* was the same marque of ship as the *Ithilien*; our cabin was identical to the one we shared on the flight

out, even down to the colour of the restraint webbing over
the bunks. Jocelyn let me help her with the straps, a timid
smile blinking on and off, as though she couldn't quite believe I was coming with her.

I gave her a quick peck on the cheek and fastened myself
down. We'd do all right on Earth, the two of us. Life would
be a hell of a lot easier for me, but then it always is when
you surrender completely. I felt a total fraud, but there was
nothing to be gained now by explaining my real reason to
her. And she was a mite more sceptical about the Church
these days. Yes, we'd be all right together. Almost like the
good old days.

I switched the bulkhead screen to a view from the spaceship's external cameras as the last commuter shuttle disengaged. Secondary drive nozzles flared briefly and brightly,
urging us away from Eden. The gap began to widen, and we
started to rise up out of the ecliptic. Eden's northern endcap
was exposed below us; with the silver-white spire of the
docking spindle extending up from the crest it resembled
some baroque cathedral dome.

I watched it slowly shrinking, while some strange emotions played around inside my skull. Regret, remorse, anger,
even a sense of relief that it was all finally over. My decision, right or wrong, stood. I had passed my judgement.

And just how do you judge the dead? For that's what
Chong is, now, dead. Or at least, beyond any justice I could
ever administer.

Chong?

Yes, Harvey?

I won't be coming back. I want you to know that.

**As always, you know more than you reveal. I did won-
der.**

**I'm not doing it for you. I'm doing it to give my three
children a chance at a life which may be worthwhile. Perhaps I even believe in what you're trying to build out**

here. You've given the people of Eden a kind of hope I
never knew existed before.

You are an honourable man, Harvey, you shame me.

There is something I want to know.

Of course.

Did Hoi Yin ever know it was you who killed Maowkavitz?

No. Like you, I deny her the truth to protect her. It is a
failing of all fathers, and I do genuinely consider her my
daughter. I was so gratified by what she has become. If
only you could have seen her the day we first met. So
beautiful, so frail, and so tragic. To blossom from that
ruined child into the sublime woman she is today is
nothing short of a miracle. I could not bear to have her
soiled again. So I withheld the knowledge, a perverted
form of dana. But I consider it to be a necessary gift.

Funny, because it was Hoi Yin who gave you away.

How so?

The day your body died, she asked me what I was
going to do with the stockpile of precious metal. I hadn't
released the information then. Which meant the two of
you had known about it all along. The only way that
could happen was if your affinity command of Eden's
personality was superior to everyone else's. A logical
assumption since you designed its thought routines to
begin with.

And that told you I was the murderer?

Not at once, but it set me to thinking. How could Wallace Steinbauer, who has only been in Eden for two
years, have developed a method of glitching the thought
routines which surpassed even your ability? Especially
given that his field of expertise was cybernetics. So then
I started to consider what he had done a little more
closely. The most obvious question was why didn't he
simply blackmail Penny Maowkavitz when it became ob-

vious she had discovered he was stealing the gold? She could hardly come running to me. So it would have resulted in a complete stand-off between them, because if he had gone to the JSKP board about her initial subterfuge they would then find out that he had been stealing the gold as well. At worst she would have to agree to let him continue substituting the Dornier's standard components with the new gold ones. Even if he had remade the entire capsule out of gold it wouldn't amount to a hundredth of a per cent of the total value of the stockpile. That would have been a very small price to pay for safeguarding the future of Boston. So I had to start looking for ulterior motives, and someone else who could manipulate the habitat's personality. The only people who qualified on the second count were you and Hoi Yin. That left me with motive. Hoi Yin had the obvious one, she hated Penny Maowkavitz, and with good reason. But she also admitted she felt cheated that Maowkavitz hadn't died from cancer. It was fairly macabre, but I believed her. That left you.

And do you have my motive, Harvey?

I think so. That was the hardest part of all to figure out. After all, everybody up here knew Maowkavitz was dying, that she would be dead in a few months at the most. So the actual question must be, why would you want her to die *now*? What was so special about the timing? Then I realized two things. One, you were also dying, but you were expected to live longer than her. And second, Penny Maowkavitz's death was fast, deliberately so. With your control over Eden you could have chosen from a dozen methods; yet you picked a bullet through the brain, which is damn near instantaneous. In other words, you made sure Penny Maowkavitz never had an opportunity to transfer her personality into the neural strata. You killed her twice, Chong, you shot her body and denied her mind immortality.

With reason, Harvey. I could not allow her to transfer herself into the neural strata before me, it would have been disastrous. And Maowkavitz had begun to think along those lines, she was not stupid. She was conferring with Eden to see if such a thing were possible. Which of course it is, it has been right from the start. As she did not reveal the existence of the precious metals, so I did not reveal the full potential of the neural strata. I had to ensure that Maowkavitz did not have the chance to experiment; and as I was already aware of Steinbauer's illegal activity, I decided to use him as my alibi. Fortunately, given his temperament his elimination was even easier to engineer than Maowkavitz's. I had only to wait until your department uncovered his theft of the gold, then goad him into panic at the prospect of discovery. The inspection tunnel was only one of a number of options I had prepared for him depending on how he reacted. Once he was dead, he could not protest his innocence, and the case would be closed.

So all this was to protect the neural strata from what you see as contamination by the unworthy?

Yes.

Does that mean you're not going to allow just anyone to transfer their personality into Eden after all?

No, I said anyone who is affinity-capable will now be welcome, and it is so. That is why I had to be the first. It is my philosophy which will ensure that others may be free to join me. I cannot do anything else, I feel great joy at such dana, the giving of immortality is a majestic gift. Who do you know that can say the same, Harvey? Would you be able to admit everyone to such a fellowship? Unquestioningly? For that is the power you would have were you to be first. I am the Eden personality now, if I wanted I could be the absolute dictator of the population. Certainly people I disapprove of could be refused transference, blocking them would be profoundly simple for me. But I chose not to, I chose dana. And in doing so, in opening the neural strata to everyone, by sharing it, I ensure that such unchecked power will not last, for I will soon become a multiplicity in which no one personality segment will have the ability to veto.

And Maowkavitz might not have been so liberally inclined?

Your investigation revealed to you the true nature of Maowkavitz's personality. A woman who prostitutes her own mirrorselves and then refuses even to acknowledge them as her own. A woman who has no regard or patience with anyone whose views differ from her own. Would you entrust such a woman to found a civilization? A whole new type of human culture?

But she wanted Eden to be free and independent.

She wanted it to be politically independent, nothing more. Boston was the ultimate California vertical. She and Harwood and the others were going to use Eden to escape from Earth. They wanted a secure, isolated, tax haven community where they would be free to practise their culture of rampant commercialism without interference. Eden was not to be culturally different from Earth, but simply an elitist enclave.

And you killed her because of it.

I was the physical agent; and I regret it, as the chimp revealed to you. But, still, Kamma rules us all. She died because of what she was.

Yeah, right. Kamma.

How do you judge the dead? You can't. Not when the living depend on them as their inspiration for the future.

On the bulkhead screen Eden had dwindled to a rusty circle no bigger than my thumbnail, the illuminated needle of its docking spindle standing proud at the centre. A nimbus of tiny blue-white lights from the tugs and capsules sparkled all around, cloaking it in a stippled halo. I would remember it like that for always, a single egg floating in the darkness. The one bright hope I had left in the universe.

Only I know that the infant society which it nurtures is flawed. Only I can tell the children playing in the garden that they are naked.

After another minute, Eden had faded from the screen. I switched cameras to the one which showed me the warm blue-white star of Earth.

Timeline

2091 . . . Lunar referendum to terraform Mars.

2094 . . . Edenists begin exowomb breeding programme coupled with extensive geneering improvement to embryos, tripling their population over a decade.

2103 . . . Earth's national governments consolidate into Govcentral.

2103 . . . Thoth base established on Mars.

2107 . . . Govcentral jurisdiction extended to cover O'Neill Halo.

2115 . . . First instantaneous translation by New Kong spaceship, Earth to Mars.

2118 . . . Mission to Proxima Centauri.

2123 . . . Terracompatible planet found at Ross 154.

2125 . . . Ross 154 planet named Felicity, first multiethnic colonists arrive.

2125–2130 . . . Four new terracompatible planets discovered. Multiethnic colonies founded.

2131 . . . Edenists germinate Perseus in orbit around Ross 154 gas giant, begin He^3 mining.

2131–2205 . . . The Great Dispersal. One hundred and thirty terracompatible planets discovered. Massive starship building programme initiated in O'Neill Halo. Govcentral begins large-scale enforced outshipment of surplus population, rising to two million a week in 2160. Civil conflict on some early multiethnic colonies. Individual Govcentral states sponsor ethnic-streaming colonies. Edenists expand their He^3 mining enterprise to every inhabited star system with a gas giant.

2139 . . . Asteroid Braun impacts on Mars.

2180 . . . First orbital tower built on Earth.

2205 . . . Antimatter production station built in orbit

around sun by Govcentral in an attempt to break the Edenist energy monopoly.

2208 . . . First antimatter drive starships operational.

2210 . . . Richard Saldana transports all of New Kong's industrial facilities from the O'Neill Halo to an asteroid orbiting Kulu. He claims independence for the Kulu star system, founds Christian-only colony, and begins to mine He³ from the system's gas giant.

2218 . . . First voidhawk gestated, a bitek starship designed by Edenists.

2225 . . . Establishment of 100 voidhawk families. Habitats Romulus and Remus germinated in Saturn orbit to serve as voidhawk bases.

2232 . . . Conflict at Jupiter's trailing Trojan asteroid cluster between belt alliance ships and an O'Neill Halo company hydrocarbon refinery. Antimatter used as a weapon; 27,000 people killed.

2238 . . . Treaty of Deimos, outlaws production and use of antimatter in the Sol system, signed by Govcentral, Lunar nation, asteroid alliance, and Edenists. Antimatter stations abandoned and dismantled.

2240 . . . Coronation of Gerrald Saldana as King of Kulu. Foundation of Saldana dynasty.

New Days Old Times

Amanda Foxon was standing right beside the smooth ebony trunk of the apple tree when she heard the pick-up van's horn being tooted in long urgent blasts. She dumped the ripe fruit into the basket at her feet, and pressed her hands hard into the small of her back. A sharp hiss of breath stole out of her mouth as her spine creaked in protest.

She'd been out in the southern orchard since first light, seven hours ago. Always the same at the end of summer. A frantic two weeks to get the big green globes picked and packed before they became overripe under the sun's fearsome summer radiance. The trees were genetically adapted so that they grew into a very specific mushroom shape, the trunk dividing into seven major boughs two and a half metres above ground. Twigs and smaller branches interlaced to form a thick circular canopy of wood which was smothered by fans of emerald leaves. Glossy apples hung from the underside, clustered as tightly as grapes. Providing they were picked early enough their re-sequenced chromosomes would ensure they didn't perish for months. So every year a race developed to get them to Harrisburg in time. The contract called for the whole crop to be at the warehouse in another eight days; she had sold the futures early in February, anxious for a guaranteed purchase. Possibly a mistake, holding out could have meant a higher price.

If I just had Arthur's nerve.

Feeling the blood pound heavily through her lowered arms, she walked out from under the shade of the tree. Blake was driving the fruit farm's ageing pick-up along the switchback track that wound down the side of the broad valley. A plume of dust fountained out from the wheels each time he swung it round a curve. Amanda's lips set in a hard line of disapproval, she'd warned him countless times about driving so fast. There would be another argument tonight.

"He'll turn the damn thing at that speed," Jane said.

All of the pickers had stopped to watch the small red vehicle's madcap approach.

"Good," Amanda grunted. "I can collect the insurance, get a decent van with the money." She flinched as she realized Guy was giving her a confused look. Her son was only nine; at that age funny was rude jokes and slapstick interactives. Lately, he'd started following Blake round the farm, eager to help out.

The pick-up's horn sounded again, blatantly distressed.

"All right," Amanda said. She pulled her wide-brimmed hat back on her head, wiping the sweat from her brow. "Jane and Lenny, with me, we'll go see what the problem is. Guy, could you make sure everyone's got a drink, please. It's very hot today."

"Yes, Mum." He started scampering across the orchard's shaggy blue-green moss that was Nyvan's grass-analogue, heading for the sheds at the far end.

"The rest of you, we've got two-thirds of the trees left, and only eight days."

The remaining pickers drifted back to their trees and the white cartons piled round them. They weren't the usual group of easygoing travellers who visited the farm for summer. Govcentral's Employment Ministry was causing them a lot of grief with new taxes and regulations concerning mobile residency permits for their caravans. Then the fishing ports had begun investing in automated plants, cutting down on the manual gutting and packing work available in the winter months. Like many communities, the travellers were beginning to feel pressured. Immigrants from Earth's diverse cultures were being deliberately compressed into the same districts by the Settlement Ministry, whose officers adhered rigidly to the approved multiethnic amalgamation policy. There were few of Nyvan's towns and cities free from strife these days, not like the first century when the pioneers shared the challenge of their new world together. Spring and summer had seen a lot of caravans heading along the main road outside the valley, rolling deeper into the continent where Govcentral's bureaucrats weren't quite so prevalent.

Blake was still doing fifty when he drove round the stone farmhouse and into the tree-lined back yard. He braked to a sharp halt outside the kitchen's open stable door.

"Give me a hand here!" he yelled.

Amanda, Jane, and Lenny were still under the big aboriginal burroughs trees when he jumped out of the driver's seat. A pair of legs were hanging over the pick-up's tailgate. The dark trouser fabric was ripped, slippery with blood.

"Hell!" Amanda started to run. The two young pickers were easily faster than her.

The man Blake had brought was in his late twenties, dressed in a green onepiece overall with an elaborate company logo on its breast pocket. A very grubby light-brown waistcoat hung loosely, containing several tool pockets. His skin was dark enough to suggest a Latino ancestry, black curly hair framed a round face with a blunt nose. He wasn't tall, shorter than Amanda, with swarthy limbs.

Amanda stared in shock at the wounds on his legs, the

bloody cloth which had been used to bandage him. "Blake, what happened?"

"Found him just off the main road. He said his horse threw him. I patched him up as good as I could." Blake gave Lenny an anxious look. "Did I do it right?"

"Yeah." Lenny nodded slowly, his hands moved down the injured man's legs, squeezing gently. He glanced up at Amanda. "This man didn't fall, these are blue marks. Some kind of dog, I'd say."

"Blake!" Amanda wanted to strike him, or perhaps just banish him from the farm. How could he have been so stupid? "For heaven's sake, what did you bring him here for?"

"What else was I supposed to do?" he demanded petulantly.

It wasn't worth the effort of arguing. Blake would never admit he was wrong about anything. His basic flaw was his inability to learn, to think ahead.

Blake was one of Arthur's more distant relatives, fostered on her by the rest of the family who were convinced a woman couldn't run the farm by herself. There are three orchards, they argued, over five hundred trees. Guy's whole future. You'll never manage to prune and fertilize and irrigate them properly, not with the other fruit fields as well, and there's the machinery, too. So Blake had come to live with her and Guy. He was twenty-two, and too quiet to be hot-headed, though he could be astonishingly stubborn. Of course, her biggest mistake was letting him into her bed. He'd interpreted that as some kind of partnership offer to give him an equal say on the way the farm was run. But the nights out here in the countryside were achingly long, and it had been nineteen months since Arthur's funeral. It wasn't even the sex she wanted, just the warmth and touch of having him there, the comfort she could draw from a warm body. So far she'd managed to contain and deflect any potential clashes over his new attitude, but this folly could not be overlooked.

"Well?" Blake insisted.

Amanda glanced at Jane and Lenny, who were waiting for her to take the lead. The stranger's blood was dripping onto the hard bare soil of the back yard, turning to black spots.

"All right. Lenny, stop the bleeding and patch him up as best you can. As soon as he's conscious again, Blake, you drive him over to Knightsville. Leave him at the station or the hospital, whatever he wants. After that he's someone else's problem."

She didn't dare look at the two pickers in case it triggered a rebellion. Don't give them the chance to refuse, she told herself. "Lenny, you and Blake take his legs, you'll need to be careful. Jane, help me with his shoulders. We'll take him into the kitchen, put him on the table. It'll be easier to treat him there."

The pickers moved hesitantly, expressing their reluctance through complete silence. Amanda climbed up into the back of the pick-up and crouched down beside the injured man. As she slid her hands under his back ready to lift him up she felt a hard lump inside the waistcoat, larger than a fist. Her hand reached automatically towards it.

The stranger's eyelids flipped open. His hand caught her wrist. "No," he grunted. "Do what you said. Patch me up. Then I will go. It is the best for us both." He glanced round at the figures clustered over him. A sharp frown appeared as soon as he saw Lenny's black and silver skull cap.

Jane and Lenny exchanged a knowing glance at that.

"I cannot help with you crushing my wrist," Amanda said levelly. It was everything she'd dreaded: his reaction to the pickers, his injuries, his weapon. What must he have done to have dogs set on him? The thought made her afraid for the first time. He wasn't an inconvenience any more, he was an active threat, to the farm, to Guy.

Between them, they hauled him into the kitchen. He made no sound during the whole process, not even when one of his legs was knocked against the doorframe. Amanda knew she would have cried out at such pain. Such control made her wonder at what electronic implants he was using. Nerve fibre regulators were not cheap, nor did ordinary citizens have any use for them.

"I'll fetch my bag," Lenny said, once the stranger was lying on the big old wooden table. He hurried out.

Amanda looked down at the man again, uncertain what to do, his eyes were tight shut again. Even Blake's confidence had ebbed in the face of such robotic stoicism.

"If I could have some water," the man said huskily.

"Who are you?" Amanda asked.

His eyes fluttered open as she filled a glass at the sink.

"My name is Fakhud. I thank you for bringing me into your home."

"I didn't." She handed him the glass.

He took a sip and coughed. "I know. But I still thank you. I have many friends in the city, influential friends, they will be grateful to you."

"I bet you've got friends," Jane muttered softly.

"It's the bank we need help with," Blake said with a dry smile. "Those bastards are bleeding us dry with their interest rates. Not just us, all the farms are suffering."

"Blake," Amanda said. He scowled, but kept quiet.

Fakhud grimaced, and took another sip of the water.

"What happened to you?" Amanda asked.

"I fell from my horse."

"And the bite wounds? Lenny said it was probably a dog."

"Your pardon, but the less you know of me, the less involved in my affairs you will be."

"Sure," she said in disgust.

Lenny returned with his bag. He started to stick small sensor disks on Fakhud's legs.

"Stay and help Lenny," Amanda told Blake. "Then come and tell me when he's ready to leave." She and Jane walked out into the heat of the farmyard. "I'm sorry," she said it so fiercely it was almost a hiss.

Jane sighed. "Not your fault."

"I can't believe Blake was so thoughtless. To put you and your friends in this position, it's . . . it's . . ."

"In a way it's rather admirable, actually. He's only interested in the farm, getting your fruit picked and the trees pruned and fertilized. Politics, race, and religion aren't part of the equation for him. That was the whole point of Nyvan, wasn't it? Our parents came here to escape their past; they wanted a land where they could put all their energies into their farms and their businesses. And your Blake, he's still living there."

"He's a fool. Times change."

"No, time doesn't change, it just goes backwards. That's the thing to be sorry for."

"I'll have Fakhud out of here by this evening, whether he's on his feet or not."

Jane gave her a sad smile. "I'm sure you will."

"Will Lenny be able to patch those wounds up? Some of them looked ugly to me."

"Don't worry about that. Lenny completed three years at medical school before we all decided to leave Harrisburg. He's as good as qualified. And he's had a lot of experience with the kind of injuries you get from clashing with the authorities."

"I can't believe you were forced out."

"Nobody can, until it happens to them. Oh, it's not that bad, not yet. But we Jews have a long history of persecution we can reference, in fact it is our history. We can see the way Harrisburg is going. Best we leave before it does spiral downwards."

"Where will you go?"

"Tasmal, most likely. A lot of our people have drifted there over the last decade, and to hell with the Settlement Ministry quotas. We're almost a majority there, the newest of the New Jerusalems."

"But that's on the Dayall continent; it has to be six thou sand kilometres away at least."

Jane laughed. "The promised land is never over the next hill. Also our history."

"I'm sorry."

"Don't be. Me and the rest will be OK. We were smart enough to start the journey early. The stubborn ones, those that stay, they'll be the ones who suffer."

Amanda glanced round the familiarity of the farmyard. The burroughs trees that waved slowly in the warm breeze were an easy five metres taller than they had been when she was a girl. Over in the eastern corner, the well pump was making its usual clatter as it topped up the cisterns. The red clay tile roof of the long barn was sagging deeper as this year's growth of purple-flowering joycevine added another heavy layer of branches.

It isn't just Blake whose mind is closed to the outside, she acknowledged reluctantly. I'm so comfortable here I share the same illusion. The only thing which matters to anyone who lives at the farm, is the farm. Until today.

"You'd better get back to the orchard," Jane said. "The apples still need picking, nothing's changed that."

"Right." Amanda took a last uneasy look at the kitchen door. "What are you going to do?"

"Tidy up here." Jane was studying the splashes of blood in the back of the pick-up van. "I'll get the hose out and wash away all the traces. Best to be careful. The Harrisburg cops are going to be searching for him, and we don't know what happened to the dogs."

Amanda didn't even feel resentful that she was being told what to do on her own farm. She walked back to the orchard, and told the pickers that Blake had found a victim of a riding accident that Lenny was now treating. They seemed to accept that with only mild curiosity.

It was another hour before Blake came out to tell her Lenny had finished. Jane had done a good job washing away the evidence from the pick-up, which was now parked in its usual place beside the gate. Amanda couldn't even see any blood spots left on the soil outside the kitchen door, just a big damp patch. Jane was busy tending a small bonfire.

The kitchen had been cleaned, too; it smelt strongly of bleach. Fakhud was sitting in one of the high-back chairs around the table. His green overalls had been replaced by a faded green T-shirt and black canvas shorts—which she recognized as belonging to Blake. Both his legs were sprayed in pale-yellow bandage foam which had hardened into a tough carapace.

A silent Lenny gave her a brief nod as he walked out.

"He doesn't say much," Fakhud said, "but he's an excellent medic. I suppose there's an irony in the situation, him tending me. We're hardly allies."

"You're humans," Amanda said.

"Ah. Indeed we are. You shame the pair of us, my dear lady."

"Well, not for any longer. You're fit to move, I'd like you to leave now."

"Of course. I have imposed too much already."

"Wait a minute," Blake said. "Amanda, you haven't heard what he's told me."

"Nor do I want to," she said wearily.

"Not about . . . you know, what he does. This is about New Balat itself, the way its society is run."

"What about New Balat?" She rounded on Fakhud. "What nonsense have you been filling his head with?"

"It's not nonsense," Blake snapped. "It's a solution to our financial problems."

"You don't have financial problems," she said. "I do. The farm does. You do not. Get that quite clear."

"All right! But it's still a solution to your problems. And if you have problems here, then so do I."

"Start getting a grip on perspective, Blake. I manage this farm just fine, thank you. The money doesn't come in regularly, because we have seasons. It's a situation I've coped with my entire life. Every farm throughout history has lived like this; we get paid for our crops when they come in and we have to make the money last throughout the rest of the year. A simple expenditure-planning program on the home terminal can see us through without any trouble. Nothing needs to change because some newcomer can't cope with that. This farm has been here for eighty years, and we've managed perfectly well up until now. If it ain't broke, don't try and fix it."

"The banks are crippling you with their interest rates. They don't care about families and people. They just want money, they want you to work your fingers to the bone for them."

"You're being simplistic. I make a profit every year. And everybody has to work for a living, even bankers."

"But it doesn't have to be like that. Fakhud says that the New Balat council gives grants to all the farms in their county so they can buy new equipment when they need it and pay workers a decent wage. And their kids have an education paid for by the state, a good education. There are no private schools, no privileged elite."

"I'm sure the New Balat council gives out thousands of

benevolent grants. But here in Harrisburg's county we get loans from the bank instead. There's no basic difference. Only the names change. Our services come from the private sector, your friend's society is paid for by the state. So what?"

"It's fairer, that's what. Can't you see that?"

"No."

"They're not dependent on the profit motive, on greed. That's the difference. That's what makes it fair! Their economic policy is controlled by democracy, with us it's the other way round."

"Heaven preserve us. Blake, I'm only going to say this once more. I am not interested. I don't want to replace our bankers with their bureaucrats, I do not want to switch from paying high interest rates to high taxes. We have a market for the fruit, we have a decent cash flow. That's all we need. This is a farming family, my only ambition is to keep it ticking over smoothly. I'm sorry if that isn't enough for you. If you don't like that, you can go. Besides, in case you haven't noticed, we're not even in New Balat county."

Blake smiled triumphantly. "But we could be."

"What?"

Fakhud coughed apologetically. "I merely pointed out that this farm is on the borderland. If you did wish to switch allegiances, then in terms of realpolitik it would be possible."

"Oh, shit." She wanted to sink into a chair and put her head in her hands. But that would be showing both of them how weak she was.

"See?" Blake said. "It can be done. We can break free if we want to."

"Break free? Are you insane or just retarded? This is a farm, that's all. We're not some big agricultural institution, not a major league economic asset. Just a family farm. We grow apples, strawberries, pears, and peaches. Once we've grown them, we sell them. That's all we do."

"Sell them to a corrupt system."

"I'm not arguing with you, Blake. This subject is now closed."

"But—"

"Blake," Fakhud said softly. "Amanda has made her choice. You should respect that."

She was too surprised to say anything. I could tell you and your kind about choices and liberty, she thought. Women must obey their husbands and aren't permitted to vote.

Blake looked from one to the other, pursing his lips in sullen resentment. "Fine, OK. Keep living in the past, then. Life's changing on Nyvan, in case you hadn't noticed; Govcentral won't always rule here. I know you haven't got as much for this year's crop as you did last year. And do you think Harrisburg's councillors care? Fat arse, do they. You have to move with the times, Amanda, move away from the old colonialist policies. Just don't complain to me when they foreclose and sell the farm from under you."

"No worries on that score." She turned to Fakhud, who even managed to look mildly embarrassed. "Time for you to go."

"You are correct. And I apologize for bringing disharmony to the lives of such decent people as yourselves. I never meant to cause any trouble."

"Not here," she said scathingly.

He bowed his head.

Jane appeared in the doorway. "People coming."

"Who?" Amanda asked.

"Dunno. They're on horses, four of them."

"Shit." Amanda glared at Fakhud. "Police?"

"I regret, that is a strong possibility."

"Oh great. Just bloody wonderful."

"All you have done is treat a man who claimed to have fallen from his horse. As I told you, it was for the best. It would go badly upon you for harbouring fugitives otherwise."

"Please, don't use your weapon. My son is here, and the pickers are completely innocent."

"In the name of Allah the compassionate, you have my word I shall not. Do you intend to turn me over to them?"

Amanda licked her lips, mind awhirl with indecision. He was too proud to plead, holding his head stiffly, though his forehead was beaded by sweat. For the first time, Blake was looking worried, his cockiness dissolving under her stare. The implications of what he'd done were finally sinking in. If nothing else, she was pleased about that.

"I don't know," she said. If Fakhud was what she suspected then she ought to run out yelling for the police. But . . . the Security Ministry was dealing out a lot of rough justice these days, all in the name of quelling and discouraging the *disturbances*. Even a criminal deserved a fair trial; she'd never abandoned that belief. "I'll see what they have to say first. Blake, at least get him out of the kitchen; they'll be able to see him from the farmyard."

"Right. The cold cellar?"

"Up to you." Don't incriminate yourself, think of Guy.

Amanda went out into the farmyard, carefully closing the bottom half of the kitchen door behind her as she went. A big hound was already trotting in through the open gate. It took a considerable effort on her part not to scurry back into the kitchen. The creature must have been genetically modified, powerful muscles flowed smoothly under a short shiny-black hide. Its ancestry was more big game cat than canine.

"Probably affinity-bonded," Jane said. "Remember, that means its master can hear and see everything it can."

Amanda didn't trust her voice, she simply nodded.

"I'll go and get the pickers." Jane turned slowly, and began walking towards the southern orchard. The hound swung its head to follow her, but didn't make any other move.

They were police. Their distinctive blue-grey tunics were visible while they were still a couple of hundred metres from the farm. Amanda waited patiently as the four horses walked unhurriedly towards her. She hated the arrogance of their approach, the way she was made to feel inferior, not worth them making an effort over.

Sergeant Derry was the leader, a black woman who must have massed nearly twice Amanda's body-weight. It wasn't fat, just muscle bulk. Amanda wondered what the woman's blood chemistry would be like to produce that kind of grotesque growth; she must have received several hormone gland implants. Her white and beige stallion was built on the same scale, carrying her without any noticeable discomfort. The three constables riding with her were normal men.

"You're the owner here?" Sergeant Derry asked.

"That's right."

"Hmm." Derry's optronic lens flashed up a file, sending minute green and red script scrolling over her right iris. "Amanda Foxon. Lived here by yourself since your husband died. Grandfather was granted full land title under first settlement law." She grinned and swivelled round to scan the farmyard and the orchards beyond. "Very nice, very cosy. Your family seems to have done all right for itself, Amanda Foxon."

"Thank you." The pickers, led by Jane, began to filter into the farmyard. Even their presence didn't do much for Amanda's confidence.

"Well, well." Derry grinned round. "Look at what we have got ourselves here. This has got to be the sorriest old collection of Jew boys and girls I've seen in a long time. I really hope you all have your ID chips."

"We have," Jane said.

It was the awful fatigue in her voice which kindled Amanda's anger, the hopelessness of the eternally beleaguered. "They're working for me," she barked up at the Sergeant. "I don't have a single complaint."

"Glad to hear it," Derry said. She was looking at each of the pickers in turn, her optronic lens imaging their faces. "But we can't be too careful with the likes of these, now can we?"

"I'm sure you can't."

"Where are you all from?"

"I'm from Harrisburg," Jane said. "The Manton suburb."

"I know it, you people turned it into a real shithole. What are you doing here, then?"

Jane smiled. "Picking fruit."

"Don't smartmouth me, bitch."

The hound growled, a low rumbling as its black rubber mouth drew back to expose long yellowed fangs. Jane flinched, but held her ground.

"They're picking fruit," Amanda said forcefully. "I asked them here to do it, and they're excellent workers. Their private lives are none of your business."

"Wrong, Amanda Foxon. What they get up to in private is always police business."

"You're being ridiculous."

"Am I? You live in Harrisburg county, an original family, so you and your son will be Christians, then?"

"No, we'll be atheists, actually."

Derry shook her head ponderously. "It doesn't work like that. You'll understand eventually. If they take a shine to this area, every neighbour you have is going to be a Jew in five years' time. It's like a goddamn invasion force; ask the decent people who used to live in Manton. They turn the local schools over to teaching their creed, their wholesalers will come in and set up a new commercial network, one that doesn't include you. This farm will get frozen out ready for a nice kosher family to take it over at way below what it's worth, because no one else will touch it. The only way your precious Guy will get to carry on here is if he gets circumcised and you hook him in for his bar mitzvah."

"You're quite pathetic. Do you know that?"

"We'll see. If you ever looked outside your little valley of paradise you'd see it's already starting. Govcentral policies don't work here, not any more. Those bastards are destroying us with their equal settlement policies. They won't listen to us when we complain, all they do is keep sending us more human xenocs who don't belong here. You'll come round to our way eventually, Amanda, and when you do, when you remember who you really belong with, we'll help each other, you and me."

The hound padded over to the pick-up, and started sniffing round the back of the vehicle.

Amanda didn't dare risk a glance at Jane. "What are you doing here? Why did you come?"

Derry was frowning at the hound. "We're assigned to Harrisburg's C15 Division."

"I'm sorry, I don't really know much about police force divisions. What does that mean?"

"C15 is responsible for counter-insurgency. Basically, we hunt down terrorists, Amanda Foxon. And right now, we're after a particularly nasty specimen. Abdul Musaf. He planted a viral vector squirt in the Finsbury arcade last night. Fifteen people are in hospital with cancer runaways sprouting inside them like mushrooms. Two have developed brain tumours. They're not going to make it. So obviously, we're rather keen to talk to him. You seen anyone like that around here?"

I should tell her, Amanda thought. A viral squirt was a terrible thing to use against innocent people. But I can't be certain she's telling the truth, a woman who thinks Jews are a plague.

"No. Why, should I have?"

"He killed one of our pursuit dogs a couple of kilometres south of your track. But he was hurt in the fight. Can't have got far."

"OK. We'll keep watch for him."

The hound had wandered over to the big patch of wet ground outside the kitchen door.

"Right." Derry pursed her lips, suspicious and ill at ease. "What about you, Jew girl? You seen him? He's a Muslim, you know, one of the Legion."

"No. I haven't seen anybody."

"Huh. Bloody typical, don't know crap about anything, you people. OK, I don't suppose you'd harbour a towel-head anyway."

"If you're a Christian, why have you got an affinity-bonded dog? I thought the Pope banned the faithful from using the bond over a century ago."

The hound raised its head swiftly, swinging round to look at Jane. The lips parted again, allowing long strands of gooey saliva to drip onto the soil.

"Don't push your luck. The only reason you're not under arrest right now is because I don't want to waste taxpayers' money on you. You get back on that road when you're done here, head for your precious Tasmal."

"Yes, sir."

Derry snorted contemptuously. "Take my advice, Amanda Foxon, kick this thieving rabble off your land the second your crop's picked. And next year, hire some decent Christians. Get in touch with the Union, they have plenty of honest casual labourers on their books."

"I'll remember what you said."

If Sergeant Derry was aware of the irony, she didn't show it. She pulled on her reins, wheeling the big stallion round. The hound trotted out of the gate ahead of the horses.

Amanda realized she was sweating, muscles down the back of her legs twitched as if she'd just run to town and back. Jane patted her gently.

"Not bad for an amateur rebel. You faced her down."

Guy pressed himself to her side, and hugged her waist. "She was horrid, Mum."

"I know. Don't worry, she's gone now."

"But she'll be back," Jane muttered. "Her kind always are. Your file's in her memory now."

"She'll have no reason to come back," Amanda said. She handed Guy over to Lenny, then went back into the farmhouse.

Blake was helping Fakhud to limp up the stairs from the cellar. Both of them were shivering.

"Did you give people cancer?"

Fakhud drew a strained breath as he reached the top of the stairs. "Is that what the police said?"

"Yes."

"They lied. I oppose many issues on this planet, but I am not a monster. I would not use weapons like that. Do you know why?"

"Tell me."

"Because we have children, too. If the Legion started a terror campaign of that nature, others would begin similar campaigns against us."

"They already are. All of you are fighting each other. All you maniacs."

"Yes. But not like that, not yet. So far we confine ourselves to sabotage and assassinations of key opponents. Allah grant that it does not move beyond that. If it does, we shall all suffer; this whole world will drown in pain."

"Why? Why do you do this?"

"To defend ourselves. To defend our way of life. Just as you would do if anything threatened this farm. We have the right to do that, to resist Govcentral's imperialism."

"Just go," she said. Tears of frustration were swelling behind her eyes. "Go, and don't come back."

The pick-up was loaded with boxes of apples for one of its regular runs to the station in Knightsville. At the same time, several of the male pickers went in and out of the house, all of them wearing wide-brimmed sunhats which obscured their faces. Fakhud, dressed in Lenny's clothes, emerged and went over to the van. He lay in a coffin-sized gap between the boxes, while more were stacked over him.

Blake drove away as the sun was less than an hour from the mountains. Amanda tried not to show any concern, keeping the rest of the farm's activities normal. The pickers remained out in the orchard, working until dusk. Their evening meal was prepared on the large solar accumulator grill in the barn. Everyone had their shower then sat around in the farmyard until the food was cooked.

Amanda stood beside the gate to eat her chicken wing. From there she would be able to see the van's headlights as it returned along the track. If Blake had kept to his schedule, he should have been back forty minutes ago.

Guy climbed up the low wall and sat on top, his skinny legs dangling over the other side. "I didn't like today," he said solemnly.

She leant forward against the wall, and put her arm round his shoulder. "Me neither."

"Was that fat woman really a police officer?"

"Yes, I'm afraid so."

"She didn't like anybody. Are all police officers like that?"

"No. You don't have to be a police officer to hate other kinds of people. Everybody on Nyvan does it."

"Everybody?"

"Well, too many of us, anyway."

"Why?"

"There's a lot of reasons. But mainly because Govcentral is forcing different kinds of people to live next to each other. They do it because they think it's fair, that people should be treated equally. Which they should be, I'm not complaining about that. The problem is, the immigrants aren't used to other cultures."

"But they all get on together on Earth."

"They get on together in different arcologies; they might be on the same planet, but they're all segregated. And the people who come here to Nyvan, especially now, are the poor ones. They don't have much education so they're very set in their ways, very stubborn, and not very tolerant."

"What do you mean, now? Haven't poor people always come here? I remember Father telling me Grandpa didn't have any money when he arrived."

"That's true, but Grandpa wanted to come. He was a pioneer who wanted to build a fresh world for himself. Most of the people of that time were. That's changed now." She pointed up at the night sky. "See those stars up there? Their planets aren't like Nyvan. The new colony worlds have ethnic streaming policies; they're all sponsored by different Govcentral states, so the only people you get emigrating to them are the ones from the same arcology. As they're all the same to start with, they don't quarrel so much."

"Then why are people still coming here?"

"Because Earth is so overcrowded, and we're close to it, only seventeen light-years away. That makes travelling here one of the cheapest starflights possible. So Govcentral sends us all the people who can't afford to pay the passage to another planet, all the unemployed and petty criminals, people who never really wanted to come here in the first place."

"Can't we stop them from doing that?" he asked indignantly. "This is our planet. Won't Govcentral wreck it?"

"We can't stop Earth dumping people on us because Govcentral is our government, too. Although a lot of people think it shouldn't be. That's another big part of the problem. Nobody here can agree on anything any more."

"Can't we go to an ethnic streaming world? A Nyvan-ethnic one, like it was before?"

Amanda was glad of the night, it meant her son couldn't see the tears forming in her eyes. That one innocent child's question reducing her every accomplishment to nothing. Three generations of labour, sacrifice, and pride had bequeathed him this farm. And for what? She couldn't even call it an island of sanctuary from the madness which raged all around. Today had extinguished that illusion.

"There aren't any Nyvan-ethnic worlds, Guy," she said slowly. "Only us. We're just going to have to stay and make the best of it."

"Oh. All right." He studied the gleaming constellations. "Which one is Earth?"

"I don't know. I never thought it was very important to find out." She gave the darkened hills one last look. There was no sign of the pick-up van returning. The bleak depression inside her was threatening to become outright despair. Not even Blake would be so stupid as to go with Fakhud, surely? Though the alternative was even worse, that Sergeant Derry had caught them.

Please let it be a puncture, or a shorted power cell, she prayed. Somewhere in the soft night air she thought she heard a mocking laugh. It was probably just an echo inside her own skull.

Amanda woke before dawn, puzzled at the silence. It was a subliminal warning of wrongness, nothing she could actually name. She also missed Blake's weight at her side. When she went into his room, he wasn't there either. His bed hadn't been used.

The wood-burning range stove in the kitchen was almost out. Amanda had to fight against the instinct to load it immediately. Instead, she pulled her house coat tight and hurried out into the farmyard. The pick-up van hadn't returned.

She closed her eyes and cursed. Blake had gone for good. No use trying to kid herself about that any more. He believed a politician's promise, that their way is better than ours. Fool, stupid country boy fool.

Now she would have to find a replacement, which wouldn't be easy in these times. For all her exasperation with him, he'd been a good worker. It was a rare quality in today's young men.

She walked towards the long barn as the sun began to rise over the horizon. A heavy dew had given the joycevine leaves a mantle of grey sparkles. The grill was still sending out small wisps of smoke from last night's fats, mingling with the thin strands of mist layering the air.

Jane or one of the others would have to drive her into Knightsville to recover the pick-up. Assuming Blake had left it at the station.

It was when she reached the end of the barn that Amanda realized what had been bothering her since she awoke. Silence. Total silence. The pickers had gone.

Amanda ran into the centre of the small paddock where their vehicles had been parked. "No!" She turned a complete circle, trying hopelessly to spot the collection of cars and trucks they'd arrived in.

But they must have left hours ago. Their departure hadn't even left any tyre tracks in the dew.

"You can't!" she yelled at the narrow brown track which wound away from the farm. "You can't leave. I haven't even paid you." It wouldn't matter to them, she knew; money versus Sergeant Derry focusing her interest and attention on their group.

Amanda sank to her knees amid the damp fur of the grass-analogue. She started sobbing as the dark fear rose to claim her thoughts. Fear of the future. Fear for Guy.

The sun rose steadily, banishing the sheets of gossamer mist which lurked among the orchards. Under its growing warmth, the rich crop of apples turned yet another shade darker as they waited for the hands of the pickers.

Timeline

2267–2270 . . . Eight separate skirmishes involving use of antimatter among colony worlds. Thirteen million killed.

2271 . . . Avon summit between all planetary leaders. Treaty of Avon, banning the manufacture and use of antimatter throughout inhabited space. Formation of Human Confederation to police agreement. Construction of Confederation Navy begins.

2300 . . . Confederation expanded to include Edenists.

2301 . . . First Contact. Jiciro race discovered, a pre-technology civilization. System quarantined by Confederation to avoid cultural contamination.

2310 . . . First ice asteroid impact on Mars.

2330 . . . First blackhawks gestated at Valisk, independent habitat.

3350 . . . War between Novska and Hilversum. Novska bombed with antimatter. Confederation Navy prevents retaliatory strike against Hilversum.

2356 . . . Kiint homeworld discovered.

2357 . . . Kiint join Confederation as "observers."

2360 . . . A voidhawk scout discovers Atlantis.

2371 . . . Edenists colonize Atlantis.

Candy Buds

Laurus is ensconced in the Regency elegance of his study, comfortable in his favourite leather chair, looking out at the world through another set of eyes. The image is coming from an affinity bond with his eagle, Ryker. A silent union produced by the neuron symbionts rooted in his medulla, which are attuned to their clone analogues in Ryker, feeding him the bird's sensorium clear and bright.

He enjoys the sensations of freedom and power he obtains from flying the big bird, they're becoming an anodyne to his own ageing body with its white hair and weakening muscles. A decay which is defeating even Tropicana's biomedical skills. Ryker, however, possesses a nonchalant virility, a peerless lord of the sky.

With wings outstretched to its full three-metre span, the duality is riding the thermals high above Kariwak. Midday heat has shrouded the coastal city in a pocket of doldrum-calm air, magnifying the teeming convoluted streets below. This is the eastern quarter, the oldest human settlement on Tropicana, where the palm-thatched bungalows cluster scant metres above the white sands of Almond Beach. Laurus is looking down on the familiar pattern of whitewashed walls crusted with a tideline of ebony solar panels. Each has a petite garden of magical colour enclosed by fences long since buried under flowering creepers, all of them locked together like the tiles on some abstract rainbow mosaic. Behind the bungalows, the streets become more ordered, the buildings sturdier. Tall trees cluster at the centre of brick-paved squares, while the pavements are lined with market barrows, channelling the dense flow of bicycles, pedestrians, horses, and carriages. No cars or taxis are permitted here, they lack the necessary grace to gain membership of such a rustic environment.

The snow-white bitek coral walls of the two-kilometre-wide harbour basin glare with a near painful intensity under the scalding sun. From Ryker's viewpoint the harbour looks like a perfectly circular crater. Its western half has bitten a chunk out of the city, allowing a dense stratum of warehouses, commercial plazas, and boatyards to spring up along its boundary. The eastern half extends out into the flawless turquoise sea, deflecting the gentle ripples which roll in from the massive shallow ocean that occupies ninety-five per cent of Tropicana's surface. Wooden quays sprout from the harbour's inner rim, home to hundreds of fishing ketches and private yachts. Trading sloops that cruise the archipelago for exotic cargo are gliding over the clean water as they visit the commercial section.

This day, Laurus has brought Ryker to the balmy air above the harbour so he may use the bird to hunt. His prey is a little girl who walks along the harbour wall, slipping easily through the press of sailors, tourists, and townsfolk thronging the white coral. She looks no more than ten or eleven to Laurus; wearing a simple mauve cotton dress, black sandals, and a wide-brimmed straw hat. There is a small leather bag with blue and scarlet tassels slung over her shoulder.

As far as Laurus can tell she is completely unaware of the enforcer squad he has tailing her. Using the squad as well as Ryker is perhaps excessive, but Laurus is determined the girl will not give him the slip.

Ryker's predatory instinct alerts him to the gull. It's twenty metres below the eagle, floating in the air, simply marking time. Laurus recognizes it, a modified bird with tiny monkey paws grafted on to replace its feet. Affinity-bonded to Silene. Laurus hurriedly searches the harbour wall around the girl for the old mock-beggar.

Silene is easy to spot, sitting cross-legged on his reed mat, silver band across his empty eye sockets. He is playing a small flute, a bowl beside him with some silver coinage inside, and a Jovian Bank credit disk available for more generous benefactors. Resting at his feet is a black cat, yawning the day away.

The girl walks past him, and his black cat turns its head to follow her, its affinity bond no doubt revealing the ripe target of her bag to the old rogue.

Laurus feels a touch of cool melancholia; Silene has been working the harbour for over twenty years. Laurus himself authorized the franchise. But nothing can be allowed to interrupt the girl, to frighten her, and maybe heighten her senses. Nothing. Not even sentiment.

Back in his study, Laurus uses his cortical chip to open a scrambled datalink to Erigeron, the enforcer squad's lieutenant. "Take out Silene," he orders curtly.

The gull has already started its descent, angling down to snatch the bag. Hundreds of tourists and starship crew have lost trinkets and credit disks to the fast greedy bird over the years.

Laurus lets Ryker's natural instincts take over. Wingtips flick casually, rolling the big bird with idle grace. Then the wings fold, and the exhilarating plummet begins.

Ryker slams into the gull, his steel talons closing, snapping the gull's neck cleanly.

Silene's head jerks up in reflex.

Two of the enforcers are already in position behind him. Erigeron bends over as if to exchange a confidential word, mouth already parted to murmur secrets to the ear of a trusted old friend. Long vampire fangs pierce the wrinkled skin of Silene's neck. Every muscle in the old man's body locks solid as the hollow teeth inject their venom into his bloodstream.

Ten metres away, the girl stops at a fruit barrow and buys some oranges. Erigeron and his squad-mate leave Silene bowed over his silent flute, the cat miaowing anxiously at his feet. Ryker pumps his wings, flying out high over the harbour wall, and drops the broken gull into the sparkling water below.

Laurus relaxes. He has devoted most of his life to establishing order in the thriving coastal city. Because only where there is order and obedience can there be control.

Kariwak's council might pass the laws, but it is Laurus's city. He runs the harbour, over fifty per cent of the maritime trade is channelled through his warehouses. His holding companies own the spaceport and license the service companies which maintain the visiting spaceplanes. It was upon his insistence fifty years ago that the founding constitution's genetic research laws were relaxed, making Tropicana the one Adamist planet in the Confederation where bitek industry prospers. This trade attracts thousands of starships, each arrival and transaction contributing further to his wealth and power. The police answer to him, as do petty malefactors such as Silene, ensuring Kariwak remains perfectly safe for the terribly mortal billionaires who visit the city's clinics that specialize in anti-ageing treatments. Nothing goes on without him knowing and approving and taking his cut. Every single citizen knows that, learning it before they can walk.

But the girl has defied him. Normally that would bring swift retribution; youth and innocence do not comprise an acceptable excuse to Laurus. She has been selling bitek devices without clearing it with his harbour master; strange devices which have never been licensed for research in Tropicana. And these sales have been made with suspicious ingenuity. The only people she has sold them to are starship crew-members.

Laurus might never have known about them if it wasn't for the captain of the blackhawk *Thaneri* who had requested a personal interview. He asked for the agency to export the candy buds across the Confederation, willing to agree to whatever percentage Laurus nominated without argument. His fusion systems officer had bought one, he explained, and the woman was driving her crew mates crazy with her lyrical accounts of mammoths and sabre-toothed tigers contained in the bud memory.

The interview worried Laurus badly, for he had no idea what the captain was talking about. Bitek is the foundation of his wealth and power, Tropicana's sole export. The research programmes which commercial laboratories pursue may be liberal, but production and distribution remains firmly under his control, especially in Kariwak. To sell on the street is to circumvent payment to Laurus. The last person in Kariwak to sell unauthorized bitek died swiftly and painfully . . .

A man called Rubus, who had grown an improved form of memory supplement nodes in a private vat. A harmless enough item. These wart-like cell clusters can store sensorium input in an ordered fashion and retrieve it on demand, allowing the recipient to relive any event. In some wealthy circles it is chic to graft on such nodes in the fashion of a necklace.

Rubus sincerely believed Laurus would overlook a couple of sales. None of them understand. It is not the inoffensive nature of memory supplement nodes; Laurus cannot countenance the thin edge of the wedge, the notion that a couple of sales isn't going to matter. Because two then becomes three, and then five. And then someone else starts.

Laurus has already fought that battle. There will be no repetition. The price of enforcing his authority over the city was his own son, killed by a rival's enforcers. So he will not tolerate any dissension, a return to factions and gang fights. There are other powerful people on Tropicana, in other cities, princelings to the Emperor, none capable of serious challenge. So Rubus was used as bait by sports fishing captains taking clients out to the archipelago in search of the planet's famed razorsquids.

Laurus calmly and politely asked the *Thaneri*'s captain if by chance he had any more of these wondrous new candy buds. And on being told that there was indeed a second, sent Erigeron and a full enforcer squad back to the hotel with the by now terrified captain to buy it from the luckless officer, who was also persuaded to tell them about the girl she'd bought it from.

Laurus has tried the candy bud, and it has given him a glimpse into the same kind of illusory world that the *Thaneri* officer experienced. The implications are as bad as he thought. It is nothing like a cortical chip's virtual reality induction; this is an actual memory of a far-gone time and place. He genuinely recalls being there. Someone has discovered how to transcribe a fantasy sensorium onto chemical memory tracers that will implant it in the brain.

If Laurus were to own the process, he would become as wealthy as the Saldana family. Visualizing the imagination, the kind of direct canvas which artists have dreamt about for centuries. Permanent memory will also have tremendous educational applications, circumventing cortical chip Technique induction. The knowledge equivalent of Norfolk Tears. That is why dear old Silene is now a huddled bundle of rags with his cat crying at his feet. That is why every day for the last week twenty-five of his best enforcers have milled with the harbour crowds, posing as visiting starship crew as they look for the girl.

And today the time and effort has paid off; she has sold another candy bud to an enforcer. The girl herself is of no real value, it is her ability to lead him to the source of this revolutionary bitek product which makes safeguarding her so essential.

Ryker is following her through the boulevards of the city centre as she heads away from the harbour. But all the time, Laurus is haunted by the candy bud's fantasyscape.

• • •

At some non-time in his past, Laurus walked through a terrestrial forest. It had a European feel, pre-industrialization, the trees deciduous, bigger than life, dark, ancient, their bark gnarled and flaking. He wandered along narrow animal paths between their trunks, exploring gentle banks and winding valleys, listening to the birdsong and smelling the blossom perfume. The air was refreshingly cool, shaded by the vast boughs arching overhead. A rain of gold-sparkle sunbeams pierced the light green leaves, dappling the ground.

This was home in the way no terracompatible world could be, however bucolic. An environment he had evolved in tandem with, his natural milieu.

He could remember his feelings of the time, preserved and treasured, undimmed. He was new to his ancient world, and each of his discoveries was accompanied by a joyful accomplishment.

There were sunny glades of tall grass sprinkled with wild flowers. Long dark lakes filled from waterfalls which burbled down bright sandstone rocks. He had dived in, whooping at the icy water which drove the breath from his lungs.

And he walked on, through a sleepy afternoon under a tumid rose-gold sun that was always halfway towards evening. He picked fruit from the trees, biting into soft flesh, thick juice dribbling down his chin. Even the taste had a vitality absent from Tropicana's adapted citrus groves. His laughter had rung around the trees, startling the squirrels and rabbits.

If Laurus went into that forest in real life he knew he wouldn't have the strength to leave. The memory segment was the most perfect part of his existence. Childhood's essence of wonder and discovery composed into a single day. He kept reliving it, dipping into the recollections with alarming frequency. In reward, they remained as fresh as if he'd walked out of the forest only minutes before.

• • •

The Longthorpe district sprawls along the eastern edge of Kariwak, curving across the wave contours of the hills which rise up behind the city. It comprises impoverished factories, abandoned heavy-plant machinery, and dilapidated habitation capsule stacks, poverty housing thrown up over a century ago. This is a slum zone where even Laurus's influence falters.

Those who have made a success of their new lives on this world clawed their way out to live closer to the ocean or out on the archipelago. Those that stay are the ones without spirit, who need the most help and receive the least.

Yet even here the vigorous vegetation human colonists brought to this planet has spread and conquered. Tenacious vines bubble over the ground between the dilapidated twenty-storey stacks, lush grass carpets the parks where barefoot children kick their footballs. It is only after the girl crosses a withered old service road and walks into a derelict industrial precinct that the greenery gives way to yellow soil smudged by occasional weeds. Faded skull-and-crossbones signs hanging on the rusty fence warn people of the dangers inside the site, but the girl carries on regardless. She threads her way between bulldozed mounds of vitrified waste blocks; treading on a rough path of stones laid down on clay stained red and blue from the chemicals which leak up from buried deposits.

Her eventual destination is an old office building whose adjacent factory was torn down over two decades earlier. The shell is a virtual wreck, brickwork crumbling, weeds and creepers growing from gutters and window ledges.

The girl slips through a gap in the corrugated sheeting nailed over a window, vanishing from Ryker's sight.

• • •

Two hours later, Laurus stands in front of the same corrugated sheet while his enforcers move into position. His presence kindles an air of nervousness among the squad, in turn producing an almost preternatural attention to detail. For Laurus to attend an operation in person is almost unheard of. He does not often venture out of his mansion these days.

Erigeron has sent his affinity-bonded ferret into the office building, scouting out the interior. The jet-black creature puts Laurus in mind of a snake with paws, but it does possess an astonishing ability to wriggle through the smallest of gaps as if its bones were flexible.

According to Erigeron, the only humans inside are the girl and a young boy who seems to be injured. He also says there is some kind of machine in the room, powered by a photosynthetic membrane hanging under the skylight. Laurus is regretting that each affinity bond is unique and impregnable. He would like to have seen for himself; all Ryker can offer him is blurred outlines through algae-crusted skylights.

The conclusion he has grudgingly arrived at is that the inventor of these candy buds is elsewhere. He could wait, mount a surveillance operation to see if the inventor shows up. But he is too near now to adopt a circumspect approach, every delay could mean someone else learning about candy buds. If this knowledge were to go elsewhere his own power would be lost. This is a matter of survival now.

Very well, the girl will simply have to provide him with the inventor's location. There are methods available for guaranteeing truth.

"Go," he tells Erigeron.

The enforcer squad penetrates the office building with deceptive efficiency; their sleek hounds racing ahead of them, sensors alert for booby traps. Laurus feels an excitement that has been missing for decades as he watches the armour-clad figures disappear into the gloomy interior.

Erigeron emerges two minutes later and pushes up his helmet visor to reveal a bleak angular face. "All secure, Mr Laurus. We've got 'em cornered for you."

Laurus strides forwards, eagerness firing his blood.

•   •   •

The room's light comes from a single soot-stained skylight high above. A pile of cushions and dirty blankets makes up a sleeping nest in one corner. There's an oven built out of loose bricks, small broken branches crackling inside, casting a dull ruby glow. The feral squalor of the den is more or less what Laurus expected, except for the books. There are hundreds of them, tall stacks of mouldering paperbacks leaning at precarious angles. Those at the bottom of the pile have already decayed beyond rescue, their pages agglutinating into a single pulp brickette.

Laurus has a collection of books at his mansion, leatherbound classics imported from Kulu. He knows of no one else on Tropicana who has books. Everyone else uses space chips.

The girl is crouched beside an ancient hospital commode, her arms thrown protectively around a small boy with greasy red hair, no more than seven or eight. A yellowing bandage is wrapped round his head, covering his eyes. Cheesy tears are leaking from the linen, crusting on his cheeks. His legs have wasted away, now little more than a layer of pale skin stretched over the bones, the waxy surface rucked by tightly knotted blue veins.

Laurus glances round at the enforcer squad. Their plasma carbines are trained on the two frightened children, hounds quiver at the ready. The girl's wide green eyes are moist from barely contained tears. Shame tweaks him. "That's enough," he says. "Erigeron, you stay. The rest of you, leave us now."

Laurus squats down next to the children as the squad clumps out. His creaky joints protest the posture.

"What's your name?" he asks the girl. Now he's face to face with her, he sees how pretty she is; ragged shoulder-length ginger hair which looks like it needs a good wash, and her skin is milk-white and gently freckled. He's curious, to retain that pallor under Tropicana's sun would require dermal tailoring, which isn't cheap.

She flinches at his closeness, but doesn't relinquish her hold on the boy. "Torreya," she says.

"Sorry if we scared you, Torreya, we didn't mean to. Are your parents around?"

She shakes her head slowly. "No. There's just me and Jante left now."

Laurus inclines his head at the boy. "Your brother?"

"Yes."

"What's the matter with him?"

"His daddy said he was ill. More ill than his daddy could cure, but he was going to learn how. Then after he cured Jante and himself we could all leave here."

Laurus looks at the blind crippled boy again. There's no telling what has ruined his legs. Longthorpe is riddled with toxicants, a whole stratum of eternity drums lying below the crumbling topsoil to provide a stable foundation for the large industrial buildings which were supposed to rejuvenate the area's economy. Laurus remembers the Council-backed development project from nearly eighty years ago. But eternity has turned out to be less than fifty years. The factories were never built. So Longthorpe remains too poor to have any clout in the Council chamber and thus insist on clean-up programmes.

Jante points upwards. "Is that your bird?" he asks in a high, curious voice.

Ryker is perched on the edge of the grubby skylight, his huge menacing head peering down.

"Yes," Laurus says. His eyes narrow with suspicion. "How did you know he was there?"

"His daddy gave us an affinity bond," Torreya says. "I see for him. I don't mind. Jante was so lonely inside his head. And it was only supposed to be until his daddy understood how to cure him."

"So where is your father now?" Laurus asks.

Her eyes drop. "I think he's dead. He was very sick. Sort of inside, you know? He used to cough up blood a lot. Then it started to get worse, and one morning he was gone. So we didn't see, I suppose."

"How was your father going to learn how to cure Jante?"

"With the candy buds, of course." She turns and gestures into the darker half of the room.

The machine is a customized life-support module. A graft of hardware and bitek; metal, plastic, and organic components fused in such an uncompromising fashion that Laurus can't help but feel its perversity is somehow intended to dismay. The globose-ribbed plant growing out of the centre has the appearance of a glochidless cactus, over a metre high, as hard and dark as teak.

At the centre, its meristem areola is a gooey gelatin patch from which the tiny candy buds emerge, growing along the rib vertices. They look like glaucous pebble cacti, a couple of centimetres in diameter, dappled by mauve rings.

One of Laurus's biotechnicians examined the candy bud obtained from the *Thaneri* officer before he ate it. The man said its cells were saturated with neurophysin proteins, intracellular carriers, but of an unknown type. Whatever they were, they would interact directly with a brain's synaptic clefts. That, he surmised, was how the memory was imparted. As to how the neurophysins were produced and formatted to provide a coherent sensorium sequence, he had no idea.

Laurus can only stare at the bizarre living machine as the forest journey memory returns to him with a vengeance.

"Are these the candy buds you've been selling?" he asks. "The ones with the forest in them?"

Torreya sniffs uncertainly, then nods.

Something like frost is creeping along Laurus's spine. There is only the one machine. "And the candy buds with the prehistoric animals as well?"

"Yes."

"Where did this device come from?" Although he's sure he knows.

"Jante's father grew it," Torreya replies. "He was a plant geneticist, he said he used to develop algae that could eat rocks to refine chemicals out of it. But the company shut down the lab after an accident; and he didn't have the money to get Jante and himself fixed in hospital. So he said he was going to put medical information into the candy buds and become his own doctor."

"And the fantasy lands?" Laurus asks. "Where did they come from?"

Torreya flicks a guilty glance at Jante. And Laurus begins to understand.

"Jante, tell me where the fantasy lands come from, there's

a good boy," he says. He's smiling at Torreya, a smile that is polite and humourless.

"I do them," Jante blurts, and there's a trace of panic in his high voice. "I've got an affinity bond with the machine's bioware processors. Daddy gave it me. He said someone ought to fill up the candy buds with something, they should-n't be wasted. So Torry reads books for us, and I think about the places in them."

Laurus is getting way out of his depth. His own biotech-nology degree is ninety years out of date. And an affinity bond with a plant is outside anything he's ever heard of be-fore. "You can put anything you want into these candy buds?" he asks hoarsely.

"Yes."

"And all you do is sell them down at the harbour?"

"Yes. If I sell enough I want to buy Jante new eyes and legs. I don't know how many that will take, though. Lots, I suppose."

Laurus is virtually trembling, thinking what would have happened if he hadn't found the children and their machine first. It must incorporate some kind of neurophysin synthe-sis mechanism, one that was programmable. Again, like nothing he's heard of.

The market potential is utterly staggering.

He meets Torreya's large green eyes again. She's curi-ously passive, almost subdued, waiting for him to say what is going to happen next. Children, he realizes, can intuitively cut to the heart of any situation.

He rests his hand on her shoulder, hoping he's doing it in a reassuringly paternal fashion. "This is very unpleasant, this room. Do you enjoy living here?"

Torreya's lips are pursed as she considers the question. "No. But nobody bothers us here."

"How would you like to come and live with me? No one will bother you there, either. I promise that."

* * *

Laurus's mansion sits astride a headland in the mountains behind Kariwak, its broad stone façade looking down on the city and the ocean beyond. He bought it for the view, all of his domain a living picture.

Torreya presses her face to the Rolls-Royce's window as they ride up the hill. She is captivated by the formal splendour of the grounds. Jante is sitting beside her, clapping his hands delightedly as she gives him a visual tour of the lawns and statues and winding gravel paths and ponds and fountains.

The gates of the estate's inner defence zone close behind the bronze car, and it trundles into the courtyard. Peacocks spread their majestic tails in welcome. Servants hurry down the wide stone steps from the front door. Jante is eased gently from the car and carried inside. Torreya stands on the granite cobblestones, turning around and around, her mouth open in astonishment.

"Did you really mean it?" she gasps. "Can we really live here?"

"Yes." Laurus grins broadly. "I meant it. This is your home now."

Camassia and Abelia emerge from the mansion to welcome him back. Camassia is twenty years old, a tall Oriental beauty with long black hair and an air of aristocratic refinement. She used to be with Kochia, a merchant in Palmetto, who has the lucrative franchise from Laurus to sell affinity bonded dogs to offworlders who want them for police-style work on stage one colony planets. Then Laurus decided he would like to see her stretched naked across his bed, her cool poise broken by the animal heat of rutting. Kochia immediately made a gift of her, sweating and smiling as she was presented.

Such whims help to keep Laurus's reputation intact. By acquiescing, Kochia sets an example of obedience to others. Had he refused, Laurus would have made an example of him.

Abelia is younger, sixteen or seventeen, shoulder-length blonde hair arranged in tiny curls, her body trim and compact, excitingly dainty. Laurus took her from her parents a couple of years ago as payment for protection and gambling debts.

The two girls exchange an uncertain glance as they see Torreya, obviously wondering which of them she is going to replace. They more than anyone are aware of Laurus's tastes.

"This is Torreya," Laurus says. "She will be staying with us from now on. Make her welcome."

Torreya tilts her head up, looking from Camassia to Abelia, seemingly awestruck. Then Abelia smiles, breaking the ice, and Torreya is led into the mansion, her bag dragging along the cobbles behind her. Camassia and Abelia begin to twitter over her like a pair of elder sisters, arguing how to style her hair once it's been washed.

Laurus issues a stream of instructions to his major-domo concerning new clothes and books and toys and softer furniture, a nurse for Jante. He feels almost virtuous. Few prisoners have ever had it so good.

• • •

Torreya bounds into Laurus's bedroom the next morning, her little frame filled with such boisterous energy that she instantly makes him feel lethargic. She has intercepted the maid, bringing his breakfast tray in herself.

"I've been up for hours," she exclaims joyfully. "I watched the sunrise over the sea. I've never seen it before.

Did you know you can see the first islands in the archipel- ago from the balcony?"

She seems oblivious to the naked bodies of Camassia and Abelia lying beside him on the bed. Such easy acceptance gives him pause for thought; in a year or two she'll have breasts of her own.

Laurus considers he has worn well in his hundred and twenty years, treating entropy's frosty encroachment with all the disdain only his kind of money can afford. But the biochemical treatments that keep his skin thick and his hair growing, the gene therapy to sustain his organs, cannot work miracles. The accumulating years have seen his sex life dwindle to practically nothing. Now he simply contents himself with watching the girls. To see Torreya's innocence lost to the skilful hands of Camassia and Abelia will be a magnificent spectacle to anticipate. It won't take that long for his technicians to solve the mystery of the candy buds machine.

"I know about the islands," he tells her expansively as Ca- massia takes the tray from her. "My company supplies the coral kernels for most of them."

"Really?" Torreya flashes him a solar-bright smile.

Laurus is struck by how lovely she looks now she's been tidied up; she's wearing a lace-trimmed white dress, and her hair's been given a French pleat. Her delicate face is aglow with enthusiasm. He marvels at that, a spirit which can find happiness in something as elementary as sunrise. How many dawns have there been in his life?

Camassia carefully measures out the milk in Laurus's cup, and pours his tea from a silver pot. If his morning tea isn't exactly right everyone suffers from his tetchiness until well after lunch.

Torreya rescues a porcelain side plate as Abelia starts to butter the toast. There's a candy bud resting on the plate. "Jante and I made this one up specially for you," she says, sucking her lower lip apprehensively as she proffers it to Laurus. "It's a thank you for taking us away from Longthorpe. Jante's daddy said you should always say thank you to people who're nice to you."

"You keep calling him Jante's father," Laurus says. "Wasn't he yours?"

She shakes her head slowly. "No, I don't know who my daddy was. Mummy would never say."

"You have the same mother, then?"

"That's right. But Jante's daddy was nice, though. I liked him lots."

Laurus holds the candy bud up, her words suddenly registering. "You composed this last night?"

"Uh huh." She nods brightly. "We know how much you like them, and it's the only gift we have."

Under Torreya's eager gaze, Laurus puts the candy bud in his mouth and starts to chew. It tastes of blackcurrant.

• • •

Laurus used to be a small boy on a tropical island, left alone to wander the coast and jungle to his heart's content. His bare feet pounded along powdery white sand. The palm-shaded beach stretched on for eternity, its waves perfect for surfing. He ran and did cartwheels for the sheer joy of it, his lithe limbs responding effortlessly. Whenever he got too warm he would dive into the cool clear water of the bay, swimming through the fantastic coral reef to sport with the dolphin shoal who greeted him like one of their own.

• • •

"You were dreaming," Camassia says. She is stroking his head as he sits in the study's leather chair.

"I was young again," he replies, and there's the feel of the lean powerful dolphin pressed between his skinny legs as he rides across the lagoon, a tang of salt in his mouth. "We should introduce dolphins here, you know. Can't think why we never did. They are to the water what Ryker is to the air."

"Sounds wonderful. When do I get to try one?"

"Ask Torreya." He shakes some life into himself, focusing on the daily reports and accounts his cortical chip has assembled. But the candy bud memory is still resonating through his mind, twisting the blue neuroiconic graphs into waves crashing over coral. And all Torreya and Jante have to go on is what she reads.

"Laurus?" Camassia asks cautiously, sensitive to his mood.

"I want you and Abelia to be very nice to Torreya, become her friends."

"We will. She's sweet."

"I mean it."

The dead tone brings a flash of fear into the girl's eyes. "Yes, Laurus."

After she leaves he still cannot bring himself to do any work. Every time he considers the candy buds another possibility is opened.

What would it feel like if Torreya was to inscribe her sexual encounters into the candy buds? His breathing is unsteady as he imagines the three girls disrobing in some softly lit bedroom, their bodies entwining on the bed.

Yes. That would be the ultimate candy bud. Not just the physical sensation, the rip of orgasm, any cortical induction can deliver that; but the mind's longing and adoration, its wonder of discovery.

Nothing, but nothing is now more important than making Torreya and Jante happy; so that in a couple of years she will slide eagerly into the arms of her lovers.

He closes his eyes, calling silently for Ryker.

The eagle finds Torreya on the south side of the estate,

busy exploring her vast new playground. He orbits overhead as she gambols about. She's a fey little creature, this untamed child. She doesn't walk, she dances.

Jante is sitting in a wicker chair on the patio outside the study, and Laurus can hear him whooping encouragement to his sister. Occasionally the boy lets out a squeal of excitement at some new discovery she makes for him.

"Stop! Stop!" Jante cries suddenly.

Laurus looks up sharply, wondering what the boy is seeing through the affinity bond, but he's smiling below his neat white bandage.

Ryker spirals lower. Torreya is standing frozen in the middle of a shaggy meadow, her hands pressed to her cheeks. A cloud of rainbow-hued butterflies is swirling around her, disturbed by her frantic passage.

"Hundreds," she breathes tremulously. "Hundreds and hundreds."

The expression on the face of both siblings is one of absolute enchantment. Laurus recalls his trip through Longthorpe, its soiled air, the stagnant puddles with their scum of dead, half-melted insects. She has probably never seen a butterfly in her life before.

His cargo agents are instructed to scan the inventory of every visiting starship in search of exotic caterpillars. The estate is going to be turned into a lepidopterist's heaven.

•   •   •

Today Torreya is all rakish smiles as she brings in Laurus's breakfast tray. He grins back at her as he takes the candy bud she holds out to him. This is going to become a ritual, he guesses.

"Another one?" Camassia asks.

"Yes!" Torreya shouts gleefully. "It's a fairy tale one. We've been thinking about it for a while, so it wasn't difficult. We just needed yesterday to make it right. The butterflies you've got here in the estate are beautiful, Laurus."

Laurus pops the candy bud in his mouth. "Glad you like them."

"I would have loved to see the forest Laurus talks about," Camassia says wistfully.

Laurus notes a more than idle interest in the girl's tone.

"Why didn't you say?" Torreya asks.

"You mean you've still got one?"

"Course. The machine keeps growing them till Jante tells it to stop."

"You mean you don't have to fill in each one separately?" Laurus asks.

"No."

He sips his tea thoughtfully. The strange machine is even more complex than he originally expected. "Do you know if Jante's father transcribed a candy bud about how the machine was built?"

Torreya screws her face up, listening to some silent voice. "No, he didn't. Sorry."

Laurus accepts that it isn't going to be easy, he never thought it would be. He will have to assemble a team of high-grade biotechnology experts, the most loyal ones he can find. They will analyse the machine's components and genetics to discover its secrets. Such research will have to be done circumspectly. If any hint of this breakthrough escapes, then every laboratory on Tropicana will launch a crash project to acquire candy-bud technology.

"What are we going to do today?" Torreya asks.

"Well, I've got a lot of work to do," Laurus says. "But Camassia and Abelia are free, why don't you all go out for a picnic."

• • • •

In his youth, Laurus had been a prince of the Eldrath Kingdom, back in Earth's dawn times when the world was flat and the oceans ended in infinite waterfalls. He lived in a city of crystal spires that was built around one of the tallest mountains in the land. The royal palace sat atop the pinnacle, from where it was said you could see halfway across the world.

When the warning of marauders reached the citadel, he led his knight warriors in defence of his father's realm. There were thirty of them, in mirror-bright armour, flying to war on the back of their giant butterflies.

The village on the edge of the Desolation was besieged by trolls and goblins, with fires raging through the wattle-and-daub cottages, and the harsh cries of battle echoing through the air.

Laurus drew his silver longsword, holding it high. "In the name of the King and our Mother Goddess, I swear none of this fellowship shall rest until the Rok lord's spawn are driven from this land," he shouted.

The other knight warriors drew their swords in unison, and shouted their accord. Together they urged their steeds down on the village.

The trolls and goblins they faced were huge scarred brutes with blue-green skin and yellow poisonous fangs. But their anger and viciousness made them cumbersome, and they had no true sword skill, just an urge to maim and kill. Their wild sword swings were always slow and inaccurate. Laurus weaved amongst them, using his longsword with terrible accuracy. A quick powerful thrust would send his enemy crashing to the ground, a dark yellow stain bubbling out of the wound.

The battle raged all day amid the black oily smoke, and flames, and muddy cobbles. Laurus eluded all injury, although the enemy directed their fiercest assaults against him; enraged by the sight of his slim golden crown denoting him a prince of the house of Eldrath.

Night was falling when the last goblin was dispatched. The village cheered their prince and his knight warriors. And a beautiful maiden with red hair falling to her waist came forward to offer him wine from a golden chalice.

Laurus could not forget the sensation of flying that incredible steed, with his long black hair flowing free, cheeks tingling in the wind, and mighty rainbow wings rippling effortlessly on either side of him.

• • •

And he's still flying. The three girls are below, resting in the long grass under the shade of a big magnolia tree. There's a little lake twenty metres away, tangerine-coloured fish sliding through the dark water.

Ryker glides to a silent halt in the branches above the girls. None of them have seen him.

"I was frightened at first," Torreya is saying, "especially at night. But after a while you get used to it, and nobody ever came into the factory site." She's reciting her life, listening to Camassia and Abelia recounting tall tales. All part of making friends.

Laurus listens to the giggles and outraged groans of disbelief, longing to be a part of the group.

"You're lucky Laurus found you," Camassia says. "He'll look after you all right, and he knows how to make the most from your candy buds."

Torreya is lying on her belly, chin resting on her hands. She smiles dreamily, watching a ladybird climb up a stalk of grass in front of her face. "Yes, I know."

Abelia jumps to her feet. "Oh, come on, it's so hot!" She slips the navy-blue dress from her shoulders, and wriggles out of the skirt. Laurus hasn't seen her naked in daylight before. He marvels at the brown skin, hair like ripe wheat, perfectly shaped breasts, strong legs. "Come on!" she taunts devilishly, and makes a dash for the lake.

Camassia follows suit; and then Torreya, completely unabashed.

For the ability to transcribe this scene into a candy bud, Laurus would sell his soul. He wants it to stretch for ever and ever. Three golden bodies racing across the ragged grass, laughing, vibrant. The shrieks and splashing as they dive into the water, sending the fish fleeing into the deeps.

This is where it will happen, Laurus decides. In the shade of the magnolia blooms, her body spread open like a star, amid the moisture and the heat.

He's not sure he can wait two years.

•   •   •

Laurus has instructed his staff to set up the machine in the mansion's coldhouse conservatory, where it is sheltered from the sun's abrasive power by darkened glass and large overhanging fern fronds. Conditioners are whining softly as they maintain a temperate climate. Spring is coming to an end for the terrestrial plants growing out of the troughs and borders. The daffodils are starting to fade, and the fuchsia flowers are popping.

Two flaccid olive-green elephant ear membranes have been draped over a metal framework above the seed beds, photosynthesizing the machine's nutrient fluids. A tube patched in to the overhead irrigation pipes supplies water to the internal systems when they run dry.

"Does it snow in here?" Torreya asks.

"No," Laurus says. "There are frosts, though. We switch them on for the winter months."

Torreya wanders on ahead, her head swivelling from side

to side as she examines the new-old shrubs and trees in the brick-lined border.

"I'd like to have some people take a look at your machine," Laurus tells her. "Will you mind that?"

"No," she says. "What is this tree?"

"An oak. They'll duplicate it for me, and I'll sell the candy buds the new machines produce. But I'd like you and Jante to stay on here. You can earn a lot of money with those fantasies of yours."

She turns off into a passage lined by dense braids of cyclamen. "I don't want to leave. They're not going to dissect the main corm, are they?"

"No, certainly not. They'll just sample a few cells to obtain the DNA, so we can understand how it works. They'll start in a week or so."

And then will come the task of setting up production lines. Selecting the information to transcribe. Finding fantasyscape artists as skilful as Torreya and Jante. The establishment of multi-stellar markets. Decades of work. And to what end, exactly? Laurus suddenly feels depressingly old.

"It's valuable, isn't it, Laurus? Our machine, I mean. Camassia says it is."

"She's quite right."

"Will there be enough money to buy Jante new eyes and legs?" Torreya asks, her voice echoing round the trellis walls of climbing plants.

Laurus has lost track of her; she's not in the cyclamen passage, nor the forsythia avenue. "One day," he calls out. The thought of giving Jante eyes is an anathema, the boy might lose his imagination.

That is something else he is going to have to research carefully. Torreya and Jante can hardly provide an endless number of different fantasies to fill the candy buds once he starts mass-producing them. Although in the three days they have been at the estate they have dreamt up three new fantasies.

Will it only be children, with their joy and uninhibited imagination, who'll be the universe's fantasyscape artists?

"Some day soon, Laurus," Torreya's disembodied voice urges. "Jante just loves the estate. With eyes and legs he can run through all of it himself. That's the very best present anyone can have. It's so gorgeous here, better than any silly candy bud land. The whole world must envy you."

Laurus is following her voice down a corridor of laburnum trees that are in full bloom. Sunlight shimmers off their flower clusters, transforming the air to a lemon haze. He turns the corner by a clump of white angels trumpets. Torreya is standing beside the machine, and even that seems to have thrived in its new home. Laurus doesn't remember its organic components as being so large.

"As soon as we can," he says.

Torreya smiles her irrepressible smile, and holds out a newly plucked candy bud. Refusing the warmth and trust in her sparkling eyes is an impossibility.

• • •

The starling is already eighty metres off the ground. Laurus thinks it must have owl-eye transplants in order to fly so unerringly in the dead of night like this.

Ryker hurtles down, and Laurus feels feathers, malleable flesh, and delicate bones captured within his talons. In his rage he wrenches the starling's head clean off. The candy bud which the little bird was carrying tumbles away, and not even Ryker can see where it falls.

Laurus contents himself with the knowledge that they are still well inside the estate's defensive perimeter. Should any animal try and recover the candy bud, the estate's hounds and kestrels will deal with them.

He drops the starling's body so he will have a rough marker when the search begins tomorrow.

Now the big eagle banks sharply and heads back towards the mansion in a fast silent swoop. The ground is a montage of misty grey shadows, trees are puffy jet-black outlines, easily dodged. He can discern no individual landmarks, speed has reduced features to a slipstream blur.

He curses his own foolishness, the satellite of vanity. He should have known, should have anticipated. The Laurus of old would have. Three days Torreya and Jante have been at the estate, and already news of the candy buds has leaked. Programmable neurophysin synthesis is too big, the stakes are now high enough to tempt mid-range players into the field. There will be no allies in this war.

Ryker soars over the last row of trees and the mansion is dead ahead, its lighted windows glaringly bright to the eagle's gloaming-acclimatized eyes. Camassia is still fifty metres from the side door. There's no urgency to her stride, no hint of furtiveness. One of his girls taking an evening stroll, nobody would question her right.

She's a cool one, he admits. Kochia's eyes and ears for eighteen months, and Laurus never knew. Only the importance of the candy buds made her break cover and risk a handover to the starling.

Laurus thinks he still has a chance to salvage his dominant position. Kochia and his Palmetto operation are small, weak. If Laurus acts swiftly the damage might yet be contained.

He activates his cortical chip's datalink. "Mine," he tells the enforcers. But first he wants the bitch to know.

Ryker's wings slap the air with a loud *fop*. Camassia jerks around at the sound. He can see the shock on her face as Ryker plunges towards her. Hand-sized steel talons stretch wide. She starts to run.

Laurus is visiting Torreya in her room to see how she is settling in. Over four days the guest bedroom has metamor-
phosed beyond recognition. Holographic posters cover the
walls, windows looking out across Tropicana's northern
polar continent. Dazzling temples of ice drift past in the sky-
blue water. Shorelines are crinkled by deep fjords. Timeless
and exquisite. But Laurus is the first to admit that the images
are feeble parodies compared to the candy bud fantasies.
The new pastel-coloured furniture is soft and puffy. Shiny
hardback books of fictional mythology from his library are
strewn all over the floor. It's nice to see them actually being
used and appreciated for once. Every flat surface is now
home to a cuddly Animate Animal. He thinks there must be
over thirty of them. There is a scuffed hologram cube on the
bedside dresser, containing a smiling woman. It seems out
of kilter with the deliberate cosiness organic to the room. He
vaguely recalls seeing it at the old office building.

Torreya clutches a fluffy AA koala to her chest, giggling
as the toy rubs its head against her, purring affectionately.

"Aren't they wonderful?" Torreya says. "All the people in
the house have given me one. They gave some to Jante, too.
You're all so kind to us."

Laurus can only smile weakly as he hands her the huge
AA panda he's brought. It's almost as tall as she is. Torreya
stands on the bed and kisses him, then bounces on the mattress as the panda hugs her, crooning with delight.

"I'm going to name him St Peter," she declares. "Because
he's your present. And he'll sleep with me at night, I'll be
safe from anything then."

The damp tingle on his cheek where she kissed him sets
off a warm contentment.

"Shame Camassia had to go," Torreya says. "I like her a
lot."

"Yes. But her family need her to help with their island plantation now her cousin's married."

"Can I go and visit her?"

"Maybe. Some time."

"And Erigeron's away as well," she says with a vexed expression. "He's nice. He helps Jante move around, and he tells funny stories, too."

The thought of his near-psychopathic enforcer reciting fairy stories to please the children is one that amuses Laurus immensely. "He'll be back in a couple of days. He's driven over to Palmetto to sort out some business contracts for me."

"I didn't know he was one of your company managers."

"Erigeron is very versatile. Who's the woman?" he asks to deflect further questions.

Torreya's face is momentarily still. She glances guiltily at the old hologram cube. The woman is young, mid-twenties, very beautiful, smiling wistfully. Her hair is a light ginger, tumbling over her shoulders.

"My mother. She died when Jante was born."

"I'm sorry." But the woman is definitely Torreya's mother; he can pick out the shared features, identical green eyes, the hair colour.

"Everyone back in Longthorpe who knew her said she was special," Torreya says. "A real lady, that's what. Her name was Nemesia."

•   •   •

After lunch, Laurus took Torreya down the hill to the city zoo. He thought it would make a grand treat, bolstering her spirits after Camassia's abrupt departure.

In all his hundred and twenty years Laurus had never found the time to visit the zoo before. But it was a lovely afternoon, and they held hands as they walked down the leafy lanes between the compounds.

Torreya pressed herself to the railings, smiling and pointing at the exhibits, asking a stream of questions. She would
often narrow her eyes and concentrate intensely on what she
was seeing, which he came to recognize as using her affinity bond with Jante, letting her brother enjoy the afternoon
as much as she did. It would be interesting to see if the visit
resulted in a new fantasyscape.

Laurus found himself enjoying the trip. Tropicana had no
aboriginal land animals, its one mountain range above water
was too small to support that kind of complex evolution. Instead its citizens had to import all their creatures, which
were chosen to be benign. Here in the zoo, terrestrial and
xenoc predators and carnivores roared and hissed and
hooted at each other.

Torreya hauled him over to one of the ice cream stalls,
and he had to borrow some coins from one of the enforcer
squad to pay for the cornets. He never carried money, never
had the need before.

Ice cream and an endless sunny afternoon with Torreya, it
was heaven.

•   •   •

Laurus wakes in the middle of the night, his body as cold as
ice. The name has connected; one of his girls was called
Nemesia. How long ago? His recollection is unclear. He
peers at Abelia, a child with a woman's body, curled up on
her side, wisps of hair lying across her face. In sleep, her
small sharp features are angelic.

He closes his eyes, and finds he cannot even sketch her
face in the blackness. In the forty years since his wife died
there have been hundreds just like her to enliven his bed.
Used then discarded for younger, fresher flesh. Placing one
out of the multitude is an impossibility. But still, Nemesia
must have been a favourite for even this tenuous yet resilient

memory to have survived so long. The Nemesia he is thinking of stood under thin beams of slowly shifting sunlight as she undressed for him, letting the gold rain lick her skin. *How long*?

• • • •

While Laurus was an entity of pure energy, he'd roamed at will across the cosmos, satisfying his curiosity about nature's astronomical spectacles. He had witnessed binary sunrises on desert worlds. Watched the detonation of quasars. Floated within the ring systems of gas giant planets. Explored the supergiant stars of the galactic core.

He had been there at the beginning when spiralling dust clouds had imploded into a new sun, seen the family of planets accrete out of the debris. He had been there at the end, when the sun cooled and began to expand, its radiance corroding first into amber then crimson.

A white pinpoint ember flared at its centre, signalling the final contraction. The neutronium core, gathering matter with insatiable greed; its coalescence generating monstrous pulses of gamma radiation.

The end came swiftly, an hour-long implosion devouring every superheated ion. Afterwards, an event horizon rose to shield the ultimate cataclysm.

He hovered above the null-boundary for a long time, wondering what lay below. Gateway to another universe. The truth.

He drifted away.

• • • •

Torreya has confessed that she's never been out on a boat before; so Laurus is taking her out onto the glassy water of the harbour basin in his magnificent twin-masted yacht. They are sailing round the crashed cargo lander in the cen-

tre of the basin, a huge conical atmospheric entry body designed to ferry heavy equipment down to the very first pioneers before the spaceport runway was built nearly two
centuries ago. The vehicle's guidance failed, allowing it to
drift away from the land. Its cargo was salvaged, but no one
was interested in the fuselage. Now its dark titanium structure towers fifty metres above the water, open upper hatches
providing a refuge for the gulls and other birds that humans
have brought to this world. At night a bright light flashes
from its nose cone, guiding ships back to the harbour.

Torreya leans over the gunwale, trailing her hand in the
warm water, her face dreamy and utterly content. "This is
lovely," she sighs. "And so was the zoo yesterday. Thank
you, Laurus."

"My pleasure." But he is distracted, haunted by a sorrow-
ful fading smile and long red hair.

Torreya frowns at the lack of response, then turns back to
the sloops and their crews bustling about on their decks. Her
eyes narrow.

Laurus orders the captain to go around again. At least Torreya will enjoy the trip.

• • •

As far as Torreya knew, the geneticist was a doctor who
wanted to run some tests. She gave him a small sample of
blood, and prowled around the study, bored within minutes
at the lack of anything interesting in that most adult of
rooms. Ryker clawed at his perch, caught up in the overspill
of trepidation from Laurus's turbulent mind.

His suspicions had been confirmed as soon as he'd accessed the major-domo's house files. Nemesia had been in
residence eleven years ago.

He sat in his high-backed leather chair behind the rose-
wood desk, unable to move from the agony of waiting. The

geneticist seemed to be taking an age, running analysis programs on his sequencer module, peering owlishly at the multicoloured graphics dancing in the compact unit's holoscreen.

Eventually the man looked up, surprise twisting his placid features. "You're related," he said. "Primary correlation. You're her father."

Torreya turned from the window, her face numb with incomprehension. Then she ran into his arms, and Laurus had to cope with the totally unfamiliar sensation of a small bewildered girl hugging him desperately, her slight frame trembling. It was one upheaval too many. She cried for the very first time.

After all she had been through. Losing her mother, living in an animal slum, the never-ending task of looking after Jante. She had coped magnificently, never giving in.

He waited until her sobs had finished, then dried her eyes and kissed her brow. They studied each other for a long poignant moment. Then she finally offered a timid smile.

Her looks had come from her mother, but by God she had his spirit.

* * *

Torreya sits cross-legged on the bed and pours out Laurus's breakfast tea herself. She glances up at him, anxious for approval.

So he sips the tea, and says: "Just right." And it really is.

Her pixie face lights with a smile, and she slurps some tea out of her own mug.

His son, Iberis, was never so open, so trusting. Always trying to impress. As a good son does, Laurus supposes. These are strange uncharted thoughts for him; he is actually free to recall Iberis without the usual icy snap of pain and shame. Forty-five years is a long time to mourn.

Now the only shame comes from his plan for Torreya's seduction, an ignominious bundle of thoughts already being suppressed by his subconscious.

The one admirable aspect to emerge from his earlier manoeuvrings is her genuine affection for Abelia. He means for Abelia to stay on, a cross between a companion and a nanny.

And now he is going to have to see about curing Jante, though how that will affect the fantasyscapes still troubles him. The idea of losing such a supreme source of creativity is most unwelcome. Perhaps he can persuade them to compose a whole series before the doctors begin their work.

So many new things to do. How unusual that such fundamental changes should come at his time of life. But what a future Torreya will have. And that's what really matters now.

She finishes her tea and crawls over the bed, cuddling up beside him. "What are we going to do today?" she asks.

He strokes her glossy hair, marvelling at its fine texture. Everything about her comes as a revelation. She is the most perfect thing in the universe. "Anything," he says. "Anything you want."

•   •   •

Laurus had tracked the lion for four days through the bush. At night he would lie awake in his tent, listening to its roar. In the morning he would pick up its spoor and begin the long trek again.

There was no more beautiful land in the galaxy than the African savanna, its brittle yellow grass, lonely alien trees. Dawn and dusk would see the sun hanging low above the horizon, streaked with thin gold clouds, casting a cold radiance. Tall mountains were visible in the distance, their peaks capped with snow.

The land he crossed teemed with life. He spent hours sitting on barren outcrops of rock, watching the animals go past. Timid gazelles, bad-tempered rhinos, graceful giraffes, nibbling at the lush leaves only they could reach. Monkeys screamed and chattered at him from their high perches, zebras clustered cautiously around muddy water holes, twitching nervously as he hiked past. There were pandas, too, a group of ten dozing on sun-baked rocks, chewing contentedly on the bamboo that grew nearby. Thinking back, their presence was very odd, but at the time he squatted down on his heels grinning at the affable creatures and their lazy antics.

Still the lion led him on; there were deep valleys, crumpled cliffs of rusty rock. Occasionally he would catch sight of his dusky prey in the distance, the silhouette spurring him on.

On the fifth day he entered a copse of spindly trees whose branches forked in perfect symmetry. The lion stood waiting for him. A fully grown adult male, powerful and majestic. It roared once as he walked right up to it, and shook its thick mane.

Laurus stared at it in total admiration for some indefinable length of time, long enough for every aspect of the jungle lord to be sketched irrevocably in his mind.

The lion shook his head again, and sauntered off into the copse. Laurus watched it go, feeling an acute sense of loss.

• • • •

Laurus is throwing a party this evening, the ultimate rare event. All his senior managers and agents are in attendance, along with Kariwak's grandees. He is hugely amused that every one of them has turned up despite the short—five hour—notice. His reputation is the one faculty which does not diminish with the passing years.

Torreya is dressed like a Victorian princess, a gown of flowering lace and chains of small flowers woven into her hair. He stands beside her under the white marble portico, immaculate in his white dinner jacket, scarlet rosebud in his buttonhole, receiving the guests as they alight from their limousines. Ryker has been watching the cars cluster at Belsize Square at the bottom of the hill, some of them were there for half an hour before beginning the journey up to the mansion, determined not to be late.

They sit around the oak table in the mansion's long-disused formal dining room. Vast chandeliers hang on gold chains above them, classical oil paintings of hunts and harvests alternate with huge garlands of flowers to decorate the walls. A string quartet plays quietly from a podium in one corner. Laurus has gone all-out. He wants to do this with style.

Torreya sits next to Jante, who is wearing a dinner jacket with an oversize velvet bow tie, a neat chrome sunshade band covering his eyes. She pauses from her own meal every so often to stare at her brother's plate, and he uses his knife and fork with quick precision.

Conversations end instantly as Laurus taps his crystal goblet with a silver dessert spoon. He rises to speak. "This is a double celebration for me. For all of us. I have found my daughter." His hand rests proudly on Torreya's shoulder.

She blushes furiously, smiling wide, staring at the tablecloth. Shocked glances fly around the table as agents and managers try to work out how they will be affected by the new order. Tentative smiles of congratulation are offered to Torreya. Laurus feels like laughing.

"Torreya will be taking over from me when she's older. And she is the best person qualified to do so, for she has brought me something which will secure all your futures. Tropicana is finally going to take its place among the Confederation's economic superpowers." He nods permission at her.

Torreya rises to her feet, and takes a big silver serving

tray from the sideboard. Candy buds are piled high upon it. She starts to walk around the table, offering them to the guests.

"This is your future," Laurus tells them. "Quite literally the fruit of knowledge. And I have a monopoly on them. You will venture out into the Confederation and establish yourselves as suppliers. I have chosen you to become this era's merchant princes; your personal wealth will increase a thousandfold. And you, like I, have Torreya to thank for bringing us this marvel."

She finishes the circle, and hands the last candy bud to Erigeron with a chirpy smile. He grimaces and rolls his eyes for her alone; observing the niceties of the formal meal has stretched his patience to breaking.

The grand guests are holding their candy buds, various expressions of unease and concern registering on their faces. Laurus chuckles, and pops his own candy bud into his mouth. "Behold, your dreams made real."

One by one, the guests follow suit.

● ● ●

Laurus holds Torreya's hand as they ascend the mansion's staircase some time after midnight. The guests have departed, some of them stumbling down the portico's stairs, dazed by the chimerical past unfolding behind their eyes.

Torreya is tired and very sleepy, but still smiling. "So many people, and they all wanted to be friends with me. Thank you, Daddy," she says as she climbs into bed.

St Peter folds his arms round the girl, and Laurus tucks the duvet up to her chin. "You don't have to thank me." The words kindle a secret delight; she has been calling him Daddy all day now, a subconscious acceptance. He has been terribly worried in case she rejected the whole notion.

"But I do," she yawns. "For finding me. For bringing me here. For making me happy."

"All part of being a father," he says softly. But she is already asleep. Laurus gazes down at her for a long time before he goes to his own bed.

•   •   •   •

After lunch Laurus took Torreya down the hill to the zoo. It was a lovely afternoon as they all were on Tropicana, and they held hands as they walked down the leafy lanes between the compounds.

Torreya pressed herself to the railings, smiling and pointing at the exhibits. "I always love it when I come to the zoo," she said. "We've been so many times I think I must know most of the animals by name now."

Together they looked down at the lions, who were lazing on flat shelves of rocks.

"Aren't they fearsome?" she said. "Legend says they're the king of all Earth's beasts. That's why the zoo has them. But they never show them when they're old and toothless and lame, do they? You only ever see kings when they're in their prime. That way the legend stays alive. But it's only ever a legend."

Laurus blinks awake, finding himself alone on his bed, gazing up at a mirror on the ceiling, seeing himself: a sickly white stick insect figure with a bloated belly. The bed's imperial-purple silk sheets have been soiled with urine and faeces. A half-eaten candy bud is wedged between his teeth, its mushy tissue smeared over his face, acidic brown juice dripping down his chin. He is starting to gag on this obscene violation.

A black ferret is poised on his chest, tiny eyes staring at

him. Its wet nose twitches, and suddenly it scurries away with a sinuous wriggle.

Laurus hears a soft click from the door.

"Erigeron?"

Erigeron's boots make no sound on the thick navy-blue carpet. From Laurus's prone position the enforcer's lanky frame appears preternaturally tall as he walks towards the bed. He smiles, fangs parting wide. Laurus has never seen a smile on that face before. It frightens him. Fear, real fear for the first time in decades.

"Why?" Laurus cries. "Why? You have everything here. Girls, money, prestige. Why?"

"Kochia promised me more, Mr Laurus. I'm going to be his partner when he starts selling candy buds."

"He can't have promised you that. You killed him for me!"

"I . . . I remember what he said."

"He said nothing! He couldn't have!"

A flicker of confusion creases Erigeron's face. It fades into determination. "He did. I remember it all very clearly. I agreed. I did, Mr Laurus. I really did."

"*No!*"

Erigeron lowers his head with its open mouth towards Laurus's neck. "Yes," and his voice is full of confidence now. "I remember."

Laurus whimpers as the fang tips break his skin. Poison shoots into his bloodstream, and blackness falls.

A tightly whorled flower opens in greeting. Each petal is a different colour, expanding, rising up towards him. Their tips begin to rotate, creating a rainbow swirl. Slowly but surely the blurred streaks begin to resolve.

Laurus and Torreya stand in the middle of the deserted zoo. The sky is grey, and the leaves on the trees are turning brown, falling to the ground in an autumn that can never be. Laurus shivers in the cold air.

"You said you'd been here before," he says.

"Yes. My daddy used to bring me all the time."

"Your daddy?"

"Rubus."

• • • •

Ryker coasts above the estate in the cool early morning air. Far below, the eagle can see someone moving slowly along one of the meandering gravel paths. A young girl pushing a wheelchair.

He banks abruptly, dropping five metres before he can regain his stability. He lets out a squawk of outrage. His new mistress has yet to learn how to exploit his natural instincts to fly with grace; her commands are too jerky, mechanical.

A quieter wish flows through him, the need to spiral down for a closer examination of the people below. Ryker dips a wing lazily, and begins his fluid descent.

He alights in a substantial magnolia tree, watching intently as she stops beside a small lake. There are water lilies mottling its black-mirror surface, swans drift amongst the fluffy purple blooms, idle and arrogant.

Torreya is indulgent with Jante, halting every few minutes so he can look around with his new eyes. His legs have been wrapped in folds of translucent membrane, their integral plasma veins pulsing slowly. The medical team she has assembled have told her the muscle implants are going to take another week to stabilize; a month should see him walking.

"It's ever so pretty here," he says, and smiles up worshipfully at her.

Torreya walks over to the shore of the lake, a gentle breeze ruffing her hair. She turns to gaze down on the city. Its rooftops are lost in a nebulous heat shimmer. Behind it she can make out the first islands of the archipelago, green dots which skip along the wavering horizon.

"Yes," she decides solemnly. "You get a marvellous view from the estate. Laurus was always one for views."

They leave the lake behind, and make their way down to the dew-splashed meadow to watch the butterflies emerge from their chrysalises.

Timeline

2395 . . . Tyrathca colony world discovered.
2402 . . . Tyrathca join Confederation.

Deathday

Today Miran would kill the xenoc. His confidence had soared to a dizzying height, driven by some subconscious premonition. He knew it was today.

Even though he was awake he could hear the ethereal wind-howl of the ghosts, spewing out their lament, their hatred of him. It seemed the whole world shared in the knowledge of impending death.

He had been hunting the xenoc for two months now. An intricate, deadly game of pursuit, flight, and camouflage, played out all over the valley. He had come to learn the xenoc's movements, how it reacted to situations, the paths it would take, its various hiding places in rocky crevices, its aversion to the steep shingle falls. He was its soul-twin now. It belonged to him.

What Miran would have liked to do was get close enough so he might embrace its neck with his own hands; to feel the life slipping from his tormentor's grotesque body. But above all he was a practical man, he told himself he wasn't going to be asinine-sentimental about it, if he could pick it off with the laser rifle he would do so. No hesitation, no remorse.

He checked the laser rifle's power charge and stepped out of the homestead. Home—the word mocked him. It wasn't a home, not any more. A simple three-room prefab shipped in by the Jubarra Development Corporation, designed for two-person assembly. Candice and himself. Her laugh, her smile, the rooms had echoed with them; filling even the glummest day with life and joy. Now it was a convenient shelter, a dry place from which to plot his campaign and strategies.

Physically, the day was no different from any other on Jubarra. Gloomy leaden-grey clouds hung low in the sky, marching east to west. Cold mist swirled about his ankles, coating grass and rocks alike in glistening dewdrops. There would be rain later, there always was.

He stood before her grave, a shallow pit piled high with big crumbling lumps of local sandstone. Her name was carved in crude letters on the largest. There was no cross. No true God would have let her die, not like that.

"This time," he whispered. "I promise. Then it will be over."

He saw her again. Her pale sweat-soaked face propped up on the pillow. The sad pain in her eyes from the knowledge there was little time left. "Leave this world," she'd said, and her burning fingers closed around his hand for emphasis. "Please, for me. We have made this world a lifeless place; it belongs to the dead now. There is nothing here for the living any more, no hope, no purpose. Don't waste yourself, don't mourn for the past. Promise me that."

So he had held back the tears and sworn he would leave to find another life on another world; because it was what she wanted to hear, and he had never denied her anything. But they were empty words; there was nowhere for him to go, not without her.

After that he had sat helplessly as the fever consumed her, watching her breathing slow and the harsh stress lines on her face smooth out. Death made her beauty fragile. Smothering her in wet earth was an unholy sacrilege.

After he finished her grave he lay on the bed, thinking only of joining her. It was deepest night when he heard the noise. A muffled knock of rock against rock. With a great effort he got to his feet. The cabin walls spun alarmingly. He had no idea how long he had lain there—maybe hours, maybe days. Looking out of the door he could see nothing at first. Then his eyes acclimatized to the pale streaks of phosphorescence shivering across the flaccid underbelly of the clouds. A dark concentration of shadows hovered over the grave, scrabbling softly at the stones.

"Candice?" he shouted, drunk with horror. Dark suppressed imaginings swelled out of his subconscious— demons, zombies, ghouls, and trolls, chilling his bones to brittle sticks of ice.

The shadow twisted at his cry, edges blurring, becoming eerily insubstantial.

Miran screamed wordlessly, charging out of the homestead, his muscles powered by outrage and vengeance-lust. When he reached the grave the xenoc had gone, leaving no trace. For a moment Miran thought he might have hallucinated the whole event, but then he saw how the limestone had been moved, the rucked mud where non-human feet had stood. He fell to his knees, panting, stroking the limestone. Nauseating fantasy images of what the xenoc would have done with Candice had it uncovered her threatened to extinguish the little flicker of sanity he had remaining. His future ceased to be a nebulous uncertainty. He had a purpose now: he would remain in this valley until he had ensured Candice was granted the dignity of eternal rest. And there was also the question of vengeance against the monster desecrator.

Miran left the grave and walked past the neglected vegetable garden, down towards the valley floor. The hills of the valley were high prison walls, steep slopes and cliffs smeared with loose stone and tough reedy grass. They reared up to create a claustrophobic universe, for ever preventing him from seeing out. Not that he had any desire to, the memory of all things good dwelt between the hills.

The river ran a crooked course ahead of him, wandering back and forth across the valley floor in great loops, fed by countless silver trickles which seeped out of secret fissures high in the forbidding massifs. Long stretches of the low meadowland below the homestead were flooded again. Skeletal branches and dead rodent-analogue creatures bobbed lazily on the slow flow of muddy water. Further down the valley, where the river's banks were more pronounced, straggly trees had established a hold, trailing weeping boughs into the turbulent water.

This was his land, the vista he and Candice had been greeted with when they struggled through the saddle in the hills at the head of the valley. They had stood together lost in delight, knowing this was right, that their gamble had paid off. They would make their life here, and grow crops for the ecological assessment team's outpost in return for a land grant of twenty thousand acres. Then when the colonists started to arrive their vast holding would make them rich, their children would be Jubarra's first merchant princes.

Miran surveyed the valley and all its wrecked phantoms of ambition, planning carefully. He had abandoned yesterday's chase at the foot of a sheer gorge on the other side of the river. Experience and instinct merged in his mind. The xenoc had been skulking along the base of the valley's northern wall for the last two days. There were caves riddling the rock of the foothills in that area, and a scattering of aboriginal fruit bushes. Shelter and food; it was a good location. Even the xenoc occasionally sought refuge from Jubarra's miserable weather.

He stared ahead. Seeing nothing. Feeling around the recesses of his mind for their perverse bond.

How it had come about he never knew. Perhaps they had shared so much suffering they had developed a mental kinship, something related to Edenist affinity. Or perhaps the xenoc possessed some strange telepathy of its own, which would account for why the ecological investigators had never caught one. Whatever the reason, Miran could sense it. Ever since that night at the grave he had known of the other's presence; moving around the valley, sneaking close, stopping to rest. Weird thoughts and confused images oozed constantly into his mind.

Sure enough, the xenoc was out there to the north, on the hummocks above the flood water, picking its way slowly down the valley.

Miran struck out across the old fields. The first crops he'd planted were potatoes and maize, both geneered to withstand Jubarra's shabby temperate climate. The night they had finished planting he carried Candice out to the fields and laid her lean body down on the new furrows of rich dark humus. She laughed delightedly at the foolishness that had come over him. But the ancient pagan fertility rite was theirs to celebrate that night, as the spring winds blew and the warm drizzle sprinkled their skin. He entered her with a fierce triumph, a primeval man appeasing the gods for the bounty of life they had granted, and she cried out in wonder.

The crops had indeed flourished. But now they were choked with aboriginal weeds. He had dug up a few of the potatoes since, eating them with fish or one of the chickens that had run wild. A monotonous diet; but food wasn't an interest, just an energy source.

The first of the morning drizzles arrived before he was halfway to his goal. Cold and insistent, it penetrated his jacket collar and crept down his spine. The stones and mud underfoot became treacherously slippery.

Cursing under his breath, he slowed his pace. Presumably the xenoc was equally aware of him. It would soon be moving on, building valuable distance between them. Miran could move faster, but unless he got within a kilometre he could never hope to catch it in a day. Yet he didn't dare take any risks, a fall and a broken bone would be the end of it.

The xenoc was moving again. Throughout the intermittent lulls in the drizzle Miran tried to match what he was sensing in his mind with what he could see.

One of the buttress-like foothills radiating out from the base of the mountain ahead of him had created a large promontory, extending for over half a kilometre out into the flood water. It was a grassy slope studded with cracked boulders, the detritus of past avalanches. The oldest stones were coated with the emerald fur of a spongy aboriginal lichen.

The xenoc was making for the promontory's tip. Trapped! If Miran could reach the top of the promontory it could never hope to get clear. He could advance towards it down a narrowing strip of solid ground, forcing it to retreat right to the water's edge. Miran had never known it to swim.

Gritting his teeth against the marrow-numbing cold, he waded through a fast icy stream which had cut itself a steep gully through the folds of peat skirting the mountain. It was after that, hurrying towards the promontory through slackening drizzle, that he came across the Bulldemon skeleton.

He paused to run his hands reverently over some of the huge ivory ribs curving above him. The Bulldemons were lumbering quadruped brutes, carnivores with a small brain and a filthy temper. Their meat was mildly poisonous to humans, and they would have played havoc amongst pioneer farming villages. A laser hunting rifle couldn't bring one down, and there was no way the Development Company would issue colonists with heavy-calibre weapons. Instead the Company had cleared them out with a geneered virus. As the Bulldemons shared a common biochemistry with the rest of the planet's aboriginal mammalian species it was tacitly assumed in the boardroom to be a multiple xenocide. Billions of fuseodollars had already been invested in exploring and investigating Jubarra, the board couldn't afford to have potential colonists scared off by xenoc dinosaur-analogues.

Too many other colony worlds were in the market for Earth's surplus population.

The virus had been ninety-nine per cent successful.

Many of Miran's dreams were of the fifty million xenoc ghosts. If he had known of the crime beforehand, he would never have taken up the Development Company's generous advance colonizer offer. Throughout history there had never been a planet so sinned against as Jubarra. The ghosts outnumbered the ecological assessment team twenty thousand to one, engulfing them in tidal waves of hatred.

Maybe it was the ghosts who had disturbed Jubarra's star. The astronomers claimed they'd never seen an instability cycle like it before. Three months after he and Candice arrived in the valley the solar observatory confirmed the abnormality; flare and spot activity was decreasing rapidly. Jubarra was heading straight for an ice age. Geologists confirmed the meagre five thousand year intervals between glacial epochs—they too had seen nothing like it. Botanists, with the wonder of hindsight, said it explained why there were so few aboriginal plant species.

The planet was abruptly declared unsuitable for colonization. The Jubarra Development Company went bankrupt immediately. All assets were frozen. The Confederation Assembly's Xenological Custodian Committee filed charges of xenocide against the board members.

Now the army of civil engineering teams designated to build a shiny new spaceport city would never arrive. No one would come to buy their crops. The ecological assessment team was winding up their research. Even the excited astronomers were preparing to fly back to their universities, leaving automatic monitoring satellites to collect data on the rogue star.

The shutdown had killed Candice. It broke her spirit. With her enhanced immunology system she should never have succumbed to the fever. But if it hadn't been the germs it would have been something else. All they had laboured over, all they had built, all their shared dreams had crumbled to dust. She died of a broken heart.

The xenoc was coming back down the promontory; moving as fast as it had ever done. It had realized its mistake. But not swiftly enough. Events were tilting in his favour. Soon now, so very soon.

Miran had reached the foot of the promontory. Now he scrambled over the deep drift of flinty stones that'd cascaded down its side from an eroded cliff higher up the mountain, hurrying for the high ground of the summit. From there he could cover both sides with the laser rifle. Small stones crunched loudly underfoot, betraying the urgency of his pounding feet.

The drizzle had stopped and the weak grey clouds were lifting, letting the sunlight through. Candice had loved the valley at moments like this. Her sweet nature prevented her from seeing it as anything other than an enclave of rugged beauty. Every time the sunbeams burst past the turbid curtains of cloud she would stop whatever task she was doing and drink in the sight. With its eternal coat of droplets the land gleamed as new.

Waiting for us to bring it to life, she said. To fill it with people and joy. A paradise valley.

He listened to her innocent sincerity, and believed as he had never believed in his life before. Never in all the months they spent alone together had they quarrelled; not even a harsh word had passed between them. There couldn't be a greater omen of a glorious future.

They worked side by side in the fields by day, using every hour of light to plant the crops. Then at night they made love for hours with a ferocity so intense it almost frightened him. Lying together in the warm darkness afterwards they shared their innermost thoughts, murmuring wondrously of the life their loving would bring to her womb.

Miran wondered about those easy days now. Had the xenoc watched them? Did it spy on their frantic rutting? Listen to their quiet simple secrets? Walk unseen through the new terrestrial plants they had infiltrated across land won in blood from its kind? Look up to see the strange lights in the sky bringing more usurpers? What were its thoughts all that time while its world was ravaged and conquered? And how would it feel if it knew all its race had suffered had turned out to be for nothing?

Miran sensed the xenoc's alarm as he reached the promontory's spine. It had stopped moving as he jogged up the last few metres of coarse, tufty grass. Now he was astride the spine, looking down the tapering spit of land.

The tip sank below the sluggish ripples of brown water six hundred metres ahead of him. There were several clumps of large boulders, and a few deep folds in the ground. But nothing which could offer secure cover.

The xenoc was retreating, slinking back to the tip. Miran couldn't see any scrap of motion; but he'd known all along it wasn't going to be easy He didn't want it to be easy. Infrared sensor goggles, or even dogs, would have enabled him to finish it within days. He wanted the xenoc to know it had been hunted. Wanted it to feel the nightmare heat of the chase, to know it was being played with, to endure the prolonged anguish and gut-wearying exhaustion of every creature that was ever cornered. Suffering as Candice had suffered. Tormented as the ghosts tormented him.

Miran began to walk forward with slow deliberate steps, cradling the laser rifle. He kept an eager watch for any sort of furtive movement—shadows flittering among the boulders, a swell of ripples gliding along the boggy shore. Perhaps a faint puff of misty breath; that was something the xenoc could never disguise. Whatever illusion it wore was of no consequence now. He had it. He would draw it into his embrace and slay it with loving tenderness. The final act of this supreme tragedy. A benevolent release for the xenoc, for the ghosts, for Candice, and for himself. The xenoc was the last thread binding them in misery. Its death would be a transcendent kindness.

With four hundred metres left to the promontory's stubby tip he began to detect the first flutterings of panic in the xenoc's thoughts. It must be aware of him, of the deadly, remorseless intent he harboured. Cool humour swept into his mind. *You will burn,* he thought at it, *your body devoured in flames and pain. This is what I bring.*

Drowning in wretchedness and loathing, that was how he wanted it to spend its last moments of life. No dignity. No hope. The same awful dread Candice had passed away with, her small golden world shattered.

He looked down into one of the narrow crinkled folds in the ground. Stagnant water was standing in the bottom. Tall reeds with magenta candyfloss seed clusters poked up through a frothy blue-green scum of algae, their lower stems swollen and splitting. Glutinous honey-yellow sap dribbled down from the wounds.

Miran tried to spot some anomaly—a bulge in the grass like a giant molehill, a blot of algae harder than the rest.

The wind set the reeds waving to and fro. A rank acidic smell of rotting vegetation rolled around him. The xenoc wasn't down there.

He walked confidently down the promontory.

Every step brought a finer clarity to the xenoc's thoughts. It was being laid bare to him. Fear had arisen in its mind, to the exclusion of almost every other thought. A chimerical sensation of wrinkling stroked his skin; the xenoc was contracting, drawing in on itself. A protective reflex, seeking to shrink into nothingness so the terrible foe would pass by unknowing. It was rooting itself into the welcoming land, becoming one with its environment.

And it was close, very close now. Bitter experience gave Miran the ability to judge.

As the day belonged to him, so the night belonged to the xenoc. It had returned to the homestead time and again. Creeping up through the dark like a malevolent wraith. Its obscene presence had corrupted the sanctuary of Miran's dreams.

Often after sleep claimed him he would find himself running down the length of the valley with Candice; the two of them laughing, shrieking and dancing through the sunlit trees. It was the valley as he had never known it—brilliant, warm, a rainbow multitude of flowers in full blossom, the trees heavy with succulent fruit. A dream of Candice's dream.

They would dive cleanly into the blue sparkling water, squealing at the cold, splashing and sporting like young naiads. Each time he would draw her to him. Her eyes closed and her neck tilted back, mouth parting in an expectant gasp. Then, as always, her skin grew coarse, darkening, bloating in his grip. He was holding the xenoc.

The first time he had woken shaking in savage frenzy, arms thrashing against the mattress in uncontrollable spasms. That was when their minds had merged, thoughts twining sinuously. His fire-rage became the ice of deadly purpose. He snatched up the laser rifle and ran naked into the night.

The xenoc was there; outside the paddock fence, a nebulous blot of darkness which defied resolution. Its presence triggered a deluge of consternation to buffet his already frail mind, although he never was quite sure whether the tumult's origin lay in himself or the monster. Miran heard the sound of undergrowth being beaten down by a heavy body as the xenoc fled. He fired after it, the needle-slim beam of infrared energy ripping the night apart with red strobe flares, illuminating the surrounding countryside in silent eldritch splendour. Puffballs of dense orange flame bloomed in front of him. Some of the drier scrub began to smoulder.

Miran had sat in the open doorway for the rest of the night, guarding the grave. A thick blanket tucked round his shoulders, taking an occasional nip from a bottle of brandy, the laser rifle lying across his lap. When dawn broke, he had set off down to the river on the trail of the xenoc.

Those first few weeks it couldn't seem to keep away. Miran almost became afraid to dream. Dreams were when the xenoc ghosts came to haunt him, slipping tortuously through his drowsy thoughts with insidious reminders of the vast atrocity humans had wrought on Jubarra. And when Candice rose to comfort him the xenoc would steal her from him, leaving him to wake up weeping from the loss.

Miran reached the downward slope at the end of the promontory. The nail of the finger, a curving expanse of gently undulating peat, wizened dwarf bushes, and a scattering of boulders. Thick brown water lapped the shore a hundred metres ahead.

The xenoc's presence in his mind was a constant babble. Strong enough now for him to see the world through its weird senses. A murky shimmer of fog with a cyclonic knot approaching gradually. Himself.

"Come out," he said.

The xenoc hardened itself, becoming one with the land.

"No?" Miran taunted, heady with the prospect of victory. "Well, we'll see about that."

There were five boulders directly in front of him. Big ochre stones which had fallen from the mountain's flanks far above. Splodges of green lichen mottled their rumpled surfaces. A sprinkling of slate-like flakes lay on the grass all around, chiselled off by a thousand winter frosts.

He lined the laser rifle up on the nearest boulder, and fired. The ruby-red beam lashed out, vividly bright even by day. A small wisp of blue smoke spurted from the stone where it struck, blackened splinters fell to the grass, singeing the blades. The thermal stress of the energy impact produced a shrill slapping sound.

Miran shifted his aim to the second boulder, and fired again.

The third boulder unfolded.

In the camp which housed the ecological assessment team they called them slitherskins, a grudging tribute to the xenocs' ability to blend flawlessly into the background. Rumours of their existence had circulated ever since the primary landing, but it wasn't until the virus was released that a specimen body had been obtained. Some of the xenobiology staff maintained their ability to avoid capture confirmed their sentience; it was an argument the Custodian Committee would rule on when the hearings began.

The few autopsies performed on decomposing corpses found that they had gristle instead of bone, facilitating a certain degree of shapeshifting. Subdermal pigment glands could secrete any colour, camouflaging them with an accuracy terrestrial chameleons could never achieve.

Miran had learned that those in the camp, too, feared the night. During the day the xenocs could be spotted; their skin texture was too rough even if they adopted human colouring, and their legs were too spindly to pass inspection. They were nature's creatures, suited to wild woods and sweeping grasslands where they mimicked inert objects as soon as they sensed danger approaching in the form of the Bulldemons, their natural predators. But at night, walking down lightless muddy tracks between the camp's prefabs, one uncertain human silhouette was indistinguishable from another.

The camp's dwindling population kept their doors securely locked after nightfall.

When it stood up, the xenoc was half a metre taller than Miran. As its knobbly skin shed the boulder's ochre, it re-

verted to a neutral damp-looking, bluish-grey. The body
abandoned its boulder guise, sagging into a pear shape
standing on two thin legs with saucer feet; its arms were
long with finger-pincer hands. Two violet eyes gazed down
at Miran.

Resignation had come to the xenoc's mind, along with a
core-flame of anger. The emotions sprayed around the inside
of Miran's skull, chilling his brain.

"I hate you," Miran told it. Two months of grief and
venom bled into his voice, contorting it to little more than a
feral snarl.

In one respect the xenoc was no different from any other
cornered animal. It charged.

Miran let off three fast shots. Two aimed at the top of the
body, one dead centre. The beam blasted fist-size holes into
the reptilian skin, boring through the subcutaneous musculature to rupture the vitals.

A vertical lipless gash parted between the xenoc's eyes to
let out a soprano warbling. It twirled with slim arms extended, thin yellow blood surging from the gaping wounds.
With a last keening gasp, the xenoc crumpled to the ground.

Miran sent another two laser pulses into what passed for
its head. The brain wouldn't be far from the eyes, he reasoned. Its pincer hands clutched once and went flaccid. It
didn't move again.

Distant thunder rumbled down the valley, a sonorous
grumble reverberating from one side to the other, announc-
ing the impending arrival of more rain. It reached Miran's
ears just as he arrived back at the homestead. There was no
elation, no sense of achievement to grip him on the long
walk back. He hadn't expected there would be. Fulfilment
was the reward gained by overcoming the difficulties which
lay in the path of accomplishment.

But Jubarra offered him no goals to strive for. Killing the
xenoc wasn't some golden endeavour, a monument to

human success. It was a personal absolution, nothing more. Ridding himself of the past so he could find some kind of future.

He stopped by the grave with its high temple of stones to prevent the xenoc from burrowing to its heart. Unbuckling his belt, he laid the laser rifle and its spare power magazines on the stones, an offering to Candice. Proof that he was done here in the valley, that he was free to leave as she'd wished.

With his head bowed he told her, "It's finished. Forgive me for staying so long. I had to do it." Then he wondered if it really was over for her. Would her ghost be lonely? A single human forced to wander amongst those her race had slaughtered indiscriminately.

"It wasn't her fault," he cried out to the xenoc ghosts. "We didn't know. We didn't ask for any of this. Forgive her." But deep down he burned from bright flames of shared guilt. It had all been done in his name.

Miran went into the homestead. The door had been left open, there was a rainwater puddle on the composite squares of the floor, and a chill dankness in the air. He splashed through the water and slipped past the curtain into the hygiene alcove.

The face which looked back from the mirror above the washbasin had changed over the last two months. It was thin, pinched with long lines running down the cheeks. Several days' worth of stubble made the jutting chin scratchy. The skin around the eyes had darkened, making them look sunken. A sorry sight. He sighed at himself, at what he had allowed himself to become. Candice would hate to see him so. He would wash, he decided, shave, find some clean clothes. Then tomorrow he would hike back to the ecological team's camp. In another six weeks there would be a starship to take them off the planet. Jubarra's brief, sorry chapter of human intervention would cease then. And not before time.

Miran dabbed warm water on his face, making inroads on the accumulated grime. He was so involved with the task his mind dismissed the scratching sounds outside, a part of the homestead's normal background noises: the wind rustling the bushes and vegetables, the door swinging on its hinges, distant gurgling river water.

The clatter which came from the main room was so sudden it made his muscles lock rigid in fright. In the mirror his face was white with shock.

It must be another xenoc. But he had felt nothing approach, none of the jumble of foreign thoughts leaching into his brain.

His hands gripped the basin in an effort to still their trembling. A xenoc couldn't do him any real harm, he told himself, those pincer fingers could leave some nasty gouges, but nothing fatal. And he could run faster. He could reach the laser rifle on the grave before the xenoc got out of the door.

He shoved the curtain aside with a sudden thrust. The main room was empty. Instead of bolting, he stepped gingerly out of the alcove. Had it gone into the bedroom? The door was slightly ajar. He thought he could hear something rustling in there. Then he saw what had made the clattering noise.

One of the composite floor tiles had been forced up, flipping over like a lid. There was a dark cavity below it. Which was terribly terribly wrong. The homestead had been assembled on a level bed of earth.

Miran bent down beside it. The tile was a metre square, and someone had scooped out all the hard-packed earth it had rested on, creating a snug cavity. The bottom was covered in pieces of what looked like broken crockery.

The xenoc. Miran knew instinctively it had dug this. He picked up one of the off-white fragments. One side was dry, smooth; the other was slimed with a clear tacky mucus. It was curved. An egg.

Rage boiled through him. The xenoc had laid an egg in *his* homestead. Outsmarting him, choosing the one place Miran would never look, never suspect treachery. Its bastard had hatched in the place intended for his own children.

He pushed the bedroom door fully open. Candice was waiting for him on the bed, naked and smiling. Miran's world reeled violently. He grabbed at the doorframe for support before his faltering legs collapsed.

She was very far away from him.

"Candice," his voice cracked. Somehow the room wasn't making sense. It had distorted, magnifying to giant proportions. Candice, beloved Candice, was too small. His vision swam drunkenly, then resolved. Candice was less than a metre tall.

"Love me," she said. Her voice was high pitched, a mousy squeak.

Yet it was her. He gazed lovingly at each part of the perfectly detailed figure which he remembered so well—her long legs, firm flat belly, high conical breasts, the broad shoulders, over-developed from months spent toiling in the fields.

"Love me."

Her face. Candice was never beautiful, but he worshipped her anyway. Prominent cheekbones, rounded chin, narrow eyes. All there, as delicate as china. Her soft smile, directed straight at him, unforgettable.

"Love me."

Xenoc. The foetus gestating under his floor. Violating his dreams, feeding on them. Discovering his all-enveloping love.

"Love me."

The first post-human-encounter xenoc; instinctively moulding itself into the form which would bring it the highest chance of survival in the new world order.

Its slender arms reached out for him. A flawless human

ribcage was outlined by supple creamy-white skin as it stretched.

Miran wailed in torment.

"Love me."

He could. That was the truth, and it was a tearing agony. He could love it. Even a pale monstrous echo was better than a lifetime without Candice. It would grow. And in the dark crushingly lonely hours it would be there for him to turn to.

"Love me."

He wasn't strong enough to resist. If it grew he would take it in his arms and become its lover. Her lover, again. If it grew.

He put his hands under the bed and tugged upwards with manic strength. Bed, mattress, and sheets cartwheeled. The xenoc squealed as it tumbled onto the floor.

"Love me!" The cry was frantic. It was squirming across the floor towards him. Feet tangled in the blankets, face entreating.

Miran shoved at the big dresser, tilting it off its rear legs. He had spent many evening hours making it from aboriginal timber. It was crude and solid, heavy.

"Love me!" The cry had become a desperate pining whimper.

The dresser teetered on its front legs. With a savage sob, Miran gave it one last push. It crashed to the floor with a hideous liquid squelch as it landed on the xenoc's upper torso.

Miran vomited, running wildly from the bedroom, blind, doubled up in convulsions. His mad flight took him outside where he tripped and sprawled on the soggy ground, weeping and pawing at the soil, more animal than human.

A strained creaking sound made him look up. Despite eyes smeared with gritty tears, he saw the rock at the top of the grave cracking open. A tiny arm punched out into the air.

Thin flakes went spinning. The hand and arm worked at enlarging the fissure. Eventually a naked homunculus emerged in jerky movements, scattering fragments of shell in all directions. Even the xenoc eggs had the ability to conform to their surroundings.

Miran watched numbly as the homunculus crawled down the pile of sandstone lumps to join the other two humanoid figures waiting at the base.

In the homestead the safest identity to adopt was a love object, cherished and protected. But outside in the valley survival meant becoming the most ruthless predator of all.

Between them, the three miniature humans lifted up the laser rifle. "Hate you," one spat venomously. Then its fist smacked into the trigger.

Miran couldn't believe his own face was capable of expressing so much anger.

Timeline

2420 . . . Kulu scoutship discovers Ruin Ring.

2428 . . . Bitek habitat Tranquillity germinated by Crown Prince Michael Saldana, orbiting above Ruin Ring.

2432 . . . Prince Michael's son, Maurice, geneered with affinity. Kulu abdication crisis. Coronation of Lukas Saldana. Prince Michael exiled.

The Lives and Loves of Tiarella Rosa

Tropicana had a distinct aura of strangeness, both in appearance and in those it gathered to itself. Eason discovered that while he was still on the flight down from orbit.

"There's a lot more islands down there than I remember from fifty years ago," said Ashly Hanson, the spaceplane's pilot. "The locals must keep on planting them, I suppose. They're still pretty keen on bitek here."

"So I hear." Tropicana wasn't Eason's ideal destination. But that was where the *Lord Fitzroy* was heading, the only starship departing Quissico asteroid for thirty hours. Time had been a critical factor. He'd been running out of it fast.

Eason paused to consider what the pilot said. "What do you mean, fifty years ago?" Ashly Hanson was a short man with a wiry build, a lax cap of brown hair flopping down over his ears, and a near-permanent smile of admiration on his lips. The universe had apparently been created with the sole purpose of entertaining Ashly Hanson. However, the pilot couldn't have been more than forty-five years old, not even if he'd been geneered.

"I time hop," he said, with the grin of someone relating his favourite unbelievable story. "I spend fifty years in zero-tau stasis, then come out for five to look around and see how things are progressing. Signing on with a starship is a good way to play tourist."

"You're kidding."

"No. I started way back in good old 2284, and now I'm on a one-way ride to eternity. There's been some changes, I can tell you. You know, I'm actually older than the Confederation itself."

"Jesus wept!" It was an incredible notion to take in.

Ashly's soft sense-of-wonder smile returned. Beyond the little spaceplane's windscreen, the planet's horizon curvature was flattening out as they lost altitude. Up ahead was the single stretch of habitable land on Tropicana. A narrow line of green and brown etched across the turquoise ocean, it straddled the equator at an acute angle, eight hundred kilometres long, though never more than fifty wide. A geological oddity on a tectonically abnormal planet. There was only one continent sharing the world, an arctic wilderness devoid of any aboriginal life more complex than moss; the rest of the globe was an ocean never deeper than a hundred and fifty metres.

Once Eason had accessed the *Lord Fitzroy*'s almanac file, his initial worry about his destination slowly dissipated. Tropicana was surrounded by thousands of small islands, its government notoriously liberal. The one Adamist planet in the Confederation which didn't prohibit bitek.

It wasn't perfect, but it was better than most.

Ashly Hanson was increasing the spaceplane's pitch sharply to shed speed as they approached the land. Eason craned forwards to see the coastline. There was a big city below, a sprawl of low buildings oozing along the beach. They were trapped between the water and the mountains whose foothills began a few kilometres inland.

"That's Kariwak, the capital," Ashly said. "Used to be run by a man called Laurus last time I was here; one bad mother. They say his daughter's taken over now. Whatever else you do while you're here, don't cross her. If she's only half as bad as her old man you'll regret it."

"Thanks, I'll remember." He actually couldn't care less about some parochial urban gangster. His immediate concern was customs. Three innocuous dull-silver globes the size of tennis balls were sitting in a small case among his luggage. He'd agonized for hours if he should keep them with him. Getting them on board the *Lord Fitzroy* was no problem, the Party had plenty of supporters in Quissico's civil service. The spheres were disguised to look like superdensity magnetic bearings used by the astronautics industry, he even had authentic documentation files confirming he was a rep for the company which made them. But if Tropicana customs had sensors capable of probing through the magnetic casing . . .

Kariwak spaceport was situated ten kilometres outside the city. It gave Eason his first taste of Tropicana's architectural aesthetics. All the buildings were designed to be as naturalistic as possible, subtle rather than ostentatious, even the maintenance hangars were easy on the eye. But it was a surprisingly big field given the size of the population. Tropicana received a lot of rich visitors, taking advantage of the relaxed bitek laws to visit specialist clinics offering rejuvenation techniques. As with the surroundings, customs were discreet and efficient, but not intrusive.

Forty minutes after landing, Eason was on an underground tube train carrying him into the city. *Lord Fitzroy* was scheduled to depart in two days' time, after that it would be extremely difficult for anyone to trace him. But not impossible, and those that would come looking were fanatical. It was that fanaticism which originally made him question the Party's aims, the doubt which started him along this road.

He left the train at a station right in the heart of the city, its escalator depositing him on a broad boulevard lined with geneered sequoias. The trees were only seventy years old but they were already towering above the department shops, restaurants, whitewashed cafés, and Mediterranean-style office blocks. He slipped easily into the crush of pedestrians that thronged its length, case held firmly in one hand, flight bag on a strap over the other shoulder.

The boulevard led directly down to the main harbour, a circular two-kilometre-wide basin, with glistening white coral walls. Half of it extended out into the shallow turquoise ocean, while the other half ate back into the city, where it had been surrounded by a chaotic mix of warehouses, taverns, marine supply shops, sportsboat hire stalls, agents' offices, and a giant fish market. Quays stabbed out into the transparent water like spokes from a wheel rim. Right at the centre a sad cone of weather-dulled titanium rose out of the soft swell, the empty shell of a cargo lander that had swung off course two and a half centuries earlier as it brought equipment down to the newly founded colony. Ships of all shapes and sizes sailed around it, bright sails drooping in the calm air.

He stared at them intently. Ranged along the horizon were the first islands of the archipelago. Out there, he could lose himself for ever among the sleeping atolls and their quiet inhabitants. The boats which docked at this harbour left no records in bureaucratic memory cores, didn't file destinations, owed no allegiances. This was a freedom barely one step from anarchy.

He started along the harbour's western wall, towards the smaller boats: the fishing ketches, coastal sampans, and traders which cruised between the mainland cities and the islands. He was sure he could find one casting off soon, although a few brief enquiries among the sailors revealed that such craft rarely took on deck hands; they were nearly all family-run concerns. Eason didn't have much money left in his bank disk, possibly enough for one more starflight if he didn't spend more than a couple of hundred fuseodollars.

He saw the girl before he'd walked halfway along the

wall. She was in her mid-teens, tall bordering on gawky, wearing a loose topaz-coloured cotton shirt and turquoise shorts. Thick gold-auburn hair fell halfway down her back, styled with an Egyptian wave; but the humidity had drawn out its lustre, leaving it hanging limply.

She was staggering under the weight of a near-paralytic old man in a sweat-stained vest. He looked as though he weighed twice as much as she did.

"Please, Ross," she implored. "Mother'll sail without us."

His only answer was an inebriated burble.

Eason trotted over. "Can I give you a hand?"

She shot him a look which was half-guilt, half-gratitude. He'd guessed her face would be narrow, and he was right: a small flat nose, full lips, and worried blue eyes were all co-cooned by her dishevelled hair.

"Are you sure?" she asked hopefully.

"No trouble." Eason put his flight bag down, and relieved her of the old man. He slung the old man's arm around his own shoulders, and pushed up. It was quite a weight to carry, the girl must be stronger than she looked.

"This way," she said, squirming with agitation.

"Take my flight bag, would you. And the name's Eason," he told her as they started off down the wall.

"Althaea." She blushed as she picked up his bag. "Shall I take your case for you as well?"

"No," he grunted. "I'll manage."

"I'm really grateful. I should have been back at the *Orphée* a quarter of an hour ago."

"Is it a tight schedule?"

"Oh no, but Mother likes to get home before dark. Visiting Kariwak takes a whole day for us."

"Should he be sailing in this condition?"

"He'll just have to," she said with a sudden flash of pique. "He does it every time we bring him. And it's always me who has to go looking in the taverns for him. I hate those places."

"Is this your father?"

She let out a guffaw, then clamped her mouth over her mouth. "I'm sorry. No, he's not my father. This is Rousseau. Ross. He lives with us, helps around the house and garden, things like that. When he's sober," she added tartly.

"Where do you live?"

"Mother and I live on Charmaine; it's an island out in the archipelago."

He hid a smile. Perfect. "Must be a tough life, all by yourselves."

"We manage. It won't be for ever, though." Her angular shoulders jerked in what he thought was supposed to be an apologetic shrug; it was more like a convulsion. Eason couldn't recall meeting someone this shy for a long while. It made her appealing, after an odd sort of fashion.

• • •

The *Orphée* was tied up to a quay near the gap in the harbour wall. Eason whistled in appreciation when he saw her. She was a trim little craft, six metres long, with a flat-bottomed wooden hull and a compact cabin at the prow. The two outriggers were smaller versions of the main hull, with room for cargo; all archipelago craft had them, a lot of the channels between islands were too shallow for keel fins.

Bitek units were dovetailed neatly into the wooden superstructure: nutrient-fluid sacs with ancillary organs in the stern compartment, a powerful-looking three metre long silver-grey serpent tail instead of a rudder, and a membrane sail whorled round the tall mast.

Althaea's mother was sitting cross-legged on the cabin roof, wearing a faded blue denim shirt and white shorts. Eason had no doubt she was Althaea's mother: her hair was much shorter, but the same colour, and though she lacked the girl's half-starved appearance her delicate features were identical. Their closeness was uncanny.

She was holding up an odd-looking pendulum, a slim gold chain that was fastened to the centre of a wooden disc, five centimetres in diameter. The disk must have been perfectly balanced, because it remained horizontal.

When Eason reached the quayside directly above the *Or phée* he saw the rim of the disc was carved with spidery hieroglyphics. It was turning slowly. Or he thought it was. When he steadied Ross and looked down properly, it was stationary.

The woman seemed absorbed by it.

"Mother?" Althaea said uncertainly.

Her gaze lifted from the disk, and met Eason's eyes. She didn't seem at all put out by his appearance.

He found it hard to break her stare; it was almost triumphant.

Rousseau vomited on the quay.

Althaea let out a despairing groan. "Oh, Ross!" She was close to tears.

"Bring him on board," her mother said wearily. She slipped the disc and chain into her shirt pocket.

With Althaea's help, Eason manhandled Ross onto a bunk in the cabin. The old man groaned as he was laid on the grey blankets, then closed his eyes, asleep at once.

Althaea put a plastic bucket on the floor beside the bunk, and shook her head sadly.

"What's the pendulum for?" Eason asked quietly. He could hear her mother moving round on the deck outside.

"Mother uses it for divining."

"On a boat?"

She pressed her lips together. "You can use divining to find whatever you wish, not just water—stones, wood, buried treasure, stuff like that. It can even guide you home in the fog, just like a compass. The disc is only a focus for your thoughts, that's all. Your mind does the actual work."

"I think I'll stick with an inertial guido."

Althaea's humour evaporated. She hung her head as if she'd been scolded.

"I'm Tiarella Rosa, Althaea's mother," the woman said after Eason stepped out of the cabin. She stuck her hand out. "Thank you for helping with Ross."

"No trouble," Eason said affably. Tiarella Rosa had a firm grip, her hand calloused from deckwork.

"I was wondering," he said. "Do you have any work available on Charmaine? I'm not fussy, or proud. I can dig ditches, pick fruit, rig nets, whatever."

Tiarella's eyes swept over him, taking in the ship's jumpsuit he wore, the thin-soled shoes, his compact but hardly bulky frame, albino-pale skin. "Why would you be interested, asteroid man?"

"I'm a drifter. I'm tired of asteroid biosphere chambers. I want the real thing, the real outdoors. And I'm just about broke."

"A drifter?"

"Yeah." Out of the corner of his eye he saw Althaea emerge from the cabin, her already anxious expression even more apprehensive.

"I can only offer room and board," Tiarella said. "In case you haven't noticed, we're not rich, either." There was the intimation of amusement in her voice.

Eason prevented his glance from slipping round the *Orphée*; she must have cost ten thousand fuseodollars at least.

"And the *Orphée* has been in the family for thirty years," Tiarella said briskly. "She's a working boat, the only link we have with the outside world."

"Right. Room and board would be fine."

Tiarella ruffled Althaea's hair. "No need to ask your opinion, is there, darling. A new face at Charmaine, Christmas come in April."

Althaea blushed crimson, hunching in on herself.

"OK, *drifter*, we'll give it a try."

•   •   •

Orphée's tail kicked up a spume of foam as she manoeuvred away from the quay. Tiarella's eyes were tight shut as she steered the boat via her affinity bond with the bitek's governing processors. Once they were clear, the sail membrane began to spread itself, a brilliant emerald sheet woven through with a hexagonal mesh of rubbery cords.

Outside the harbour walls they picked up a respectable speed. Tiarella headed straight away from the land for five kilometres, then slowly let the boat come round until they were pointing east. Eason went into the cabin to stow his flight bag. Rousseau was snoring fitfully, turning the air toxic with whisky and bad breath.

He unlocked the case to check on the spheres it contained. His synaptic web established a datalink with them, and ran a diagnostic. All three superconductor confinement systems were functioning perfectly, the drop of frozen anti-hydrogen suspended at the centre of each one was completely stable. The resulting explosion should one of them ever rupture would be seen from a million miles away in space. It was a destructive potential he considered too great.

The Quissico Independence Party had other ideas. It was the blackmail weapon they were going to use against the development company administration to gain full political and economic freedom for the asteroid. They had spent three years establishing contact with one of the black syndicates which manufactured antimatter. Three years of a gradually escalating campaign of propaganda and harassment against the development company.

Eason had joined the cause when he was still in his teens. Quissico was a highly successful settlement, with dozens of industrial stations and rich resources of minerals and organic chemicals. Its people worked hard and manufactured excellent astronautics equipment and specialist microgee compounds. That they were not allowed a greater say in how the wealth they created was spent was a deliberate provocation. They had made the founding consortium rich, paying off investment loans ahead of schedule. Now they should be permitted to benefit as the money cartels had.

It was a just cause. One he was proud to help. He was there giving beatings to company supervisors, taking an axe to finance division processor networks, fighting the company police. At twenty he killed his first enemy oppressor, an assistant secretary to the Vice-Governor. After that, there was no turning back. He worked his way through the Party ranks until he wound up as quartermaster for the movement's entire military wing. Over ten years of blood and violence.

He was already tiring of it, the useless pain and suffering he inflicted on people and their families. Gritting his teeth as the authorities launched their retaliations, erasing his friends and comrades. Then came the grand scheme, the Party's master plan for a single blow that would break the chains of slavery for good. Planned not by the military wing, those who knew what it was to inflict death; but by the political wing, who knew only of gestures and theoretical ideology. Who knew nothing.

A threat would never be enough for them. They would detonate some of the antimatter. To show their determination, their strength and power. In a distant star system, thousands would die without ever knowing why. He, the killer, could not allow such slaughter. It was insanity. He had joined to fight for people; to struggle and agitate. Not for this, remote-controlled murder.

So he stopped them in the simplest way he could think of.

Eason came back up on deck, and leant on the taffrail, allowing himself to relax for the first time in a fortnight. He was safe out here. Safe to think what to do next.

He'd never thought much past the theft itself; a few vague notions. That was almost as crazy as the Party's decision to acquire the stuff in the first place. Far too many people were acting on impulse these days.

Tropicana's ocean looked as if it had been polished smooth. The only disturbance came from *Orphée*'s wake, quiet ripples which were quickly absorbed by the mass of water. He could see the bottom five metres below the boat, a carpet of gold-white sand. Long ribbons of scarlet weed and mushroomlike bulbs of seafruit rose up out of it, swaying in the languid currents. Schools of small fish fled from the boat like neon sparks. Out here, tranquillity was endemic.

Althaea sat on *Orphée*'s prow, letting the breeze of their passage stream her hair back, a sensual living figurehead. Tiarella was standing amidships, staring at the islands ahead, straight-backed and resolute. Totally the ship's mistress.

Eason settled down in the stern, looking from one to the other, admiring them both, and speculating idly on which would be best in bed. It was going to be enjoyable finding out.

• • • •

For three hours they moved deeper into the archipelago. Families had been planting the coral kernels around the mainland coast for over two centuries, producing their little island fiefdoms. They numbered in the tens of thousands now.

The larger, inhabited, islands were spaced two or three

kilometres apart, leaving a broad network of channels to navigate through. Tiarella navigated *Orphée* around innumerable spits and reefs without even reducing speed.

Eason gripped the gunwale tightly as vicious jags of coral flashed past the outriggers. Most of the islands he could see had tall palm trees growing above the beaches. Some had just a few grand houses half-concealed through the lush vegetation, while others hosted small villages of wooden bungalows, whitewashed planks glowing copper in the sinking sun.

"There it is," Althaea called excitedly from the prow. She was on her feet, pointing ahead in excitement. "Charmaine." She gave Eason a shy smile.

The island was a large one, with a lot more foliage than the others; its trees formed a veritable jungle. Their trunks were woven together with a dense web of vines; grape-cluster cascades of vividly coloured flowers, fluoresced by the low sun, bobbed about like Chinese lanterns.

Eason couldn't see any beaches on this side. Several low shingle shelves were choked by straggly bushes which extended right down to the water's edge. Other than that, the barricade of pink-tinged coral was a couple of metres high.

Orphée was heading for a wooden jetty sticking out of the coral wall.

"What do you do here?" he asked Tiarella.

"Scrape by," she said, then relented. "Those trees you can see are all geneered citrus varieties, some of them are actually xenoc. We used to supply all the nearby islands with fruit, and some coffee beans, too; it gave the community a sense of independence from the mainland. Fishing is the mainstay in this section of the archipelago. Trees have a lot of trouble finding the right minerals to fruit successfully out here, even with geneering. There's never enough soil, you see. But my grandfather started dredging up seaweed almost as soon as the island's original kernel grew out above the water. It took him thirty years to establish a decent layer of loam. Then Dad improved it, he designed some kind of bug which helped break the aboriginal seaweed down even faster. But I'm afraid I've allowed the groves to run wild since my husband died."

"Why?"

She shrugged, uncoiling a mooring rope. "I didn't have the heart to carry on. Basically, I'm just hanging on until Althaea finds herself someone. It's her island really. When she has a family of her own, they can put it back on its feet."

• • • •

The house was set in a dishevelled clearing about a hundred metres from the jetty. It was a two-storey stone building with climbing roses scrambling around the ground-floor windows and a wooden balcony running along its front. Big precipitator leaves hung under the eaves, emerald valentines sucking drinking water out of the muggy air. When he got close, Eason could see the white paint was flaking from the doors and window frames, moss and weeds clogged the guttering, and the balcony was steadily rotting away. Several first-floor windows were boarded up.

His situation was looking better by the minute. Two women, a drunk, and an isolated, rundown island. He could stay here for a century and no one would ever find him.

As soon as they walked into the clearing, birds exploded from the trees, filling the air with beating wings and a strident screeching. The flock was split between parrots and some weird blunt-headed thing which made him think of pterodactyls. Whatever they were, they were big, about thirty centimetres long, with broad wings and whiplike tails; their colours were incredible—scarlet, gold, azure, jade.

Rousseau clamped his hands over his ears, belching wetly.

"What the hell are those?" Eason shouted above the din.

Althaea laughed. "They're firedrakes. Aren't they beautiful?"

"I thought Tropicana didn't have any aboriginal animals; there isn't enough dry land for them to evolve."

"Firedrakes didn't evolve. They're a sort of cross between a bat, a lizard, and a parrot."

He gawped, using his retinal amps to get a better look at one; and damn it, the thing did look like a terrestrial lizard, with membranous wings where the forepaws should be.

"My father spliced the original ones together about forty years ago," Tiarella said. "He was a geneticist, a very good one."

"You could make a fortune selling them," Eason said.

"Not really. They can't fly very far, they only live for about three years, only a third of the eggs ever hatch, they're prone to disease, and they're not very sociable. Dad was going to improve them, but he never got round to it."

"But they're ours," Althaea said proudly. "Nobody else has them. They help make Charmaine special."

• • •

Eason walked into the ground-floor study the next morning. He was still kneading kinks out of his back; the bed in the fusty little back room they'd given him was incredibly hard. It was only for one night; Tiarella had told him he would be living in one of the grove workers' chalets.

The study, like the rest of the house, had dull-red clay floor tiles and whitewashed plaster walls. Several black and white prints of various sizes were hanging up. A big brass fan was spinning slowly on the ceiling.

Tiarella was sitting behind a broad teak desk. The only objects on the polished wood surface in front of her were a century-old computer slate, and a pack of cards with a fan-

ciful design printed on the back—from what he could see it
looked like a star map.

He sat in an austere high-backed chair facing her.

"About your duties," she said. "You can start by repairing
the grove worker chalets. We have a carpentry shop with a
full set of tools. Ross doesn't use them much these days. Are
you any good with tools?"

He checked the files stored in his synaptic web. "I couldn't build you an ornamental cabinet, but cutting roofing timbers to length is no trouble."

"Good. After that I'd like you to start on the garden."

"Right."

Tiarella picked up the pack of cards and started to shuffle
them absently. She had the dexterity of a professional
croupier. "We are getting a little bit too overgrown here.
Charmaine might look charmingly rustic when you sail by,
but the vines are becoming a nuisance."

He nodded at one of the big prints on the wall. It was of
three people, a formal family pose: Tiarella when she was
younger, looking even more like Althaea, a bearded man in
his late twenties, and a young boy about ten years old. "Is
that your husband?"

The cards were merged with a sharp burring sound. "Yes,
that's Vanstone, and Krelange, our son. They died eighteen
years ago. It was a boating accident. They were outside the
archipelago when a hurricane blew up. They weren't found
until two days later. There wasn't much left. The razorsquids . . ."

"It must have been tough for you."

"Yes. It was. I loved him like nobody else. Ours was a
genuine till death do us part marriage. If it hadn't been for
Althaea I would probably have killed myself."

He glanced up sharply, meeting a hard-set smile.

"Oh yes, it is possible to love someone that much.

Enough so their absence is pure torture. Have you ever experienced that kind of love, Eason?"

"No."

"I don't know whether to envy you or pity you for that lack. What I felt for Vanstone was like a tidal force. It ruled my life, intangible and unbreakable. Even now it hasn't let go. It never will. But I have my hopes for Charmaine and Althaea."

"She's a nice girl. She should do well with this island, there's a lot of potential here. It's a wonderful inheritance."

"Yes, she has a beautiful future ahead of her. I read it in the cards."

"Right."

"Are you a believer in tarot, Eason?"

"I like to think I can choose my own destiny."

"We all do at first. It's a fallacy. Our lives are lived all at once, consciousness is simply a window into time. That's how the cards work, or the tea leaves, or palmistry, or crystals for that matter. Whatever branch of the art you use, it simply helps to focus the mind."

"Yes, I think I've heard that already on this planet."

"The art allows me to see into the future. And, thank God, Althaea isn't going to suffer like I have done."

He stirred uncomfortably, for once feeling slightly out of his depth. Bereavement and isolation could pry at a mind, especially over eighteen years.

"Would you like to know what your future has in store?" she asked. The pack of cards was offered to him. "Cut them."

"Maybe some other time."

• • •

Rousseau walked him over to the chalet, following a path worn through an avenue of gloomy trees at the back of the house. The old man seemed delighted at the prospect of male company on the island. Not least because his share of the work would be considerably lessened. Probably to around about zero if he had his way, Eason guessed.

"I've lived here nearly all my life," Rousseau said. "Even longer than Tiarella. Her father, Nyewood, he took me on as a picker in the groves when I was younger than you. About fifteen, I was, I think." He looked up at the tangle of interlocking branches overhead with a desultory expression pulling at his flabby lips. "Old Nyewood would hate to see what's happened to the island. Charmaine's success was all down to him, you know, building on his father's vision. Half of these trees are varieties he spliced together, improvements on commercial breeds. Why, I planted most of them myself."

Eason grunted at the old man's rambling reminiscences. But at the same time he did have a point. There was a lot of fruit forming on the boughs in this part of the jungle, oranges, lemons, and something that resembled a blue grapefruit, most of them inaccessible. The branches hadn't been pruned for a decade, they were far too tall, even on those trees that were supposedly self-shaping. And the snarl of grass and scrub plants which made up the undergrowth was waist-high. But that was all superficial growth. It wouldn't take too much work to make the groves productive again.

"Why stay on, then?" Eason asked.

"For little Althaea, of course. Where would she be without me to take care of things? I loved Vanstone when he was alive, such a fine man. He thought of me as his elder brother, you know. So I do what I can for his daughter in honour of his memory. I have been as a father to her."

"Right." No one else would take on the old soak.

There were twelve chalets forming a semicircle in their own clearing. Rousseau called it a clearing; the grass came up over Eason's knees.

"My old chalet, the best of them all," Rousseau said, slapping the front door of number three.

"Shack, not a chalet," Eason mumbled under his breath. Two rooms and a shower cubicle built out of bleached planking that had warped alarmingly, a roof of thick palm thatch which was moulting, and a veranda along the front. There was no glass in the windows, they had slatted shutters to hold back the elements.

"I fixed up the hinges and put in a new bed last week," Rousseau said, his smile showing three missing teeth. "Tiarella, she told me fix the roof as well. With my back! That woman expects miracles. Still, now you're here, I'll help you."

Eason paused on the threshold, a gelid tingling running down his spine. "What do you mean, last week?"

"Last Thursday, it was, she told me. Ross, she said, get a chalet fixed up ready for a man to live in. It was a mess, you know. I've done a lot of work here for you already."

"Ready for *me* to live in?"

"Yes." Rousseau shifted unhappily from foot to foot as Eason stared at him.

"Did she mention me by name?"

"No. How could she? Listen, I made sure the toilet works. You don't have to run back to the house every time."

Eason reached out and grasped the front of Rousseau's vest. "What did she say, exactly?"

Rousseau gave him a sickly grin, trying to prise his hand loose. Sweat broke out on his forehead when he found just how implacable that grip was.

"She said there would be a man coming. She said it was the time and we should get ready. That's all, I swear."

Eason let go of his vest. "The time? What did she mean?"

"I don't know." Rousseau stroked the front of his vest down. "Tiarella, she's not . . . you know. Since Vanstone's death I have to make allowances. Half of what she says is mad. I wouldn't worry about it."

• • •

After Eason finished sweeping the chalet's floor and washing fungal colonies from the walls he sat on the cot-style bed and opened his case. The three confinement spheres were still functioning perfectly. Of course, there were only two modes, working and not working. If one of them ever did suffer a glitch, he'd never know about it. That still didn't stop him from checking. Their presence was heightening his sense of paranoia.

Tiarella worried him. How the hell could she know he would be coming out to Charmaine? Unless this was all some incredibly intricate trap. Which really was crazy. More than anyone he knew how the Party members operated. Sophistication was not part of the doctrine.

It was no good terrorizing Rousseau, that drunken fart didn't know anything.

"I brought you some cups and things," Althaea said. She was standing in the doorway, wearing a sleeveless mauve dress that had endured a lot of washes. A big box full of crockery was clutched to her chest. Her face crumpled into misery when he looked up, the heat of surprise in his eyes.

He closed the case calmly and loaded an access code into its lock. "It's all right, come in. I'm just putting my things away."

"I'm sorry, I didn't think. I always walk straight in to Mother's room."

"No trouble." He put the case into his flight bag and slipped the seal, then pushed the whole bundle under the bed.

"I knew Ross would never think to bring anything like this for you," she said as she began placing the dishes and cups on a shelf above the sink. "He doesn't even know how to wash up. I can bring some coffee beans over later. We still dry our own. They taste nice. Oh, you'll need a kettle, won't you. Is the electricity on here?"

He reached out and touched her long bare arm. "Leave that. Why don't you show me round the island?"

"Yes," she stammered. "All right."

Charmaine's central lagoon was a circle seven hundred metres across, with a broad beach of fine pink sand running the whole way round. Eason counted five tiny islands, each crowned with a clump of trees festooned in vines. The water was clear and warm, and firedrakes glided between the islands and the main jungle.

It was breathtaking, he had to admit, a secret paradise.

"The sand is dead coral," Althaea said as they walked along the beach. Her sandals dangled from her hand, she'd taken them off to paddle. "There's a grinder machine which turns it to powder. Mother says they used to process a whole batch of dead chunks every year when Father was alive. It took decades for the family to make this beach."

"It was worth it."

She gave him a cautious smile. "The lagoon's chock full of lobsters. It fills up through a vent hole, but there's a tidal turbine at the far end to give us all our power. They can't get past it so they just sit in there and breed. I dive to catch them, it's so easy."

"You must have been very young when your father died."

"It happened before I was born." Her lower lip curled anxiously under her teeth. "I'm seventeen."

"Yes, I'd worked that out. Seventeen and beautiful, you must knock the boys dead when you visit Kariwak."

Althaea turned scarlet.

"And you've lived here all your life?"

"Yes. Mother says the family used to have a plantation on Earth, somewhere in the Caribbean. We've always grown exotic crops." She skipped up on an outcrop of smooth yellow coral and gazed out across the lagoon. "I know Charmaine must look terribly ramshackle to you. But I'm going to wake it up. I'm going to have a husband, and ten children, and we'll have teams of pickers in the groves again, and boats will call every day to be loaded with fruit and coffee beans, and we'll have our own fishing smacks, and a new village to house everyone, and big dances under the stars." She stopped, drastically self-conscious again, hunching up her shoulders. "You must think I'm so stupid talking like that."

"No, not at all. I wish I had dreams like yours."

"What do you dream of?"

"I don't know. Somewhere small and quiet I can settle down. Definitely not an asteroid, though."

"But it could be an island?" She sounded hopeful.

"Yes. Could be."

• • • •

Starship fusion drives twinkled brighter than stars in the night sky as Eason walked across the garden to the house. Only one of Tropicana's pair of small moons was visible, a yellow-orange globe low above the treetops and visibly sinking.

He went into the silent house, taking the stairs two at a time. When he reached Tiarella's bedroom door he turned the handle, ready to push until the lock tore out of the frame. It wasn't locked.

Moonlight shone in through the open window, turning the world to a drab monochrome. Tiarella was sitting cross-legged on the double bed, wearing a blue cotton nightshirt. The eccentric pendulum was held out at arm's length. She didn't show the slightest surprise at his presence.

Eason closed the door, aroused by the scene: woman waiting calmly on a bed. "You have something to tell me."

"Do I?"

"How did you know I was coming? Nobody could know that. It was pure chance I bumped into Althaea back in the harbour."

"Chance is your word. Destiny is mine. I read it in the cards. Now is the time for a stranger to appear."

"You expect me to believe that crap?"

"How do you explain it, then?"

He crossed the room in three quick strides, and gripped her arms. The pendulum bounced away noisily as she dropped it.

"That hurts," she said tightly.

He increased the pressure until she gasped. "How did you know I was coming?" he demanded.

"I read it in the cards," she hissed back.

Eason studied her eyes, desperate for any sign of artfulness. Finding none. She was telling the truth, or thought she was. Cards! Crazy bitch.

He shoved her down on the bed, and glared down at her, angry at himself for the growing sense of vulnerability, the suspicion he was being manipulated. All this astrology shit was too far outside his experience.

The nightshirt had ridden up her legs. He let his eyes linger on the long provocative expanse of exposed thigh.

"Take it off," he said softly.

"Fuck off."

He knelt on the bed beside her, smiling. "You knew exactly what you were doing when you asked me out here, didn't you? Eighteen years is a long time." He stroked her chin, receiving another glimpse into that steely reserve, but this time there was a spark of guilt corroding the composure. "Yes," he said. "You knew what you were doing." His hand slipped down inside the nightshirt to cup her left breast. He enjoyed the fullness he found, the warmth.

"Don't push your luck," she said. "Remember, the only way off this island is the *Orphée*, and she's affinity-bonded to me. If you want to clear out ahead of whoever is hunting you, you do what you're told."

"What makes you think someone's after me?"

"Oh, please. Fresh off a starship, no money, desperate to get out of the city. I believe you're drifting."

"And you still let me on board."

"Because you were meant to be. It's your time."

"I've had enough of this crap. I think I'll go see Althaea. How do tall handsome strangers fit into her horoscope today?" He let go of her and stood up.

"Bastard. Don't you touch my daughter."

Eason laughed. "Give me a reason."

He waited until she started to unbutton the nightshirt, then tugged off his jeans and T-shirt.

• • •

Charmaine's daily routine was insidiously somnolent. Eason soon found himself lapsing into the same unhurried rhythm Rousseau used to approach any task. After all, there was nothing which actually needed doing urgently.

The old man showed him the outhouse which was fitted out as a carpentry shop. Its roof leaked, but the tools and bench jigs were in good condition, and there was plenty of power from the tidal turbine (Tropicana's moons were small, but they had a close orbit, producing a regular fluctuation in the ocean). It took him three days to fix up the chalet's frame properly, and repair the thatch roof. He had to junk a lot of the planking, cutting new wood from a stack of seasoned lengths. After that, he began to survey the remaining chalets. Two of them had rotted beyond repair, but the others were salvageable. He started to measure up, surprised to find himself enjoying the prospect of restoring them.

He decided it was because the work he was doing on Charmaine was practical. The first time in his life he had constructed rather than destroyed.

Althaea brought him an endless supply of fruit drinks when he was working on the chalets. She was eager to hear stories of life in the Confederation, gossip about the Kulu abdication, what asteroid settlements were like, details of a starship flight, the new colony worlds, wicked old Earth. The chilled fresh juice, the sweltering heat, Rousseau's continuing laziness, and her interest were good enough excuses to down tools.

He accompanied her when she went across to the lagoon, and watched her dive for lobsters. It was a ridiculous way to catch the things; a couple of pots would have brought an overnight bounty. But that wasn't the way of Charmaine. Besides, he enjoyed the sight of her stripping down to a bikini, almost unaware of her own sexuality. She was an excellent swimmer, long limbs propelling her sleekly through the water. Then she'd emerge glistening and smiling as she held up two new snapping trophies.

Tiarella took *Orphée* out sailing every two or three days, visiting the neighbouring islands. She and Ross would pick a couple of crates full of fruit from the accessible trees around the lagoon to trade, returning with fish, or cloth, or flour. She told him they only visited Kariwak every couple of weeks, carrying a cargo of lobsters to sell at the harbour's market, and buying essentials only available in the city.

She spent most of her days working on the *Orphée*. A lot of effort went into keeping the boat seaworthy.

Eason kept returning to her at night, though he was beginning to wonder why. After a week he was still no closer to understanding her. Island life had given her a great body, but she was lifeless in bed; appropriately, for she fantasized she was making love to a dead man. On the two occasions he had managed to rouse her, she called out Vanstone's name.

On the tenth day he turned down an invitation to sail with the three of them on a circuit of the nearby islands. Instead he spent the morning overhauling a mower tractor which he found in the cavernous shed used to garage Charmaine's neglected agricultural machinery. After he'd stripped down and reassembled the gearbox, and charged the power cell from the tidal turbine, he got to work on the lawn. Driving round and round the house, grass cuttings shooting out of the back like a green geyser.

When Althaea emerged from the trees late in the afternoon she gawped at the lawn in astonishment, then whooped and hugged him. "It looks wonderful," she laughed. "And you've found the lily pond!"

He'd nearly driven straight into the damn thing; it was just a patch of emerald swamp, with a statue of Venus in the centre, concealed by reeds. If it hadn't been for the frogs fleeing the tractor's blades he would never have guessed what it was in time.

"Will you get the fountain working again? Please, Eason!"

"I'll have a look at it," he said. Pressed against him, her lean body left an agreeable imprint through the thin fabric of her dress. Tisrella was giving him a stern frown, which he replied with a silent mocking smile.

Althaea took a step back, face radiant. "Thank you."

• • •

That night, Eason jerked awake as Tiarella's hand jabbed into his side.

"Get up," she hissed urgently.

It was gone midnight; a storm had risen to batter the archipelago. Huge raindrops pelted the windowpanes; lightning flares illuminated the garden and its palisade of trees in a stark chiaroscuro. Thunder formed an almost continuous grumble.

"They're here," she said. "They're docking at the jetty, right now."

"Who's here?" His thoughts were still sluggish from sleep.

"You tell me! You're the one they're after. No one with honest business would try to sail tonight."

"Then how do you know anyone's here?"

Tiarella had closed her eyes. "*Orphée* has a set of dolphin-derived echo receptors fitted under her hull. I can see their boat, it's small. Ah, they've hit the jetty. It's wobbling. They must be getting out. Yes . . . yes, they are."

The Party! It couldn't be anyone else, not creeping up in the middle of the night. Conceivably it was comrades he'd once fought with, although contract killers were more likely.

Eason's training took over: assess, plan, initiate. He cursed violently at being caught out so simply. Ten days was all it had taken for Charmaine's cosy existence to soften him. He should have moved on immediately, broken his trail into chaotic segments which no one could piece together.

"There's three of them," Tiarella said, her eyes still tight shut.

"How do you know that?"

"Three!" she insisted.

"Oh, for fuck's sake. Stay here," he ordered. "You'll be safe. They only want me." He rolled out of bed and shoved the window open, climbing out on to the balcony, still naked. Retinal amps scanned the freshly cut garden. Nothing was moving.

At least the rain and wind would hinder them slightly. But it still didn't look good.

Eason scrambled down one of the balcony pillars, rust

flakes scratching his palms and thighs. He raced across the lawn, desperate to reach the cover of the trees, slipping three times on the sodden grass. Thorns tore at his legs as he sprinted into the undergrowth. There was no sign of the intruders yet.

He forced his way through the mass of clawing vegetation until he was ten metres from the path to the jetty, then started to climb the gnarled trunk of an orange tree. The branches were dense, unyielding, but he twisted and wriggled his way through them, feeling them snap and bend against his ribs. He finally stopped when he'd manoeuvred himself above the path.

Thunder and lightning swamped his senses. He was totally dependent on his retinal amps now, praying they could compensate for the storm. The infra-red function rewarded him with a large hot-spot creeping along the sombre tunnel formed by the overgrown trees. It resolved into a human shape, a man. He held his breath. If he could see the man, then he was visible, too. It had been a stupid move; he'd gambled on the attackers being closer to the house by now.

But the man was only a couple of metres away, and showed no awareness of Eason. He was wearing dark oilskins and a broad-brimmed hat, cradling some kind of rifle. Hick-boy out hunting.

This wasn't any kind of professional operation. Which made even less sense.

Someone else was floundering through the undergrowth parallel to the path, making enough noise to be heard above the thunder and the rain. The man on the path walked directly under Eason, and kept on going. There was a commotion away towards the ocean. Someone screamed. It choked off rapidly, but not before Eason got an approximate fix.

"Whitley? Whitley, where the hell are you?"

That was the one Eason had heard blundering about, shouting at the top of his voice.

"Come on, let's get out of these bloody trees," the one on the path yelled in answer. "Now shut up, he'll hear us."

"I can't fucking hear us! And what happened to Whitley?"

"I don't bloody know. Tripped most likely. Now come on!"

The figure on the path started to advance again. Eason landed behind him as thunder shook the creaking trees. He focused, and punched. Powered by an augmented musculature, his fist slammed into the back of the man's neck, snapping the spinal cord instantly, shoving fractured vertebrae straight into his trachea, blocking even a reflex grunt from emerging.

The body pitched forward, squelching as it hit the muddy path. Eason snatched up the rifle, checking it in a glance. His synaptic web ran a comparison search through its files, identifying it as a Walther fluxpump. Basically, a magnetic shotgun which fired a burst of eighty steel pellets.

The breech was fully loaded with twenty-five cartridges. Satisfied, Eason plunged back into the undergrowth, crouching low as he closed the gap on the second intruder.

The man was leaning against a tree trunk at the edge of the lawn, peering through the branches at the house. Eason stood three metres behind him, pointed the fluxpump at his legs, and fired.

"Who are you?"

"Jesus God, you shot me! You fucking shot me. I can't feel my legs!"

It was another bovine islander, same as the first. Eason shook his head in wonder, and moved the fluxpump's barrel slightly. "In three seconds you won't feel your prick if you don't answer me. Now who are you?"

"Don't! God, I'm called Fermoy. Fermoy, OK?"

"Right. Well done, Fermoy. So what are you and where do you come from?"

"I'm a shipwright over on Boscobel."

"Where's Boscobel?"

"An island, nine kilometres away. God, my legs!"

"What are you doing here, Fermoy?"

"We came for the man. You."

"Why?"

"You're wanted. There must be money for you."

"And you thought you'd collect?"

"Yes."

"Who were you going to give me to, Fermoy?"

"Torreya."

"Why her?"

"You were running from Kariwak. We thought she must want you. You wouldn't be running, else."

"Who told you I was running?"

"Ross."

Eason stared down at him, teeth bared in rage. That drunken *shithead*. He'd been safe on Charmaine, home dry. He made an effort to calm down. "When did he tell you?"

"This morning. We were drinking. It came out. You know what he's like."

"How many of you came?"

"Three, just three."

So Tiarella had been right about that. "And how many people on Boscobel know I'm here?"

"Only us."

"Right. Well, thanks, I think that's covered everything."

The third bounty hunter, Whitley, was easy to find. He lay, strangely motionless, in the centre of a broad circle of mangled undergrowth. Eason took a couple of cautious steps towards him, fluxpump held ready.

A vivid lightning bolt sizzled overhead.

Whitley was wrapped from his neck downwards in what

looked like a spiral of tubing, thirty centimetres thick, jet black, glistening slickly. He was gurgling weakly, drooling blood. Eason squinted forward, every nerve shrieking in protest, and switched his retinal amps to infra-red. The coil of tubing glowed pale crimson, a length of it meandered through the broken grass.

"*Jesus!*"

The snake's head reared up right in front of him. It was a demonic streamlined arrowhead seventy centimetres long, the jaw open to show fangs the size of fingers. A blood-red tongue as thick as his forearm shot out, vibrating eagerly.

Training or not, Eason lurched back in terror.

"Solange won't hurt you," Tiarella shouted above the storm. "He's affinity-bonded to me."

She was standing behind him, her rain-soaked nightshirt clinging like a layer of blue skin.

"That *thing* is yours?"

"Solange? Yes. He's another of my father's designs. But I'm not sure he was supposed to grow this big. He does eat rather a lot of firedrakes, you see."

The real horror was the lightness of her tone. So matter-of-fact. Crazy bitch!

Eason took another couple of steps back. The snake had been on the island the whole time. She could have set it on him whenever she wanted and he would never have known. Not until the very last instant when it came rustling out of the thick concealing undergrowth.

"Do you want to question this one?" Tiarella asked, gesturing at Whitley.

"No."

Her eyes fluttered shut.

Whitley started screaming again as the coils round him flexed sinuously. The sound was swallowed up by the crack of snapping bones, a sickeningly wet squelching. Eason looked away, jaw clenched.

"I'll take their boat out and scuttle it," Tiarella said. "Everyone will think the storm capsized them. You can bury the bodies. Somewhere where Althaea won't find them, please."

• • •

"She asked me how old I thought you were," Rousseau slurred, then burped. "I said thirty, thirty-five. Around there."

"Thanks a lot," Eason said. He was sitting with the old man, their backs against a fallen tree trunk on the lagoon's beach as the gloaming closed in. A bottle of Rousseau's dreadful home-brew spirits had been passed to and fro for over an hour. Eason wasn't drinking any more, though he made it look like he was.

"You're a good man. I see that. But Althaea, I love her. The two of you together, it's not right. Who knows how long you're gonna stay, eh? These people, your enemies, they could find you. Even here."

"Right."

"She would cry if you left her. She would cry more if you were taken away from her. You understand? I couldn't stand to see her cry. Not my little Althaea."

"Of course. Don't worry. I like Tiarella."

"Ha!" He coughed heavily. "That's a mistake, too, my friend. She's a harsh, cold woman, that Tiarella. Cracked up completely after her Vanstone died. Never shown a single emotion since, not one. She won't be interested in you."

Eason grunted his interest and passed the bottle back. A sheet of low cloud hid the stars and moons. Balmy warmth and serenity were a profound contrast to the storm of the previous night. "She loves Althaea, that's an emotion."

Rousseau took a long swig, his eyelids drooping. "Crap. Loves nobody else, not even her own children." He took another swig, the liquid running down his stubble. "Gave one away. Said she couldn't afford to keep it here. I pleaded, but she wouldn't listen. Damn ice woman. Never thanks me for what I do, you know. Kept Charmaine going, I have. All for my little Althaea, not her." He started to slide over, the bottle slipping from his fingers.

Eason put out a hand to steady him. "Gave one what away?"

Rousseau only mumbled, saliva bubbling from his mouth. His eyes had closed.

"Gave what away?" Eason shook him.

"Twins. She had twins," Rousseau sighed. "Beautiful twins." Then every muscle went limp; he sprawled on the sand as Eason let go.

Eason looked at him for a long moment. Pathetic and utterly harmless. But he was a liability.

He scanned his retinal amps round the edge of the lagoon, searching for the tell-tale rosy glow that would reveal Solange watching him. All he could see was the black and grey of the tangled trees.

Rousseau was so drunk he didn't even react to having his head immersed in the water. Eason held him under for two minutes, then waded out and started to sweep away the incriminating tracks in the sand.

*   *   *

They held the funeral two days later. A dozen people attended from the neighbouring islands, staid men and women in sturdy clothes gathered round the grave. Althaea leant against her mother the whole time, sobbing softly. The ceremony was conducted by Lucius, a forty-year-old deacon from Tropicana's Orthodox Church, an archipelago-based sect which had split from the Unified Christian Church a century and a half earlier. He was a broad-shouldered, powerful man who captained the *Anneka*, one of the Church's traders.

Along with three men from the islands, Eason lowered the coffin he had built into the hole while Lucius led the singing of a hymn. The coffin came to rest on a bedrock of coral one and a half metres down.

After the mourners departed, Eason shovelled the rich loam back in, two of the men helping him. Nobody questioned his presence. He was the new labourer Tiarella had taken on, that was enough for them.

It started him thinking. He'd only possessed the most generalized notion for the future when he stole the Party's antimatter. Dump it harmlessly in interstellar space, start over somewhere else. No destination in mind, simply a place where he could live without ever having to watch his back.

Looking around, he didn't think he could find a more Arcadian location than the archipelago to live. It was just the lifestyle which was the problem, this vaguely sanctimonious poor-but-proud kick which the islanders shared. That and a snake which even hell would reject.

But changes could be made, or paid for, and snakes were not immortal.

The wake was a mawkish, stilted ordeal. Conversation between the islanders was limited to their fishing and the minutiae of large family genealogies. Althaea sat in a corner of the lounge, her mouth twitching in a kind of entreating helplessness if anyone offered their condolences. Even Tiarella allowed her relief to show when it limped to its desultory conclusion.

"I've arranged with Lucius for a picking team to visit us next month," Tiarella told Eason after they saw off the last of the boats. "They'll be coming from Oliviera, that's one of the Church's parish islands about twelve kilometres away. They usually come about twice a year to pick whatever fruit is ripe. Some of the crop is handed round to other parishes, the remainder is sold to a trader in Kariwak and we split the proceeds."

"Couldn't you find yourself a better partner than the Church?" he asked.

She cocked her head to one side, and gave him a derisive look. "It was the Church which looked after Vanstone when he was a boy, he grew up in their orphanage."

"Right." He gave up. Rousseau had been right, she was too odd.

"I don't accept their doctrine," she said. "But they make decent neighbours, and they're honest. Oliviera also has several parishioners who are Althaea's age. Their company will be good for her; she deserves something to cheer her up right now."

• • • •

Both moons were in the sky that night, casting an icy light that tinted Charmaine's trees and foliage a dusky grey. Eason found Althaea arranging a garland of scarlet flowers on Rousseau's grave, a quiet zephyr twirling her loose mane of hair. The dark blouse and skirt she had worn for the funeral seemed to soak up what little light there was, partially occluding her with shadows.

She stood up slowly when he arrived, making no attempt to hide her dejection. "He wasn't a bad man," she said. Her voice was husky from crying.

"I know he wasn't."

"I suppose something like this was bound to happen."

"Don't dwell on it. He really loved you. The last thing he'd want was for you to be unhappy."

"Yes."

He kissed her brow, and began to undo the buttons on her blouse.

"Don't," she said. But even that was an effort for her.

"Shush." He soothed her with another kiss. "It's all right, I know what I'm doing."

She simply stood there with her shoulders slumped, as he knew she would. He finished unbuttoning her blouse, and pushed the fabric aside to admire her breasts. Althaea looked back at him, numb with grief.

"I can't make you forget," he said. "But this will show you your life has more to offer than grief."

He led her, unresisting, back through the unruly trees to his chalet.

•   •   •

The parishioners from Oliviera were a chirpy, energetic bunch. There were twenty of them, trooping down the jetty from *Anneka*'s deck: teenagers and adolescents, loaded up with backpacks and wicker baskets. After Charmaine's usual solitude they were like an invading army.

Eason had prepared a section of the island ready for them, determined the harvesting arrangement would be a prosperous one for both sides. It'd been a hectic, happy time for him since the funeral.

After the sun fell, Althaea would slip away from the house, returning night after night to the darkness and heat of his chalet. She was a sublime conquest—youthful, lithe, obedient. Taking her as his lover was sweet revenge on Tiarella. Replaced by her own daughter. She must have known, lying alone in her own bed as Althaea was ruthlessly corrupted in his.

By day, the two of them set about righting Charmaine. Eason renovated a rotary-scythe unit which fitted on the front of the mower tractor. He and Althaea took it in turns to drive the vehicle through the grove of citrus trees which was fruiting, blades hacking at the thick tangle of vines and low bushes, terrorizing the parrots and firedrakes. The chips were cleared away and piled high, making bonfires which burned for days at a time. Now they were left with broad clear avenues of trunks to walk down. That one section of island, two hundred metres long, stretching right across the saddle of coral between the lagoon and the ocean, was almost back to being a proper grove instead of a wilderness. Crooked branches still knotted together overhead, but all the fruit was accessible. Pruning could wait until later; his synaptic web didn't have any files on that at all.

"We'll need another boat to cope with the load," Lucius said after they'd filled the *Anneka*'s outrigger holds by the middle of the afternoon on the first day. "We normally only get three or four boatloads out of the whole week. I wish I'd brought a bigger team now, as well. You've done a good job improving things here, Eason."

Eason tipped back the straw hat which Althaea had woven for him, and smiled. "Thank you. Can you get hold of another boat?"

"I'll put in at the cathedral island this evening, ask the Bishop to assign us a second. It shouldn't be a problem."

At night the picking team gathered on the lawn. Tiarella had set up a long open-range charcoal grill. They ate lobsters and thick slices of pork, washed down with juice and wine. After the meal they sang as a moon arched sedately across the sky, and the fountain sent a foaming white jet seven metres up into the air.

Althaea was in her element as she moved between the groups with a tray, her face animated in a way Eason had never seen before. Still later, when they had stolen away to make love in the jungle beyond the restored grove, he lay back on his blanket and watched her undressing, skin stippled by moonlight filtering through the thick canopy of leaves, his resolve crystallized. Her body, a rewarding challenge, beautiful location, it didn't get any better. He was going to stay.

Eason didn't see them together until the third day. It was a lunch break, and he'd just walked back from the jetty to help himself to the sandwiches Tiarella had made in the kitchen. Through the window he could see most of the garden.

Althaea was sitting in the shade of a eucalyptus tree with one of the parishioners, a lad in his teens. They were talking avidly, passing a chillflask to and fro. Her easiness with the lad irritated Eason. But he made a conscious effort to keep his feelings in check. The last thing he wanted was a scene which would draw attention and comment.

When his retinal amp focused on the lad's face, Eason could see a disturbing amount of adoration written there. Fair enough, she was divine after all. But there was something about his features which was familiar: he had a broad face, strong jaw, longish blond hair, clear blue eyes—a real charmer. Faces were Eason's business, and he'd seen that face once before, recently. Yet offhand he couldn't even point in the direction Oliviera lay.

It was Althaea who introduced him to the lad. His name was Mullen, he was seventeen, polite and respectful, if slightly overeager. It was an engaging combination. Eason found himself warming to him.

The three of them sat together for the meal that night, biting into broad slices of pineapple coated in a tart sauce, drinking a sweet white wine. Tiarella sat on the other side of the grill, her outline wavering in the heat shimmer given off by the glowing charcoal. Her gaze was locked on them.

"So how many times have you come here to pick?" Eason asked.

Mullen tore his attention away from Althaea. "This is my first time. It's wonderful. I've never seen a firedrake before."

"Where were you living before Oliviera?"

"Nowhere. I've always lived there. This is the first time I've been anywhere except for other parish islands, and they're pretty much the same."

"You mean you've never been on the mainland?" he asked, surprised.

"Not yet, no. I'm probably going to go next year, when I'm eighteen."

"You've got a real treat in store," Althaea said. "Kariwak's a riot; but just make sure you count your fingers after you shake hands."

"Really?" Mullen switched his entire attention back to her.

Eason felt lonely, out of it. The truth was, their conversation had been incredibly boring all evening. They talked about nothing—the antics of the firedrakes, weather, which fish they liked best, how the picking was progressing. Every word was treated as though it had been spoken by some biblical prophet.

He was also very aware of the way Mullen's eyes roamed. Althaea was wearing just her turquoise shorts and a cotton halter top. It was distracting enough for him, so Heaven knew what it was doing to Mullen's hormones—the other boys from the parish, too, for that matter. He ought to have a word with her about it.

When he looked round the garden, Tiarella was still staring at him; her face sculpted, immobile. Maybe she was finally realizing her time was coming to an end. After eighteen years of stagnation and inertia it would be a jolt for any personality.

He allowed Mullen and Althaea to babble on for another ten minutes, then plucked at her halter strap. "Come on."

She glanced at him, frowning as he rose to his feet, slapping sand and grass from his jeans. "Oh . . . not just yet."

"Yes. We need to get some sleep afterwards." He let an impish grin play over his lips, and picked up their blanket.

Althaea blushed as she glanced at Mullen, lips twitching into an embarrassed smile.

"Come on." Eason clicked his fingers impatiently.

"I'll see you both tomorrow," the lad mumbled.

"Sure. Good night." He steered Althaea towards the black picket of trees. He liked Mullen, but the lad had to understand exactly who she belonged to.

"That was very rude," Althaea whispered.

His free arm went round her shoulder. "Not as rude as what I'm about to show you in a minute."

Althaea fought against a grin as he tickled her ribcage. Her finger poked him in retaliation. "Rude!"

"Was not."

"Was too."

He looked back as he reached the trees. The glowing charcoal was spilling a pool of tangerine radiance over the lawn. It showed him Mullen covering his face with his hands, shoulder muscles knotted. And Tiarella, who hadn't been staring at him after all, because her eyes had never moved when he and Althaea departed. She was watching Mullen.

When the lad's hands slipped back down to reveal a crest-fallen expression, the corners of her mouth lifted into a serene smile.

• • •

Eason stood on the jetty, his arm around Althaea as they waved goodbye to the *Anneka*. The parishioners were leaning over the gunwale, waving back, shouting farewells which were scrambled by the wavelets lapping against the coral.

Tiarella started walking back to the house. Eason turned to follow, and gave Althaea a reassuring hug, noting a certain wistfulness in her eyes. "Don't worry, I'm sure your new boyfriend will be in touch. He's madly in love with you, after all." He grinned broadly to show he understood.

Althaea shot him a look of pure venom, then her face became the identical blank mask which defended Tiarella from the world.

"Hey, listen—" he began.

But she shook herself free and ran off down the jetty. He stared after her in consternation.

"What did I say?"

Tiarella arched her eyebrow. "It's not what you say, it's what you are."

"You make me out as some kind of ogre," he snapped, suddenly exasperated with her, the unending stream of oblique remarks.

"In medieval times that's exactly what you would be."

"Name one thing I've done to hurt her."

"You wouldn't dare. We both know that."

"With or without your threats, I wouldn't hurt her."

Her lips compressed as she studied him. "No, I don't suppose you would. I never really thought about how you would be affected by your time here. I should have done."

"My time? You make it sound finite."

"It is. I told you that the day you came."

"Your fucking cards again!" Crazy bitch!

Tiarella shrugged and sauntered off down the path to the house.

He slept alone that night, for the first time since the funeral. Guilt soaked his mind as he lay on the cot, yet he still didn't know what it was he'd done.

The next morning over breakfast she gave him a timid smile, and he glossed over any awkwardness with an enthusiastic account of how he intended to clear all the island's old service tracks with the mower tractor. Then they'd be able to start attending to the coffee bushes.

That night he welcomed her back to his bed. It wasn't the same; she had become reserved. Not physically, as always her body was defenceless against his skill and strength. But somewhere deep inside her thoughts she was holding herself back from him. No matter how exquisite their lovemaking was she no longer surrendered completely.

* * *

It took a certain amount of nerve to walk into the Kulu Embassy carrying three antimatter-confinement spheres. Eason was pleased to find himself perfectly calm as the glass doors of the reception area closed behind him. He asked the girl behind the desk for an interview with the military attaché, only to be told the Kingdom had no military ties with Tropicana.

"What about a police or security liaison officer?" he asked. "Surely you cooperate in tracking down criminals?"

She agreed they did, and asked for his name.

He handed over his passport, proving if nothing else that he was a bona fide citizen of Quissico. "And could you also say I'm a senior member of the Independence Party." He smiled warmly at her flustered expression.

Three minutes later he was in a plain second-floor office with a window wall overlooking Kariwak's eastern quarter. The man sitting on the other side of the marble desk introduced himself as Vaughan Tenvis, of indistinct age, but certainly under fifty. He wore a conservative green suit, but filled it out in a way that suggested he spent a lot of time away from the office performing more physical tasks than accessing files.

"I need to speak to a representative of the Kingdom's External Security Agency," Eason said. "And please, I don't want the bullshit stalling routine."

"Sounds reasonable," Vaughan Tenvis said with a dry

smile. "If you're quite sure you want that much honesty. Suppose you tell me why I should allow a known terrorist organization's quartermaster to walk out of here alive?"

"Because I don't want to be the quartermaster any more. And I've done you a favour."

"Ah. And there I was thinking you were going to threaten me with whatever it is you have in your case. Our sensors couldn't quite get through the magnetic covering."

"No threats. I just want to do a deal."

"Go on."

"The Kulu Corporation is one of the major investors in the Quissico Development Company, that makes it a target for my Party. I came to you because the ESA is more than capable of neutering the Party if it has sufficient reason."

"Very flattering. But contrary to rumour, we don't go around terminating everyone who has a quarrel with the Kingdom. Bluntly, you're too small and petty to warrant any effort. We monitor you, that's all."

"Not very well. Our Party acquired some antimatter. The Kulu Corporation's administrative centre on StAlbans is the first intended target."

"Antimatter . . ." Vaughan Tenvis stared in shock at the case resting on Eason's lap, his hands gripping the side of his chair. "Holy shit!"

The risk of coming to the embassy was worth it, just to see the horror cracking the suave agent's face.

"As I said, I've done you a favour." Eason put the case on Vaughan Tenvis's desk. "That's all of it. I'm sure the Kingdom has the appropriate facilities to dispose of it."

"Holy shit."

"I would appreciate two things in return."

"Holy shit."

"One, your agency's gratitude."

Vaughan Tenvis let out a long breath, and swallowed hard. "Gratitude?"

"I expect to be left alone by you in future, Mr Tenvis."

"Sure. OK, I can swing that."

"I'd also like a reward. That antimatter cost the Party eight million fuseodollars. I'll settle for one million. You can pay me in Kulu pounds if you like; and I'll throw in the codes for the confinement systems. I'd hate you to have any accidents with them now we're friends."

● ● ●

Tenvis paid him in Kulu pounds. With the current conversion rate, he wound up with eight hundred thousand in his bank disk. Not bad for forty minutes' work. Forty minutes to erase his life.

Eason was back on board the *Orphée* an hour later, after a shopping expedition through the fancy shops of Kariwak's main boulevard. He picked Althaea up, and spun her around, kissing her exuberantly. Tiarella gave him a sour glance as she cast off. He even smiled at her.

The department store's big carrier bag was slapped down on the roof of the cabin with considerable panache. "I bought some essentials," he said as they were passing the ancient landing craft in the middle of the harbour. Althaea gasped in delight as he pulled out a couple of bottles of champagne, and three crystal glasses. Packs of honey-roast ham followed, then steaks, imported cheeses, exotic chocolates, ice-cream cartons cloaked in frost.

"You'll be sick if you eat all that lot," Tiarella grunted.

He pulled a face at Althaea, who bit back on her giggles.

"I got something for you, too," he said. "Actually, for us." He held out the flat red leather jewellery case.

Althaea opened it cautiously. There were two platinum lockets resting on the black velvet inside.

"It's for hair," he told her. "You snip off a few strands of your hair for mine, and I do the same for you. If you want."

She nodded eagerly. "I do."

"Good." Finally, he produced a square box, and gave Tiarella a pointedly dubious look before he eased the lid off a fraction to show Althaea what was inside. Her eyes flashed as she saw the tiny white-silk negligée. She hugged him tightly, and licked his ear mischievously. Closer than she had been for a week.

They sat together on the cabin roof, back to back, sipping champagne as *Orphée* cut through the water. He could feel the tension slipping away as the mainland fell behind.

It wouldn't be long, a month at most, before there was nothing left of the hardliners of the Quissico Independence Party. Vaughan Tenvis was right to say the ESA's main activity was collecting information; but if it ever found a threat to the Kingdom it acted with terrifying efficiency to eliminate it. Nobody would come for him now.

The just cause would go on, of course, led by whoever survived. Moderates and compromisers, those who lacked fire. And in another thirty-five years Quissico would be an independent state, just as the founding charter promised.

One chapter of his life had closed irrevocably. He was free to embrace the new. Tiarella was now nothing more than an annoying irrelevance, one he could ignore with impunity. She was deranged, reading portents in the sky. Althaea belonged to him, and through her Charmaine. *Fait accompli*. If Tiarella continued to object . . . well, there had already been one boating accident in the family.

It was for the best. He could do wonders with Charmaine; a smart tough new master with plenty of money to invest was exactly what it needed. In a few years the old place would be up and jumping.

"More champagne?" Althaea asked.

He grinned and kissed her. "I think so."

•   •   •

Tiarella sat behind the desk in her study, dealing from her pack of tarot cards. She was aligning them in the shape of a cross, each one pushed down firmly on the dark wooden surface with a distinct snick.

"I'm going to live here permanently," Eason told her.

Another card was dealt. "You wouldn't enjoy it, not full-time. Oh, granted you're riding a crest with all these improvements you're making right now. It's all new and thrilling for you. But forty years of hard labour. I don't think you're quite cut out for that, now are you?"

"I wasn't proposing to do it all myself. I'm offering to buy in. I've cashed in my starship ticket, and liquidated some other investments. There's enough money."

"A dowry. How quaint." The arms of the cross were laid down methodically, five cards on each side. "The man Althaea chooses won't have to buy his way in. I'll greet him with open arms. He will have Charmaine because she has Charmaine. It's that simple, Eason. Have you asked her if she wants to share it with you?"

"We're virtually engaged. She's mine, and you know it."

"Quite the opposite. She is not yours. She never will be. Her destiny is with another."

The sly attitude of superiority infuriated him. He leant over the desk and caught her wrist as the last card was slapped down.

Tiarella didn't flinch at the pressure he exerted.

"Maybe you're jealous," he said harshly.

"Of you two being lovers? Good God, no! You can never replace Vanstone. I thought you knew that by now."

He bit back a furious retort.

"Would you mind letting go of me now, please?" she asked grimly.

He released her, slouching back in his own chair. "The money would make an incredible difference," he said, refusing to give up. "We could buy some more tractors, clean out the rest of the groves, restore the coffee bushes, hire some labourers to prune the trees. Then there's the house to fix up properly."

"That's the short cut, Eason, the easy option. You want to be a manager, the grand plantation owner living in his mansion while others bring in the crop. That's not the way to do it, not here. Life is about cycles; you can't fight what nature has ordained. And now we've come round to the time when Charmaine is passed on to Althaea just as it was passed to me all those years ago. I haven't done very well with it, but Althaea and her husband will. They'll rebuild Charmaine slowly. Every day there will be some new accomplishment for them to rejoice about. Their whole life is going to be rich with genuine satisfaction, not this cheaply bought gratitude you offer."

"Then I'll give the bloody money away. She can have me just the way I was when we met, a destitute drifter."

Tiarella's mask of indifference cracked for the very first time. She gave him a tired smile, compassion lurking in flecked emerald irises. "I never expected you to fall in love with her. I really didn't."

"I . . ." He clenched his fists. Admitting that to her would be a defeat in this war, he knew.

"The money won't make any difference to Althaea's answer or mine," she said weakly. "Believe me, I'm being kind to you. Just go, Eason. If you truly love her. Go now. You'll be hurt by her if you don't."

"Is that a threat?"

"No. Listen to me, I had a lover before I met Vanstone. He was a good man, he adored me passionately, and I did him. But then Vanstone arrived, and I dropped him. Just like that. I never thought about how he felt. Girls that age can be unknowingly cruel. I don't want that to happen to you."

"Althaea's not like you. She has a heart."

Tiarella laughed. "And you believe I don't? I suppose I

can't blame you for thinking that. I am a bitch these days, I admit. But I used to, Eason, I used to have a heart just like hers."

"I don't get it. I really don't. You brought me here, you and that monstrosity snake helped me snuff the bounty hunters. You screwed with me. You stand by and let me screw your daughter. Now you tell me you don't want me here. *Why?*"

"Your time is over."

"Don't give me that card shit again. You realize she's probably pregnant by now. I didn't exactly hold back."

"Don't get excited, she's not pregnant. I made quite sure she was using a contraceptive."

He stared at her, shocked. "You . . ."

"Bitch? I'm her mother, Eason."

"Jesus Christ."

"You're welcome to stay here as long as you like, although I expect you won't want to. But you must understand, neither Althaea nor Charmaine is ever going to belong to you."

"We'll see." He was so furious he didn't trust himself to say anything else to her.

Althaea was in the kitchen, preparing their lunch. She looked up when he came in and gave him a happy smile. He kissed her, and took her hand. "Come along."

She skipped after him as he went out into the hall. Tiarella was standing in the study's doorway, watching. Althaea automatically stiffened, glancing sheepishly at her mother.

"Althaea and I are going upstairs," Eason said levelly. "That cot in my chalet is too small for the kind of sex I prefer. So from now on we'll be using the bed in her room. OK?"

Althaea drew a loud, astonished breath.

Tiarella shrugged indifferently. "Whatever."

Eason grinned victoriously, and tugged a confounded Althaea up the stairs.

"Oh God, she'll kill me," Althaea wailed as soon as the door shut behind them. "She'll kill both of us."

"No, she won't." He imprisoned her head between his palms, putting his face centimetres from hers. "She must learn to accept that you're a grown woman now, and that you and I are in love. We have a perfect right to be together in your bed. I did this for you. Everything I do is for you now."

"You love me?" She sounded even more frightened than before.

"Yes. Now you and I are going to take the rest of the afternoon and evening off, and spend it in here. If your mother doesn't like that, then she should seriously start to think about leaving the island."

• • •

Eason had never been in Althaea's bedroom before. When he woke up the next morning he looked round blearily. Wan white walls were hung with holographic posters, one of which gave the bed a panoramic view over rugged snow-capped mountains and a magical Bavarian castle. He turned over. Althaea was missing. Her ageing Animate Animal bear was on the floor along with the white silk negligée. Last night she hadn't quite dropped her reserve completely, but he was definitely making progress. And the seeds of rebellion against her witch mother had been firmly planted. Another pleasurable day at Charmaine.

He pulled on his jeans and went down to the kitchen. Althaea wasn't there either, which was unusual. She normally made breakfast for everyone.

He started opening cupboards, then he heard her screaming for help. Tiarella was already charging down the stairs as he rushed out of the back door. It sounded as though she was down at the jetty. He pounded along the path, wishing to Christ that the fluxpump wasn't back at his chalet. If that damn snake had run amok . . .

When Eason burst out of the trees, the scene he found was nothing like what he expected. Althaea was lying on the grass right on top of the coral wall, stretching out desperately. There was a wooden dinghy in the water, being tossed about by the current. It smacked into the coral wall with a nasty crunch. Althaea tried to grab the arm of the single occupant, but the dinghy twisted and surged backwards.

Eason ran forwards and threw himself down beside her. The dinghy had been holed on the vicious coral teeth surrounding the wall, and was sinking fast. Another swell rose, pitching it forward again. His synaptic web came on-line, calculating the approach vector and projecting the impact point. He shifted round fractionally, stretching out—

A wrist slapped into his waiting palm. He grabbed tight and pulled. The dinghy was dragged back, sharp spears of coral punching through the hull as it sank below the foam. Tiarella landed on the grass beside him with a hefty thump, reaching out to grasp the shoulder of the lad Eason was holding. Together, the three of them hauled him up over the top of the wall.

Eason blinked in surprise. It was Mullen.

"You idiot!" Tiarella yelled. "You could have been killed." She flung her arms round the dazed lad. "Dear God, you could have been killed."

"I'm sorry," Mullen stammered. He was shaking badly. There was blood oozing from his palms.

Tiarella let go, as self-conscious as Althaea had ever been, then sniffed and wiped away what Eason swore were tears. "Yes. Well, OK. It's a tricky approach, you'll have to learn about the currents round the island."

"Yes, miss," Mullen said meekly.

Eason took one of the lad's hands and turned it over. The skin on the palm had been rubbed raw. "What happened?"

"It was the rowing. I'm not used to it."

"Rowing? You mean you rowed here from Oliviera?"

"Yes."

Eason's immediate response died in his throat. He glanced at Althaea who was looking at Mullen with an expression of surprise and wonder.

"Why?" she asked timidly. "Why did you come?"

"I wanted . . ." He glanced round at Eason and Tiarella, panic-stricken.

"Go on," Tiarella said gently. "The truth never hurts in the long run." She smiled encouragement.

Mullen took a nervous breath. "I wanted to see you again," he blurted to Althaea.

"Me?"

"Uh-huh."

Her delicate face betrayed a universe of delight. Then it crumpled to guilt, and she looked at Eason, almost fearful.

His own emotions were almost as confused. What a ridiculous romantic the lad was. Small wonder Althaea was flattered. However, right now he was not prepared to tolerate a rival.

"Eason," Tiarella said sharply. "You and I have to talk. Right now."

"We do, yes, but now is not the time." He said it politely, making an effort to keep his temper in check.

"I insist. Althaea."

"Yes, Mother?"

"I want you to treat Mullen's hands. You know where the first aid kit is. Do it in the kitchen, I expect he'll want something to eat after that voyage." She patted the surprised lad's head. "Silly boy. Welcome back."

• • •

Eason closed the study door, cutting off the sound of Althaea and Mullen chattering in the kitchen. When he faced Tiarella he knew that somehow she'd undermined him. Mullen's arrival had changed everything. Yet he didn't see how that was possible.

"Just what the fuck is going on?" he asked.

Tiarella's expression was glacial. "I warned you. I told you your time was up, but you wouldn't listen."

"My time is just beginning."

"No it isn't. And as from now, you're not to sleep with Althaea again. I mean that, Eason. And I will enforce it if you make me. Solange is quite capable of dealing with you, and that's just the creature you know about."

"You're bluffing."

"Am I? Then it's your call." She opened a drawer in the desk and pulled out a finger-length cylinder with wires trailing from one end. "This is out of the fluxpump. I visited your chalet yesterday evening, just in case."

"You would seriously set that snake on me for loving your daughter?"

"I would now, yes. Force is all you know, Eason. It's what you'll use if you think Mullen threatens you. I won't tolerate any violence against him."

"Oh, come on! You honestly think she's going to choose that boy-child over me?"

"She chose him before she was born."

"This is your cards shit again, isn't it?"

"Far from it." She walked round the desk and pointed up at the big family print. "Who is this?" A finger tapped impatiently on Vanstone.

He gave an exasperated sigh. Crazy bitch. Then he looked, really looked at the man's features. All the confidence, all the anger inside him started to chill. "It's . . . But it can't be."

"Yes, it is," she said wistfully. "It's Mullen. About ten years older than he is now."

"What have you done? What is going on here?"

Tiarella grinned ruefully. "Small wonder he frightened the life out of me in that dinghy this morning." She cocked her head to one side, looking up at Eason. "There's just one last thing to show you."

He hadn't even known the house had a cellar. Tiarella took a torch to lead him down the slippery stone steps. There was a metal airlock door at the bottom. It was open, leading into a small decontamination chamber. The door at the far end was shut.

"This is Dad's old lab," Tiarella said as she pumped the manual handle to open the inner door. "The electrics fused in a storm years ago, but it's all still functional, I think."

Inside, Eason found a world completely removed from the rest of Charmaine. Benches of glassware glinted and sparkled as Tiarella swept the torch beam round. Dead electronic modules sprouted wires and optical fibres to mingle with the tubes, bulbs, and dishes. Autoclaves, freezers, synthesis extruders, and vats stood around the walls, along with cabinets he couldn't begin to understand. Two large computer terminals occupied the central desk, a high-resolution holographic projector on the ceiling above them.

"Most of Charmaine's foliage was spliced together in here," Tiarella said. "And those pesky firedrakes."

"Right."

She came to a halt in front of a large stack of machinery. "What I'm trying to show you, Eason, is that Dad knew what he was doing. He took his master's degree at Kariwak University. Several bitek research labs offered him a position, but he came back here."

"OK, I believe you. Nyewood was good."

"Yes. So have you worked it out yet?"

"Tell me."

"He cloned Vanstone for me. A parthenogenetic clone, identical to the original. There was enough of him left after the accident."

"Oh Jesus wept. Rousseau said you gave one of your babies away. Twins! He said you had twins." *Then* he realized.

"That's right. Dad cloned me as well. He engendered them in here." She tapped the stack of machinery. "And I nurtured the pair of them in my womb. A second little me, a second little Vanstone, growing together even then. After they were born I kept Althaea here, and gave Mullen to the Church orphanage. He grew up in exactly the same environment as Vanstone did."

"You really think she's going to fall in love with him, don't you?"

"She already has; she couldn't do anything else. The love between us is too strong, too beautiful. I couldn't let something that wonderful die, not when I had a chance to see it renewed."

"You used me. You crazy bitch, you used me. You had a lover before Vanstone. That's why you let me come here; to make the conditions for Althaea as close as possible to your time."

"Of course I did. As you used us to escape whatever it was you were fleeing. Althaea had to learn the difference between a meaningless sexual infatuation and the true love which only Mullen can provide."

"Crazy bitch! You can't dictate her life like this."

"But it's *my* life. And you know she doesn't belong to you. You saw the effect Mullen had on her, and her on him." She smiled, distant with recollection. "Just like me and my Vanstone. He sneaked back to Charmaine from his parish, you know. Only he did it on a regular trader."

"It's different this time," he snarled. "This time, I'm here. She loves me, I know she does."

Tiarella started to put her hand out towards him, then drew back. "Oh, Eason, I never meant for you to get hurt. What the hell is someone like you doing falling in love anyway?"

"Someone like me?"

"Yes. I thought you were perfect when you turned up at the harbour. A thug on the run; selfish and iron-hearted. Why couldn't you treat her the way you treated everyone else in your life?"

He glared at her, helpless against her sympathy, then ran from the laboratory.

"Don't touch her!" Tiarella shouted after him. "I mean it. You leave her alone."

• • •

Eason didn't need the warning. It was obvious within hours that he'd lost. Althaea and Mullen were so besotted with each other it was scary. The one person he'd ever loved was gloriously happy, and anything he did to stop that happiness would make her hate him for ever.

He didn't know whether to call it destiny or history.

They went to bed together on the second night, the two of them bounding up the stairs after supper. Althaea was in front, carefree and eager.

He watched them go, remembering that night after the funeral, the wretched difference. Tiarella was watching him, her face showing compassion.

"If it means anything, I am sorry," she said.

"Right." He rose and went out into the gloaming. Rousseau's stock of despicable home-brew was where he'd left it.

Althaea found him the next morning, sitting on the jetty, looking down at the water. A few scraps of the dinghy's timbers were still wedged between the coral spikes.

She settled down beside him, her face anxious. "Are you all right?"

"Sure. I'm just amazed Ross survived as long as he did. That stuff really is dangerous."

"Eason. Mullen and I are going to get married."

"Tough decision, was it?"

"Don't. Please."

"OK. I'm happy for you."

"No, you're not."

"What the hell else can I say?"

She stared out across the ocean. "I'm almost frightened of myself, the way I'm behaving. I know how stupid this is, I've only known him for two days. But I feel it's right. Is it?"

"Know what I think."

"Tell me."

"I think that your body is the focus for your mind on this journey. It's guided you home through an awful lot of fog, and now it's time to make a safe landing."

"Thank you, Eason."

He put a finger under her chin, and turned her head to face him. "I want to know one thing. And I want you to be completely honest. Did you ever love me?"

"Of course I did."

• • •

Tiarella gave him a quizzical glance as he came into the kitchen and flopped down at the table.

"You'll be happy to hear I'm leaving," he announced.

Her blatant relief made him laugh bitterly.

"I'm not that heartless," she protested.

"Oh, yes you are."

"*Orphée* and I will take you wherever you want to go."

"How very conscientious of you; but it's not that simple."

"What do you mean?" The old suspicion resonated through the question.

"I've thought this through. Wherever I am, I will always think of Althaea. You know that. Which means you and I will always worry that I might come back. Because I know

I'll never be able to trust myself, not completely. So what I propose is that I go somewhere that I can't come back from. I'll pay you to take me there, give Charmaine a proper contract to maintain the ride. God knows you can do with the money despite all those ridiculous ideals of yours; it'll be a nice dependable income for Althaea and Mullen to start with, too."

"What are you talking about? Where do you want to go?"

"The future."

* * *

The zero-tau field was nothing more than a grey eyeblink. An eyeblink that was giddily disorientating. The laboratory instantly changed to a dark, cool room with an uneven polyp ceiling.

Where Tiarella was leaning over him to switch on the pod a moment before, another figure now straightened up as her finger left the control panel. They looked at each other suspiciously. The girl was about twenty, undoubtedly related to Althaea. He could never mistake that fragile, narrow chin; her skin was ebony, though, with flaming red hair trimmed to a curly bob. Geneering trends had changed a lot, apparently.

"Hi," he said.

She managed a strong echo of Althaea's shy grin. "I never quite believed it," she said. "The man in the basement. You're a family legend. When we were little Dad told us you were like a sleeping knight ready to defend Charmaine from evil. Then after I grew up I just thought they were using the zero-tau pod to store botanical samples or something."

"I'm afraid I'm not a knight, nothing like." He swung his feet out of the pod, and stepped down. The floor was raw coral. Large cases and plastic boxes were stacked up all around. "Where am I?"

"The basement. Oh, I know what you're thinking. They dismantled the old lab fifty or sixty years ago. The family has membership in an agronomy consortium back on Kariwak. They provide upgrades for Charmaine's groves these days." She gestured at the stairs.

"What's the date?"

"April nineteenth, 2549."

"Jesus Christ, a hundred and two years. Is the Confederation still intact?"

"Oh yes." She gave him an awkward grimace. "Mr Eason, Grandma's waiting."

"Grandma?" he asked cautiously.

"Althaea."

He stopped at the foot of the stairs. "That wasn't the deal."

"I know. She says she'll understand if you want to jump back into the pod for another few days. She doesn't have long to live, Mr Eason."

He nodded thoughtfully. "Always knew what she wanted, did Althaea. I never said no to her back then."

The girl smiled, and they started up the stairs.

"So you're her granddaughter, are you?"

"Great-great-granddaughter, actually."

"Ah."

He recognized the layout of the house, but nothing more. It was full of rich furnishings and expensive artwork. Too grand for his taste.

Althaea was in the master bedroom. It was painful for him to look at her. Two minutes ago she'd been a radiant seventeen-year-old a week from her wedding day.

"Almost made a hundred and twenty," she said from her bed. Her chuckle became a thin cough.

He bent over and kissed her. Small black plastic patches were clinging to the side of her wrinkled neck. He could see the outline of more beneath her shawl.

"Still want to fight dragons for me?" she asked.

"'Fraid not. I was rather impressed by that great-great-granddaughter of yours."

She laughed and waved him into a seat beside the bed. "You haven't changed. Mind you, you haven't had the time."

"How's Mullen?"

"Oh, him. Been gone five years, now."

"I'm sorry."

"We had a century together. That's why I wanted to see you again. I wanted to thank you."

"What for?"

"For doing what you did. For leaving us alone." She tilted her head towards the open window. "I loved him, you know. All the time he was alive, and even now, a whole century of love. It was an excellent life, Eason, truly excellent. Oh, I wasn't a saint; I had my share of fooling around when I was younger, so did he. But we stayed together for a hundred years. How about that?"

"I'm glad."

"I lied to you about the children. Remember the day after you arrived I said I wanted ten."

"I remember."

"Course you do; it's only been two months for you. Well, I only had eight."

"That's a shame."

"Yes. But, ah, what they achieved. Take a look." She flicked a pale finger at the window. "Go on."

So he did. And there was his dream waiting outside. The neat ordered ranks of fruit trees stretching right round the island, a fleet of tractors buzzing down the grassy avenues, and Edenist-style servitor chimps scampering through the branches in search of the bright globes. The red-clay rooftops of a small fishing village; boats bobbing at their moorings along the seven jetties. People walking and cycling everywhere. Adults and children setting up tables and parasols in the garden ready for a party. And, as ever, the firedrakes, noisy flocks of them spiralling and wheeling overhead.

"That's all thanks to you," she said. "I don't know what would have happened if you'd stayed around. I was so torn. I loved Mullen for a century, but I kept the guilt, too."

"It's beautiful," he said.

"You can stay if you want. I'd like you to enjoy it."

"No. My time here is over."

"Ha! That's Mother talking."

"She told you?"

"Oh yes. Mind you, I never told Mullen. It was too weird."

"She was right, though, wasn't she? You two were made for each other."

"Yes, damn her, she was right. But that guilt always made me wonder."

• • • •

It was called the Torreya Memorial Clinic, a mansion sitting astride the foothills above Kariwak. Long since converted from a private residence, its main wings provided free health care for the city's poor. Of course, such charity was expensive, so the foundation which ran it also provided first-class treatment for those who could afford it. As well as standard medical facilities there was an excellent rejuvenation centre, and for those who wished to give their offspring the best start in life, a geneering department.

Eason waited for Dr Kengai to complete his credit checks, remembering the last time he was in an office, facing down agent Tenvis. The doctor had a much better view over Kariwak than the old Kulu Embassy provided. Although the city was much the same size as it had been a century ago, he was disappointed to see the number of skyscrapers that had sprung up. The sequoias were still there along the central boulevard, and prospering, tall green spires waving gently high above the clutter of white buildings.

"Your financial status appears quite impeccable, Mr Eason," Dr Kengai said happily.

Eason grinned back with equal sincerity. "Thank you. And you'll have no trouble providing the service I want?"

"A parthenogenetic clone is a relatively straightforward procedure. It poses no difficulty."

"Good." He unclipped the silver chain around his neck, and handed over the locket. "Is there sufficient genetic material here?"

Dr Kengai removed the tuft of gold-auburn hair it contained. "You could reproduce several million of her from this." He teased a single strand loose, and returned the locket.

"I only want one," Eason said.

"I understand you don't intend to raise the girl yourself?"

"That is correct. I'm going to be away travelling again for a few more years, my ride isn't quite finished."

"Unfortunately, we do have to reassure ourselves that the child will have a viable home to go to once she is removed from the exowomb. The clinic is not in the business of producing orphans."

"Don't worry. My lawyer is currently seeking a suitable set of foster parents. A trust fund will pay for her to be brought up out in the archipelago for seventeen years."

"Then what will happen to her?"

"I'll come back, and she'll marry me. That's when she loves me, you see."

Timeline

2550 . . . Mars declared habitable by Terraforming office.

2580 . . . Dorado asteroids discovered around Tunja, claimed by both Garissa and Omuta.

2581 . . . Omutan mercenary fleet drops twelve antimatter planet-busters on Garissa, planet rendered uninhabitable. Confederation imposes thirty-year sanction against Omuta, prohibiting any interstellar trade or transport. Blockade enforced by Confederation Navy.

2582 . . . Colony established on Lalonde.

Escape Route

Marcus Calvert glanced at the figures displayed on the account block, and tried not to make his relief too obvious. The young waitress wasn't so diplomatic when she read the amount he'd shunted over from his Jovian Bank credit disk and saw he hadn't included a tip. She turned briskly and headed back to the *Lomaz* bar, heels clicking their disapproval on the metal decking.

It was one of life's more embarrassing ironies that the owner of a multi-million fuseodollar starship didn't actually have any spare cash. Marcus raised his beer bottle ruefully to his two crew-members sitting at the table with him. "Cheers."

Bottle necks were clinked together.

Marcus took a long drink, and tried not to grimace at the taste. Cheap beer was the same the Confederation over. He was quite an expert on the subject now.

Roman Zucker, the *Lady Macbeth*'s fusion engineer, shot a mournful look at the row of elegant bottles arranged behind the bar. The *Lomaz* had an impressive selection of expensive imported beers and spirits. "I've tasted worse."

"You'll taste a lot better once we get our cargo charter," said Katherine Maddox, the ship's node specialist. "Any idea what it is, Captain?"

"The agent didn't say; apart from confirming it's private, not corporate."

"They don't want us for combat, do they?" Katherine

asked. There was a hint of rebellion in her voice. She was in her late forties, and like the Calverts her family had ge-neered their offspring to withstand both free fall and high acceleration. The dominant modifications had given her thicker skin, tougher bones, and harder internal membranes; she was never sick or giddy in free fall, nor did her face bloat up. Such changes were a formula for blunt features, and Katherine was no exception.

"If they do, we're not taking it," Marcus assured her.

Katherine exchanged an unsettled glance with Roman, and slumped back in her chair.

The combat option was one Marcus had considered re-grettably possible. *Lady Macbeth* was combat-capable, and Sonora asteroid belonged to a Lagrange-point cluster with a strong autonomy movement. An unfortunate combination. But having passed his sixty-seventh birthday two months ago he sincerely hoped those kind of flights were behind him. His present crew deserved better, too. He owed them ten weeks' back pay, and not one of them had pressed him for it yet. They had faith in him to deliver. He was deter-mined not to let them down.

Part of his predicament was due to the ruinous cost of cryogenic fuels these days. Starflight was not a cheap ven-ture, consuming vast quantities of energy. Maintenance, too, cut savagely into profit margins. Flying to Sonora without a cargo had been a severe financial blow. It was a position Marcus had constantly reacquainted himself with through-out his career; the galaxy didn't exactly shower favours on independent starships.

"This could be them," Roman said, glancing over the rail. One of Sonora's little taxi boats was approaching their big resort raft.

Marcus had never seen an asteroid cavern quite like this one before. The centre of the gigantic rock had been hol-lowed out by mining machines, producing a cylindrical cavity twelve kilometres long, five in diameter. Usually the floor would be covered in soil and planted with fruit trees and grass. In Sonora's case, the environmental engineers had simply flooded it. The result was a small freshwater sea that no matter where you were on it, you appeared to be at the bottom of a valley of water.

Floating around the grey surface were innumerable rafts, occupied by hotels, bars, and restaurants. Taxi boats whizzed between them and the wharfs at the base of the two flat cavern walls. The trim cutter curving round towards the *Lomaz* had two people sitting on its red leather seats.

Marcus watched with interest as they left the taxi. He ordered his neural nanonics to open a fresh memory cell, and stored the pair of them in a visual file. The first to alight was a man in his mid-thirties; a long face and a very broad nose gave him a kind of imposing dignity. He wore expensive casual clothes, an orange jacket and turquoise trousers, with a bright scarlet sash that was this year's fashion on Avon.

His partner was less flamboyant. She was in her late twenties, obviously geneered; Oriental features matched with white hair that had been drawn together in wide dreadlocks and folded back aerodynamically. Her slate-grey office suit and prim movements made her appear formidably unsympathetic.

They walked straight over to Marcus's table, and introduced themselves as Antonio Ribeiro and Victoria Keef. Antonio clicked his fingers at the waitress, who took her time sauntering over. Her mood swung when Antonio slapped down a local 5,000 peso note on her tray and told her to fetch a bottle of Norfolk Tears.

"Hopefully to celebrate the success of our business venture, my friends," he said. "And if not, it is a pleasant time of day to imbibe such a magical potion. No?"

Marcus found himself immediately distrustful. It wasn't just Antonio's phoney attitude; his intuition was scratching

away at the back of his skull. Some friends called it his paranoia program, but it was rarely wrong. A family trait, like
the wanderlust which no geneering treatment had ever erad-
icated.

"Any time of day will do for me," Roman said.

Antonio smiled brightly at him.

"The cargo agent said you had a charter for us," Marcus
said. "He never mentioned any sort of business deal."

"If I may ask your indulgence for a moment, Captain
Calvert. You arrived here without a cargo. You must be a
very rich man to afford that."

"There were . . . circumstances requiring us to leave Ayacucho ahead of schedule."

"Yeah," Katherine muttered darkly. "Her husband."

Marcus was expecting it, and smiled serenely. He'd heard
very little else from the crew for the whole flight.

Antonio received the tray and its precious pear-shaped
bottle from the waitress, and waved away the change. She
gave him a coy smile, eyes flashing gamely.

"If I may be indelicate, Captain, your financial resources
are not optimum at this moment," Antonio suggested.

"They've been better. But I'm not desperate. Any financial institution would fall over themselves to advance me a
loan against my next charter if I asked them for it."

Antonio handed him a glass. "And yet you don't. Why is
that, Captain?"

"I might not have a good cash flow, but I'm hardly bankrupt. I own *Lady Mac*, and it took me a long time to achieve
that. That means I fly her as I want to, how she's meant to
be flown. I've taken her on scouting missions beyond the
Confederation boundaries to find new terracompatible planets, risked my own money on cargos, and even piloted her
into battle for dubious causes. If I want commercial
drudgery I'll sign on with a line company. Which is what I'd
be doing if I took out a loan."

"Bravo, Captain!" Antonio raised his glass in salute. "May the grey men be consigned to hell for all eternity." He sipped his Norfolk Tears, and grinned in appreciation. "For myself, I was born with the wrong amount of money. Enough to know I needed more."

"Mr Ribeiro, I've heard all the get-rich-quick schemes in existence. They all have one thing in common, they don't work. If they did, I wouldn't be sitting here with you."

"You are wise to be cautious, Captain. I was, too, when I first heard this proposal. However, if you would humour me a moment longer, I can assure you this requires no capital outlay on your part. At the worst you will have another mad scheme to laugh about with your fellow captains."

"No money at all?"

"None at all, simply the use of your ship. We would be equal partners sharing whatever reward we find."

"Jesus. All right, I can spare you five minutes. Your drink has bought you that much attention span."

"Thank you, Captain. My colleagues and I want to fly the *Lady Macbeth* on a prospecting mission."

"For planets?" Roman asked curiously.

"No. Sadly, the discovery of a terracompatible planet does not guarantee wealth. Settlement rights will not bring more than a couple of million fuseodollars, and even that is dependent on a favourable biospectrum assessment, which would take many years. We have something more immediate in mind. You have just come from the Dorados?"

"That's right," Marcus said. The system had been discovered six years earlier, comprising a red-dwarf sun surrounded by a vast disc of rocky particles. Several of the larger chunks had turned out to be nearly pure metal. Dorados was an obvious name; whoever managed to develop them would gain a colossal economic resource. So much so that the governments of Omuta and Garissa had gone to war over who had that development right.

It was the Garissan survivors who had ultimately been awarded settlement by the Confederation Assembly. There weren't many of them. Omuta had deployed twelve anti-matter planet-busters against their homeworld. "Is that what you're hoping to find, another flock of solid metal asteroids?"

"Not quite," Antonio said. "Companies have been searching similar disc systems ever since the Dorados were discovered, to no avail. Victoria, my dear, if you would care to explain."

She nodded curtly and put her glass down on the table. "I'm an astrophysicist by training," she said. "I used to work for Mitchell-Courtney; it's a company based in the O'Neill Halo that manufactures starship sensors, although their speciality is survey probes. It's been a very healthy business recently. For the last five years commercial consortiums, Adamist governments, and the Edenists have all been flying survey missions through every catalogued disc system in the Confederation. As Antonio said, none of our clients found anything remotely like the Dorados. That didn't surprise me, I never expected any of Mitchell-Courtney's probes to be of much use. All our sensors did was run broad spectroscopic sweeps. If anyone was going to find another Dorados cluster it would be the Edenists. Their voidhawks have a big advantage; those ships generate an enormous distortion field which can literally see mass. A lump of metal fifty kilometres across would have a very distinct density signature; they'd be aware of it from at least half a million kilometres away. If we were going to compete against that, we'd need a sensor which gave us the same level of results, if not better."

"And you produced one?" Marcus enquired.

"Not quite. I proposed expanding our magnetic anomaly detector array. It's a very ancient technology; Earth's old nations pioneered it during the twentieth century. Their military maritime aircraft were equipped with crude arrays to track enemy submarines. Mitchell-Courtney builds its array into low-orbit resource-mapping satellites; they produce quite valuable survey data. Unfortunately, the company turned down my proposal. They said an expanded magnetic array wouldn't produce better results than a spectroscopic sweep, not on the scale required. And a spectroscopic scan would be quicker."

"Unfortunate for Mitchell-Courtney," Antonio said wolfishly. "Not for us. Dear Victoria came to me with her suggestion, and a simple observation."

"A spectrographic sweep will only locate relatively large pieces of mass," she said. "Fly a starship fifty million kilometres above a disc, and it can spot a fifty-kilometre lump of solid metal easily. But the smaller the lump, the higher the resolution you need or the closer you have to fly, a fairly obvious equation. My magnetic anomaly detector can pick out much smaller lumps of metal than a Dorado."

"So? If they're smaller, they're worth less," Katherine said. "The whole point of the Dorados is that they're huge. Believe me, I've been there and seen the operation those ex-Garissans are building up. They've got enough metal to supply their industrial stations with specialist microgee alloys for the next two thousand years. Small is no good."

"Not necessarily," Marcus said carefully. Maybe it was his intuition again, or just plain logical extrapolation, but he could see the way Victoria's thoughts were flowing. "It depends on what kind of small, doesn't it?"

Antonio applauded. "Excellent, Captain. I knew you were the right man for us."

"What makes you think they're there?" Marcus asked.

"The Dorados are the ultimate proof of concept," Victoria said. "There are two possible origins for disc material around stars. The first is accretion; matter left over from the star's formation. That's no use to us, it's mostly the light elements, carbonaceous chondritic particles with some silica aluminium thrown in if you're lucky. The second type of disc is made up out of collision debris. We believe that's what the Dorados are, fragments of planetoids that were large enough to form molten metal cores. When they broke apart the metal cooled and congealed into those hugely valuable chunks."

"But nickel iron wouldn't be the only metal," Marcus reasoned, pleased by the way he was following through. "There will be other chunks floating about in the disc."

"Exactly, Captain," Antonio said eagerly. "Theoretically, the whole periodic table will be available to us, we can fly above the disc and pick out whatever element we require. There will be no tedious and expensive refining process to extract it from ore. It's there waiting for us in its purest form; gold, silver, platinum, iridium. Whatever takes your fancy."

* * *

Lady Macbeth sat on a docking cradle in Sonora's spaceport, a simple dull-grey sphere fifty-seven metres in diameter. All Adamist starships shared the same geometry, dictated by the operating parameters of the ZTT jump, which required perfect symmetry. At her heart were four separate life-support capsules, arranged in a pyramid formation; there was also a cylindrical hangar for her spaceplane, a smaller one for her Multiple Service Vehicle, and five main cargo holds. The rest of her bulk was a solid intestinal tangle of machinery, generators, and tanks. Her main drive system was three fusion rockets capable of accelerating her at eleven gees, clustered round an antimatter intermix tube which could multiply that figure by an unspecified amount; a sure sign of her combat-capable status. (By a legislative quirk it wasn't actually illegal to have an antimatter drive, though possession of antimatter itself was a capital crime throughout the Confederation.)

Spaceport umbilical hoses were jacked into sockets on her lower hull, supplying basic utility functions. Another expense Marcus wished he could avoid; it was inflicting further pain on his already ailing cash flow situation. They were going to have to fly soon, and fate seemed to have decided what flight it would be. That hadn't stopped his intuition from maintaining its subliminal assault on Antonio Ribeiro's scheme. If he could just find a single practical or logical argument against it . . .

He waited patiently while the crew drifted into the main lounge in life-support capsule A. Wai Choi, the spaceplane pilot, came down through the ceiling hatch and used a stikpad to anchor her shoes to the decking. She gave Marcus a sly smile that bordered on teasing. There had been times in the last five years when she'd joined him in his cabin, nothing serious, but they'd certainly had their moments. Which, he supposed, made made her more tolerant of him than the others.

At the opposite end of the spectrum was Karl Jordan, the *Lady Mac*'s systems specialist, with the shortest temper, the greatest enthusiasm, and certainly the most serious of the crew. His age was the reason, only twenty-five; the *Lady Mac* was his second starship duty.

As for Schutz, who knew what emotions were at play in the cosmonik's mind; there was no visible outlet for them. Unlike Marcus, he hadn't been geneered for free fall; decades of working on ships and spaceport docks had seen his bones lose calcium, his muscles waste away, and his cardiovascular system atrophy. There were hundreds like him in every asteroid, slowly replacing their body parts with mechanical substitutes. Some even divested themselves of their human shape altogether. At sixty-three, Schutz was still humanoid, though only twenty per cent of him was biological. His body supplements made him an excellent engineer.

"We've been offered a joint prize flight," Marcus told them. He explained Victoria's theory about disc systems and the magnetic anomaly array. "Ribeiro will provide us with consumables and a full cryogenics load. All we have to do is take *Lady Mac* to a disc system and scoop up the gold."

"There has to be a catch," Wai said. "I don't believe in mountains of gold just drifting through space waiting for us to come along and find them."

"Believe it," Roman said. "You've seen the Dorados. Why can't other elements exist in the same way?"

"I don't know. I just don't think anything comes that easy."

"Always the pessimist."

"What do you think, Marcus?" she asked. "What does your intuition tell you?"

"About the mission, nothing. I'm more worried about Antonio Ribeiro."

"Definitely suspect," Katherine agreed.

"Being a total prat is socially unfortunate," Roman said. "But it's not a crime. Besides, Victoria Keef seemed level-headed enough."

"An odd combination," Marcus mused. "A wannabe playboy and an astrophysicist. I wonder how they ever got together."

"They're both Sonoran nationals," Katherine said. "I ran a check through the public data cores, they were born here. It's not that remarkable."

"Any criminal record?" Wai asked.

"None listed. Antonio has been in court three times in the last seven years; each case was over disputed taxes. He paid every time."

"So he doesn't like the taxman," Roman said. "That makes him one of the good guys."

"Run-ins with the tax office are standard for the rich," Wai said.

"Except he's not actually all that rich," Katherine said. "I also queried the local Collins Media library; they keep tabs on Sonora's principal citizens. Mr Ribeiro senior made his money out of fish breeding, he won the franchise from the asteroid development corporation to keep the biosphere sea stocked. Antonio was given a fifteen per cent stake in the breeding company when he was twenty-one, which he promptly sold for an estimated eight hundred thousand fuseodollars. Daddy didn't approve, there are several news files on the quarrel; it became very public."

"So he is what he claims to be," Roman said. "A not very rich boy with expensive tastes."

"How can he pay for the magnetic detectors we have to deploy, then?" Wai asked. "Or is he going to hit us with the bill and suddenly vanish?"

"The detector arrays are already waiting to be loaded on board," Marcus said. "Antonio has several partners; people in the same leaky boat as himself, and willing to take a gamble."

Wai shook her head, still dubious. "I don't buy it. It's a free lunch."

"Victoria Keef's star disc formation theory sounds plausible, and they're willing to invest their own money in the array hardware. What other guarantees do you want?"

"What kind of money are we talking about, exactly?" Karl asked. "I mean, if we do fill the ship up, what's it going to be worth?"

"Given its density, *Lady Mac* can carry roughly five thousand tonnes of gold in her cargo holds," Marcus said. "That'll make manoeuvring very sluggish, but I can handle her."

Roman grinned at Karl. "And today's price for gold is three and a half thousand fuseodollars per kilogram."

Karl's eyes went blank for a second as his neural nanonics ran the conversion. "Seventeen billion fuseodollars' worth!"

He laughed. "Per trip."

"How is this Ribeiro character proposing to divide the proceeds?" Schutz asked.

"We get one-third," Marcus said. "Roughly five-point-eight billion fuseodollars. Of which I take thirty per cent. The rest is split equally between you, as per the bounty flight clause in your contracts."

"Shit," Karl whispered. "When do we leave, Captain?"

"Does anybody have any objections?" Marcus asked. He gave Wai a quizzical look.

"OK," she said. "But just because you can't see surface cracks, it doesn't mean there isn't any metal fatigue."

•   •   •

The docking cradle lifted *Lady Macbeth* cleanly out of the spaceport's crater-shaped bay. As soon as she cleared the rim her thermo-dump panels unfolded, and sensor clusters rose up out of their recesses on long booms. Visual and radar information was collated by the flight computer, which datavised it directly into Marcus's neural nanonics. He lay on the acceleration couch at the centre of the bridge with his eyes closed as the external starfield blossomed in his mind. Delicate icons unfurled across the visualization, ship status schematics and navigational plots sketched in primary colours.

Chemical verniers fired, lifting *Lady Mac* off the cradle amid spumes of hot saffron vapour. A tube of orange circles appeared ahead of him, the course vector formatted to take them in towards the gas giant. Marcus switched to the more powerful ion thrusters, and the orange circles began to stream past the hull.

The gas giant, Zacateca, and its moon, Lazaro, had the

same apparent size as *Lady Mac* accelerated away from the spaceport. Sonora was one of fifteen asteroids captured by their Lagrange point, a zone where their respective gravity fields were in equilibrium. Behind the starship Lazaro was a grubby grey crescent splattered with white craters. Given that Zacateca was small for a gas giant, barely forty thousand kilometres in diameter, Lazaro was an unusual companion. A moon nine thousand kilometres in diameter, with an outer crust of ice fifty kilometres deep. It was that ice which had originally attracted the interest of the banks and multistellar finance consortia. Stony-iron asteroids were an ideal source of metal and minerals for industrial stations, but they were also notoriously short of the light elements essential to sustain life. To have abundant supplies of both so close together was a strong investment incentive.

Lady Mac's radar showed Marcus a serpentine line of one-tonne ice cubes flung out from Lazaro's equatorial mass driver to glide inertly up to the Lagrange point for collection. The same inexhaustible source which allowed Sonora to have its unique sea.

All the asteroids in the cluster had benefited from the plentiful ice, their economic growth racing ahead of equivalent settlements. Such success always bred resentment among the indigenous population, who inevitably became eager for freedom from the founding companies. In this case, having so many settlements so close together gave their population a strong sense of identity and shared anger. The cluster's demands for autonomy had become increasingly strident over the last few years. A situation agitated by numerous violent incidents and acts of sabotage against the company administration staff.

Ahead of the *Lady Mac*, Marcus could see the tidal hurricane Lazaro stirred up amid the wan amber and emerald stormbands of Zacateca's upper atmosphere. An ocean-sized hypervelocity maelstrom which followed the moon's orbit faithfully around the equator. Lightning crackled round its fringes, five hundred kilometre long forks stabbing out into the surrounding cyclones of ammonia cirrus and methane sleet.

The starship was accelerating at two gees now, her triple fusion drives sending out a vast streamer of arc-bright plasma as she curved around the bulk of the huge planet. Her course vector was slowly bending to align on the star which Antonio intended to prospect, thirty-eight light-years distant. There was very little information contained in the almanac file other than confirming it was a K-class star with a disc.

Marcus cut the fusion drives when the *Lady Mac* was seven thousand kilometres past perigee and climbing steadily. The thermo-dump panels and sensor clusters sank down into their jump recesses below the fuselage, returning the ship to a perfect sphere. Fusion generators began charging the energy-patterning nodes. Orange circles flashing through Marcus's mind were illustrating the slingshot parabola she'd flown, straightening up the further the planet was left behind. A faint star slid into the last circle.

An event horizon swallowed the starship. Five milliseconds later it had shrunk to nothing.

• • •

"OK, try this one," Katherine said. "Why should the gold or anything else congeal into lumps as big as the ones they say it will? Just because you've got a planetoid with a hot core doesn't mean it's producing the metallic equivalent of fractional distillation. You're not going to get an onion layer effect with strata of different metals. It doesn't happen on planets, it won't happen here. If there is gold, and platinum, and all the rest of this fantasy junk, it's going to be hidden away in ores just like it always is."

"So Antonio exaggerated when he said it would be pure," Karl retorted. "We just hunt down the highest-grade ore particles in the disc. Even if it's only fifty per cent, who cares? We're never going to be able to spend it all anyway."

Marcus let the discussion grumble on. It had been virtually the only topic for the crew since they'd departed Sonora five days ago. Katherine was playing the part of chief sceptic, with occasional support from Schutz and Wai, while the others tried to shoot her down. The trouble was, he acknowledged, that none of them knew enough to comment with real authority. At least they weren't talking about the sudden departure from Ayacucho any more.

"If the planetoids did produce ore, then it would fragment badly during the collision which formed the disc," Katherine said. "There won't even be any mountain-sized chunks left, only pebbles."

"Have you taken a look outside recently?" Roman asked. "The disc doesn't exactly have a shortage of large particles."

Marcus smiled to himself at that. The disc material had worried him when they arrived at the star two days ago. *Lady Mac* had jumped deep into the system, emerging three million kilometres above the ecliptic. It was a superb vantage point. The small orange star burnt at the centre of a disc a hundred and sixty million kilometres in diameter. There were no distinct bands like those found in a gas-giant's rings, this was a continuous grainy copper mist veiling half of the universe. Only around the star itself did it fade away; whatever particles were there to start with had long since evaporated to leave a clear band three million kilometres wide above the turbulent photosphere.

Lady Mac was accelerating away from the star at a twentieth of a gee, and curving round into a retrograde orbit. It was the vector which would give the magnetic arrays the best possible coverage of the disk. Unfortunately, it increased the probability of collision by an order of magnitude. So far, the radar had only detected standard motes of interplanetary dust, but Marcus insisted there were always two crew on duty monitoring the local environment.

"Time for another launch," he announced.

Wai datavised the flight computer to run a final systems diagnostic through the array satellite. "I notice Jorge isn't here again," she said sardonically. "I wonder why that is?"

Jorge Leon was the second companion Antonio had brought with him on the flight. He'd been introduced to the crew as a first-class hardware technician, who had supervised the construction of the magnetic array satellites. As introverted as Antonio was outgoing, he'd shown remarkably little interest in the arrays so far. It was Victoria who'd familiarized the crew with the systems they were deploying.

"We should bung him in our medical scanner," Karl suggested cheerfully. "Be interesting to see what's inside him. Bet you'd find a whole load of weapon implants."

"Great idea," Roman said. "You ask him. He gives me the creeps."

"Yeah, Katherine, explain that away," Karl said. "If there's no gold in the disc, how come they brought a contract killer along to make sure we don't fly off with their share?"

"Karl!" Marcus warned. "That's enough." He gave the open floor hatch a pointed look. "Now let's get the array launched, please."

Karl's face reddened as he began establishing a tracking link between the starship's communication system and the array satellite's transponder.

"Satellite systems on-line," Wai reported. "Launch when ready."

Marcus datavised the flight computer to retract the satellite's hold-down latches. An induction rail shot it clear of the ship. Ion thrusters flared, refining its trajectory as it headed down towards the squally apricot surface of the disc.

Victoria had designed the satellites to skim five thousand kilometres above the nomadic particles. When their operational altitude was established they would spin up and start to reel out twenty-five gossamer-thin optical fibres. Rotation insured the fibres remained straight, forming a spoke array parallel to the disc. Each fibre was a hundred and fifty kilometres long, and coated in a reflective, magnetically sensitive film.

As the disc particles were still within the star's magnetosphere, every one of them generated a tiny wake as it traversed the flux lines. It was that wake which resonated the magnetically sensitive film, producing fluctuations in the reflectivity. By bouncing a laser pulse down the fibre and measuring the distortions inflicted by the film, it was possible to build up an image of the magnetic waves writhing chaotically through the disc. With the correct discrimination programs, the origin of each wave could be determined.

The amount of data streaming back into the *Lady Macbeth* from the array satellites was colossal. One satellite array could cover an area of two hundred and fifty thousand square kilometres, and Antonio Ribeiro had persuaded the Sonora Autonomy Crusade to pay for fifteen. It was a huge gamble, and the responsibility was his alone. Forty hours after the first satellite was deployed, the strain of that responsibility was beginning to show. He hadn't slept since the first satellite launch, choosing to stay in the cabin which Marcus Calvert had assigned to them, and where they'd set up their network of analysis processors. Forty hours of his mind being flooded with near-incomprehensible neuroiconic displays. Forty hours spent fingering his silver crucifix and praying.

The medical monitor program running in his neural nanonics was flashing up fatigue toxin cautions, and warning him of impending dehydration. So far he'd ignored them, telling himself discovery would occur any minute now. In his heart, Antonio had been hoping they would find what they wanted in the first five hours.

His neural nanonics informed him the analysis network was focusing on the mass/density ratio of a three-kilometre particle exposed by satellite seven. The processors began a more detailed interrogation of the raw data.

"What is it?" Antonio demanded. His eyes fluttered open to glance at Victoria, who was resting lightly on one of the cabin's flatchairs.

"Interesting," she murmured. "It appears to be a cassiterite ore. The planetoids definitely had tin."

"Shit!" He thumped his fist into the chair's padding, only to feel the restraint straps tighten against his chest, preventing him from sailing free. "I don't fucking care about tin. That's not what we're here for."

"I am aware of that." Her eyes were open, staring at him with a mixture of contempt and anger.

"Sure, sure," he mumbled. "Holy Mother, you'd expect us to find some by now."

"Careful," she datavised. "Remember this damn ship has internal sensors."

"I know how to follow elementary security procedures," he datavised back.

"Yes. But you're tired. That's when errors creep in."

"I'm not that tired. Shit, I expected results by now; some progress."

"We have had some very positive results, Antonio. The arrays have found three separate deposits of pitchblende."

"Yeah, in hundred kilogram lumps. We need more than that, a lot more."

"You're missing the point. We've proved it exists here; that's a stupendous discovery. Finding it in quantity is just a matter of time."

"This isn't some fucking astrological experiment you're running for that university which threw you out. We're on an assignment for the cause. And we cannot go back empty-handed. Got that? Cannot."

"Astrophysics."

"What?"

"You said astrological, that's fortune-telling."

"Yeah? You want I should take a guess at how much future you're going to have if we don't find what we need out here?"

"For Christ's sake, Antonio," she said out loud. "Go and get some sleep."

"Maybe." He scratched the side of his head, unhappy with how limp and oily his hair had become. A vapour shower was something else he hadn't had for a while. "I'll get Jorge in here to help you monitor the results."

"Great." Her eyes closed again.

Antonio deactivated his flatchair's restraint straps. He hadn't seen much of Jorge on the flight. Nobody had. The man kept strictly to himself in his small cabin. The Crusade's council wanted him on board to ensure the crew's continuing cooperation once they realized there was no gold. It was Antonio who had suggested the arrangement; what bothered him was the orders Jorge had received concerning himself should things go wrong.

"Hold it." Victoria raised her hand. "This is a really weird one."

Antonio tapped his feet on a stikpad to steady himself. His neural nanonics accessed the analysis network again. Satellite eleven had located a particle with an impossible mass/density ratio; it also had its own magnetic field, a very complex one. "Holy Mother, what is that? Is there another ship here?"

"No, it's too big for a ship. Some kind of station, I suppose. But what's it doing in the disc?"

"Refining ore?" he said with a strong twist of irony.

"I doubt it."

"OK. So forget it."

"You are joking."

"No. If it doesn't affect us, it doesn't concern us."

"Jesus, Antonio; if I didn't know you were born rich I'd be frightened by how stupid you were."

"Be careful, Victoria, my dear. Very careful."

"Listen, there's two options. One, it's some kind of commercial operation; which must be illegal because nobody has filed for industrial development rights." She gave him a significant look.

"You think they're mining pitchblende?" he datavised.

"What else? We thought of the concept, why not one of the black syndicates as well? They just didn't come up with my magnetic array idea, so they're having to do it the hard way."

"Secondly," she continued aloud, "it's some kind of covert military station; in which case they saw us the moment we emerged. Either way, they will have us under observation. We have to know who they are before we proceed any further."

•   •   •

"A station?" Marcus asked. "Here?"

"It would appear so," Antonio said glumly.

"And you want us to find out who they are?"

"I think that would be prudent," Victoria said, "given what we're doing here."

"All right," Marcus said. "Karl, lock a communication dish on them. Give them our CAB identification code, let's see if we can get a response."

"Aye, sir," Karl said. He settled back on his acceleration couch.

"While we're waiting," Katherine said, "I have a question for you, Antonio."

She ignored the warning glare Marcus directed at her.

Antonio's bogus smile blinked on. "If it is one I can answer, then I will do so gladly, dear lady."

"Gold is expensive because of its rarity value, right?"

"Of course."

"So here we are, about to fill *Lady Mac*'s cargo holds with five thousand tonnes of the stuff. On top of that you've developed a method which means people can scoop up millions of tonnes any time they want. If we try and sell it to a dealer or a bank, how long do you think we're going to be billionaires for, a fortnight?"

Antonio laughed. "Gold has never been that rare. Its value is completely artificial. The Edenists have the greatest known stockpile. We don't know exactly how much they possess because the Jovian Bank will not declare the exact figure. But they dominate the commodity market, and sustain the price by controlling how much is released. We shall simply play the same game. Our gold will have to be sold discreetly, in small batches, in different star systems, and over the course of several years. And knowledge of the magnetic array system should be kept to ourselves."

"Nice try, Katherine," Roman chuckled. "You'll just have to settle for an income of a hundred million a year."

She showed him a stiff finger, backed by a shark's smile.

"No response," Karl said. "Not even a transponder."

"Which, technically, is illegal," Marcus said. "Though *Lady Mac*'s own transponder has been known to glitch at unfortunate moments."

"*Un*-fortunate?" Wai challenged.

"Keep trying, Karl," Marcus told him. "OK, Antonio, what do you want to do about it?"

"We have to know who they are," Victoria said. "As Antonio has just explained so eloquently, we can't have other people seeing what we're doing here."

"It's what they're doing here that worries me," Marcus

said; although, curiously, his intuition wasn't causing him any grief on the subject.

"I see no alternative but a rendezvous," Antonio said.

"We're in a retrograde orbit, thirty-two million kilometres away and receding. That's going to use up an awful lot of fuel."

"Which I believe I have already paid for."

"OK, your call. I'll start plotting a vector."

"What if they don't want us there?" Schutz asked.

"If we detect any combat-wasp launch, then we jump out-system immediately," Marcus said. "The disc's gravity field isn't strong enough to affect *Lady Mac*'s patterning-node symmetry. We can leave any time we want."

•   •   •

For the last quarter of a million kilometres of the approach, Marcus put the ship on combat status. The nodes were fully charged, ready to jump. Thermo-dump panels were retracted. Sensors maintained a vigilant watch for approaching combat wasps.

"They must know we're here," Wai said when they were eight thousand kilometres away. "Why don't they acknowledge us?"

"Ask them," Marcus said sourly. *Lady Mac* was decelerating at a nominal one gee, which he was varying at random. It made their exact approach vector impossible to predict, which meant their course couldn't be seeded with proximity mines. The manoeuvre took a lot of concentration.

"Still no electromagnetic emission in any spectrum," Karl reported. "They're certainly not scanning us with active sensors."

"Sensors are picking up their thermal signature," Schutz said. "The structure is being maintained at thirty-six degrees Celsius."

"That's on the warm side," Katherine observed. "Perhaps their environmental system is malfunctioning."

"Shouldn't affect the transponder," Karl said.

"Captain, I think you'd better access the radar return," Schutz said.

Marcus boosted the fusion drives up to one and a half gees, and ordered the flight computer to datavise him the radar feed. The image which rose into his mind was of a fine scarlet mesh suspended in the darkness, its gentle ocean-swell pattern outlining the surface of the station and the disc particle it was attached to. Except Marcus had never seen any station like this before. It was a gently curved wedge-shaped structure, four hundred metres long, three hundred wide, and a hundred and fifty metres at its blunt end. The accompanying disc particle was a flattened ellipsoid of stony iron rock measuring eight kilometres along its axis. The tip had been sheered off, leaving a flat cliff half a kilometre in diameter, to which the structure was clinging. That was the smallest of the particle's modifications. A crater four kilometres across, with perfectly smooth walls, had been cut into one side of the rock. An elaborate unicorn-horn tower rose nine hundred metres from its centre, ending in a clump of jagged spikes.

"Oh, Jesus," Marcus whispered. Elation mingled with fear, producing a deviant adrenalin high. He smiled thinly. "How about that?"

"This was one option I didn't consider," Victoria said weakly.

Antonio looked round the bridge, a frown cheapening his handsome face. The crew seemed dazed, while Victoria was grinning with delight. "Is it some kind of radio astronomy station?" he asked.

"Yes," Marcus said. "But not one of ours. We don't build like that. It's xenoc."

Lady Mac locked attitude a kilometre above the xenoc

structure. It was a position which made the disc appear uncomfortably malevolent. The smallest particle beyond the
fuselage must have massed over a million tonnes; and all of
them were moving, a slow, random three-dimensional cruise
of lethal inertia. Amber sunlight stained those near the disc's
surface a baleful ginger, while deeper in there were only
phantom silhouettes drifting over total blackness, flowing in
and out of visibility. No stars were evident through the dark,
tightly packed nebula.

"That's not a station," Roman declared. "It's a ship-
wreck."

Now that *Lady Mac*'s visual-spectrum sensors were providing them with excellent images of the xenoc structure,
Marcus had to agree. The upper and lower surfaces of the
wedge were some kind of silver-white material, a fuselage
shell which was fraying away at the edges. Both of the side
surfaces were dull brown, obviously interior bulkhead walls,
with the black geometrical outline of decking printed across
them. The whole structure was a cross-section torn out of a
much larger craft. Marcus tried to fill in the missing bulk in
his mind; it must have been vast, a streamlined delta fuselage like a hypersonic aircraft. Which didn't make a lot of
sense for a starship. Rather, he corrected himself, for a starship built with current human technology. He wondered
what it would be like to fly through interstellar space the
way a plane flew through an atmosphere, swooping round
stars at a hundred times the speed of light. Quite something.

"This doesn't make a lot of sense," Katherine said. "If
they were visiting the telescope dish when they had the accident, why did they bother to anchor themselves to the asteroid? Surely they'd just take refuge in the operations
centre."

"Only if there is one," Schutz said. "Most of our deep
space science facilities are automated, and by the look of it
their technology is considerably more advanced."

"If they are so advanced, why would they build a radio telescope on this scale anyway?" Victoria asked. "It's very impractical. Humans have been using linked baseline arrays for centuries. Five small dishes orbiting a million kilometres apart would provide a reception which is orders of magnitude greater than this. And why build it here? Firstly, the particles are hazardous, certainly to something that size. You can see it's been pocked by small impacts, and that horn looks broken to me. Secondly, the disc itself blocks half of the universe from observation. No, if you're going to do major radio astronomy, you don't do it from a star system like this one."

"Perhaps they were only here to build the dish," Wai said. "They intended it to be a remote research station in this part of the galaxy. Once they had it up and running, they'd boost it into a high-inclination orbit. They had their accident before the project was finished."

"That still doesn't explain why they chose this system. Any other star would be better than this one."

"I think Wai's right about them being long-range visitors," Marcus said. "If a xenoc race like that existed close to the Confederation we would have found them by now. Or they would have contacted us."

"The Kiint," Karl said quickly.

"Possibly," Marcus conceded. The Kiint were an enigmatic xenoc race, with a technology far in advance of anything the Confederation had mastered. However, they were reclusive, and cryptic to the point of obscurity. They also claimed to have abandoned starflight a long time ago. "If it is one of their ships, then it's very old."

"And it's still functional," Roman said eagerly. "Hell, think of the technology inside. We'll wind up a lot richer than the gold could ever make us." He grinned over at Antonio, whose humour had blackened considerably.

"So what were the Kiint doing building a radio telescope here?" Victoria asked.

"Who the hell cares?" Karl said. "I volunteer to go over, Captain."

Marcus almost didn't hear him. He'd accessed the *Lady Mac*'s sensor suite again, sweeping the focus over the tip of the dish's tower, then the sheer cliff which the wreckage was attached to. Intuition was making a lot of junctions in his head. "I don't think it is a radio telescope," he said. "I think it's a distress beacon."

"It's four kilometres across!" Katherine said.

"If they came from the other side of the galaxy, it would need to be. We can't even see the galactic core from here there's so much gas and dust in the way. You'd need something this big to punch a message through."

"That's valid," Victoria said. "You believe they were signalling their homeworld for help?"

"Yes. Assume their world is a long way off, three or four thousand light-years away if not more. They're flying a research or survey mission in this area and they have an accident. Three-quarters of their ship is lost, including the drive section. Their technology isn't good enough to build the survivors a working stardrive out of what's left, but they can enlarge an existing crater on the disc particle. So they do that; they build the dish and a transmitter powerful enough to give God an alarm call, point it at their homeworld, and scream for help. The ship can sustain them until the rescue team arrives. Even our own zero-tau technology is up to that."

"Gets my vote," Wai said, giving Marcus a wink.

"No way," said Katherine. "If they were in trouble they'd use a supralight communicator to call for help. Look at that ship, we're centuries away from building anything like it."

"Edenist voidhawks are pretty sophisticated," Marcus countered. "We just scale things differently. These xenocs might have a more advanced technology, but physics is still the same the universe over. Our understanding of quantum relativity is good enough to build faster than light starships, yet after four hundred and fifty years of theoretical research we still haven't come up with a method of supralight communication. It doesn't exist."

"If they didn't return on time, then surely their homeworld would send out a search and recovery craft," Schutz said.

"They'd have to know the original ship's course exactly," Wai said. "And if a search ship did manage to locate them, why did they build the dish?"

Marcus didn't say anything. He knew he was right. The others would accept his scenario eventually, they always did.

"All right, let's stop arguing about what happened to them, and why they built the dish," Karl said. "When do we go over there, Captain?"

"Have you forgotten the gold?" Antonio asked. "That is why we came to this disc system. We should resume our search for it. This piece of wreckage can wait."

"Don't be crazy. This is worth a hundred times as much as any gold."

"I fail to see how. An ancient, derelict starship with a few heating circuits operational. Come along. I've been reasonable indulging you, but we must return to the original mission."

Marcus regarded the man cautiously, a real bad feeling starting to develop. Anyone with the slightest knowledge of finance and the markets would know the value of salvaging a xenoc starship. And Antonio had been born rich. "Victoria," he said, not shifting his gaze, "is the data from the magnetic array satellites still coming through?"

"Yes." She touched Antonio's arm. "The Captain is right.

We can continue to monitor the satellite results from here, and investigate the xenoc ship simultaneously."

"Double your money time," Katherine said with apparent innocence.

Antonio's face hardened. "Very well," he said curtly. "If that's your expert opinion, Victoria, my dear. Carry on by all means, Captain."

• • •

In its inert state the SII spacesuit was a broad sensor collar with a protruding respirator tube and a black football-sized globe of programmable silicon hanging from it. Marcus slipped the collar round his neck, bit on the tube nozzle, and datavised an activation code into the suit's control processor. The silicon ball began to change shape, flattening out against his chest, then flowing over his body like a tenacious oil slick. It enveloped his head completely, and the collar sensors replaced his eyes, datavising their vision directly into his neural nanonics. Three others were in the preparation compartment with him: Schutz, who didn't need a spacesuit to EVA, Antonio, and Jorge. Marcus had managed to control his surprise when they'd volunteered. At the same time, with Wai flying the MSV he was glad they weren't going to be left behind in the ship.

Once his body was sealed by the silicon, he climbed into an armoured exoskeleton with an integral cold-gas manoeuvring pack. The SII silicon would never puncture, but if he was struck by a rogue particle the armour would absorb the impact.

When the airlock's outer hatch opened, the MSV was floating fifteen metres away. Marcus datavised an order into his manoeuvring pack processor, and the gas jets behind his shoulder fired, pushing him towards the small egg-shaped vehicle. Wai extended two of the MSV's three waldo arms in greeting. Each of them ended in a simple metal grid, with a pair of boot clamps on both sides.

Once all four of her passengers were locked into place, Wai piloted the MSV in towards the disc. The rock particle had a slow, erratic tumble, taking a hundred and twenty hours to complete its cycle. As she approached, the flattish surface with the dish was just turning into the sunlight. It was a strange kind of dawn, the rock's crumpled grey brown crust speckled by the sharp black shadows of its own rolling prominences, while the dish was a lake of infinite black, broken only by the jagged spire of the horn rising from its centre. The xenoc ship was already exposed to the amber light, casting its bloated sundial shadow across the featureless glassy cliff. She could see the ripple of different ores and mineral strata frozen below the glazed surface, deluding her for a moment that she was flying towards a mountain of cut and polished onyx.

Then again, if Victoria's theory was right, she could well be.

"Take us in towards the top of the wedge," Marcus datavised. "There's a series of darker rectangles there."

"Will do," she responded. The MSV's chemical thrusters pulsed in compliance.

"Do you see the colour difference near the frayed edges of the shell?" Schutz asked. "The stuff's turning grey. It's as if the decay is creeping inwards."

"They must be using something like our molecular-binding-force generators to resist vacuum ablation," Marcus datavised. "That's why the main section is still intact."

"It could have been here for a long time, then."

"Yeah. We'll know better once Wai collects some samples from the tower."

There were five rectangles arranged in parallel, one and a half metres long and one metre wide. The shell material below the shorter edge of each one had a set of ten grooves leading away down the curve.

"They look like ladders to me," Antonio datavised. "Would that mean these are airlocks?"

"It can't be that easy," Schutz replied.

"Why not?" Marcus datavised. "A ship this size is bound to have more than one airlock."

"Yeah, but five together?"

"Multiple redundancy."

"With technology this good?"

"That's human hubris. The ship still blew up, didn't it?"

Wai locked the MSV's attitude fifty metres above the shell section. "The micro-pulse radar is bouncing right back at me," she informed them. "I can't tell what's below the shell, it's a perfect electromagnetic reflector. We're going to have communication difficulties once you're inside."

Marcus disengaged his boots from the grid and fired his pack's gas jets. The shell was as slippery as ice, neither stik-pads nor magnetic soles would hold them to it.

"Definitely enhanced valency bonds," Schutz datavised. He was floating parallel to the surface, holding a sensor block against it. "It's a much stronger field than *Lady Mac*'s. The shell composition is a real mix; the resonance scan is picking up titanium, silicon, boron, nickel, silver, and a whole load of polymers."

"Silver's weird," Marcus commented. "But if there's nickel in it our magnetic soles should work." He manoeuvred himself over one of the rectangles. It was recessed about five centimetres, though it blended seamlessly into the main shell. His sensor collar couldn't detect any seal lining. Halfway along one side were two circular dimples, ten centimetres across. Logically, if the rectangle was an airlock, then these should be the controls. Human back-ups were kept simple. This shouldn't be any different.

Marcus stuck his fingers in one. It turned bright blue.

"Power surge," Schutz datavised. "The block's picking up several high-voltage circuits activating under the shell. What did you do, Marcus?"

"Tried to open one."

The rectangle dilated smoothly, material flowing back to the edges. Brilliant white light flooded out.

"Clever," Schutz datavised.

"No more than our programmable silicon," Antonio retorted.

"We don't use programmable silicon for external applications."

"It settles one thing," Marcus datavised. "They weren't Kiint, not with an airlock this size."

"Quite. What now?"

"We try to establish control over the cycling mechanism. I'll go in and see if I can operate the hatch from inside. If it doesn't open after ten minutes, try the dimple again. If that doesn't work, cut through it with the MSV's fission blade."

The chamber inside was thankfully bigger than the hatch: a pentagonal tube two metres wide and fifteen long. Four of the walls shone brightly, while the fifth was a strip of dark-maroon composite. He drifted in, then flipped himself over so he was facing the hatch, floating in the centre of the chamber. There were four dimples just beside the hatch. "First one," he datavised. Nothing happened when he put his fingers in. "Second." It turned blue. The hatch flowed shut.

Marcus crashed down onto the strip of dark composite, landing on his left shoulder. The force of the impact was almost enough to jar the respirator tube out of his mouth. He grunted in shock. Neural nanonics blocked the burst of pain from his bruised shoulder.

Jesus! They've got artificial gravity.

He was flat on his back, the exoskeleton and manoeuvring pack weighing far too much. Whatever planet the xenocs came from, it had a gravity field about one and a half times that of Earth. He released the catches down the side of his exoskeleton, and wriggled his way out. Standing was an effort, but he was used to higher gees on *Lady Mac*; admittedly not for prolonged periods, though.

He stuck his fingers in the first dimple. The gravity faded fast, and the hatch flowed apart.

"We just became billionaires," he datavised.

The third dimple pressurized the airlock chamber; the fourth depressurized it.

The xenoc atmosphere was mostly a nitrogen/oxygen blend, with one per cent argon and six per cent carbon dioxide. The humidity was appalling, pressure was lower than standard, and the temperature was forty-two degrees Celsius.

"We'd have to keep our SII suits on anyway, because of the heat," Marcus datavised. "But the carbon dioxide would kill us. And we'll have to go through biological decontamination when we go back to *Lady Mac*."

The four of them stood together at the far end of the airlock chamber, their exoskeleton armour lying on the floor behind them. Marcus had told Wai and the rest of the crew their first foray would be an hour.

"Are you proposing we go in without a weapon?" Jorge asked.

Marcus focused his collar sensors on the man who alleged he was a hardware technician. "Jesus. That's carrying paranoia too far. No, we do not engage in first contact either deploying or displaying weapons of any kind. That's the law, and the Assembly regulations are very specific about it. In any case, don't you think that if there are any xenocs left after all this time they're going to be glad to see someone? Especially a spacefaring species."

"That is, I'm afraid, a rather naive attitude, Captain. You keep saying how advanced this starship is, and yet it suffered catastrophic damage. Frankly, an unbelievable amount of damage for an accident. Isn't it more likely this ship was engaged in some kind of battle?"

Which was a background worry Marcus had suffered right from the start. That this starship could ever fail was unnerving. But like physical constants, Murphy's Law would be the same the universe over. He'd entered the airlock because intuition told him the wreck was safe for him personally. Somehow he doubted a man like Jorge would be convinced by that argument.

"If it's a warship, then it will be rigged to alert any surviving crew or flight computer of our arrival. Had they wanted to annihilate us, they would have done so by now. *Lady Mac* is a superb ship, but hardly in this class. So if they're waiting for us on the other side of this airlock, I don't think any weapon you or I can carry is going to make the slightest difference."

"Very well, proceed."

Marcus postponed the answer which came straight to mind, and put his fingers in one of the two dimples by the inner hatchway. It turned blue.

The xenoc ship wasn't disappointing, exactly, but Marcus couldn't help a growing sense of anticlimax. The artificial gravity was a fabulous piece of equipment, the atmosphere strange, the layout exotic. Yet for all that, it was just a ship; built from the universal rules of logical engineering. Had the xenocs themselves been there, it would have been so different. A whole new species with its history and culture. But they'd gone, so he was an archaeologist rather than an explorer.

They surveyed the deck they had emerged onto, which was made up from large compartments and broad hallways. Marcus could just walk about without having to stoop, there was a gap of a few centimetres between his head and the ceiling. The interior was made out of a pale-jade composite, slightly ruffled to a snakeskin texture. Surfaces always curved together, there were no real corners. Every ceiling emitted the same intense white glare, which their collar sensors compensated for. Arching doorways were all open, though they could still dilate if you used the dimples. The only oddity was fifty-centimetre hemispherical blisters on the floor and walls, scattered completely at random.

There was an ongoing argument about the shape of the xenocs. They were undoubtedly shorter than humans, and they probably had legs, because there were spiral stairwells, although the steps were very broad, difficult for bipeds. Lounges had long tables with large rounded stool-chairs inset with four deep ridges.

After the first fifteen minutes it was clear that all loose equipment had been removed. Lockers, with the standard dilating door, were empty. Every compartment had its fitted furnishings and nothing more. Some were completely bare.

On the second deck there were no large compartments, only long corridors lined with grey circles along the centre of the walls. Antonio used a dimple at the side of one, and it dilated to reveal a spherical cell three metres wide. Its walls were translucent, with short lines of colour slithering round behind them like photonic fish.

"Beds?" Schutz suggested. "There's an awful lot of them."

Marcus shrugged. "Could be." He moved on, eager to get down to the next deck. Then he slowed, switching his collar focus. Three of the hemispherical blisters were following him, two gliding along the wall, one on the floor. They stopped when he did. He walked over to the closest, and waved his sensor block over it. "There's a lot of electronic activity inside it," he reported.

The others gathered round.

"Are they extruded by the wall, or are they a separate device?" Schutz asked.

Marcus switched on the block's resonance scan. "I'm not

sure, I can't find any break in the composite round its base, not even a hairline fracture; but with their materials technology that doesn't mean much."

"Five more approaching," Jorge datavised. The blisters were approaching from ahead, three of them on the walls, two on the floor. They stopped just short of the group.

"Something knows we're here," Antonio datavised.

Marcus retrieved the CAB nexus interface communication protocol from a neural nanonics memory cell. He'd stored it decades ago, all qualified starship crew were obliged to carry it along with a million and one other bureaucratic lunacies. His communication block transmitted the protocol using a multi-spectrum sweep. If the blister could sense them, it had to have some kind of electromagnetic reception facility. The communication block switched to laserlight, then a magnetic pulse.

"Nothing," Marcus datavised.

"Maybe the central computer needs time to interpret the protocol," Schutz datavised.

"A desktop block should be able to work that out."

"Perhaps the computer hasn't got anything to say to us."

"Then why send the blisters after us?"

"They could be autonomous, whatever they are."

Marcus ran his sensor block over the blister again, but there was no change to its electronic pattern. He straightened up, wincing at the creak of complaint his spine made at the heavy gravity. "OK, our hour is almost up anyway. We'll get back to *Lady Mac* and decide what stage two is going to be."

The blisters followed them all the way back to the stairwell they'd used. As soon as they started walking down the broad central hallway of the upper deck, more blisters started sliding in from compartments and other halls to stalk them.

The airlock hatch was still open when they got back, but the exoskeletons were missing.

"Shit," Antonio datavised. "They're still here, the bloody xenocs are here."

Marcus shoved his fingers into the dimple. His heartbeat calmed considerably when the hatch congealed behind them. The lock cycled obediently, and the outer rectangle opened.

"Wai," he datavised. "We need a lift. Quickly, please."

"On my way, Marcus."

"Strange way for xenocs to communicate," Schutz datavised. "What did they do that for? If they wanted to make sure we stayed, they could have disabled the airlock."

The MSV swooped over the edge of the shell, jets of twinkling flame shooting from its thrusters.

"Beats me," Marcus datavised. "But we'll find out."

* * *

Marcus called his council of war five hours later, once everyone had a chance to wash, eat, and rest. Opinion was a straight split: the crew wanted to continue investigating the xenoc ship, Antonio and his colleagues wanted to leave. For once Jorge had joined them, which Marcus considered significant. He was beginning to think young Karl might have been closer to the truth than was strictly comfortable.

"The dish is just rock with a coating of aluminium sprayed on," Katherine said. "There's very little aluminium left now, most of it has boiled away. The tower is a pretty ordinary silicon/boron composite wrapped round a titanium load structure. The samples Wai cut off were very brittle."

"Did you carbon-date them?" Victoria asked.

"Yeah." She gave her audience a laboured glance. "Give or take a decade, it's thirteen thousand years old."

Breath whistled out of Marcus's mouth. "Jesus."

"Then they must have been rescued, or died," Roman said. "There's nobody left over there. Not after that time."

"They're there," Antonio growled. "They stole our exoskeletons."

"I don't understand what happened to the exoskeletons. Not yet. But any entity who can build a ship like that isn't going to go creeping round stealing bits of space armour. There has to be a rational explanation."

"Yes! They wanted to keep us over there."

"What for? What possible reason would they have for that?"

"It's a warship, it's been in battle. The survivors don't know who we are, if we're their old enemies. If they kept us there, they could study us and find out."

"After thirteen thousand years, I imagine the war will be over. And where did you get this battleship idea from anyway?"

"It's a logical assumption," Jorge said quietly.

Roman turned to Marcus. "My guess is that some kind of mechanoid picked them up. If you look in one of the lockers you'll probably find them neatly stored away."

"Some automated systems are definitely still working," Schutz said. "We saw the blisters. There could be others."

"That seems the most remarkable part of it," Marcus said. "Especially now we know the age of the thing. The inside of that ship was brand new. There wasn't any dust, any scuff marks. The lighting worked perfectly, so did the gravity, the humidity hasn't corroded anything. It's extraordinary. As if the whole structure has been in zero-tau. And yet only the shell is protected by the molecular-bonding-force generators. They're not used inside, not in the decks we examined."

"However they preserve it, they'll need a lot of power for the job, and that's on top of gravity generation and environmental maintenance. Where's that been coming from uninterrupted for thirteen thousand years?"

"Direct mass-to-energy conversion," Katherine speculated. "Or they could be tapping straight into the sun's fusion. Whatever, bang goes the Edenist He^3 monopoly."

"We have to go back," Marcus said.

"NO!" Antonio yelled. "We must find the gold first. When that has been achieved, you can come back by yourselves. I won't allow anything to interfere with our priorities."

"Look, I'm sorry you had a fright while you were over there. But a power supply that works for thirteen thousand years is a lot more valuable than a whole load of gold which we have to sell furtively," Katherine said levelly.

"I hired this ship. You do as I say. We go after the gold."

"We're partners, actually. I'm not being paid for this flight unless we strike lucky. And now we have. We've got the xenoc ship, we haven't got any gold. What does it matter to you how we get rich, as long as we do? I thought money was the whole point of this flight."

Antonio snarled at her, and flung himself at the floor hatch, kicking off hard with his legs. His elbow caught the rim a nasty crack as he flashed through it.

"Victoria?" Marcus asked as the silence became strained. "Have the satellite arrays found any heavy metal particles yet?"

"There are definitely traces of gold and platinum, but nothing to justify a rendezvous."

"In that case, I say we start to research the xenoc wreck properly." He looked straight at Jorge. "How about you?"

"I think it would be prudent. You're sure we can continue to monitor the array satellites from here?"

"Yes."

"Good. Count me in."

"Thanks. Victoria?"

She seemed troubled by Jorge's response, even a little bewildered, but she said: "Sure."

"Karl, you're the nearest thing we've got to a computer expert. I want you over there trying to make contact with whatever control network is still operating."

"You got it."

"From now on we go over in teams of four. I want sensors put up to watch the airlocks when we're not around, and I want some way of communicating with people inside. Start thinking. Wai, you and I are going to secure *Lady Mac* to the side of the shell. OK, let's get active, people."

• • •

Unsurprisingly, none of the standard astronautics industry vacuum epoxies worked on the shell. Marcus and Wai wound up using tether cables wrapped round the whole of the xenoc ship to hold *Lady Mac* in place.

Three hours after Karl went over, he asked Marcus to join him.

Lady Mac's main airlock tube had telescoped out of the hull to rest against the shell. There was no way it could ever be mated to the xenoc airlock rectangle, but it did allow the crew to transfer over directly without having to use exoskeleton armour and the MSV. They'd also run an optical fibre through the xenoc airlock to the interior of the ship. The hatch material closed around it forming a perfect seal, rather than slicing it in half.

Marcus found Karl just inside the airlock, sitting on the decking with several processor blocks in his lap. Eight blisters were slowly circling round him; two on the wall were stationary.

"Roman was almost right," he datavised as soon as Marcus stepped out of the airlock. "Your exoskeletons were cleared away. But not by any butler mechanoid. Watch." He lobbed an empty recording flek case onto the floor behind the blisters. One of them slid over to it. The green composite became soft, then liquid. The little plastic case sank through it into the blister.

"I call them cybermice," Karl datavised. "They just scurry around keeping the place clean. You won't see the exoskeletons again, they ate them, along with anything else they don't recognize as part of the ship's structure. I imagine they haven't tried digesting us yet because we're large and active; maybe they think we're friends of the xenocs. But I wouldn't want to try sleeping over here."

"Does this mean we won't be able to put sensors up?"

"Not for a while. I've managed to stop them digesting the communication block which the optical fibre is connected to."

"How?"

He pointed to the two on the wall. "I shut them down."

"Jesus, have you accessed a control network?"

"No. Schutz and I used a micro SQUID on one of the cybermice to get a more detailed scan of its electronics. Once we'd tapped the databus traffic it was just a question of running standard decryption programs. I can't tell you how these things work, but I have found some basic command routines. There's a deactivation code which you can datavise to them. I've also got a reactivation code, and some directional codes. The good news is that the xenoc program language is standardized." He stood and held a communication block up to the ceiling. "This is the deactivation code." A small circle of the ceiling around the block turned dark. "It's only localized, I haven't worked out how to control entire sections yet. We need to trace the circuitry to find an access port."

"Can you turn it back on again?"

"Oh yes." The dark section flared white again. "The codes

work for the doors as well; just hold your block over the dimples."

"Be quicker to use the dimples."

"For now, yes."

"I wasn't complaining, Karl. This is an excellent start. What's your next step?"

"I want to access the next level of the cybermice program architecture. That way I should be able to load recognition patterns in their memory. Once I can do that I'll enter our equipment, and they should leave it alone. But that's going to take a long time; *Lady Mac* isn't exactly heavily stocked with equipment for this kind of work. Of course, once I do get deeper into their management routines we should be able to learn a lot about their internal systems. From what I can make out the cybermice are built around a molecular synthesizer." He switched on a fission knife, its ten-centimetre blade glowing a pale yellow under the ceiling's glare. It scored a dark smouldering scar in the composite.

A cybermouse immediately slipped towards the blemish. This time when the composite softened the charred granules were sucked down, and the small valley closed up.

"Exactly the same thickness and molecular structure as before," Karl datavised. "That's why the ship's interior looks brand new, and everything's still working flawlessly after thirteen thousand years. The cybermice keep regenerating it. Just keep giving them energy and a supply of mass and there's no reason this ship won't last for eternity."

"It's almost a von Neumann machine, isn't it?"

"Close. I expect a synthesizer this small has limits. After all, if it could reproduce anything, they would have built themselves another starship. But the principle's here, Captain. We can learn and expand on it. Think of the effect a unit like this will have on our manufacturing industry."

Marcus was glad he was in an SII suit, it blocked any giveaway facial expressions. Replicator technology would be a true revolution, restructuring every aspect of human society, Adamist and Edenist alike. And revolutions never favoured the old.

I just came here for the money, not to destroy a way of life for eight hundred star systems.

"That's good, Karl. Where did the others go?"

"Down to the third deck. Once we solved the puzzle of the disappearing exoskeletons, they decided it was safe to start exploring again."

"Fair enough, I'll go down and join them."

• • • •

"I cannot believe you agreed to help them," Antonio stormed. "You of all people. You know how much the cause is depending on us."

Jorge gave him a hollow smile. They were together in his sleeping cubicle, which made it very cramped. But it was one place on the starship he knew for certain no sensors were operational; a block he'd brought with him had made sure of that. "The cause has become dependent on your project. There's a difference."

"What are you talking about?"

"Those detector satellites cost us a million and a half fuseodollars each; and most of that money came from sources who will require repayment no matter what the outcome of our struggle."

"The satellites are a hell of a lot cheaper than antimatter."

"Indeed so. But they are worthless to us unless they find pitchblende."

"We'll find it. Victoria says there are plenty of traces. It's only a question of time before we get a big one."

"Maybe. It was a good idea, Antonio, I'm not criticizing. Fusion bomb components are not easily obtainable to a novice political organization with limited resources. One mistake, and the intelligence agencies would wipe us out. No, old-fashioned fission was a viable alternative. Even if we couldn't process the uranium up to weapons quality, we can still use it as a lethal large-scale contaminate. As you say, we couldn't lose. Sonora would gain independence, and we would form the first government, with full access to Treasury. Everyone would be reimbursed for their individual contribution to the liberation."

"So why are we fucking about in a pile of xenoc junk? Just back me up, Jorge, please. Calvert will leave it alone if we both pressure him."

"Because, Antonio, this piece of so-called xenoc junk has changed the rules of the game. In fact we're not even playing the same game any more. Gravity generation, an inexhaustible power supply, molecular synthesis, and if Karl can access the control network he might even find the blueprints to build whatever stardrive they used. Are you aware of the impact such a spectrum of radical technologies will have upon the Confederation when released all together? Entire industries will collapse from obsolescence overnight. There will be an economic depression the like of which we haven't seen since before the invention of the ZTT drive. It will take decades for the human race to return to the kind of stability we enjoy today. We will be richer and stronger because of it; but the transition years, ah . . . I would not like to be a citizen in an asteroid settlement that has just blackmailed the founding company into premature independence. Who is going to loan an asteroid such as that the funds to re-equip our industrial stations, eh?"

"I . . . I hadn't thought of that."

"Neither has the crew. Except for Calvert. Look at his face next time you talk to him, Antonio. He knows, he has reasoned it out, and he's seen the end of his captaincy and freedom. The rest of them are lost amid their dreams of exorbitant wealth."

"So what do we do?"

Jorge clamped a hand on Antonio's shoulder. "Fate has smiled on us, Antonio. This was registered as a joint venture flight. No matter we were looking for something different. By law, we are entitled to an equal share of the xenoc technology. We are already trillionaires, my friend. When we get home we can *buy* Sonora asteroid; Holy Mother, we can buy the entire Lagrange cluster."

Antonio managed a smile, which didn't quite correspond with the dew of sweat on his forehead. "OK, Jorge. Hell, you're right. We don't have to worry about anything any more. But . . ."

"Now what?"

"I know we can pay off the loan on the satellites, but what about the Crusade council? They won't like this. They might—"

"There's no cause for alarm. The council will never trouble us again. I maintain that I am right about the disaster which destroyed the xenoc ship. It didn't have an accident. That is a warship, Antonio. And you know what that means, don't you? Somewhere on board there will be weapons just as advanced and as powerful as the rest of its technology."

•   •   •

It was Wai's third trip over to the xenoc ship. None of them spent more than two hours at a time inside. The gravity field made every muscle ache, walking round was like being put on a crash exercise regimen.

Schutz and Karl were still busy by the airlock, probing the circuitry of the cybermice, and decrypting more of their programming. It was probably the most promising line of research; once they could use the xenoc program language they should be able to extract any answer they wanted from the ship's controlling network. Assuming there was one. Wai was convinced there would be. The number of systems operating—life-support, power, gravity—had to mean some basic management integration system was functional.

In the meantime there was the rest of the structure to explore. She had a layout file stored in her neural nanonics, updated by the others every time they came back from an excursion. At the blunt end of the wedge there could be anything up to forty decks, if the spacing was standard. Nobody had gone down to the bottom yet. There were some areas which had no obvious entrance; presumably engineering compartments, or storage tanks. Marcus had the teams tracing the main power lines with magnetic sensors, trying to locate the generator.

Wai plodded after Roman as he followed a cable running down the centre of a corridor on the eighth deck.

"It's got so many secondary feeds it looks like a fishbone," he complained. They paused at a junction with five branches and he swept the block round. "This way." He started off down one of the new corridors.

"We're heading towards stairwell five," she told him, as the layout file scrolled through her skull.

There were more cybermice than usual on deck eight; over thirty were currently pursuing her and Roman, creating strong ripples in the composite floor and walls. Wai had noticed that the deeper she went into the ship the more of them there seemed to be. Although after her second trip she'd completely ignored them. She wasn't paying a lot of attention to the compartments leading off from the corridors, either. It wasn't that they were all the same, rather that they were all similarly empty.

They reached the stairwell, and Roman stepped inside. "It's going down," he datavised.

"Great, that means we've got another level to climb up when we're finished."

Not that going down these stairs was easy, she acknowledged charily. If only they could find some kind of variable gravity chute. Perhaps they'd all been positioned in the part of the ship that was destroyed.

"You know, I think Marcus might have been right about the dish being an emergency beacon," she datavised. "I can't think of any other reason for it being built. Believe me, I've tried."

"He always is right. It's bloody annoying, but that's why I fly with him."

"I was against it because of the faith gap."

"Say what?"

"The amount of faith these xenocs must have had in themselves. It's awesome. So different from humans. Think about it. Even if their homeworld is only two thousand light-years away, that's how long the message is going to take to reach there. Yet they sent it believing someone would still be around to receive it, and more, act on it. Suppose that was us; suppose the *Lady Mac* had an accident a thousand light-years away. Would you think there was any point in sending a lightspeed message to the Confederation, then going into zero-tau to wait for a rescue ship?"

"If their technology can last that long, then I guess their civilization can, too."

"No, our hardware can last for a long time. It's our culture that's fragile, at least compared to theirs. I don't think the Confederation will last a thousand years."

"The Edenists will be here, I expect. So will all the planets, physically if nothing else. Some of their societies will advance, possibly even to a state similar to the Kiint; some will revert to barbarism. But there will be somebody left to hear the message and help."

"You're a terrible optimist."

They arrived at the ninth deck, only to find the doorway was sealed over with composite.

"Odd," Roman datavised. "If there's no corridor or compartment beyond, why put a doorway here at all?"

"Because this was a change made after the accident."

"Could be. But why would they block off an interior section?"

"I've no idea. You want to keep going down?"

"Sure. I'm optimistic enough not to believe in ghosts lurking in the basement."

"I really wish you hadn't said that."

The tenth deck had been sealed off as well.

"My legs can take one more level," Wai datavised. "Then I'm going back."

There was a door on deck eleven. It was the first one in the ship to be closed.

Wai stuck her fingers in the dimple, and the door dilated. She edged over cautiously, and swept the focus of her collar sensors round. "Holy shit. We'd better fetch Marcus."

• • •

Decks nine and ten had simply been removed to make the chamber. Standing on the floor and looking up, Marcus could actually see the outline of the stairwell doorways in the wall above him. By xenoc standards it was a cathedral. There was only one altar, right in the centre. A doughnut of some dull metallic substance, eight metres in diameter with a central aperture five metres across; the air around it was emitting a faint violet glow. It stood on five sable-black arching buttresses, four metres tall.

"The positioning must be significant," Wai datavised. "They built it almost at the centre of the wreck. They wanted to give it as much protection as possible."

"Agreed," Katherine replied. "They obviously considered it important. After a ship has suffered this much damage, you don't expend resources on anything other than critical survival requirements."

"Whatever it is," Schutz reported, "it's using up an awful lot of power." He was walking round it, keeping a respectful distance, wiping a sensor block over the floor as he went. "There's a power cable feeding each of those legs."

"Is it radiating in any spectrum?" Marcus asked.

"Only that light you can see, which spills over into ultraviolet, too. Apart from that, it's inert. But the energy must be going somewhere."

"OK." Marcus walked up to a buttress, and switched his collar focus to scan the aperture. It was veiled by a grey haze, as if a sheet of fog had solidified across it. When he took another tentative step forward the fluid in his semicircular canals was suddenly affected by a very strange tidal force. His foot began to slip forwards and upwards. He threw himself backwards, and almost stumbled. Jorge and Karl just caught him in time.

"There's no artificial gravity underneath it," he datavised. "But there's some kind of gravity field wrapped around it." He paused. "No, that's not right. It pushed me."

"Pushed?" Katherine hurried to his side. "Are you sure?"

"Yes."

"My God."

"What? Do you know what it is?"

"Possibly. Schutz, hang on to my arm, please."

The cosmonik came forward and took her left arm. Katherine edged forward until she was almost under the lambent doughnut. She stretched up her right arm, holding out a sensor block, and tried to press it against the doughnut. It was as if she was trying to make two identical magnetic poles touch. The block couldn't get to within twenty centimetres of the surface, it kept slithering and sliding through the air. She held it as steady as she could, and datavised it to run an analysis of the doughnut's molecular structure.

The results made her back away.

"So?" Marcus asked.

"I'm not entirely sure it's even solid in any reference frame we understand. That surface could just be a boundary effect. There's no spectroscopic data at all, the sensor couldn't even detect an atomic structure in there, let alone valency bonds."

"You mean it's a ring of energy?"

"Don't hold me to it, but I think that thing could be some kind of exotic matter."

"Exotic in what sense, exactly?" Jorge asked.

"It has a negative energy density. And before you ask, that doesn't mean anti-gravity. Exotic matter only has one known use, to keep a wormhole open."

"Jesus, that's a wormhole portal?" Marcus asked.

"It must be."

"Any way of telling where it leads?"

"I can't give you an exact stellar coordinate; but I know where the other end has to emerge. The xenocs never called for a rescue ship, Marcus. They threaded a wormhole with exotic matter to stop it collapsing, and escaped down it. That is the entrance to a tunnel which leads right back to their homeworld."

•　•　•

Schutz found Marcus in the passenger lounge in capsule C. He was floating centimetres above one of the flatchairs, with the lights down low.

The cosmonik touched his heels to a stikpad on the decking beside the lower hatch. "You really don't like being wrong, do you?"

"No, but I'm not sulking about it, either." Marcus moulded a jaded grin. "I still think I'm right about the dish, but I don't know how the hell to prove it."

"The wormhole portal is rather conclusive evidence."

"Very tactful. It doesn't solve anything, actually. If they could open a wormhole straight back home, why did they build the dish? Like Katherine said, if you have an accident of that magnitude then you devote yourself completely to survival. Either they called for help, or they went home through the wormhole. They wouldn't do both."

"Possibly it wasn't their dish, they were just here to investigate it."

"Two ancient unknown xenoc races with FTL starship technology is pushing credibility. It also takes us back to the original problem: if the dish isn't a distress beacon, then what the hell was it built for?"

"I'm sure there will be an answer at some time."

"I know, we're only a commercial trader's crew, with a very limited research capability. But we can still ask fundamental questions, like why have they kept the wormhole open for thirteen thousand years?"

"Because that's the way their technology works. They probably wouldn't consider it odd."

"I'm not saying it shouldn't work for that long, I'm asking why their homeworld would bother maintaining a link to a chunk of derelict wreckage?"

"That is harder for logic to explain. The answer must lie in their psychology."

"That's too much like a cop-out; you can't cry alien at everything you don't understand. But it does bring us to my final query. If you can open a wormhole with such accuracy across God knows how many light-years, why would you need a starship in the first place? What sort of psychology accounts for that?"

"All right, Marcus, you got me. Why?"

"I haven't got a clue. I've been reviewing all the file texts we have on wormholes, trying to find a solution which pulls all this together. And I can't do it. It's a complete paradox."

"There's only one thing left, then, isn't there?"

Marcus turned to look at the hulking figure of the cosmonik. "What?"

"Go down the wormhole and ask them."

"Yeah, maybe I will. Somebody has to go eventually. What does our dear Katherine have to say on that subject? Can we go inside it in our SII suits?"

"She's rigging up some sensors that she can shove through the interface. That grey sheet isn't a physical barrier. She's already pushed a length of conduit tubing through. It's some kind of pressure membrane, apparently, stops the ship's atmosphere from flooding into the wormhole."

"Another billion-fuseodollar gadget. Jesus, this is getting too big for us, we're going to have to prioritize." He datavised the flight computer, and issued a general order for everyone to assemble in capsule A's main lounge.

* * *

Karl was the last to arrive. The young systems engineer looked exhausted. He frowned when he caught sight of Marcus.

"I thought you were over in the xenoc ship."

"No."

"But you . . ." He rubbed his fingers against his temples. "Skip it."

"Any progress?" Marcus asked.

"A little. From what I can make out, the molecular synthesizer and its governing circuitry are combined within the same crystal lattice. To give you a biological analogy, it's as though a muscle is also a brain."

"Don't follow that one through too far," Roman called.

Karl didn't even smile. He took a chocolate sac from the dispenser, and sucked on the nipple.

"Katherine?" Marcus said.

"I've managed to place a visual-spectrum sensor in the wormhole. There's not much light in there, only what soaks through the pressure membrane. From what we can see it's a straight tunnel. I assume the xenocs cut off the artificial gravity under the portal so they could egress it easily. What I'd like to do next is dismount a laser radar from the MSV and use that."

"If the wormhole's threaded with exotic matter, will you get a return from it?"

"Probably not. But we should get a return from whatever is at the other end."

"What's the point?"

Three of them began to talk at once, Katherine loudest of all. Marcus held his hand up for silence. "Listen, everybody, according to Confederation law if the appointed commander or designated controlling mechanism of a spaceship or free-flying space structure discontinues that control for one year and a day then any ownership title becomes null and void. Legally, this xenoc ship is an abandoned structure which we are entitled to file a salvage claim on."

"There is a controlling network," Karl said.

"It's a sub-system," Marcus said. "The law is very clear on that point. If a starship's flight computer fails, but, say, the fusion generators keep working, their governing processors do not constitute the designated controlling mechanism. Nobody will be able to challenge our claim."

"The xenocs might," Wai said.

"Let's not make extra problems for ourselves. As the situation stands right now, we have title. We can't not claim the ship because the xenocs may or may not return at some time."

Katherine rocked her head in understanding. "If we start examining the wormhole they might come back, sooner rather than later. Is that what you're worried about?"

"It's a consideration, yes. Personally, I'd rather like to meet them. But, Katherine, are you really going to learn how to build exotic matter and open a wormhole with the kind of sensor blocks we've got?"

"You know I'm not, Marcus."

"Right. Nor are we going to find the principle behind the artificial-gravity generator, or any of the other miracles on board. What we have to do in ontologue as much as we can, and identify the areas that need researching. Once we've done that we can bring back the appropriate specialists, pay them a huge salary, and let them get on with it. Don't any of you understand yet? When we found this ship, we stopped being starship crew, and turned into the highest-flying corporate executives in the galaxy. We don't pioneer any more, we designate. So, we map out the last remaining decks. We track the power cables and note what they power. Then we leave."

"I know I can crack their program language, Marcus," Karl said. "I can get us into the command network."

Marcus smiled at the weary pride in his voice. "Nobody is going to be more pleased about that than me, Karl. One thing I do intend to take with us is a cybermouse, preferably more than one. That molecular synthesizer is the hard evidence we need to convince the banks of what we've got."

Karl blushed. "Uh, Marcus, I don't know what'll happen if we try and cut one out of the composite. So far we've been left alone; but if the network thinks we're endangering the ship, well . . ."

"I'd like to think we're capable of something more sophisticated than ripping a cybermouse out of the composite. Hopefully, you'll be able to access the network, and we can simply ask it to replicate a molecular synthesizer unit for us. They have to be manufactured somewhere on board."

"Yeah, I suppose they do. Unless the cybermice duplicate themselves."

"Now that'd be a sight," Roman said happily. "One of them humping away on top of the other."

•   •   •

His neural nanonics time function told Karl he'd slept for nine hours. After he wriggled out of his sleep pouch he air-swam into the crew lounge and helped himself to a pile of food sachets from the galley. There wasn't much activity in the ship, so he didn't even bother to access the flight computer until he'd almost finished eating.

Katherine was on watch when he dived into the bridge through the floor hatch.

"Who's here?" he asked breathlessly. "Who else is on board right now?"

"Just Roman. The rest of them are all over on the wreck. Why?"

"Shit."

"Why, what's the matter?"

"Have you accessed the flight computer?"

"I'm on watch, of course I'm accessing."

"No, not the ship's functions. The satellite analysis network Victoria set up."

Her flat features twisted into a surprised grin. "You mean they've found some gold?"

"No, no fucking way. The network was reporting that satellite three had located a target deposit three hours ago. When I accessed the network direct to follow it up I found out what the search parameters really are. They're not looking for gold, those bastards are here to get pitchblende."

"Pitchblende?" Katherine had to run a search program through her neural nanonics encyclopedia to find out what it was. "Oh Christ, uranium. They want uranium."

"Exactly. You could never mine it from a planet without the local government knowing; that kind of operation would be easily spotted by the observation satellites. Asteroids don't have deposits of pitchblende. But planetoids do, and out here nobody is going to know that they're scooping it up."

"I knew it! I bloody knew that fable about gold mountains was a load of balls."

"They must be terrorists, or Sonoran independence fronkra, or black syndicate members. We have to warn the others, we can't let them back on board *Lady Mac*."

"Wait a minute, Karl. Yes, they're shits, but if we leave them over on the wreck they'll die. Even if you're prepared to do that, it's the Captain's decision."

"No it isn't, not any more. If they come back then neither you, me, nor the Captain is going to be in any position to make decisions about anything. They knew we'd find out about the pitchblende eventually when *Lady Mac* rendezvoused with the ore particle. They knew we wouldn't take it on board voluntarily. That means they came fully prepared to force us. They've got guns, or weapons implants. Jorge is exactly what I said he was, a mercenary killer. We can't let them back on the ship, Katherine. We can't."

"Oh, Christ." She was gripping the side of her acceleration couch in reflex. Command decision. And it was all hers.

"Can we datavise the Captain?" he asked.

"I don't know. We've got relay blocks in the stairwells now the cybermice have been deactivated, but they're not very reliable; the structure plays hell with our signals."

"Who's he with?"

"He was partnering Victoria. Wai and Schutz are together; Antonio and Jorge made up the last team."

"Datavise Wai and Schutz, get them out first. Then try for the Captain."

"OK. Get Roman, and go down to the airlock chamber; I'll authorize the weapons cabinet to release some maser carbines . . . Shit!"

"What?"

"I can't. Marcus has the flight computer command codes. We can't even fire the thrusters without him."

•   •   •

Deck fourteen appeared no different from any other as Marcus and Victoria wandered through it. The corridors were broad, and there were few doorways. None they did find were closed.

"About sixty per cent is sealed off," Marcus datavised. "This must be a major engineering level."

"Yeah. There's so many cables around here I'm having trouble cataloguing the grid." She was wiping a magnetic sensor block slowly from side to side as they walked.

His communication block reported it was receiving an encrypted signal from the *Lady Mac*. Sheer surprise made him halt. He retrieved the appropriate code file from a neural nanonics memory cell.

"Captain?"

"What's the problem, Katherine?"

"You've got to get back to the ship. Now, Captain, and make sure Victoria doesn't come with you."

"Why?"

"Captain, this is Karl. I accessed the analysis network; the satellites are looking for pitchblende, not gold or platinum. Antonio's people are terrorists, they want to build fission bombs."

Marcus focused his collar sensors on Victoria, who was waiting a couple of metres down the corridor. "Where's Schutz and Wai?"

"On their way back," Katherine datavised. "They should be here in another five minutes."

"OK, it's going to take me at least half an hour to get back." He didn't like to think about climbing fourteen flights of stairs fast, not in this gravity. "Start prepping the ship."

"Captain, Karl thinks they're probably armed."

Marcus's communication block reported another signal coming on-line.

"Karl is quite right," Jorge datavised. "We are indeed armed; and we also have excellent processor blocks and decryption programs. Really, Captain, this code of yours is at least three years out of date."

Marcus saw Victoria turn to face him. "Care to comment on the pitchblende?" he asked.

"I admit, the material would have been of some considerable use to us," Jorge replied. "But of course, this wreck has changed the Confederation beyond recognition, has it not, Captain?"

"Possibly."

"Definitely. And so we no longer require the pitchblende."

"That's a very drastic switch of allegiance."

"Please, Captain, do not be facetious. The satellites were left on purely for your benefit; we didn't wish to alarm you."

"Thank you for your consideration."

"Captain," Katherine datavised. "Schutz and Wai are in the airlock."

"I do hope you're not proposing to leave without us," Jorge datavised. "That would be most unwise."

"You were going to kill us," Karl datavised.

"That is a hysterical claim. You would not have been hurt."

"As long as we obeyed, and helped you slaughter thousands of people."

Marcus wished Karl would stop being quite so blunt. He had few enough options as it was.

"Come now, Captain," Jorge said. "The *Lady Macbeth* is

combat-capable; are you telling me you have never killed people in political disputes?"

"We've fought. But only against other ships."

"Don't try and claim the moral high ground, Captain. War is war, no matter how it is fought."

"Only when it's between soldiers; anything else is terrorism."

"I assure you, we have put our old allegiance behind us. I ask you to do the same. This quarrel is foolish in the extreme. We both have so much to gain."

And you're armed, Marcus filled in silently. Jorge and Antonio were supposed to be inspecting decks twelve and thirteen. It would be tough if not impossible getting back to the airlock before them. But I can't trust them on *Lady Mac*.

"Captain, they're moving," Katherine datavised. "The communication block in stairwell three has acquired them, strength one. They must be coming up."

"Victoria," Jorge datavised. "Restrain the Captain and bring him to the airlock. I advise all of you on the ship to remain calm, we can still find a peaceful solution to this situation."

Unarmed combat programs went primary in Marcus's neural nanonics. The black, featureless figure opposite him didn't move.

"Your call," he datavised. According to his tactical analysis program she had few choices. Jorge's order implied she was armed, though a scan of her utility belt didn't reveal anything obvious other than a standard fission blade. If she went for a gun he would have an attack window. If she didn't, then he could probably stay ahead of her. She was a lot younger, but his geneered physique should be able to match her in this gravity field.

Victoria dropped the sensor block she was carrying, and moved her hand to her belt. She grabbed the multipurpose power tool and started to bring it up.

Marcus slammed into her, using his greater mass to throw her off balance. She was hampered by trying to keep her grip on the tool. His impact made her sway sideways, then the fierce xenoc gravity took over. She toppled helplessly, falling fast. The power tool was swinging round to point at him. Marcus kicked her hand, and the unit skittered away. It didn't slide far, the gravity saw to that.

Victoria landed with a terrible thud. Her neural nanonics medical monitor program flashed up an alert that the impact had broken her collarbone. Axon blocks came on-line, muting all but the briefest pulse of pain. It was her programs again which made her twist round to avoid any follow-on blow, her conscious mind was almost unaware of the fact she was still moving. A hand scrabbled for the power tool. She snatched it and sat up. Marcus was disappearing down a side corridor. She fired at him before the targeting program even gave her an overlay grid.

"Jorge," she datavised. "I've lost him."

"Then get after him."

Marcus's collar sensors showed him a spray of incendiary droplets fizzing out of the wall barely a metre behind him. The multipurpose tool must be some kind of laser pistol. "Katherine," he datavised. "Retract *Lady Mac*'s airlock tube. Now. Close the outer hatch and codelock it. They are not to come on board."

"Acknowledged. How do we get you back?"

"Yes, Captain," Jorge datavised. "Do tell."

Marcus dodged down a junction. "Have Wai stand by. When I need her, I'll need her fast."

"You think you can cut your way out of the shell, Captain? You have a fission blade, and that shell is held together by a molecular bonding generator."

"You touch him, shithead, and we'll fry that fucking wreck," Karl datavised. "*Lady Mac*'s got maser cannons."

"But do you have the command codes, I wonder. Captain?"

"Communication silence," Marcus ordered. "When I want you, I'll call."

• • •

Jorge's boosted muscles allowed him to ascend stairwell three at a speed which Antonio could never match. He was soon left struggling along behind. The airlock was the tactical high ground, once he had secured that, Jorge knew he'd won. As he climbed his hands moved automatically, assembling the weapon from various innocuous-looking pieces of equipment he was carrying on his utility belt.

"Victoria?" he datavised. "Have you got him?"

"No. He broke my shoulder, the bastard. I've lost him."

"Go to the nearest stairwell, I expect that's what he's done. Antonio, go back and meet her. Then start searching for him."

"Is that a joke?" Antonio asked. "He could be anywhere."

"No, he's not. He has to come up. Up is where the airlock is."

"Yes, but—"

"Don't argue. And when you find him, don't kill him. We have to have him alive. He's our ticket out. Our only ticket, understand?"

"Yes, Jorge."

When he reached the airlock, Jorge closed the inner hatch and cycled the chamber. The outer hatch dilated to show him the *Lady Macbeth*'s fuselage fifteen metres away. Her airlock tube had retracted, and the fuselage shield was in place.

"This is a no-win stand-off," he datavised. "Captain, please come up to the airlock. You have to deal with me, you have no choice. The three of us will leave our weapons over here, and then we can all go back on board together. And when we return to a port none of us will mention this unfortunate incident again. That is reasonable, surely?"

· • • ·

Schutz had just reached the bridge when they received Jorge's datavise.

"Damn! He's disconnected our cable from the communication block," Karl said. "We can't call the Captain now even if we wanted to."

Schutz rolled in midair above his acceleration couch and landed gently on the cushioning. Restraint webbing slithered over him.

"What the hell do we do now?" Roman asked. "Without the command codes we're bloody helpless."

"It wouldn't take that long for us to break open the weapons cabinet," Schutz said. "They haven't got the Captain. We can go over there and hunt them down with the carbines."

"I can't sanction that," Katherine said. "God knows what sort of weapons they have."

"Sanction it? We put it to the vote."

"It's my duty watch. Nobody votes on anything. The last order the Captain gave us was to wait. We wait." She datavised the flight computer for a channel to the MSV. "Wai, status, please?"

"Powering up. I'll be ready for a flight in two minutes."

"Thank you."

"We have to do something!" Karl said.

"For a start you can calm down," Katherine told him. "We're not going to help Marcus by doing anything rash. He obviously had something in mind when he told Wai to get ready."

The hatchway to the Captain's cabin slid open. Marcus air-swam out and grinned round at their stupefied expressions. "Actually, I didn't have any idea what to do when I said that. I was stalling."

"How the fuck did you get back on board?" Roman yelped.

Marcus looked at Katherine and gave her a lopsided smile. "By being right, I'm afraid. The dish is a distress beacon."

"So what?" she whispered numbly.

He drifted over to his acceleration couch and activated the webbing. "It means the wormhole doesn't go back to the xenoc homeworld."

"You found out how to use it!" Karl exclaimed. "You opened its other end inside the *Lady Mac*."

"No. There is no other end. Yes, they built it as part of their survival operation. It was their escape route, you were right about that. But it doesn't go somewhere; it goes some-*when*."

•   •   •

Instinct had brought Marcus to the portal chamber. It was as good as any other part of the ship. Besides, the xenocs had escaped their predicament from here. In a remote part of his mind he assumed that winding up on their homeworld was preferable to capture here by Jorge. It wasn't the kind of choice he wanted to make.

He walked slowly round the portal. The pale violet emanation in the air around it remained constant, hazing the dull surface from perfect observation. That and a faint hum were the only evidence of the massive quantity of power it consumed. Its eternal stability a mocking enigma.

Despite all the logic of argument he knew Katherine was wrong. Why build the dish if you had this ability? And why keep it operational?

That factor must have been important to them. It had been

built in the centre of the ship, and built to last. They'd even reconfigured the wreck to ensure it lasted. Fine, they needed reliability, and they were masters of material science. But a one-off piece of emergency equipment lasting thirteen thousand years? There must be a reason, and the only logical one was that they knew they would need it to remain functional so they could come back one day.

The SII suit prevented him from smiling as realization dawned. But it did reveal a shiver ripple along his limbs as the cold wonder of the knowledge struck home.

• • •

On the *Lady Mac*'s bridge, Marcus said: "We originally assumed that the xenocs would just go into zero-tau and wait for a rescue ship; because that's what we would do. But their technology allows them to take a much different approach to engineering problems."

"The wormhole leads into the future," Roman said in astonishment.

"Almost. It doesn't lead anywhere but back to itself, so the length inside it represents time not space. As long as the portal exists you can travel through it. The xenocs went in just after they built the dish and came out again when their rescue ship arrived. That's why they built the portal to survive so long, it had to carry them through a great deal of time."

"How does that help you get here?" Katherine asked. "You're trapped over in the xenoc wreckage right now, not in the past."

"The wormhole exists as long as the portal does. It's an open tube to every second of that entire period of existence, you're not restricted which way you travel through it."

• • •

In the portal chamber Marcus approached one of the curving black buttress legs. The artificial gravity was off directly underneath the doughnut so the xenocs could rise into it. But they had been intent on travelling into the future.

He started to climb the buttress. The first section was the steepest; he had to clamp his hands behind it, and haul himself up. Not easy in that gravity field. It gradually curved over, flattening out at the top, leaving him standing above the doughnut. He balanced there precariously, very aware of the potentially lethal fall down onto the floor.

The doughnut didn't look any different from this position, a glowing ring surrounding the grey pressure membrane. Marcus put one foot over the edge of the exotic matter, and jumped.

He fell clean through the pressure membrane. There was no gravity field in the wormhole, although every movement suddenly became very sluggish. To his waving limbs it felt as if he was immersed in some kind of fluid, though his sensor block reported a perfect vacuum.

The wormhole wall was insubstantial, difficult to see in the meagre backscatter of light from the pressure membrane. Five narrow lines of yellow light materialized, spaced equidistantly around the wall. They stretched from the rim of the pressure membrane up to a vanishing point some indefinable distance away.

Nothing else happened. Marcus drifted until he reached the wall, which his hand adhered to as though the entire surface was one giant stikpad. He crawled his way back to the pressure membrane. When he stuck his hand through, there was no resistance. He pushed his head out.

There was no visible difference to the chamber outside. He datavised his communication block to search for a signal. It told him there was only the band from one of the relay blocks in the stairwells. No time had passed.

He withdrew back into the wormhole. Surely the xenocs

hadn't expected to crawl along the entire length? In any case, the other end would be thirteen thousand years ago. Marcus retrieved the xenoc activation code from his neural nanonics, and datavised it.

The lines of light turned blue.

He quickly datavised the deactivation code, and the lines reverted to yellow. This time when he emerged out into the portal chamber there was no signal at all.

* * *

"That was ten hours ago," Marcus told his crew. "I climbed out and walked back to the ship. I passed you on the way, Karl."

"Holy shit," Roman muttered. "A time machine."

"How long was the wormhole active for?" Katherine asked.

"A couple of seconds, that's all."

"Ten hours in two seconds." She paused, loading sums into her neural nanonics. "That's a year in thirty minutes. Actually, that's not so fast. Not if they were intending to travel a couple of thousand years into the future."

"You're complaining about it?" Roman asked.

"Maybe it speeds up the further you go through it," Schutz suggested. "Or more likely we need the correct access codes to vary its speed."

"Whatever," Marcus said. He datavised the flight computer and blew the tether bolts which were holding *Lady Mac* to the wreckage. "I want flight-readiness status, people, please."

"What about Jorge and the others?" Karl asked.

"They only come back on board under our terms," Marcus said. "No weapons, and they go straight into zero-tau. We can hand them over to Tranquillity's serjeants as soon as we get home." Purple course vectors were rising into his mind. He fired the manoeuvring thrusters, easing *Lady Mac* clear of the xenoc shell.

• • •

Jorge saw the sparkle of bright dust as the explosive bolts fired. He scanned his sensor collar round until he found the tethers, narrow grey serpents flexing against the speckled backdrop of drab orange particles. It didn't bother him un- duly. Then the small thrusters ringing the starship's equator fired, pouring out translucent amber plumes of gas.

"Katherine, what do you think you're doing?" he datavised.

"Following my orders," Marcus replied. "She's helping to prep the ship for a jump. Is that a problem for you?"

Jorge watched the starship receding, an absurdly stately movement for an artifact that big. His respirator tube seemed to have stopped supplying fresh oxygen, paralysing every muscle. "Calvert. How?" he managed to datavise.

"I might tell you some time. Right now, there are a lot of conditions you have to agree to before I allow you back on board."

Pure fury at being so completely outmanoeuvred by Calvert made him reach automatically for his weapon. "You will come back now," he datavised.

"You're not in any position to dictate terms."

Lady Macbeth was a good two hundred metres away. Jorge lined the stubby barrel up on the rear of the starship. A green targeting grid flipped up over the image, and he ze- roed on the nozzle of a fusion-drive tube. He datavised the X-ray laser to fire. Pale white vapour spewed out of the noz- zle.

"Depressurization in fusion drive three," Roman shouted. "The lower deflector coil casing is breeched. He shot us, Marcus, Jesus Christ, he shot us with an X-ray."

"What the hell kind of weapon has he got back there?" Karl demanded.

"Whatever it is, he can't have the power capacity for many more shots," Schutz said.

"Give me fire control for the maser cannons," Roman said. "I'll blast the little shit."

"Marcus!" Katherine cried. "He just hit a patterning node. Stop him."

Neuroiconic displays zipped through Marcus's mind. Ship's systems coming on-line as they shifted over to full operational status, each with its own schematic. He knew just about every performance parameter by heart. Combat-sensor clusters were already sliding out of their recesses. Maser cannons powering up. It would be another seven seconds before they could be aimed and fired.

There was one system with a faster response time.

"Hang on," he yelled.

Designed for combat avoidance manoeuvres, the fusion-drive tubes exploded into life two seconds after he triggered their ignition sequence. Twin spears of solar-bright plasma transfixed the xenoc shell, burning through deck after deck. They didn't even strike anywhere near the airlock which Jorge was cloistered in. They didn't have to. At that range, their infra-red emission alone was enough to break down his SII suit's integrity.

Superenergized ions hammered into the wreck, smashing the internal structure apart, heating the atmosphere to an intolerable pressure. Xenoc machinery detonated in tremendous energy bursts all through the structure, the units expending themselves in spherical clouds of solid light which clashed and merged into a single wavefront of destruction. The giant rock particle lurched wildly from the ex-

plosion. Drenched in a cascade of hard radiation and sub-
atomic particles, the unicorn tower at the centre of the dish
snapped off at its base to tumble away into the darkness.

Then the process seemed to reverse. The spume of light
blossoming from the cliff curved in on itself, growing in
brightness as it was compressed back to its point of origin.

Lady Mac's crew were straining under the five-gee acceleration of the starship's flight. The inertial-guidance systems
started to flash priority warnings into Marcus's neural
nanonics.

"We're going back," he datavised. Five gees made talking
too difficult. "Jesus, five gees and it's still pulling us in."
The external sensor suite showed him the contracting fire-
ball, its luminosity surging towards violet. Large sections of
the cliff were flaking free and plummeting into the confla-
gration. Black lightning cracks were splitting open right
across the rock.

He ordered the flight computer to power up the nodes and
retract the last sensor clusters.

"Marcus, we can't jump," Katherine datavised, her face
pummelled into frantic creases by the acceleration. "It's a
gravitonic emission. Don't."

"Have some faith in the old girl." He initiated the jump.

An event horizon eclipsed the *Lady Macbeth*'s fuselage.

Behind her, the wormhole at the heart of the newborn
micro-star gradually collapsed, pulling in its gravitational
field as it went. Soon there was nothing left but an expanding cloud of dark snowdust embers.

• • •

They were three jumps away from Tranquillity when
Katherine ventured into Marcus's cabin. *Lady Mac* was accelerating at a tenth of a gee towards her next jump coordinate, holding him lightly in one of the large black-foam

sculpture chairs. It was the first time she'd ever really noticed his age.

"I came to say sorry," she said. "I shouldn't have doubted."

He waved limply. "*Lady Mac* was built for combat, her nodes are powerful enough to jump us out of some gravitonic field distortions. Not that I had a lot of choice. Still, we only reduced three nodes to slag, plus the one dear old Jorge damaged."

"She's a hell of ship, and you're the perfect captain for her. I'll keep flying with you, Marcus."

"Thanks. But I'm not sure what I'm going to do after we dock. Replacing three nodes will cost a fortune. I'll be in debt to the banks again."

She pointed at the row of transparent bubbles which all held identical antique electronic circuit boards. "You can always sell some more Apollo command module guidance computers."

"I think that scam's just about run its course. Don't worry, when we get back to Tranquillity I know a captain who'll buy them from me. At least that way I'll be able to settle the flight pay I owe all of you."

"For Heaven's sake, Marcus, the whole astronautics industry is in debt to the banks. I swear I never could understand the economics behind starflight."

He closed his eyes, a wry smile quirking his lips. "We very nearly solved human economics for good, didn't we?"

"Yeah. Very nearly."

"The wormhole would have let me change the past. Their technology was going to change the future. We could have rebuilt our entire history."

"I don't think that's a very good idea. What about the grandfather paradox for a start? How come you didn't warn us about Jorge as soon as you emerged from the wormhole?"

"Scared, I guess. I don't know nearly enough about quantum temporal displacement theory to start risking paradoxes. I'm not even sure I'm the Marcus Calvert that brought this particular *Lady Macbeth* to the xenoc wreck. Suppose you really can't travel between times, only parallel realities? That would mean I didn't escape into the past, I just shifted sideways."

"You look and sound pretty familiar to me."

"So do you. But is my crew still stuck back at their version of the wreck waiting for me to deal with Jorge?"

"Stop it," she said softly. "You're Marcus Calvert, and you're back where you belong, flying *Lady Mac*."

"Yeah, sure."

"The xenocs wouldn't have built the wormhole unless they were sure it would help them get home, their true home. They were smart people."

"And no mistake."

"I wonder where they did come from?"

"We'll never know, now." Marcus lifted his head, some of the old humour emerging through his melancholia. "But I hope they got back safe."

PETER F. HAMILTON was born in Rutland, England, in 1960 and still lives near Rutland Water. He began writing in 1987 and has published short stories in a number of magazines and anthologies. His other works include the Greg Mandel novels: *Mindstar Rising*, *A Quantum Murder*, and *The Nano Flower*. The epic story begun in *The Reality Dysfunction* and *The Neutronium Alchemist* concludes in *The Naked God*, which Warner Aspect published in 1999.